THE SCARLET RIBBON

Center Point
Large Print

Also by Naomi Stephens and available from Center Point Large Print:

The Burning of Rosemont Abbey

The SCARLET Ribbon

NAOMI STEPHENS

CENTER POINT LARGE PRINT
THORNDIKE, MAINE

This Center Point Large Print edition
is published in the year 2025 by arrangement with
WhiteFire Publishing.

The text of this Large Print edition is unabridged.
In other aspects, this book may vary
from the original edition.
Printed in the United States of America
on permanent paper sourced using
environmentally responsible foresting methods.
Set in 16-point Times New Roman type.

ISBN: 979-8-89164-656-8

The Library of Congress has cataloged this record
under Library of Congress Control Number: 2025938789

For those who feel broken.

Comfort, comfort ye my people,
speak ye peace, thus saith our God;
comfort those who sit in darkness,
mourning ’neath their sorrow’s load.
Speak ye to Jerusalem
of the peace that waits for them;
tell her that her sins I cover,
and her warfare now is over.

(*Lutheran Service Book*, Hymn 347)

PROLOGUE

New York, February 1776

The sign balanced between Rebekah's dry, cracked fingers had been inscribed with a single word—*Harlot*.

Peter Nelson, the local magistrate, had forced her to paint the word herself, to hold the sign as high as she could as she stood upon a barrel outside the church doors. The word bore down on her, a crushing weight that was twice as heavy as the plank of wood it had been painted on, but Rebekah held fast. Her arms burned above her as the magistrate, a lumbering gollompus of a man, paced like a beast at her feet. With each turn of his wide shoulders, she counted down the seconds until her sentence was over.

"*Please* . . ." Such a pitiful word, pulled not from Rebekah's lips, but from Reverend Wainwright, who stood a short way off. "Might she be permitted to eat something?"

Rebekah's stomach cramped in agreement. Twelve hours had passed without food or drink of any kind. Dizziness curled the edges of her vision as she listened, numbly, to the reverend's quiet intercession.

"I think not," came Nelson's oily reply. "How else is she to learn?"

At that, the reverend's tone sharpened. "Surely, she might come into the church. To pray. To confess."

Nelson laughed. He acted the part of puritan but was nothing of the sort, as Rebekah had lately discovered through a series of unsavory advances. "I appreciate your tactics, Reverend, but they are not the ways of good government. If we allow one bawd into our midst, we will soon have a dozen. It pains me, of course, but we must make a public example of her."

Rebekah would have scoffed, but her chest was too tight as she swallowed against another press of tears. She was, as far as she could remember, the only woman to be made an example of in such a way. Haverstraw's illicit markets, such as they were, were of a trifling nature, and so most women faced few repercussions as long as they were discreet.

As for Rebekah, one night in Mason's bed had been enough to ruin her. She'd been barely seventeen at the time. Twenty-three and charming, Mason was the kind of man who appealed to a motherless girl with a stern, forbidding father. Rebekah had cared for him, truly, and trusted him enough that, when she learned he was leaving, she'd stepped into his arms and let him show her all the ways he wanted to love her. Mason had promised to return, to write to her, and she'd believed him. Yet, that was all well over a year ago, and she'd had no word.

Her father had since taken great pains to conceal his daughter's situation, swearing the household staff to secrecy with threats of dismissal. When at last her son was born, he told the servants the baby had died, then deposited him with the reverend and prayed this would be an end of it.

But someone somewhere wagged a loose tongue, for rumors soon made their way through town. When Peter Nelson heard them, it never occurred to him that a girl like Rebekah, already compromised in name, might refuse him.

Now, he prowled at her feet, exacting his vengeance, watching the hours carve slowly away at her. She ignored his disheveled wig and puffed-up chest and stared instead at those who'd stopped to watch, wondering what they gained from the spectacle, what satisfaction there was in watching another person suffer.

By the following morning, she balanced on the verge of delirium, head lolling from side to side as she struggled to remain upright. The sign, which she'd held high above her head the first day, now hovered near her hips. Still, she did not speak. She did not cry. Whenever she felt the urge to moan in quiet anguish, she tightened her grip on the sign until the wood felt ready to crack beneath her fingertips.

A small crowd gathered in her final hour. Listless, she squinted into the pale, upturned faces, half dreaming she might find Mason among them. If only he would see her, she thought. Perhaps he would curse Peter Nelson as he helped her down from the barrel, assure her the worst was over, and marry her after all.

She searched for him in vain. And, of all the curious onlookers, only one person dared to meet her eyes fully—

Her father.

She nearly fainted when she saw him. He'd always been an ardent Anglican, but now he looked as solemn as a Quaker. The lines in his face had become more pronounced of late, his chestnut hair graying about the temples. His black coat, which she'd seen him wear to numerous funerals, formed a rigid line from shoulder to shoulder.

Though he didn't speak, she could hear his silent laments. After all he'd done to protect her reputation, after all the sacrifices he'd made and the hours he'd wasted worrying about her future, and there was that horrible word—*harlot*—written in black for everyone to see.

He valued strength and honesty above all else, and so she stood a little taller as she met his eyes. Silently, she pleaded for him to intervene. Could he really bear to see his flesh and blood—his own child—subjected to such agony? She prayed his heart would be turned at the sight of her suffering, that he would bring her back home despite the ugly scrawl of that terrible word.

At first, he set his jaw as if his thoughts matched hers exactly. But he was principled, both high-minded and unmoving. He'd done all he could to bury Rebekah's past, but it had been resurrected against her will, and they both knew there would never be an end to it. She'd shamed him publicly, smeared his good name. Perhaps, to him, this was the foulest sin of all.

She recognized the flicker of pride in his dark eyes—they were deep-set like hers—a half second before he turned and strode away, washing his hands of his only daughter as he left her to finish the rest of her sentence alone.

CHAPTER 1

Three Years Later
June 13, 1779

From her place on the bed, Rebekah watched the drunken fool fumble back into his clothes. He straightened his collar and smoothed his hair, then smacked a handful of coins on the table on his way out. She stared at the ceiling as he went, counting in her mind all the steps it would take for him to stumble down the stairs—*twelve*—across the parlor—*six*—and into the road.

Gone.

Releasing a tight breath, Rebekah wrenched herself up from the bed. Shadows dappled her bare shoulders as she ghosted across the narrow room and tugged her petticoat up over her rumpled shift. She washed in the basin, despairing a moment about the defiant state of her unruly hair before scraping the man's coins into her palm. Without bothering to cinch her stays, she took up her candle and abandoned the chamber.

The usual stairs creaked on her way down, but no one was awake to notice. The halls were empty, lines of moonlight slanting through the squat casements and illuminating the faded rugs beneath her bare feet.

At last, she pushed through the front door and stepped onto a ramshackle porch. She perched on the top step beneath a wooden sign with faded letters that had once clearly read: PENDERGRASS HOUSE. Running her hands up and down her arms, she willed herself to forget the young man's face as she'd forgotten all the others who came before, but it was becoming harder to do so.

She'd been only twelve days out of her father's house—hungry and tired and already ashamed—when she'd sold herself to a man for the first time. She'd vomited in the alley as soon as it was done and vowed never again. But by the time she found herself outside Pendergrass House, a boardinghouse with a well-known reputation for harlotry, she was too cold and tired to resist, well past the point of hesitation. Everyone already thought she was a harlot. First in name, and now in deed. At the time, it hardly seemed to matter.

As far as mistresses went, Mrs. Pendergrass wasn't brutal, but she kept sharp eyes on her girls, always suspicious they were cheating her. She had every reason to be shrewd.

Pendergrass House, which was left to her following her husband's death, was *all* she'd been left. Two stories high, the creaky, weather-beaten building was brimming with extra bedrooms that had been stuffed into every nook and closet. From the road, the outer walls appeared the slightest bit slanted, as if the whole structure was as tired as the women working within, wishing it could but lean and rest against the woods beside it.

Rebekah sat on her usual step until the skies faded to their darkest and a cool mist rolled off the Hudson River and spilled across the yard. Once, a handsome young boarder had found her sitting in that very spot and stopped to tell her how well the midnight skies became her. It was the loveliest compliment she'd ever received, so gentlemanly, but then he handed her a sovereign and pulled her behind the stable.

Rebekah laughed bitterly.

Perhaps it was best her mother died in childbirth. It would have killed any mother, surely, to see her child in such a place.

And her father?

She clenched her jaw. She'd written to him only once, nearly a year ago, but fed the letter to the fire before she could bring herself to send it. She would not crawl back to him. Not then. Not now.

Brushing off her skirt, Rebekah pulled herself up from the step. The cool mist curled around her nape and exposed shoulders as a wayward wind blew a rustling gust through the trees. She paused to watch, frowning when an unfamiliar horse—a black gelding, fully saddled—plodded out of the woods to stare at her. Confused, she stepped down into the grass, her bare feet squelching in the muddy dew.

After a moment's consideration, she decided that the horse must have belonged to a British soldier. Stony Point, the nearest fort, had been taken by the British a few weeks prior, and several of the officers had been in the parlor that evening for supper. She turned to go back inside but paused when another gust of wind blew directly behind her.

Or was it something else?

It sounded more like the haggard draw of an uneven breath.

Too late to react, she heard shuffling to the right, and there was no mistaking them now—footsteps!

Rebekah spun to confront the newcomer, but her arm was seized from behind. Before she could draw enough breath to shriek, a hand clamped hard over her mouth, smothering the sound of her scream to the faintest yelp of surprise.

Rebekah's chest burned as she was yanked sideways. Blindly, she threw up a hand to strike, but the man grunted and pulled her into the shadows at the side of the house. For a moment, her mind whirred, fearing he was one of those who had no interest in paying for his pleasure but would beat it out of her instead. She twisted hard to the right, trying to upset his balance, but then the moonlight glanced upon his features, and her terror waned.

The man standing before her bled from the

temple and, judging by what she could see of his collar, from the shoulder as well. He was young and pale, as concentrated as any man she'd ever seen. As soon as they were concealed beneath the trees, he released her and staggered sideways, tumbling to the ground where he groaned at her feet.

Trembling from the tussle, Rebekah fetched her candle from the porch step and crouched beside the stranger, splaying a hand against his chest. Her search was answered by a heartbeat. It pulsed strong, thank heavens, but was unnervingly erratic.

Before she could think what to do, the man gripped her arm. "Is anyone in the parlor?" he asked in a hoarse whisper.

She considered lying to make him go away, but his eyes were feverish, cornered. If she left him there, she had no doubt he'd be dead by morning. "No."

The man nodded. Then, summoning some extra store of strength, he wrenched himself up from the ground, swaying before he propelled her up the porch and into the front room. He closed the door silently behind them, then turned hard eyes on her. "Where's your room?" he demanded.

Struggling to find her voice, she glanced at the stairs.

"Go now," he said. "Quickly."

Rebekah obeyed, but she hesitated on the

landing when she realized a gun had appeared in his hand. This man could be about to accost her. He could be about to *kill* her. Would anyone, save Mrs. Pendergrass, even notice? Terror renewed, she shoved sideways, trying to knock him back down the stairs.

His hand turned into a vice, anchoring her against him.

Burying the urge to scream, Rebekah surrendered, leading him to her chamber at the end of the hall and opening the door. It was a cramped space, though she kept it clean enough. In the corner, there was her bed with strewn covers. By the door, a small round table and a rickety chair where gentlemen stopped long enough to toss their hats. As soon as the door was closed, the stranger released her with a grimace and would have fallen to the floor had she not swept forward out of instinct and offered her shoulder.

"Water," he ordered throatily as, with a heave, she slumped him against the bed.

She jumped to pour the water as the man set his pistol on the table, well within reach, and shouldered out of his coat. He snatched the cup from her fingers when she offered it, his hands clenching to fists as Rebekah tore open the top of his shirt to examine the extent of his injuries.

He didn't flinch at what she found beneath, but Rebekah did. "Someone shot you," she observed in a strangled voice.

The man drank the whole cup of water without answering, then fell backward on the bed. His face, growing paler by the moment, was sheened with sweat.

Rebekah found yesterday's shift discarded in a basket and ripped a few strips from the hem. As she approached the bed, she faltered, wondering if the man might wake the whole house with his howls when she touched the wound.

"Don't spare me," he heaved, beads of sweat trailing down his temples. "Get on with it."

Squaring her jaw, she nodded and pressed her shift firmly to his wound, watching his complexion turn from white to gray. A hideous oath hissed past his teeth, but his hand closed over hers to steady it when she might have shrunk back.

"Who are you?" she whispered.

He writhed, his eyes rolling up in his head, but somehow talked through the pain. "Doesn't matter," he muttered. "I'll be gone by morning."

Rebekah tied off part of her shift as a tourniquet at his shoulder, working quickly as his breath rattled in his chest like an old, rusty hinge. "You can't travel in this state."

He gave the barest thread of a laugh. "The devil I can't."

A muffled sound disturbed the silence at the back of the house. The man recaptured Rebekah's hand, but she merely tilted her head, listening.

Was it the man's runaway horse padding around the property, or was it something else—*someone* else?

She felt the man's gaze on her face as she listened. He was being hunted, like a fox that had slipped its way through an unlikely hole. But who, exactly, was the hunter?

He might have been shot by soldiers, or perhaps he'd gotten in deep with vagabonds who could easily trace his flight directly to her chamber. Skin prickling, she pulled her hand out of his and stepped to the window, inching the curtain back with one finger to scan the yard below.

At first, she saw the same patch of grass. The same misty moon. But then clusters of shadow broke from the tree line behind the boarding-house. As soon as they reached the yard, the moon-light betrayed them.

Soldiers—a dozen strong, and sweeping steadily toward the house.

"Good heavens," Rebekah whispered, her hand at her throat.

"What?" the man demanded. "What is it?"

"Redcoats."

She didn't think he would be able to stand, but he was on his feet before she'd even finished uttering the word, using her bedpost as leverage as he found his footing. "How many?"

"Too many."

He grabbed his pistol and edged over to the

window, brushing the curtain aside as he scanned the lawn below. "I'll have to make a run for it."

Rebekah stooped, collecting the thin scraps of cloth she'd used to wash the blood from his shoulder. "You can't," she said, tossing the whole wad beneath her bedcovers. She rushed to her basin, scrubbing the rest of the blood from her shaking fingers. "They might already have the house surrounded."

The man lifted a brow as she poured the bloodied water into her chamber pot. "If you have a better plan," he said, "by all means share it."

She dried her hands on her skirt as she studied him. He was a rebel, of course, perhaps even a spy, which meant lying for him in any respect was dangerous beyond measure. Yet there was something in his grim smile, something in the hitch of his brow as he awaited her answer.

The redcoats would kill him. Of this, she was certain. Rebekah hardly considered herself a Loyalist like her father, but neither was she by any stretch a Patriot like many who lived in Haverstraw. She'd long since discovered that men were men whatever the color of their uniform, and there she was.

As the stranger swayed on his feet, the last scraps of color fading from his cheeks, she strode to the bed and threw back the covers, unwilling that any man should perish as a result of her indecision.

"Climb in," she ordered.

He settled his eyes on her more narrowly. They were blue, she realized, the same bright hue of a Continental uniform. "That's not quite the kind of plan I was expecting."

She laughed. "I promise you, no one will question it. Nor can it ruin whatever is left of my reputation."

At that, his gaze dipped to her loose shift, which had slipped past the slope of her shoulder. He set his jaw, though she couldn't tell if it was because he was offended by her livelihood or because he was in the painful process of shrugging back into his torn shirt. Tucking his pistol somewhere beneath, he rolled over onto the bed, leaning down on his wounded side as she flung her covers over him.

CHAPTER 2

Writhing lantern light shone through the windows, breathing the black casements to life with a tawny glow. A moment later, footsteps thundered as soldiers barreled through the front door and up the stairs, their boots pounding the floors as they pushed from room to room, upsetting all manner of furniture and patrons as they went.

Mrs. Pendergrass welcomed them in her most sanguine voice. "Search all you'd like, gentlemen. You will find everyone here most obliging."

A moment later, vigorous pounding rattled Rebekah's door. She gave her room one last cursory glance. All seemed normal except for a small slip of folded paper that had fallen beside the bed. Crumpling it quickly in her hand, she slipped a shawl around her shoulders, covering a stray splatter of blood near her neckline, and opened her door. "Yes?"

A powdered wig appeared in the gap and a set of dark, important eyes. "Move aside. We're searching for a rebel spy."

Though Rebekah had already suspected as much, she gasped audibly for effect. In many areas, Haverstraw remained a Patriot stronghold. Recent rumors even favored a militia counterstrike to take back the fort and drive out the

British for good. As such, the British regiments kept almost entirely to the fort, except for the officers who enjoyed the usual amusements at the nearby tavern and boardinghouse. Though their presence there was tolerated by the locals, it was a tense, unspoken truce, and so the redcoats had never imposed hard jurisdiction.

But if a spy hid on the premises, this was another matter entirely.

Several locals sniffing much too near the fort had already been seized and questioned, one of them hanged shortly after, screaming his innocence even as they spurred his horse out from under him.

Rebekah swallowed her terror to answer in a straight, even voice. "I'm afraid I'm with a customer at present."

The officer smiled mildly, but there was something serpentine about his lips and nose, a tapered look, and so the smile hung uncomfortably between them. Without further coaxing, he shoved the door open so roughly she tripped back and cracked a rib against the table.

Rebekah hissed in pain as Mrs. Pendergrass released an angry shriek. But if Rebekah thought her mistress was about to defend her, she was swiftly disenchanted of the notion. "This girl works for me," Mrs. Pendergrass said, with umbrage. "If you damage her, Captain Haggerty, you'll owe me her wages for the next two weeks."

Ignoring this less-than-sentimental plea, the officer stared expectantly down at Rebekah, his eyes touching every inch of her thin chemise. “Your customer is a heavy sleeper.”

“He’s drunk,” Rebekah answered flatly, pulling herself up. “I’ve been trying to wake him for nearly twenty minutes.”

At the captain’s nod, one of the soldiers cut across the room and nudged the stranger in the shoulder with the butt of his musket. The man shifted as if in sleep and grunted, slurring his words as he swatted him away.

The soldier stepped back. At Haggerty’s order, he crouched to search beneath her bed as another inspected her wardrobe, every inch. The men worked quickly and methodically. As Rebekah waited for them to finish their inspection, a thin tendril of blood seeped from beneath the stranger’s chest onto the sheet. She crushed the paper in her fist, so hard her nails cut into her palm, and could only hope the captain wouldn’t notice.

“There’s no sign of him, sir.”

Hands clasped behind his back, the captain strode to the window. He stared down at the woods, searching the shadows, then offered Rebekah another slippery smile. “You’ll have to forgive me for interrupting your . . . work.”

“It was no trouble at all,” Mrs. Pendergrass assured.

Rebekah massaged her rib and scowled.

The captain gestured his men from the room. Then, donning his hat with a flourish, he spun on his heel and left.

Mrs. Pendergrass moved to follow the small parade but paused with one hand on Rebekah's doorframe. She glanced at the man senseless in the bed, then at Rebekah. "Did he pay?"

Rebekah pulled the previous man's coins from her pocket and held them up.

"Double the usual," the older woman noted, her fingers brushing Rebekah's palm as she plucked the coins up in her hand. "Must have made him think it would be worth his time."

"After all that ale," Rebekah answered. " 'Tis remarkable he could see straight, let alone count."

Mrs. Pendergrass laughed. "Heartless wench," she called Rebekah, then swept out of the room.

As her door closed, some of the tension eased from Rebekah's shoulders, but not all. She'd just lied to His Majesty's men. If the man was who they claimed—a spy—it would be well within the captain's rights to drag her from the premises and have her flogged for all to see. Granted, the redcoats didn't control all of Haverstraw, but this didn't mean they wouldn't make an example of her, if only to draw out the man she'd aided.

As if hearing her thoughts, the man in question rolled onto his back, gasping as though the pain itself was enough to drown him from within.

Relief shot through Rebekah as she jumped to his side and helped him sit up. “Thank heavens,” she said, shakily. “I was afraid you might die in my bed.”

“That makes two of us,” he muttered, his hazy eyes struggling to focus on her face. “You aren’t hurt, are you? I heard him shove you.”

She crossed the room and pushed open her window, wincing at the tweak of pain in her rib. “I’ll mend. But you must go. Now.”

He came and stood beside her, hoisting one leg through the casement as he prepared to leave. “What do they call you?” he asked, already lingering far longer than she would have expected.

Rebekah paused. Throughout the years, she’d been called many crass and common names, by men whose faces converged as a single sneer in her mind. When she didn’t answer straight out, the man leaned closer, and she betrayed herself by stepping back. He was, without a doubt, the most imposing man to enter her chamber, gruff and bloodied as he was. But then he met her eyes, and there was the faintest glint of gratitude as he took her hand. After all the men who’d pawed and pulled at her, the quiet gesture carried her breath away.

“Rebekah,” she said at last. “My name is Rebekah.”

She waited for him to return the courtesy, but he didn't.

He pressed her fingers, then released her. "I'm in your debt," was all he said before he sprung down from her casement, onto the roof below, and vanished into the night.

Alone again, Rebekah became aware of the tension she'd been holding in both hands. Breathing slowly through her nose, she loosened her fists one finger at a time, until she remembered the small square of paper she'd found beside the bed. There it was now in the center of her palm. She ought to set it directly to her candle flame. After all, reading its contents, even keeping it, could make her a party to treason.

Instead, she pulled her candle closer.

She opened the letter.

And she read.

Shielded by fog and darkness, Ben lumbered from tree to tree. It was a miracle his pistol was steady in his hand because the stitching between mind and body had become severed by what he could only assume was shock. He saw and heard things he knew weren't there.

Clang! Clang! Clang! A bell clamored in his head like the one which had called him to prayer at school, cruel and shrill at four thirty each morning.

Then he heard the fiddle music, the same jolly

tune his father played on Christmas mornings. Shaking, he crammed his hands to his ears and reminded himself his father was dead, had been for years.

"I hope you go to the devil," Ben had cursed him at their final parting. Though he'd meant it at the time, he trembled to hear that ghostly fiddle play, wondering if his curse had caught up to him at last.

"Get a hold of yourself," he muttered, but the fever scorched up his neck, hot as hellfire as he stumbled through the woods.

For a moment, he spotted mangled bodies beneath the trees, but then he blinked, and they were gone. All the while, the desperation he'd heard in Jotham Eldridge's voice dogged him. *"I tell you I won't do it,"* he'd said that evening. *"They've hung a man since taking Stony Point. I have no intention of being next, and that's if the Patriots don't come for me first . . ."*

Ben ground his teeth until the phantom words faded. For several weeks, his friend had been gathering intelligence from soldiers who came into his uncle's tavern. Stony Point was a prize Washington wasn't ready to abandon. Because whoever held the ferry likewise held access to the Hudson and could control and choke supplies and correspondence moving to and from the south. He certainly wasn't about to trust the efforts of the local militia, who by all accounts were a ragtag ensemble, lacking both organization and discipline despite the efforts of a certain Lt. Colonel Hay to subdue them.

No, if Washington was to regain Stony Point, he needed to move deftly, discreetly, and so General Wayne had enlisted Jotham at Ben's recommendation, who swore his old schoolfellow would prove both willing and inconspicuous. The arrangement was casual, but dangerous. After only two weeks, Jotham, already scared and paranoid, wanted nothing more than to return to a regular, civilian life.

What had Ben told him?

That he had no choice.

Wayne needed him there.

"I'll stay here," Ben had promised. *"In Haverstraw, until the fort is ours. I swear nothing will happen to you."*

His vow was tested a second later when passing redcoats stopped to ask what they were about. He and Jotham might have kept to their covers, except one of the redcoats demanded they empty their pockets. They'd had no choice but to kill them, though a third had gotten away in the skirmish. Ben could only hope the fog had shielded him well enough to obscure his face—and that Jotham had escaped safely out of those infernal woods.

He mumbled another prayer to this end as he trailed a meandering stream. To the right, he spotted a worn footpath. He followed it, staggering up a low incline and stumbling from the shelter of shadows. Wheezing slightly, he stared across the moonlit yard. On the other side, a thin ribbon of smoke curled upward from a stone chimney. And there, opposite the house, was a patchwork graveyard laid out beneath the stronghold of a nearby steeple.

Sanctuary.

Ben ordered himself to move forward, but his aching body refused the first few tries. The pain in his shoulder had twisted into a sharp, stabbing sensation. He could scarcely breathe, but he wasn't dead. Not yet.

His finger resting on the groove of the trigger, he lurched across the yard, his boots upsetting a young row of cabbages in his stumbling haste through the garden. He made it to the back door and leaned against the jamb, battling an inner darkness as his vision teetered sideways. He struck the door with a white fist, which left a streak of blood upon the wood. Was it his blood, or the blood of a redcoat—?

The door was pulled open before he could decide. Heat from a busy fireplace wafted outward as a tall, slender man in a faded wrapping gown stepped into the night. The man's eyes widened, but his hand gripped Ben's arm to steady him.

Vision clouded again, Ben blinked, warring

with his senses, but it was no use. The man's face had already transformed, and his father stared back in his place, a living corpse riddled with bullets.

Ben swayed forward, grasping at his pistol as if clutching at consciousness. It wasn't real. His father was dead. He would have known this even in the blackest of oblivions, yet the fiddle music crept into his ears as he clung to the man's arm with his bloodied hand.

"Hello, Father." Ben murmured the feverish words with an arch, rebellious smile, then collapsed, motionless upon the stone.

CHAPTER 3

Boston, Summer of 1775

Ben never felt as out of place as he did in the cobblestone parsonage at the end of White Oak Street, but there he was. His father sat, as he always did, in the seat nearest the fire, and his mother beside him with her starched white kerchief pinned in an elegant swoop around her neck.

Rain had been falling for more than an hour, the casements framing a dismal scene of the street beyond. His mother, trained to smooth awkward creases out of an otherwise uncomfortable silence, glanced out the window and sighed. "My, but the roads will be washed away in all this mess. I had thought to go to market in the morning, but now I think not."

"I only pray the rains put out the flames of this wretched rebellion." This from Corporal Haskins, who sat at the far end of the table, across from Ben's sister, Meg. The dandy had made himself up in full uniform, his wig impeccably powdered, the rolls resting at the top of his high cheekbones.

"Oh, but then you will be obliged to leave us." Meg's lips pushed out into a newly practiced pout. "And *that* would not be pleasant at all."

Ben nearly groaned. His sister had taken to wearing only her finest dresses for supper, and he knew why. No doubt the corporal noticed as well, for he smiled fondly and set his hand over hers on the table. "Rest yourself on that account, Miss Renshaw. It doesn't sound like I'll be leaving any time soon."

"Are things really as bad as that?" she asked, though she already knew the answer. Though their father disliked her dabbling in politics, Ben had caught her rifling through his newspapers again that morning.

"A lot of impudence, though nothing we can't handle. We've heard of young men in taverns saying they want to behead statues of our king, can you believe it?" The corporal's dark eyebrows furrowed. "If the rumors are true, they want to melt them all down for bullets."

His father speared a bite of veal. "A bunch of bad-mannered ruffians."

"Really?" Ben disagreed mildly. "Some, I've heard, are rather well educated."

His father grunted. He knew a number of Ben's classmates—his friends—had recently joined the Continentals. "What a lot of good that education did," he said. "To make them so self-important they would deny their God-appointed rulers."

Ben's mother darted a glance between them. If she'd noticed a change in her son's political leanings, she never spoke of it, perhaps hoping he might grow out of it as a child would outgrow a new pair of breeches. She'd taken to observing in recent weeks how young people often joined causes early, in the impetuosity of youth, and were first to leave off and return to the security of their roots.

His father was not so hopeful.

He harbored nothing but disdain for the so-called Sons of Liberty and had grown frosty with his son in recent months. Sometimes, Ben wondered if he suspected the full depth of his son's political fervor. Twice now, Ben had sent coded information, gleaned from the contents of Corporal Haskins's desk, to a contact in the city. On this, he had to tread carefully. If his father ever found out, he would not hesitate to turn him in.

From the other side of the table, Meg straightened her hair and sent her brother a hopeless, pleading look. Attempting to shift the conversation, she flashed a smile at Haskins. "Would you like more tea, Corporal Haskins?"

Ben glanced down at his cup, which remained full. When his mother poured, he always accepted, but he refused to drink the stuff until the taxes were lifted. His father certainly noticed but hadn't mentioned it. Not in front of the corporal, at any rate.

Haskins extended his cup, matching Meg's smile. "Thank you, Miss Renshaw. You are very accommodating."

Accommodating, Ben scoffed inwardly. As if they had any choice in the matter. Redcoats had been quartered in homes across the city, and no family had the right to deny them entrance. Ben had watched Haskins carefully in the early days and grudgingly acknowledged the man was gentlemanly enough toward his sister, albeit a bit of a dandy. Some women were not so fortunate as to be spared unwanted advances from their temporary houseguests.

Haskins shifted his gaze back to Ben. "You must miss your classmates," he observed, trying, and failing, to strike up a brotherly tone. "Eager for the new term to begin?"

"Oh, I keep to myself much of the time." Ben smiled again. "My studies keep me busy."

This was a lie, and everyone at that table, except the corporal, knew it. Schoolwork had always come easily to Ben, and so he spent a good amount of time on extracurriculars, some of which were unsanctioned and had nearly gotten him expelled. He'd been actively involved in debating clubs—which, admittedly, pleased his father—and taken part in a number of theatricals, for which his father was not likely to forgive him, should ever he learn of it.

Haskins smiled. "And at the end of the year? Still planning to settle into a parish of your own?"

"I know a quiet village to the north of here," his father put in quickly. "They've been looking for a vicar for some time. Ben will fit in nicely there."

Ben stifled a laugh. His father had chosen a quiet parish for his son, all right. One that had recently driven out any and all Patriot sympathizers. The man was more conniving than a general. "Nothing is decided," Ben said after a moment. "After all, these are uncertain times."

His father shot him a look. "There's nothing uncertain about it. This war doesn't change what you've been preparing for."

"I only mean I ought not limit myself to the clergy. I could enlist."

His father's eyes gleamed. No doubt, he was trying to divine the color of his son's hypothetical uniform. "You've sworn to me that you would join the ministry," he said. " 'Tis the only reason we sent you to Yale."

"Forgive me, but I take my vows to God more seriously. Would you have me pledge myself half-heartedly?"

His father's brows rose to the middle of his forehead. "You think a man can accomplish more on the battlefield than in a pulpit?"

"That would depend on the man, I suppose."

His father's complexion shifted, paling in the low light.

"Benjamin." His mother spoke his name firmly, not sharply, and Ben fell silent as he always did when faced with her particular censure.

Haskins smiled in sympathy to what likely seemed a fairly common family squabble. "I understand your indecision, Ben, I really do. Why, I shared similar sentiments when I first put on the uniform. Where is a man best put to use? It seems a question only God can answer."

Though it rankled to be talked down to in such a way by a man who was no more than four years his senior, Ben forced himself not to speak.

Haskins sat back in his chair, tipping his glass toward Ben. "But it's uncertain times like these when people need a righteous, sensible voice guiding them forward. Men like your father, Ben. Men like *you*."

Present Day
June 15, 1779

Soaked in sweat, Ben rolled over in the bed and nearly retched.

For hours, his senses returned to him piece-meal, obscured by nightmares and unpleasant memories. He smelled smoke and pine and, far more potent, the metallic zing of his blood coupled with vinegar. From time to time, an unfamiliar voice disturbed the silence, muted, disembodied, as if speaking up to him from beneath a great expanse of water.

When at last Ben's eyes blinked open, it took several minutes to make any sense of his surroundings. He was tucked into a narrow bed as tightly as a corpse, his left shoulder grinding with merciless pain. A decanter of water rested on the table beside him and a bowl of clear broth. The room itself was narrow, clean, and sparsely trimmed. The only light came from a fire popping in the grate, shadows and light flickering over a wooden cross hanging above the door. In a chair beside him, an elderly man in spectacles read from a tattered volume, his neck cricked at a thoughtful angle.

Ben licked his lips and tried to address the stranger, but only a low gurgle emerged from his throat.

The man lifted his head, resting an unnervingly placid set of eyes on him. "It seems you've returned to the land of the living." He snapped his book closed and poured a glass of water. "I certainly hope it treats you more favorably this time."

Ben quaffed the contents of the glass, coughing until he found his voice. "How long have I been out?"

"Nearly two days."

Ben groaned, kicking his legs free of the blanket. He glanced down and found a damp poultice tied against his bare shoulder. The wet herbs smelled of yarrow, a familiar, heady aroma. He'd seen similar treatments used in battle to help slow bleeding. Whoever his rescuer was, he certainly knew his way around a bullet wound.

"You're lucky," the man went on. "Bullet went straight through. I'd have had to send for the doctor if it hadn't."

Ben's head fell back on the pillow. "Forgive me for coming to you like this. I saw the church, and I thought . . . well, I thought—"

"Quite right," the man answered. "I am Reverend Wainwright."

Out of instinct, Ben almost provided his usual alias—Benjamin Clarke—but felt he did not wish to lie to a reverend straight out. "Does anyone know I'm here?"

"Not a soul." The reverend took the empty glass from Ben's hand and set it on the table, then fixed him with a steady, searching gaze. "You talk in your sleep, you know. Seems an unfortunate habit for someone in your position."

Ben stiffened. In his delirium, he might have let anything slip. He might have exposed the Eldridges. He might have revealed Washington's interest in taking back the fort. He might have told this unassuming reverend that he was, in fact, a spy.

"What did I say?"

"You recited the Yale regulations." A slight smile accompanied this observation. "In Latin, no less. Impressive, I must say, for a vagrant."

Grunting through the agony in his shoulder, Ben pushed up from the bed. He had to see

Jotham. He had to make sure his friend was alive, his cover secure. If anything had gone wrong, if his friend had been recognized or captured or . . .

The reverend gripped Ben's elbow, holding him steady. "What are you doing? My friend, you must rest."

"I need my bag."

The reverend's eyes narrowed, but he proved an obliging fellow by fetching Ben's canvas haversack without asking any questions.

Wordlessly, Ben rifled inside, moving aside the spare clothes he'd brought along with a few other accoutrements. He checked twice, three times, his heart pounding double rate.

"Is everything all right?" asked the reverend.

Unable to answer, Ben tossed the bag upon the bed, rumpling his hair in his hand. The letter was gone. It had been coded, of course, but this was small consolation. Codes were cracked all the time. Men were captured and questioned until the pieces came together. This particular missive provided detailed instructions for Jotham and his uncle as they worked undercover.

Ben had sworn to Wayne that he could convince Jotham to stay at his post. To a point, all had gone to plan. He'd summoned Jotham to the meeting place, given him every assurance he would be protected, but those cursed redcoats had stolen upon them before Ben could hand Wayne's letter off to Jotham.

How the blazes had the letter been lost since then?

Suspicion swirled as Ben swiveled his attention back on the reverend. With a snarl of pain, he leapt to his feet and seized the man roughly by the arm, staring down into the whites of his startled eyes. “Where is it?” he growled, shaking the man by the collar. “I swear if you’ve turned it over to—”

The reverend held up both of his hands. “I’ve taken *nothing* from you,” he insisted sharply, the lines in his brow crumpling with disdain.

Ben had a special propensity for reading people. In his younger years, at Yale, this skill gave him a suitable edge when gambling. Now he lied for a living, often enough and well enough to know when he was being lied to.

And when he wasn’t.

He released the reverend with a shudder and sank back onto the bed as he struggled to collect his thoughts. The night of the attack was a blur. He remembered meeting Jotham. He remembered shooting the soldiers and moving the bodies away from the meeting place. He’d been in and out of consciousness after that, keeping to the shadows whenever possible, except, of course . . .

A laugh slipped out as the truth dawned.

The woman from the boardinghouse.

Good heavens, he’d been gulled by a woman. Rebekah, she called herself, if that was her true name. In the short time they'd been together, he'd detected her wide range of emotions—terror, of course, and distrust, followed by an eventual willingness to help though he hadn't been able to account for it.

Of course, some prostitutes had been known to work for rebels and redcoats alike. The beautiful ones were especially useful, commissioned to service drunken soldiers who talked too much or else talked in their sleep. Perhaps she was an informant, a pretty piece in an officer's pocket, or perhaps she'd simply been curious. Either way, she had deft hands and remarkable poise, and if he wasn't so wretchedly furious about it, he might have commended her for her raw nerve.

"Where are you going?" asked the reverend as Ben pulled himself back to his feet.

Without looking up, Ben reached for his pistol then his clothes. "To take back what's mine."

CHAPTER 4

Heavy clouds loomed outside Rebekah's window as she lay in bed turning the small square of parchment over and over. Two days had passed since the young stranger had fled her chamber, and she couldn't make heads or tails of his letter. The margins were crowded with numbers, coded in some way, the creases worn and faded as if his hands had turned it over twice as many times as hers.

She still thought she ought to toss it in the fire. After all, she sometimes entertained redcoats in her chamber and couldn't risk one of them discovering it. But there was something powerful about the note. It could say anything, mean anything, and because she didn't know what that might be, she held onto it all the longer.

"Rebekah!"

She sighed at the sound of her name and tucked the letter back in her pocket before venturing downstairs. Hattie and Martha were both overseeing the midday meal, gossiping together as they delivered steaming bowls and platters from the kitchen. They nodded when Rebekah passed through but knew better than to pull her from her errand when Mrs. Pendergrass beckoned.

Miss Ward—Mrs. Pendergrass's older sister—was tucked in by the fire, polishing her way through a basket of cutlery. The rumpled, middle-aged spinster had witnessed enough depravity in her years to have formed indestructible nerves, yet she still called for her smelling salts when randy young soldiers boasted of their exploits in her presence.

Rebekah ducked her head, avoiding the woman's notice as she slipped through the side door, down a narrow hall which led to the back of the house. At the far end was a cramped room lined with faded portraits of former Pendergrasses. In the corner, the estate's current namesake stooped over her desk, counting the money in the box for what was likely the fifth time that morning.

When Rebekah entered, the older woman spoke without looking up. "Nicholas Browne requests your services this evening."

"Yes, Mrs. Pendergrass."

Before Rebekah could make her escape, Mrs. Pendergrass glanced up and clicked her tongue. "Oh, but surely you can find something more suitable to wear than that old rag? Mr. Browne is one of our finer clients, don't forget."

Rebekah, who already had spent an hour primping for customers, fought a stab of annoyance, but she did as Mrs. Pendergrass ordered. Once retired to her room, she stripped off her linen gown and threw open the door to her wardrobe, searching briefly among the garments. There wasn't much of a selection. Since coming to Pendergrass House, Rebekah's tight, tawdry gowns had been remade a few times over to fit the shifting fashions. All except the lilac one, which had taken her nearly two years to afford.

She rarely wore it since she thought it a terrible waste to wear such a pretty thing for men who would sooner see her undressed anyway. Yet again, Mr. Browne was the kind of man easily charmed by such vanities and paid well for them, so she set at once to making herself ready, draping her curves in lengths of fine satin. Cut in the French "sack-back" style, the gown draped like a cape down her back and cutaway in front to reveal a sumptuous olive-green petticoat. The neckline was low and square, per the fashion, and she prevailed upon no neckerchief to conceal her womanly charms.

Adjusting a few pins to heighten her stack of curls, as close as she could come to a fashionable high roll, Rebekah tipped her head and inspected her reflection. She'd been called a comely lass since the age of thirteen and wasn't too humble to own to it now. She had her father's dark eyes and her mother's thick tangle of chestnut hair. Most of the other women at the brothel flaunted beauty patches and the like, but Rebekah had a deep dimple in her right cheek that could turn twice as many heads when she smiled.

And it was pathetically easy to turn the head of a man like Mr. Nicholas Browne. He was nearly twice her age, but he flirted well enough and readily, and so Rebekah's work wasn't as awkward as it sometimes was with drunkards. Still, he was nothing if not predictable.

As she stood from her toilette, thunder rolled in the distance. She sighed, snatching up her cloak as she stepped through the door. Since coming to Pendergrass House, she'd endured many soakings. A customer was a customer, as Mrs. Pendergrass was in the habit of observing, and so it mattered very little if Rebekah must wade through mud to entertain him.

Pendergrass House nestled at a woodsy crossroads a few miles south of Stony Point. In many respects, the village of Haverstraw wasn't much to write home about. It had an old Anglican church—run-down, with poor attendance—and a tavern near the ferry, which had been more or less claimed by the British when they took control of the fort. Though a few people ran businesses out of their homes, the rest were farmers who altogether were barely enough to fill the stalls on market day. Most families traveled into surrounding counties for their goods and to attend churches of a more Reformed persuasion.

From Pendergrass House to Browne's estate was a thirty-minute walk. Rebekah had only passed the halfway point when the first ominous drop of rain struck her skirt. Lifting up a prayer for her fine satin, she pulled her cloak tighter and quickened the pace, but her prayer went unheeded when, several minutes later, the skies opened and baptized all her fine things in a hard, unforgiving rain.

Bunching her skirt in one hand, she tented her cloak over her hair with the other and ran. For a while, she struggled to see through the rain. But then, as she rounded a bend in the road, a flash of red stood stark against the misty path ahead. By the time Rebekah reached the soldiers—who were some half dozen in number—damp satin clung to every limb, and her skirts were weighted with so much rain she expected to sink six inches into the mud. The fort was near enough that the soldiers needn't have been so much on their guard, but they surveyed the woods beyond her as if she was but the distraction before an ambush.

The one in front strode forward.

Rebekah stared down at his boots as she waited for him to speak. In her sodden gray cloak, she must have appeared a curious creature, like a half-drowned sparrow lost in the woods.

Head bent, the officer stepped forward, bellowing hard over the rain. "What are you doing out in this squall?"

At the sound of his voice, Rebekah's hand crept up, clutching her drab cloak closer about her neck, each of her senses overwhelmed by a sudden dizzying nausea. *No.*

Impossible. If there was one thing she knew to be true, one thing in all the world, it was that Mason was gone. Four years gone. It had been long enough for Rebekah to cast aside their child, to be cast aside herself time and again by men who neither loved nor respected her. She closed her eyes, willing herself to remain upright when her trembling legs might have propelled her down into the mud.

The man stepped closer. "Did you hear me?"

Rebekah had heard, and though she fairly quaked to hear his address, she pulled the hood of her cloak down from her hair, fastening her gaze defiantly to his. All the curls she'd spent an hour arranging drooped against her neck, sending thin rivulets of cold rain between her shoulders.

She couldn't help but think that Mason was still a handsome blade, with bright green eyes and a commanding presence. He'd removed his hat at some point, and so his blond hair was slick with rain, pulled back in a tight queue and held fast with a black ribbon. He wore a curious expression as he waited for her to present herself, but then his eyes lit on her face. He flinched back. His eyes narrowed, then widened.

At last, he found his voice. "Miss Stanton?"

“Lieutenant Davies.” She fixed a smile upon her lips, as primly as if fixing a pretty new hat upon her head, refusing to appear at all unsettled though her skin fairly burned. “How long it has been.”

His face suffused with color at this less-than-veiled rebuke.

She wondered if, like her, he was remembering their final embrace, which had only ended when she’d climbed back out of his bed.

Clearing his throat abruptly, Mason tugged her a few paces away from his men. “I can hardly believe it’s you,” he murmured.

His touch flustered Rebekah, which made her all the more determined to stand firm in his presence. “I assure you I’m very real,” she answered, a shallow laugh falling from her lips.

He bowed his head slightly at her words, raindrops racing down the slope of his nose. He shook his head once, then scuffed his boot heel back through the mud. It was a familiar gesture, one she’d seen him carry out dozens of times. Since they’d both grown up in Haverstraw, she couldn’t help but know him well. He was somewhat older than her, enough so that for most of Rebekah’s school years he’d been little more to her than the tip of a gentlemanly hat as he passed her on the road.

And now?

Despite it all, she fought the urge to grasp his hand. She wasn’t sure how much he might have heard during his time abroad, if he knew of her situation or not. He certainly wasn't looking at her as though she was a prostitute, though she supposed it might not have mattered to him whether or not she was.

Forcing herself to breathe, she clasped her hands tightly in front of her stomach and hunched her shoulders against the driving rain. "I didn't realize you'd returned to Haverstraw."

"I was brought in to help hold the fort." He looked into her face and smiled mildly. "A local's perspective is invaluable, or so I'm told." When she failed to return his smile, he straightened. "I confess I ought to have called on you sooner and heartily beg your pardon. Have you been well?"

Rebekah could have told him everything.

She wanted to.

She wanted to tell him of their child—their son—how he'd been lifted out of her arms when she was too weak and too frightened to cling to him. She wanted to tell him how Peter Nelson had shamed her, tortured her, how she'd turned to Pendergrass House for refuge when no one else would have her.

She couldn't bring herself to speak a word of it because Mason was looking down at her as he always had, as if nothing had changed between them, and she could not stand for him to cringe away from her, to recoil as so many others had done.

"I've been well enough," she said, the rain nearly washing away her words.

"And your father?"

"He keeps much to himself," she answered, not untruthfully. "But I believe him to be well."

Mason glanced back in the direction from which she'd come. "What brings you out in weather such as this?"

His men were paying her a bit more attention now, squinting through the rain for a better look. Rebekah turned her face away from them. Though most of the soldiers kept to the fort, some of the officers ventured to the boardinghouse for the occasional supper and were likely to recognize her.

"I am just on my way back from visiting a friend," she explained quickly. "Admittedly, I was not expecting the rain. I'm afraid my new gown will never forgive me for my carelessness."

She peeled back the bottom of her cloak, offering him a passing glimpse of her satin hem. Here was proof that she was well enough, a respectable lady despite it all.

Mason's eyes dipped to her sopping skirt, and his smile returned, a tentative twist to his lips as he reached forward and took her hand. "And are you *Miss* Stanton still?" he asked in a lower voice. "I ought to have asked before."

Rebekah nearly wept when the familiar warmth of his hand curled around her fingers. If only she'd waited for him, she thought. If only she'd waited, his return might have been a moment worthy of jubilant tears. In all the time he'd been away, she'd never stopped imagining what it would be like if he returned to marry her. It was the ending to a story which had been unraveling within her for many years.

"I'm unmarried," she whispered.

Yes! her conscience hissed. *And a harlot!*

Rebekah staggered back, pulling her hand from his, but not before his fingers moved over her knuckles, brushing against a thin gold band he'd given her at one of their final meetings.

"Wear it and think only of me," he'd said that night, and though she'd been tempted to sell it a time or two, she'd worn it faithfully, or else foolishly, ever since.

Mason dropped his eyes, twisting the ring once around her slender finger before releasing her hand. "One of my men will escort you home," he said with a bit more formality.

Rebekah stiffened down the whole length of her spine, surprised by his gallantry, and a good deal panicked. She couldn't allow them to return her home. As soon as her father stepped onto the porch, all of her lies would be exposed.

"I thank you kindly for the offer." She forced herself not to speak too quickly. "But that isn't necessary. I walk this road all the time, you see, and—"

Mason shook his head. "Rebels ambushed a few of our men in the woods," he explained. "It isn't safe to be roving about unaccompanied."

Rebekah's heartbeat bounded as she thought of the bleeding man she'd allowed into her chamber. "You mean they *killed* them?"

"No need to panic," he said. "We've apprehended one of their horses, you see. It's possible the owner might have remained in the area. I'm merely taking a few precautions."

His smile did nothing to ease her terror. The man from her chamber might have been a murderer, willing to kill her like he had those soldiers if she'd proven difficult. Belatedly, she remembered his coded note. She ought to tell Mason about it, ought to set him on his guard. Indeed, she would have done as much had a new fear not arisen.

Four years had passed since last she'd laid eyes on Mason, and here he was. What might he do if he knew she'd abetted a criminal? Surely, if she told him the man had been armed, he'd understand, but this wasn't entirely the truth. She could have screamed for the soldiers at any moment, and they'd have apprehended the man with little commotion.

What if Mason thought she was suspect?

She laughed to disguise her distress. "Excepting my father, as you know, this area leans heavily toward the Patriot cause. Whichever rebels may have shot your men are likely neighbors of mine in some respect."

"Is that supposed to set me at ease?"

"It is a matter of fact. Even you have to admit that I would be an unlikely mark."

He slanted a brow as he considered her words. "Are you being disagreeable on purpose?"

"I've always had a talent for it, if you'll remember."

He laughed. "Very well, Miss Stanton. We shall leave you at your liberty. Though I do hope you won't be *so* disagreeable as to refuse to see me again?"

His question took her breath and spirited it away. He still wanted her. It was unthinkable. Unthinkable, too, that he should stand so near and not know the horror of what had happened to her in his absence. Even as she thought it, an unlikely plan unfolded in her mind. If she could but ease him quietly into the truth, if she could rekindle his affections before he became too appalled by her profession—

His warm smile encouraged her all the more.

Perhaps it wasn't too late. Perhaps he might propose while it was possible for him to love her as she was. And as she'd always been.

"I often walk this road," she remarked, turning at the hip so he might follow the direction of her gaze. "Up to the old grove near Heston's place. Do you remember?"

The rain had pattered to a stop. Mason's eyes shone brighter now, clear and full of meaning.

The grove had once been a secret spot of theirs. Rebekah recalled standing beneath an orange palette of autumn trees, waiting for a few stolen moments. The crisp air had turned her cheeks pink that day. Or perhaps it had been Mason's doing when he folded her in his arms beneath the foliage and told her how deeply he adored her.

"I remember," he said at last.

"I'll be there on Sunday. A little after six. If that's agreeable to you."

Mason's gaze swept to his men, who were speaking among themselves. Meeting alone with a single woman was risky for any officer, riskier still if one of the locals exposed her to them as a prostitute. Rebekah had no wish to jeopardize Mason's position, but she saw no alternative. She couldn't risk him calling on her at home in the meantime. If he spoke to her father, that would be the end. She told herself, if they were careful, no harm would come from it. That is, if Mason was willing to take the chance.

Apprehension turned her to stone as Mason looked down at his feet.

He tipped his hat as if to leave, but then, in a brusque undertone, said, "Yes."

Her heart soared as he gestured to his men. They assembled around him at once, speaking together in muted tones before making their way up the road.

Rebekah waited until they'd vanished from sight, then moved fast in the direction of Mr. Browne's house.

All around, the marshy forest was shot through with a heavy fog. She squinted against the haze, thinking again of the brash young stranger who'd escaped through her window covered in blood. Perhaps it was a trick of the mind, but for one second she thought she spied another shadow moving in the trees, tall as a man. She stumbled to a halt and blinked, but the shadow was gone.

Rebekah held her breath as she watched the trees. The rain had ceased, but traces dropped from the heavy leaves onto the rocks below, filling the woods with faint, pattering echoes.

The stranger from her chamber had killed Mason's men. She knew it and now hadn't the faintest idea where he'd gone. What might a murderer have done to her—or still do, she wondered with trepidation—if he suspected the woman who'd seen his face was entangled with a British lieutenant?

She cinched her cloak tighter about her neck and walked faster. With each sprinting step, she imagined a pistol trained on her from behind that formidable veil of fog and almost wished she'd accepted Mason's escort.

She could feign confidence all she wanted, but

it didn't change facts. With two angry armies drumming in the distance, even she knew it was far safer to cast two shadows in the forest instead of one.

CHAPTER 5

Shortly after Rebekah returned to Pendergrass House, the rain returned with double vengeance. It beat hard against the shutters and melted the roads beyond into a veritable swamp. The supper hours presented no customers and a steady increase in grumbling on the part of Mrs. Pendergrass, who viewed the abysmal weather as a personal slight against her suffering pocketbook.

Though the other girls walked up and down the halls at will, chatting together as they relished a few quiet hours, Rebekah kept to her room until well after midnight, her blankets pulled up to her ears as she stared at the rivulets running down her dirty window—

Bang!

As the violent crack of sound dashed her welcome repose, she jumped out of bed.

"Whiskey!" shouted an unfamiliar voice downstairs.

To which Miss Ward shrilly replied, "Merciful heavens, but *look* at the *state* of you!"

The front door slammed on the end of her screech, followed by the thud of many footsteps. Curiosity prodding her forward, Rebekah crept out of bed, her blanket trailing like a cape from around her shoulders. She tiptoed down the hall and lowered herself onto the step above the landing. Tucking her knees beneath her shift, she peered between the banister rungs, down into the parlor.

Redcoats.

Six or so, covered in mud and shaking rain from their hats.

Through a door to the right of them, Miss Ward bustled in and out of the kitchen, wearing nothing but her shift, stays, and a faded green petticoat. "Never in my life have I seen such a mess," she exclaimed, stepping around their muddy tracks with a tray of pewter tankards propped upon her bulbous hip. "Drenched to your bones, the lot of you. Come, please, sit by the fire, and I shall have my girl bring some vittles at once. I only wonder what could have brought so many of you out in such a storm."

"We caught a few rebels sniffing around the fort," one of the lower officers answered, removing his hat and setting it on the table. "We tracked them as far as Parker's farm but can't see through this infernal rain."

Tugging out of his gloves, another cursed the militia under his breath.

Miss Ward's hand was at her bosom, her eyes rolling heavenward in exaggerated horror. "Stony Point is safe, though, surely?"

Thoughts shifting to Mason, Rebekah leaned closer, but the officer gestured offhand and smiled for the first time. "Rest yourself on that account, ma'am. Stony Point is a fortress. It will never again fall into the hands of vermin."

Miss Ward pursed her lips and nodded stoutly. "Right glad I am to hear it, sir!"

She turned and barked a quick order through a side door, which summoned the boardinghouse cook, a young woman named Coffey, who emerged with a tray piled high with her usual midnight provisions: brown bread, cold smoked bacon, and a heaping pile of pickled oysters.

Coffey didn't say anything when she entered the room. In fact, she rarely did. Rebekah only knew, after a shared cup of punch one dreary Christmas Eve, that Coffey had once been enslaved by a wealthy family in New Jersey. Then the British marched in, purging the area of all Patriot sympathizers. Unwilling for any of their property to fall into the enemy's hands, the family had torched their own house and freed all their slaves, including Coffey, for spite.

Now, the soldiers watched the cook with inquiring, if not interested, eyes. She dressed plainly as a rule, so as not to be mistaken for one of the working girls, but her dark skin gleamed handsomely in the amber light, her thick black tresses concealed within the elaborate twists and tucks of a bright, scarlet wrap.

"Hurry up, girl," Miss Ward snapped. "They're hungry, can't you see?"

Coffey bowed her head and finished her work, empty tray tucked against her chest as she stepped away. All peevishness melted off the soldiers as they gathered eagerly around the table she'd set.

The officer in charge stood back, ensuring his men were fed first. "We thank you heartily," he said, the words directed only to Miss Ward. "But we would also prefer to lodge here for the night. I hope you can accommodate us, late as it is?"

"We have three empty rooms," Mrs. Pendergrass interrupted, entering the parlor with a gold satin dressing gown wrapped around her middle. "Unless your men are looking for some companionship, in which case I have a few girls who would gladly share their beds." She gestured grandly toward the staircase.

Before Rebekah could flee, the officer's eyes moved in her direction, and he spotted her. Though Rebekah was tempted to jump away, she offered the man a slow, attractive smile. She must have looked less than enticing, if not downright ridiculous, huddled beneath the blanket, her only adornments a rumpled shift and a frizzy, sleep-mussed braid.

One thin brow rose as the captain considered her, but he dropped his gaze a second later. "Let your girls sleep," he said to Mrs. Pendergrass. "I will be lodging alone tonight. As will my men."

At this veiled order, a few soldiers grumbled behind him, but Rebekah felt a quiet gust of gratitude. Sometimes, she forgot what it felt like to be protected, that there were actually men who cared for more in life than an hour spent in a woman's bed.

The Next Morning

When Rebekah was twelve, her father hired a music tutor to come into the house. Rebekah had taken to the harpsichord well enough, but she hated to practice, and, so, like many things, it had faded.

A harpsichord stood in the parlor of Pendergrass House. It was a rickety, old instrument, as out of tune as it was out of use. Rebekah rarely heard anyone play it save the occasional drunkard, but she often sat upon the bench and stared at the keys, skeleton white beneath her fingertips, trying to recollect a handful of notes.

The soldiers were still sleeping upstairs when Mrs. Pendergrass found her sitting there in the morning. "Come!" she cried, sweeping her arm toward the stairs with a grating laugh. "Play a ditty, and maybe the men will *dance* their way into your bed!"

Like a startled creature, Rebekah stood and backed away from the instrument, nearly colliding with Miss Ward as the woman pushed out of the kitchen with a basket of mending.

Mrs. Pendergrass smirked when she spotted her

sister. "Aha!" she called, delightedly. "Now we shall have a *duet!*"

"Oh, I'll play any old tune those soldiers like," Miss Ward quipped, giving her petticoat a suggestive swish.

Cackling laughter followed Rebekah as she trudged upstairs, but she stopped short of entering her chamber when she noticed a tricorn hat on her bed, which had not been there when she left the room that morning. She leaned against the doorframe, glancing this way and that, searching for a customer who had not announced himself, but her chamber was otherwise empty.

Leaving the door open, she stepped cautiously inside. When no one appeared, she took up the hat, sliding its brim slowly between her fingers. "Show yourself at once," she commanded, gripping the hat.

The door snapped shut behind her. She rounded fast as the stranger from the other night, the man who'd been shot, advanced.

"You!" Rebekah gasped.

More than once, she'd imagined him sleeping in some miserable hole somewhere, covered in rats and wretched, or perhaps lying dead in some forgotten patch of forest. Seeing him in daylight quashed these suspicions and made her question her senses. She scanned him carefully, but aside from being a bit pale, he showed no proof of having been shot, neither was he the least bit shabby. He wore a fine brown coat with copper buttons and a waistcoat of forest green. His dark hair, scraggly with sweat the last time she'd seen him, was pulled away from his face.

"Where is it?" he demanded.

The letter burned within Rebekah's pocket. She hadn't meant to steal it, exactly, but now that it was in her possession, she wasn't entirely sure she was ready to hand it over. She had no way of knowing what this man or his associates might be plotting or who might get hurt along the way. Tipping her head, she set down his hat and affected a look of mild interest. "Where's what?"

He rebuked her with a dismissive smile, then crossed to the wardrobe and threw open the door. He rummaged briefly among her dresses, taking special care as he felt about their hems. Unnerved, Rebekah studied him, wondering if he had his pistol, if he would use it if she proved unobliging.

"Don't play games with me," he cautioned, tossing a few garments upon the ground. He lifted a shoe and reached into the toe. Threw it aside. Then the next. "You know what you took, and I will have it back."

"And if I say I can't help you? Shall I be shot for the trouble?"

"What put that idea into your head?"

"You shot two redcoats, didn't you? In the woods?"

His smile sharpened as he turned to face her. “Well now, who told you that?”

“Not all the gossips are sympathetic to traitors.”

“Neither are lieutenants.”

Rebekah’s fingers curled. He knew about Mason. At first, she wasn’t sure how he could have figured it out when she’d been so careful, but the truth dawned eerily within her, like an unworldly whisper. This man had been in the woods that day, the shadow she’d seen moving in the distance—

He’d been watching her all along.

Breathing sharply, she darted toward the door and yanked on the handle, but the man pressed a hand against it, forcing it closed before she could make her escape. “My men will be far less pleasant with you once they realize they’ve been compromised. I’m generally a patient man, but I warn you I have my limit.”

“I haven’t a clue what you mean.”

“Really? Then empty your pocket.”

She lifted both brows, trying to look scandalized by the suggestion, but he grabbed her by the arm, pulling her within a finger’s breadth of his chest. “Shall I *search* you for it?”

Despite a tremor of panic, Rebekah settled into a provocative smile. “If you pay enough,” she challenged in a slow, cool voice. “You can do whatever you’d like with me.”

He pressed her back against the door so

abruptly her shoulder blades thrummed. His eyes were fierce, furious, a glacial shade of blue. She didn't trust those eyes, not for a second, and so she abandoned her earlier challenge and clouted him in the left shoulder, hard, right where she knew he'd been shot.

The man snarled like a beast, flinching away when she lifted her fist to strike again. Seizing upon his distraction, Rebekah lurched back and danced beyond his grip, skirting the bed to put a safer distance between them. "If you don't leave at once," she threatened. "I shall scream for the soldiers."

She could hardly believe it, but her voice barely shook.

The stranger lifted his head and met her eyes. His face was calmer, more controlled despite the pain. She wasn't sure, but she thought she saw the slightest flash of appreciation in his eyes, as if he'd met with an adversary who interested him.

"Have you given it to Lieutenant Davies?" he asked.

"Why should I tell you?" Rebekah taunted, refusing to forfeit now that she held the upper hand. "You're a traitor, aren't you?"

"About to lecture me on the state of my moral character?" He huffed a laugh. "Forgive me, but I don't have that much time. Answer me. Did you give him my letter?"

"There are at least a dozen redcoats in the

rooms next door. Aren't you afraid they might discover you here?"

He smiled even as someone knocked at the door. A moment later, Mrs. Pendergrass floated into the room. "Well, my girl, orders or not, it seems you've caught the notice of one of those—"

Surprise stifled her words as she spotted the man in Rebekah's chamber, but then her mouth curled into a thin-lipped smile. "Ah, but it seems you are already with a customer," she remarked with more cordiality. She measured the man by his fine coat and hat. Then, extending a hand, "Two guineas, sir. A pound if you wish to reserve her for the night."

The man's eyes flicked to Mrs. Pendergrass's empty palm. "Two guineas?" he repeated. "That's more than a bit steep."

Mrs. Pendergrass smiled, but her hand didn't waver. "Two guineas," she said again, far more than Rebekah's usual two shillings. "Unless it is your intention to cheat me in a house filled with His Majesty's men?"

The man lifted a brow, slowly, then reached into his pocket, proffering a two-guinea coin.

With a triumphant smirk, Mrs. Pendergrass pocketed his payment. "It is very good of you, sir." Then, turning on Rebekah, she said, "One of the soldiers is asking about you downstairs. You'll want to do something with your face, I'm sure, before you see to him. You're looking a bit drawn, my dear."

Rebekah glanced sideways at the mysterious stranger. He was studying her more closely, and, for the first time in many years, she blushed. Why, after everything she'd already done, she should feel embarrassed in his presence, she hadn't the dimmest idea. But as he donned his hat and moved to the door, she hoped he wouldn't have to pass the soldier, whoever he was, on his way down the stairs.

CHAPTER 6

After retreating from Pendergrass House, Ben made his way to The King's Ferry Tavern, where a number of His Majesty's finest were enjoying an early lunch. Though the presence of a few British officers had never concerned him in the past, his bullet wound, still fresh, ached in silent warning as he pushed into the room.

The place must have seen its fair share of travelers, as his arrival drew only a perfunctory glance from the room's occupants. One table quibbled about a lost shipment of provisions, likely beset by a band of privateers. Another discussed the fine attributes of a certain lady about town. The last table he passed was crowded with gentlemen officers, their ribald conversation inspired by more than a few bottles of shared spirits. Ben's blood boiled to hear Washington's name bastardized by every tongue, but he ignored the tired, familiar epithets and searched the room for Jotham.

He knew there was a chance that his friend might have been captured or shot. Thus far, he'd had no way of finding out. After the skirmish in the woods, he hadn't dared go near the meeting place. And though he trusted the reverend, he couldn't risk revealing any interest in the tavern, nor ask after his friend by name, without exposing the both of them.

Claiming an empty seat by the fire, he drummed his fingers on the table, giving every appearance of an impatient customer in need of a drink. The room teemed with locals and redcoats alike, though—like water and oil—the two groups knew far better than to mix. Since taking the fort, the British had all but claimed the tavern as their own, connected as it was to King's Ferry. As long as none of the local customers spoke loudly against the king, they were permitted to remain. And while most knew better than to shoot down a redcoat for fear of widespread reprisal, the whole arrangement simmered like a pot doomed to boil over at the slightest provocation.

Silas Eldridge, the tavern's elderly proprietor, tossed out any man who threatened the status quo. He was by all appearances an ardent opportunist. In the early days of the war, his tables were crowded with hot-blooded Patriots. As soon as the British took the fort, however, he made a spectacle of surrendering himself to their cause by tacking a gaudy portrait of King George above the bar. From this place of apparent prominence, the bewigged king looked forward with a closed-mouthed smile. To Ben, everything about the monarch conveyed wealth and self-importance, from his golden suit and billowing robe to a dainty pair of ivory satin shoes.

Ben stared upward at the shrine, matching his so-called-sovereign's lofty gaze with a dissenting twitch of his lips, but his fingers, which had been drumming the table all this time, froze when he looked sideways and saw Jotham slipping into the room with a few logs tucked beneath his arm. Relief quickened Ben's pulse. Then, almost immediately, he set to plotting.

His first task was to establish a suitable cover with the redcoats. Though there was little time, he could develop a decent enough rapport if he had something to offer. Ben dabbled in trade for this very reason, so he might always have a suitable cache of goods and money in his pocket. Reimbursements from Washington were a pittance and often delivered late, if at all. Smuggling proved the easiest way to finance a career that required him to rove about. Besides that, it was not an uncommon side business for otherwise respectable merchants.

They had the war to thank for that.

Many in the city enjoyed luxurious imports—Spanish olives, Scottish salmon, spices from India—but rebel farmers in the country hoarded basic provisions like milk and beef, which made them hard to come by in British-held cities and exorbitantly expensive. Fresh produce was often traded for imported goods. While soldiers at Stony Point were well supplied with rations, officers bred for better living might be eager to get their hands on some rare bit of finery, not part of the usual shipments, and here was Ben's best chance at slipping in.

Jotham tossed a log onto the fire, raining sparks upon the hearth. If the man had been at all worried about Ben after the ambush, he didn't show it. There might have been a tightening at his jaw when he spotted Ben. Yet again, there might not have been. It was always hard to tell with Jotham. In their school days, he'd been a moody boy with wide, tragic eyes and disheveled hair. He was sturdier about the shoulders now, his former lankiness outgrown, but as far as Ben had been able to see, the passing of four years had altered little else about him.

Ben removed his hat and tossed it on the table.

A few seconds later, Jotham appeared at his shoulder. "What will you have, sir?"

Angling back in his chair, Ben made a small show of mulling this over. "A glass of your best sherry," he decided at last. "And a bit of snuff."

Ordering, in this case, was a particular business. Whereas sherry signaled an emergency, requesting snuff indicated they needed to meet, in twenty minutes or so, in the cellar. Jotham dismissed Ben's order cuttingly. "All out."

"Out of sherry, you say?"

"And snuff."

Ben glowered. He recognized the familiar fury hidden within Jotham's insipid expression, and, after their close scrape in the woods, had no doubt his sour friend had dumped all the sherry in the Hudson just to get back at him. But even if Jotham wanted out of the game, Ben couldn't let him go—not until he warned him that their note had fallen into Rebekah's hands.

He had no idea what, if anything, she intended to do with it. As soon as he'd realized it was missing, he'd gone to the brothel to speak with her. She was already on the road by then, and so he'd followed at a short distance that he might confront her privately.

Then the soldiers had come.

He'd ducked behind a tree, shielded by the rain, and seen a good deal to set him ill at ease. The lieutenant had history with her. Of this, Ben was certain. But whether that same man held her loyalty—well, this was another matter entirely.

Ben glanced carefully at a few officers who had all stood at once. "A pity," he mused, "for sherry does sound the *very* thing . . ."

Jotham dropped a hand to Ben's shoulder—the left one, where he'd been shot—and clenched. A nondescript gesture, friendly enough, yet viciously deliberate. "Choose something else or be on your way."

His breath shallow with pain, Ben bit out a strangled reply, "Ale, then."

Jotham released his hold, slinking off to fill the order. A moment later, his uncle shuffled into the room, his lean frame stooped over a walking stick. Silas Eldridge had a cadaverous appearance on his best days, with eyes slightly sunken and bones extending from beneath his papery skin. Ben, privy to the man's true political inclinations, knew there was nothing rickety about the fellow. Those eyes, though sunken, were remarkably sharp and calculating. Without a British audience, Ben had an inkling the older man might have tossed that cane aside and skipped all the way down the stairs.

Instead, he released a long, phlegmy cough. "Build up the fire," he scolded his nephew, hacking into his handkerchief. "I feel a distinct draft in this old wretched catacomb of a parlor. For shame, but the colonel's drink is nearly empty. Don't you see? Fill it. Fill it now!"

Jotham scowled but did as he was bid. His parents had died when he was too young to have known them. His uncle, an entrepreneur by nature, had no children, so he'd taken the boy under his protection and paid for his education, with the transactional understanding that Jotham would one day return the favor.

Apologizing on his nephew's behalf, Silas slipped in with the table of redcoats. Ben couldn't hear every word beneath the ruckus, but, within minutes, the men were guffawing loudly, their drinks refilled twice at the old proprietor's urging. Silas had a marked talent for setting men at their ease. He prodded and flattered, encouraging them to share their grandest battlefield triumphs. As he listened to their tales, his eyes watered with a faraway look, as if he would join their ranks in an instant if he could but scrub away the inconvenient weathering of some thirty-five years.

Jotham cut the tableau by plunking down a tankard of ale before tossing a small scrap of paper beside Ben's fingers. Ben prayed it was a hidden message, something to indicate that Jotham wasn't lost to the cause but was simply being more careful. But, no. All Ben found, as he slid the paper into his hand, was a receipt for a single ale.

Deciding it best to retreat for the moment, he drank the contents of his tankard, then felt for his pockets. "Forgive me, but I seem to have misplaced my pocketbook. Confounded nuisance, but I'm sure a few of my personal effects have gone *missing* as well. Do you mind if I pay you tomorrow?"

He didn't wait for Jotham's reaction but donned his hat and slipped through the crowd, cursing the whole fiasco in his mind as he went. His assignment in Haverstraw had been fairly straightforward—to ensure Jotham and his uncle remained useful assets and to keep lines of communication open with Wayne.

So far, both missions were in grave peril.

He could turn them back around. He had to. It didn't do to imagine otherwise.

For if the redcoats didn't see him strung up from the nearest tree, then General Wayne—who was not called Mad Anthony without reason—would certainly find cause to do so.

CHAPTER 7

Three Years Before

All Rebekah's pain, the hideous, splitting pain, was nothing to the numbness that followed. The pain of broken promises, the pain of self-imposed excommunication—yes, even the pain of labor—none of it came close to that cold, silent walk to the church.

Skin nipped raw by rough wind, Rebekah watched the snow gather on her father's hat. Within her sleeves, her fingernails sliced into her palms as she willed him to turn around, to look at her. Just one glance, she thought. One glance, and he would see the empty look in her eyes. Surely then he'd change his mind.

Shoulders stiff, he pushed through the gate, his boots crunching buried leaves and sticks as they circled the building. There, to the right, was the graveyard, a garden of mismatched headstones guarded on all four sides by stiff white fence. As they approached a small side door, her father took a moment to straighten his hat, then turned, holding out his arms.

"Give him here."

With vacant eyes, Rebekah stared at his hands, then at the tiny bundle in her arms. She folded down the top corner of the blanket, revealing a smooth, pale cheek and the thin curve of a blond eyebrow. She drew herself up, waiting to feel something. Piercing pain, perhaps, or regret, or even fear. But the seconds gathered like the snow, one on top of the other, and not a single emotion stole upon her.

Perhaps her mind knew her body couldn't endure the truth of what she was doing. She'd become so small, so frail those past few months, had been sick twice as often as she wasn't. Perhaps the numbness was only the result of feeling too much, of hurting more than she could handle.

Or perhaps she really was a wretched mother.

Her father must have sensed her indecision, for his voice softened. "It's for the best." He drew the blanket back up to cover the baby's cheek, shrouding him from her sight. "He's better off here. You know he is." He met her eyes and attempted a smile. "You have to trust me."

Trust me. Mason had told her that, too, and she had, with everything.

Anger reared like a serpent within her. Clenching her teeth, she bit down on her tongue for fear she would scream.

Her father translated her silence as compliance and took the baby from her arms, ignoring his daughter's empty, fisted hands as he pounded upon the sacristy door.

Reverend Wainwright must have been expecting

them. The door swung open immediately, and there he stood, a thin, spectacled man, the kind who greeted everyone he met with a bright, broad smile. Everyone, that is, except for Rebekah, who squirmed beneath his scrutiny because he was certainly *not* smiling now.

Without prelude, her father held out the child. "As we discussed."

Reverend Wainwright removed his glasses and tucked them in his pocket. As he held out his arms, Rebekah couldn't help wondering if he'd done this before.

How many babies?

How many mothers?

She wrung her hands and shifted away from him, stifling the scream gathering in her chest.

Just as quickly as the reverend had reached out his hands, he slowly drew them back. "Are you . . . certain?" He asked the question falteringly, as if he'd never thought to ask it before.

"Of course she's certain," snapped her father, thrusting the baby toward him.

The reverend did not move.

Rebekah tipped her head, her eyes tracing the narrow steeple towering behind his bony shoulders. Nearly a year had passed since she dared enter the church. Since her father had permitted her to leave the house at all, lest news of the baby get out. In the early days, before she'd had no choice but to tell her father the truth of her condition, she sat beside him in their family box, head bowed, praying again and again that Mason would return for her. If only he would claim the child, if only he would marry her—

Amen, amen, she'd said with fervor.

Yes, yes, it shall be so.

"Tell the reverend," her father insisted.

"I'm certain," she echoed quietly.

Rebekah's father placed a hand upon her shoulder. To Reverend Wainwright, it might have seemed a supportive gesture, meant to steady her, but Rebekah knew better. How could she ever provide for her baby if her father cast her out for keeping him?

The reverend swooped forward and lifted the baby from her father's arms. "Have you named him?"

Eli.

Rebekah clamped her lips together to keep from speaking the name. She'd whispered it to her son so many times. As she fed him, as she clothed him, she impressed his name upon him, hoping he might someday be struck by the remembrance of it. Once her son was given to another family, his name would be all she had left, all that was hers and hers alone, and so she shook her head.

"I'll find a good home for him," promised the reverend. "He will be safe."

Her father spoke his thanks when Rebekah would not. He shook the reverend's hand with a grateful smile. As he turned away to lead her home, not once did he look back at the baby he'd left in the reverend's arms.

Rebekah vowed never to forgive him.

Present Day
June 19, 1779

The trees in the grove were unchanged. So, too, the heady musk of moss blanketing the damp rocks. Yet, as Rebekah paced from one end of the clearing to the other, none was as she remembered, least of all herself.

Four years ago, Mason had left behind a young admirer with twinkling memories of a long winter romance. Rebekah's edges had been roughened since then, the bloom nearly scoured from her cheeks. Now, she never trusted men, never felt anything for them, only survived off their piggishness and loose purse strings. Normally, she never thought too hard about what she did for a living—tried not to care—but she worried Mason knew her well enough to spot the changes in her, to wonder what they meant. And while she couldn't stand the thought of lying to him any more than she already had, she was far too terrified to tell him the truth. If she did, she had no doubt he would leave her again, as any sensible man would.

She banished these thoughts with a shake of

her head, reminding herself that he might come to love her before he knew the truth. Such a nasty deception, she knew, unlikely to work, and yet—

"You're twice as beautiful as I remember."

Rebekah turned. She tried for a cheerful smile, but this was already one lie too many, for she nearly flinched when she saw him.

Mason was as striking as ever in his dazzling red uniform, his tall boots glistening beneath a sheen of dew. His smile was warm, flattering, but even this did not settle her thoughts. It reminded her of all the men who thought of her beauty as a commodity, something to be used up and spent.

She tamped down the thought, forcing herself to speak. "I wasn't sure you'd come."

"I said I would."

His words sounded sincere, absolute, yet Rebekah questioned his dependability. He'd promised to write to her too, to return for her. He'd done neither.

She shook her head again, wrenching free that thorn of bitterness. Now was not the time to rake him over the coals. Flirtation was a language all its own, one she'd mastered long ago, but even as she told herself to be charming, her tongue sat heavy as stone.

Mason shifted closer. He moved a stray hair away from her face. "You're pale as a ghost. Tell me your thoughts, I beg you."

"I waited for you," she whispered, feeling very

like a ghost, indeed. "For four years, I waited."

The accusation building in her chest, which a moment before had carried but a quiet wisp of foreboding, took form and stood between them.

Mason drew back. He opened his mouth, then snapped it shut, shaking his head until he and Rebekah were both struck dumb by his silence. "I never meant to leave off as I did. I swear to you I didn't. I was young and foolish."

"*You* were young?" She let slip a resentful laugh. "I'd never been with a man before you, and I'd certainly never been jilted by one."

His left brow dipped defensively low. "You'll have to forgive me the indelicacy of pointing out that you didn't write me either."

All opposition fell dead within her. Of course, she should have written. Even her father had told her as much, though at the time fear had commanded her silence. She worried she was nothing to Mason but an amusing distraction, that he would scorn her pleas when he learned of the child or else be furious that she'd given him away. She could see now that she was mistaken, that Mason still felt something for her. Whether he would prove faithful enough to act on it, she had no idea, but she couldn't tell him of the child now without appearing false and duplicitous.

His voice softened to a caress. "My position was much too unpredictable to have taken on a wife, which we both know is what would have happened if we'd kept on. In truth, I thought you'd be married by now."

She laughed again, an empty, brittle sound. If known, the time she'd spent in his bed would have made her unmarriageable to any man of her standing. Mason's hopes were foolish at best. At worst, a practiced rebuttal.

Mason had never been one to fidget, but he fidgeted now. "Is this why you agreed to meet with me? To rail at me? Put me in my place? Give as good as I gave to you?"

"If that is what you think, Lieutenant Davies, then you do not know me at all."

Her formal tone fooled no one, least of all Mason, who took her chin and angled her face. He had the piercing eyes of a keen officer, sharp and searching. "Then what?" he demanded.

"I wish only to know where we stand with one another."

He dropped his hand, guarded still, though one blond brow rose in consideration of her words. "Where, exactly, should you like to stand with me, Miss Stanton?"

Here was the moment for truth, if Rebekah could be brave enough to speak it. With a grave show of dignity, she perched on the nearest rock, her satin skirt draping her knees, and forced herself to speak plainly. "I've missed you, Mason. More than I care to admit, and yet 'tis the truth. We mattered to each other once. At least, you mattered to me, very much, and so I wondered, or rather hoped, that you might feel the same, that we might pick up where we left off. That is, if you're inclined to."

She feared he might laugh in her face, that he might beg his excuses and be off, but he took her hand at the end of this little speech, his fingers circling her wrist very gently, like a bracelet. Rebekah's breath hitched at his touch. She lifted her chin, unnerved by the depth of unspoken feeling in his eyes, which he softened with the slightest curl of a smile.

"I'm inclined," came his answer.

CHAPTER 8

Rebekah and Mason didn't dally long.

With each passing moment, she expected him to move closer, to kiss her at least, but he had transformed himself into propriety incarnate. He inquired about her family, to which she replied with vague disinterest, and when he asked if she'd entertained any other suitors in his absence, she sought to distract him with a compliment by saying none of her suitors had been able to hold a candle to him in her estimation. This pleased him. In turn, he spoke to her about his undertakings in Pennsylvania, how he'd been involved in the Battle of Paoli, how he'd never stopped thinking about her in the midst of it all.

"Can I call upon you again?" he asked when at last he stood to leave. "Perhaps somewhere a bit more . . . chaperoned?"

Rebekah nearly laughed to hear such caution given to protecting her reputation, and yet it only made her feel all the more wretched for lying. She had no way of knowing how Mason would react if he learned how many men she'd serviced, some of them likely his subordinates. Her reputation would be worth very little once the truth came out, far less than the usual two shillings.

"I don't see how that's possible," she replied. "My father never much cared for you, you know."

"Some things don't change, I take it?" He laughed ruefully, staring out at the trees. "Well, if I can't be received at your father's house, I suppose I shall have to receive you at my family's."

At this suggestion, Rebekah dropped her gaze. Mason's parents had died almost a decade ago, after which their property had passed to Mason's elder brother, Jacob. Rebekah had been to their home only once—four years ago, when she first received word that Mason was being sent from Haverstraw. That day, Mason had been looking after things while his brother was away on business, and so he and Rebekah had found themselves alone. She ached to remember his crushing embrace. It seemed impossible that one encounter could have redefined her so completely.

Since then, Mason's brother had married a fine young woman from the city who had little patience with a place as remote as Haverstraw—or as Patriot-minded, for that matter—and so the old Davies home had remained vacant for the last several years.

And would be vacant still if Rebekah agreed to meet with Mason there . . .

He took her hand when she didn't speak and pressed her fingers. "I've made arrangements to set a few things in order there, next week on

Tuesday. Would you chance to meet me there in the afternoon? Say, three o'clock?"

Rebekah's toes curled into the bottoms of her shoes. Most of her customers were philanderers, adulterers. Some were drunkards who couldn't help themselves or else restless young soldiers who snatched at every bit of pleasure in case they perished on the field. Mason was nothing like them. He didn't deserve to be lied to, to be manipulated into a marriage he might not want. She ought to speak the truth before her lies yanked her any deeper, but guilt and dread warred within her stomach, silencing her.

If she told Mason about Eli, there was a chance he would marry her out of a sense of duty. Yet again, he might just as easily rage at her for lying to him, for manipulating him, for turning to a life of debauchery after tossing away their child. If he was angry enough, he might hand her off to the likes of Peter Nelson, to be made an example of for her depravity. Or, if he truly wanted to punish her, he might dig out two shillings and have her on the usual terms.

"I'll be there."

Mason's smile broadened at her answer. He touched her cheek but kept an otherwise respectable distance. Rebekah closed her eyes. She'd forgotten how pleasant it was to have even the smallest of formalities observed by a proper suitor, and so she swayed closer, leaning into his touch a moment before he stepped back, into the mist, and was gone.

By the time Rebekah left the grove, the sun hovered on the horizon, casting long, spindly shadows in front of her. The evening air was uncommonly still. She passed Haverstraw Bay, where British ships drifted powerfully along the Hudson.

Before the British had occupied the fort, they'd carried out a campaign of raids and incursions along the shore. Stealing aground in the thick of night, they would raid a handful of homes, perhaps lift a few pigs, and then duck back onto their ships before the rebels could intercept them. Some nights, they simply glided up and down the water, firing along the shoreline, pluming the air with heavy smoke. One woman, whose home was much too near the water, had been forced to crawl through the woods with her infant son in her arms, seeking shelter at a neighbor's house out of range of their firing.

Since taking Stony Point, nearly all such raids had ceased, and so the bay was serene, albeit under the constant, watchful eye of British warships. A few local men felt so at ease as to sit upon the shore, fishing lines cast far out in the water. Rebekah paused to rest her legs, studying the mix of fair and swarthy faces gathered there.

In that moment she spotted her father walking

on the other side of the road. He was too tall to miss, with broad shoulders and a wide gait, and he wore the same fine green coat she'd seen him wear a hundred times to church.

He must have felt her gaze, for he turned at exactly the same moment and met her eyes.

Rebekah's pulse pounded in her throat.

Her father looked much the same, wealthy and well. Working in merchant circles, he'd once been a sociable type, attending every church function, every weekly market, and dining with various families throughout the county. The gossips said he'd long since made a hermit of himself because of Rebekah, because he could no longer stand the sight of his profligate daughter.

A rider and horse trotted up the road between them, but still they stared, until Rebekah felt the urge to rush forward, to throw herself at his feet. *Oh, Father, perhaps I could forgive you, if only you would forgive me . . .*

But even if she spoke the words, nothing would change between them. Mrs. Pendergrass had made sure no one from her old life would ever want her again.

And Rebekah had let her.

Her father removed his hat. He turned it once over in his hands and walked the other way.

CHAPTER 9

June 20, 1779

Ben entered the tavern an hour before closing. Raucous laughter in the parlor masked his arrival, allowing him to slip upstairs without being seen.

Jotham's chamber was at the end of the unlit hall. With a backward glance to ensure only empty shadows followed him, Ben slunk inside, leaving the door open a taunting inch. The room, he discovered, was as nondescript as its occupier and impeccably ordered. Comb and brush were arranged on the table an even inch apart. Hat and coat had both been brushed free of hair and hung neatly on pegs to the side of the door. The desk drawers were nearly empty, save for an account book and a thick parcel of letters, which was bound with a pale pink ribbon.

Ben chuckled, considering the feminine hue of this bit of trimming. If nothing else, it suggested his ornery friend was not as stiff and noncommittal as he otherwise seemed. Loosening his collar, Ben closed the drawer and sank into a chair in the corner to await his friend.

All the while, the British carried on downstairs, laughing and sporting, oblivious to the spy lurking right above their heads.

Not for the first time, Ben's thoughts shuffled to another schoolfellow, Nathan Hale, who had been recruited as a spy early in the war. While most reconnaissance missions at that point were mad dashes across enemy lines, Nathan had been planted with a cover story, as a schoolteacher seeking work, and tasked with raking in useful information. This new form of espionage might have worked had the savage ranger, Robert Rogers, not recognized him.

Nathan had swung for his crimes.

His death was a constant source of grief for those who knew him and a stiff reminder to Ben that a spy could never afford to misplace his trust.

Scorn twisting within him, he waited until the last customers had withdrawn for the evening. He imagined Jotham putting out the fire, sweeping beneath the chairs, counting the money in the till. Nearly an hour passed before footsteps echoed on the landing, followed by the scuff of boots shuffling tiredly down the hall.

A punctuated silence settled when the footsteps neared the chamber where Ben was hiding. A moment later, the door was eased open by a careful hand, drawing barely a creak from the cranky, old hinges. For a moment, the newcomer stood framed in the doorway, straight backed, suspicious, the soft glow of a lantern illuminating the glint of a gun in his other hand.

When Ben chuckled, Jotham pivoted with an

oath, hoisting his lantern higher. "How the devil did you get in here?"

"No need to get chuffy," Ben said, straightening in his chair. "I wouldn't have come if it wasn't important."

Jotham shut the door, the lantern's glass panes rattling as he set it roughly on the table.

The gun, Ben noticed, was still in his hand.

"Well?" snapped Jotham. "Get on with it."

"It's about the letter I tried to pass to you the other evening. Someone's lifted it off me."

Jotham's face turned a corpselike shade of gray. "Do you know who took it?"

Ben nodded, which was all the reassurance Jotham needed. "Well good!" he said, gesturing impatiently. "Either he gives it back, or you have to silence him. 'Tis as simple as that."

Ben struggled. He knew this would be Jotham's solution. The man was cautious to be sure, but no slouch when the time came to be decisive. Neither was Ben. If they'd been dealing with a man, he might have suggested the same solution himself, but he wasn't so hardened to the cause as to shoot any woman, however meddlesome, in cold blood.

"Not *so* simple," he answered.

Jotham stared at him a moment before his lips curled in a scornful sneer. "Ah, it's a woman, is it? Very well. Tell me who she is."

"Why? What are you going to do?"

"Whatever needs to be done."

Before Ben could reply to that cryptic threat, voices sounded from close outside the tavern. Jotham edged away from the window, a muscle in his neck twitching. Ben wondered if, like him, Jotham had been thinking too much of Hale lately, of all the men they'd lost along the way because someone noticed something, some trifling detail that didn't make sense, and talked.

When Jotham spoke again, the anger was stripped from his voice. All that remained was undiluted fear. "Ben, please. I tell you, that letter *can't* be turned over to the British."

"What is it?" Ben stood. "What has you so uneasy?"

Jotham avoided his gaze, fiddling with the comb on the table. Then he muttered, "I'm getting married."

"Married!" Ben's voice was lodged halfway between a laugh and a scoff of disbelief. "Good heavens, man, I had no idea."

"It's been a fairly recent decision."

Well, this certainly changed matters. Nothing was more dangerous for a spy, especially one stationed in his hometown, than to have a family. Risks were more easily undertaken by men who had nothing to lose, no loved ones who could be turned or else used against them. For this very reason, Ben had once sworn to himself that he wouldn't marry until the worst of the war was over.

"Does she know what you are?" Ben asked.

"She's safer not knowing."

"I see. And what of your contact in the city? Any word there?"

"Not for months."

Which meant that Jotham's contact was either scared, compromised, or dead.

"All right," said Ben, bracingly. "Just listen, will you? Listen to me. You don't have to meet the courier. You don't even have to gather intelligence. But I need a cover. I have some goods I can trade with the redcoats, but I need an associate to connect me with them. Someone they already trust. Will you help me?"

"The British will never loosen their fist from around Stony Point. I tell you the devil's in it."

"Really? I can't help wondering if your uncle would be more cooperative."

This proposal was answered with a frosty silence, then grudgingly. "Suppose I can help you. What of the woman? The one who stole the letter?"

Again, Ben hesitated. Since getting swept up in the war, he'd engaged with many dangerous, unpredictable men. He'd been forced to shoot a few when they would have shot him first. He'd watched the life trickle out of them, sometimes slowly. War was ugly, made men do ugly things, and he'd accepted that. As a spy, it was in his best interest, and in the interest of his country, to use every method at his disposal to get Rebekah to hand the note over before she could betray him to Davies.

And yet, against every impulse of self-preservation, he wanted to protect her.

When Ben didn't answer, Jotham snorted. "She's a pretty one, I take it? Well, that doesn't matter. Until that letter's back in our possession, we have to assume she intends to hand it over to the redcoats."

Ben put up his hands. "What would you have me do?"

"Would anyone notice terribly if she disappeared?"

"You can't expect me to murder her."

"You have to do something," Jotham snapped, scowling again. "And quickly. Get her out of the way if you must, or else secure her trust. If you can do that, I'll do whatever you want. I swear it. Whoever she is, I don't care—just take care of that blasted woman."

CHAPTER 10

June 27, 1779

The Sawyers lived on the farthest outskirts of Haverstraw.

The husband was a farmer. The wife was a brickmaker's daughter. By all accounts, they were decent, hardworking people. They'd been married nearly ten years when, three years ago, they adopted an infant son of unknown parentage.

Rebekah never saw their child, nor heard his name, but as soon as she heard about the adoption she knew. Her first instinct had been to go to them, to see the child for herself so she might know exactly where her son lived and who was raising him.

She never found the courage.

Instead, she'd spent the better part of those three years imagining Mason's return. She would tell him of the child, and he would take her at once to Reverend Wainwright. They would be married. And then they would ride to the Sawyers' homestead and knock upon the door. "He's mine," Rebekah would say, taking up her child in her arms—

This was as far as she ever allowed her fancies to go.

Mrs. Sawyer had waited ten years for a baby, and now she was the only mother Eli, or whatever they'd named him, had known. Rebekah had not wept when she gave up her child, but Mrs. Sawyer was a good mother, the kind who *would* weep, and so Rebekah had never dared go near the woman's house.

But after her meeting with Mason in the grove, Rebekah knew it was only a matter of time. The following Sunday, she stood across the road from the old Anglican church, her eyes narrowed as a small exodus of stiff coats and prim hats exited the tall doors. The church was an old relic, as was Reverend Wainwright, who'd lived there as a bachelor all his life and served a thinning flock, most of whom were closet Loyalists like her father.

Rebekah spun Mason's ring around her knuckle, studying the reverend, who stood in his usual place in the doorway, genial as ever. As he shook hands and greeted his few remaining parishioners, she fought the impulse to march up to him, to demand to know what the Sawyers had named her baby.

And was he healthy? Was he tall for his age, or clever, or funny?

Who, exactly, had her son become?

As if sensing her scrutiny, the reverend shifted his eyes toward her side of the road. He'd been in the middle of an animated conversation with a handsome young couple, newly married by the looks of them, but his smile weakened when he noticed Rebekah standing there.

She'd not gone near the church since the day she'd stood upon the barrel, but sometimes she spied the steeple through the trees and felt that someday soon she'd have to pay for what she'd done—for the kind of woman she'd allowed herself to become. She stared at Reverend Wainwright in his black coat and collar, still fighting the urge to march up to him and wanting nothing more than to strike him in front of all the people who trusted him most.

How could you take him? she wanted to ask, but this was not fair, for she herself had told him to.

Reverend Wainwright spoke a hasty farewell to the smiling couple then stepped down into the road, his eyes pleading with Rebekah to wait for him to reach her—

She turned away, disappearing down the nearest path, and raced back to the boardinghouse. With every step she imagined going back to ask him the question that plagued her more than all the rest.

How could you not know I was afraid?

Later that evening, Rebekah descended the boardinghouse stairs, intending to fill a plate to bring back to her room. This was not unusual, as she usually kept to herself at mealtimes. The other girls were friendly enough, but something about their company unsettled her; too much like peering into a mirror, perhaps.

Hattie was going up the stairs as Rebekah was coming down. Younger than Rebekah by a few years, she was popular among soldiers on leave. Every morning, she applied a small beauty patch to the corner of her mouth, in the shape of a heart, to conceal a scar she'd inherited from a childhood case of smallpox. As she and Rebekah met at the center of the landing, Hattie's fingers curled around the banister, and the heart patch lifted as she flashed a pert smile. "Have you heard who came around asking for you?"

Rebekah became keenly aware of Mason's ring on her finger and resisted the urge to touch it. What if Mason had already learned the truth? What if he'd come looking for her?

The fear was only silenced when Hattie scrunched up her little nose and answered in her most scandalized whisper. "The *reverend*."

Certain she'd misunderstood, Rebekah forced a polite smile. "What about the reverend?"

"On my life, he came in asking for you. Mrs. Pendergrass told him you were seeing to a customer, but he insisted you be sent to him straightaway. That's what Martha told me." Hattie's heart patch jumped again as she grinned. "And who'd have thought it? Such an upright man, and old enough to be your father, I'm sure. Well, I suppose even holy men have their predilections. Mrs. Pendergrass says you're to go see him at once."

Though Rebekah didn't think much of the Reverend Wainwright, there was simply no reconciling Hattie's suggestion with the man she knew. After all, Rebekah had been in the trade for nearly three years and hadn't heard two words put together against him. He preached decency from his pulpit and never gave the impression of hypocrisy, at least not publicly. "There must be some mistake," she decided.

"I'm only telling you what Martha said. She was supposed to tell you herself, except she got caught up with a customer at the last minute."

Rebekah faltered. It had to be some kind of misunderstanding. Perhaps he only wanted to speak with her, to make sure she was all right; this certainly made sense after their brief encounter outside the church. "I'll speak to Mrs. Pendergrass."

"She's out," Hattie reminded her, climbing the last few stairs with a swish of her skirt. "You're more than welcome to wait for her, but there will be the devil to pay if she comes back and you've not followed orders."

Rebekah tried to think up another excuse. She hated the idea of returning to the church. It was the last place she'd seen her son, the last place she'd held him against her breast. And the reverend had been there. It wasn't his fault, yet it was, and now she was too confused to work any of it out in her mind. Of course, there was a chance that Hattie was right about the reverend's intentions, a chance he was as lecherous as all the rest.

After all, Rebekah thought miserably, he *was* a man.

But could she really go through with it?

Through the years, she'd crossed many lines within herself. For the most part, each line had been easier to cross than the last. But the thought of sharing the reverend's bed soured Rebekah's stomach. It made her think that someday she would cross a line from which there would be no returning, and no decent man would ever want her when she did.

CHAPTER 11

From the front room of the parsonage, which served as kitchen and dining room, Ben watched a line of redcoats finish their slow progression up the road.

"Come away from the window," scolded the reverend from behind him. "You're making me nervous."

"Just making sure none of my friends are planning on joining us for supper," Ben answered with a vague, half-interested smile.

The reverend hummed his amusement.

He'd been back and forth across the room for nearly an hour, hovering busily at the mammoth fireplace on the far side of the room. Various pots and trammels hung from an iron bar beneath the mantel, and the poor man kept nearly bumping his head as he maneuvered various dishes in steaming crockery. "Here I thought I was your only friend," he jested, grabbing a plate from one of the cluttered shelves near Ben.

Ben laughed without taking his eyes from the empty road, his thoughts stuck on the soldiers though they'd already turned out of sight. More than likely, they were retiring to the fort, but he couldn't help thinking they might just as easily make their way to Pendergrass House for supper.

He imagined them shuffling through the front door, glutting themselves on food and drink before they set to perusing the women . . .

As soon as he thought it, Rebekah's slow, scornful smile unfurled in his mind. He shook his head and stepped away, letting the curtain fall back in place. "I think I've stayed too long," he admitted, a bit more soberly.

"You've been careful," said the reverend. "Not a soul knows you're here."

"When I think of the danger I might have put you in—"

"Never mind the danger. Come and eat."

Ben turned and found that the reverend had plated a modest cut of veal accompanied by a loaf of bread and sauerkraut. A man of little means, perhaps, but Ben had been pleased to discover he was a more than proficient cook.

As Ben slid obediently into his seat, the reverend bowed his graying head, spoke the usual mealtime prayer, and set to slicing the veal in silence. He'd been quiet all afternoon, from the moment he'd returned from services, with more than his usual air of distraction. Ben wasn't sure if the presence of a spy was beginning to weigh on him or if it was another matter entirely. Given the nature of the reverend's calling, Ben hadn't wanted to pry.

Even so, if the man harbored any misgivings about their arrangement, it was best to know now.

From past experience, Ben knew it was never safe to stay with those who feared to share his company. "Is anything the matter, Reverend?"

The reverend shook his head, dropping a serving of sauerkraut on Ben's plate. "Worrying about a parishioner is all. Though I have been meaning to speak with you on another matter."

"I'm listening."

"You may not be aware, but I hire someone to see to some of the parsonage needs throughout the week—cooking, cleaning, that sort of thing."

Ben glanced around. "I've never seen anyone about the place."

"A young woman. Her father's one of the Hessian soldiers, and she has an ailing mother who lives in the city. Dreadfully poor family. When you came upon me that night, I sent her off to stay with her mother for a little holiday. I had a feeling, given your condition, you might wish to go unnoticed."

"And you're sharing this now because—?"

"I received word this morning. Her mother has died. I expect she will return any day."

Ben's chair legs clashed against the floor as he pushed up to his feet. Still sitting, the reverend lifted his hand as if calming a spooked horse. "Come, now. 'Tis nothing as dire as that. She's a quiet girl, keeps mostly to herself."

"I don't care how quiet she is. If her father's a

Hessian, then he answers to British command. I can't chance it."

Ben studied the reverend carefully for a reaction. Thus far, he'd never openly admitted to the man that he was a spy, and the reverend had never asked him outright. These were untested waters for both of them.

The reverend's eyes merely narrowed. "May I ask what your plans are from here?"

Ben glanced out the window again. Instinct told him he could trust the reverend implicitly, but that didn't mean he wished to put a holy man in any position that would require him to lie more than absolutely necessary. His answer was suitably vague. "I have business in Haverstraw which makes it imperative I stay. I'm waiting on a few resources, after which I should be able to set myself up in a position."

"I have no doubt you'll be hanged if you're discovered."

Ben smiled grimly. A strange way to live one's life, he sometimes thought, knowing if he was captured, if he was hanged, his death would be met with loud, triumphant *huzzahs*.

The reverend removed his spectacles, his lips withering. Then, with a sigh of resignation, said, " 'Tis getting much too late for you to go off tonight. You must take time to think, to plan. Stay one more night. In the sacristy, if that makes you more comfortable."

"In the church, you mean?"

"Until you've had time to think through your next steps, yes, I think it for the best. Though you must stay out of the sanctuary, unless to pray. On that point, I am quite firm. Too many churches have been desecrated in the mad pursuit of winning this war." For the first time, a note of resentment crept into the reverend's voice.

Ben understood. He'd heard of churches used for hospitals, for barracks, to lodge passing soldiers who wanted nothing more than a warm place to get cross-eyed drunk as they waited for orders. Some churches had been ransacked, their pulpits destroyed. One closer to home had all the windows smashed out and cannons rolled in their place. Ben hadn't stepped foot inside an actual church since his father's death, but, even to him, this was sacrilege.

"You don't seem a particularly political man," Ben observed at last, suspicious despite himself. "Why go out of your way to help me like this if you know, or at least suspect, what I'm about?"

The reverend smiled tiredly, then gestured Ben back to the table, where their supper was growing cold. "I have my reasons," he replied.

Her cloak folded around her like a pair of gray wings, Rebekah trudged the long way to the church. The lights in the parsonage were out by the time she arrived, which made her wonder if the reverend was already in bed. The sacristy window was lit, so she changed directions, circling the graveyard fence.

Here, she found the same narrow path she and her father had traveled the night Eli was lifted out of her arms. This made her feel as though she was haunting the memory of her younger self. If she closed her eyes, she could nearly hear her father's boots crushing sticks and leaves as he directed her forward. She could feel the warmth of her son's tiny body as she tucked him close to her breast.

Her father had been ashamed of her then, of the child she carried in her arms, but she shuddered to imagine what he would think if ever he learned the reason for her visit to the church that night.

Rebekah shook her head, refusing her father entrance into her conscience, and pushed through the front door, trailing through the hallowed hush of the sanctuary. When she reached the sacristy, she pulled down her hood, the better to face the reverend directly. She rapped on the door then shrunk back on impulse, amazed by what she'd done, plenty horrified.

Seconds passed before the door inched open and a tall man stood framed in the doorway, his eyes flashing with a spark of astonishment which Rebekah felt mirrored within herself.

For Reverend Wainwright's eyes were not the ones which greeted her—

They were the spy's.

CHAPTER 12

"What the dev—" he began, then seemed to remember where he stood, for he snapped his mouth shut. "Forgive me. I was expecting someone else."

"Likewise."

Her trite answer brought him the rest of the way to his senses. Darting a glance over her shoulder, he seized her by the hand and pulled her inside. Shutting the door roughly behind her, he demanded, "No one's with you?"

Nerves strung tight, Rebekah glanced around the room. A stub of a candle was lit on the table, its glow flickering over a tankard and an open book. Had the man broken into the church without Reverend Wainwright's knowledge? She could hardly believe the reverend would willingly hide a spy; yet again, Rebekah had done as much in her own way.

"What are you doing here?" she asked as he slipped a coat over his loose shirt. "Does Reverend Wainwright know you're here?" Another thought forced itself upon her, far more sinister. "You haven't hurt him, have you?"

"I should think not."

She turned to find the reverend standing in the doorway, a stack of folded blankets in his arms.

"Though your presence, Miss Stanton, I cannot account for in the slightest."

Rebekah's face burned as she remembered her disgraceful commission. "Mrs. Pendergrass told one of the girls you'd come by the house asking for me . . . ?" She tried to sound confident, unaffected, but her voice trailed into a question, after which a hideous silence descended.

The reverend's eyes boggled. The young stranger, whoever he was, coughed under his breath and turned away. Rebekah couldn't begrudge either man for floundering. Even she could hardly believe what she'd just implied.

"You thought that I—" The poor reverend shook his head. He could go no further.

Though Rebekah wanted nothing more than to sink through the floorboards, she'd been trained to handle embarrassments of this nature. "In truth, I didn't know what to think." She lifted her chin. "I was merely minding Mrs. Pendergrass, you understand."

"I can assure you I meant nothing untoward. I saw you outside the church today, and I wondered—well, I wondered if I might speak with you privately. Though I am *quite* sure I asked that you be sent by in the morning."

He glanced at the spy, who cleared his throat and, snatching up his book, slid through the door, presumably to wait in the sanctuary. As soon as he was gone, Rebekah felt more at ease, but then

Reverend Wainwright closed the door. “It seems you’ve met Ben,” he said.

Learning the spy’s name, or else his alias, touched a raw nerve which had been growing tenderer for days. “He’s a spy,” she blurted, relieved to finally speak the words. “For the rebels.”

“Really?” The reverend smiled mildly. “How surprising.”

Rebekah stared at him, aghast. “Have you any idea the risk you’re taking? Good heavens, sir, you answer to the crown.”

“No. I don’t.”

He’d spoken the words steadily enough, but Rebekah swayed back on her feet as if he’d shouted them. She never would have thought to hear such a response from Reverend Wainwright. He was as traditional an Anglican as they came, nothing like the so-called “Black Robe Regiment,” the Presbyterian pastors who preached openly against the crown from their pulpits. In awe, she watched as he removed his spectacles and laid them on the table between them. “The church will always be a place of sanctuary for those who need it.”

“Even for a spy?”

“I certainly hope so.”

A strange calm settled over Rebekah as vengeance came within an inch of her grasp. She could ruin the reverend. All she had to do was tell Mason she'd seen the spy in the sacristy, and the man's fate would be sealed. She closed her eyes and willed the anger to consume her as she often wished it would.

The anger did not come.

Yes, her arms were empty, far too empty, but this was as much her doing as his.

When she opened her eyes, the reverend had moved a few steps closer. "I did not come to talk with you about my guest, Miss Stanton, such as he is. I came to speak with you—well, about you."

"Really?" She lowered herself into a chair and turned her face away. "I can't imagine why."

"You're angry with me. I saw it outside the church. I see it now. And I understand. To be honest, when I think of that night, I'm just as angry with myself."

This admission surprised Rebekah. As far as she was concerned, Reverend Wainwright had rescued a child from the arms of an unfit mother and given him to the kind of family who deserved him. She thought he'd be pleased. Why should he give a woman like Rebekah a second thought? Unless—

She stood so fast her head swam. "Has something happened to my son?" she rasped.

"Not a thing," he assured. "He is well cared for, and, what is more, well loved by a good Christian family."

Relief swept Rebekah's body as she stumbled back into her seat. Moving slowly, as though expecting her to jump away, the reverend sat in the chair beside hers. "I believed you when you said you wanted to give him up. But that wasn't the truth, was it?"

Rebekah stared at her hands and imagined another woman—another mother—loving her son in all the ways she couldn't. "The truth hardly matters," she answered. "My child has a family, which is more than I could have given him."

"I did not realize then that it wasn't what you wanted, and for that I must apologize."

"Apologize to *me?*" She laughed. "You know what I presumed the nature of my visit tonight to be, good reverend. There is no need to prostrate yourself on my account."

"But your child—"

"He's not mine."

"Of course he is."

"What's done is done," she said, with far more conviction than she felt. "And, if I linger much longer, Mrs. Pendergrass will wonder why I return to her *without* payment from you."

She raised her brows and smiled scornfully, but if she thought she could fluster him she was mistaken.

"My door is always open," he said, "should you need counsel."

"What would the rest of your flock think to

see you speaking with someone like me on the regular?"

" 'Tis not too late to come back to us, Rebekah." His voice was soft but steady, answering a question she would never have dared to ask him otherwise. "It never is, you know."

Rebekah covered her eyes with her hand. Like flipping rapidly through the pages of a book, she remembered every man who'd ever touched her, who had followed her to her chamber and made her feel the full worth of two shillings—

She banished the memories with a slight shake of her head and settled inquisitive eyes upon the reverend. "I confess I do wonder what kind of sermon I might hear preached from your pulpit. Do you preach revolution, as your new friend might expect? Or submission to authority, as I'm sure your congregation demands?"

"I preach the Gospel," he answered drolly, then gestured her to be on her way.

CHAPTER 13

Rebekah didn't make it far. Ben saw to that. He circled the church while she was in counsel with the reverend and waited on the other side of the graveyard fence until he spied her shadow moving along the church wall.

"I can't help feeling you and I have gotten off to a bad start," he observed as she passed.

She stiffened in the darkness, then turned. She hadn't been able to hide her embarrassment in the sacristy, not even from him, but she betrayed no trace of it now. "What do you want?"

He took his time in answering as he studied her face. Of course, she was beautiful. She had fine, melancholy features and an elegant scowl, and all the powder in the world would never conceal the stray freckles around her nose, which made her appear slightly younger than her grave eyes otherwise suggested. Her beauty may already have caught his attention, but something else entirely held it now, for she showed both dignity and presence of mind as she stared at him, coolly, in unmasked challenge.

"I must be assured of your silence," he said. "It pains me to suggest it, but if you breathe a word about the reverend to anyone—"

"I would never turn him in."

Ben believed her, but there was also no overlooking her wording. She might not turn in the reverend, but she'd made no such promises where he was concerned.

"In that case, I have a proposal. A trade, if you will. For my letter."

"A loyal subject would hand any such letter over at once."

"Ah. So, you mean to say you *have* turned it in to Davies?"

"Of course I have."

Though Rebekah had thus far proven herself a capable liar, there was no missing the tick of agitation at the corner of her mouth. Ben tucked his knuckles beneath her chin, lifting her head to match his gaze. "If you're going to keep lying to me," he said in a low voice, "then you'd better look me in the eye—make me believe it."

Though he tried to soften his counsel with a slight smile, she stepped back out of his reach and set her jaw. "You said something about a trade?"

"I have useful connections in the city. I could get you silk. Perfume. Or, if you'd rather, thirty pounds would go a long way in setting you up away from Pendergrass House."

She laughed at that.

"Fifty, then," he haggled. "With the added caution that my associates would suggest I use far less diplomatic means to sway you."

This was more money than Rebekah could imagine acquiring in a single night, but she didn't accept.

"I've read stories of your militia," she said. "Homes and churches burned. Entire families cast out with nothing but the clothes on their backs. Men tied to their horses and dragged through the center of town. Tell me, is this what Haverstraw can expect of you?"

"Why should you be so protective of Haverstraw?" he parried. "Has Haverstraw been so protective of you?"

She didn't answer that. Neither did she laugh.

He changed tactics. "Let me put things to you another way. You've heard stories. Fair enough. But so have I. How do you think things will go for you if that letter is found on your person by, say, Lieutenant Davies? Little leniency is afforded a captured spy, no decency, even if she is a woman. Are you really so loyal to the crown that you'd risk it?"

She waved a frustratingly flippant hand. "It matters little to me who puppets the strings of this country. My life will look much the same as it does now regardless of the outcome."

Ben frowned as he considered her words. Of course, there was no easy way to determine a person's true political allegiances, regardless of any claims they made. There were those whose loyalty shifted like the wind, following whichever side seemed most likely to win. There were those who swore loyalty to the crown to cover a past of dormant revolutionary principles. Ben himself had once sworn such an oath to finagle himself out of prison.

In other areas, closet Loyalists remained silent for fear of being labeled a Tory by their neighbors. No one really knew the full measure of their neighbor, and so no one ever dared assume. Men's homes, their businesses could be burned at the slightest slip.

Then there were those rare few who fundamentally lacked any political conviction—mercenaries, most of them, who served the highest bidder—but Rebekah had never struck him as that kind of person. He wasn't sure what might have happened in her life to mark her with such ambivalence, or if, more likely, it was a mask she wore to protect herself. Perhaps she merely needed to be rattled, made angry. Angry like Ben had once been. Angry enough to care.

"I could give you enough money for a fresh start," he suggested. "Unless, of course, you enjoy letting pathetic men bed you for a living."

She gasped as if he'd struck her.

He hated to press her at her weakest, but he saw no other choice. "One hundred pounds," was his final barter. "British currency, of course."

Cold vehemence sharpened her features. "You

may pay for my services at the boardinghouse, sir, but I am otherwise *not* for sale."

She sidestepped him before he could counter and hurried away. Her refusal vexed him, as she, no doubt, intended, but even he had to admit—that time she'd been convincing.

Ben slipped into the sacristy and set at once to packing. He traveled light by rule—a few spare clothes, some bread, a knife, a book of prayers he'd lifted from his father's library on one of his last visit's home.

When Reverend Wainwright stepped into the room, he observed the scene before him with a woeful sigh. "You're leaving."

Ben closed up his haversack and shouldered it. "If she tells anyone what she's seen, you'll hang for treason."

"She won't."

"How can you be so sure?"

"For the same reason you are, I suppose, or else I'm sure you'd have detained her."

In Ben's line of work, trusting anyone, least of all a stranger, was rarely worth the risk. He'd already made himself a nuisance with Wayne by working only with men he knew intimately from previous experience. Schoolmates. Friends. He *never* worked outside his circle.

"I'll contact you as soon as I can," he said, cutting toward the door.

"And should Miss Stanton return? If she presses me for answers about our connection?"

"I'll deal with her," said Ben.

"And tell her what, exactly?"

"Best leave the lying to me, Reverend. I'm a bit better at it than you, I should imagine."

The reverend smiled wistfully. "I suppose you would be, Benjamin Renshaw."

Renshaw.

A nasty, dangerous impulse nearly prompted Ben to draw his pistol. His name—his *true* name—was his most dangerous secret, one he dared share with no man. To keep from doing something he might regret, he went very still, hand on the doorjamb, and whispered hoarsely. "Who told you that name?"

"No one told me. I merely suspected."

Ben puzzled over these words until the truth struck a blow. Winded by the force of it, he rounded on the reverend. "You knew my father?"

There was that droll smile again. "We were schoolfellows. We kept on through the years, until he died. I know some time has passed, but I do offer my sincerest condolences to you."

Ben could not accept the man's condolences, which were a distraction from far more pressing matters. "How did you know who I was?"

"I've suspected for some time. You look rather like him when you're irritated. Then I remembered what he told me of you."

"What was that, exactly?"

"That you had a particular penchant for Latin. And for gambling."

Ben nearly laughed to hear his younger years summarized so correctly. Yale had a strict policy where gambling was concerned—three strikes before one faced expulsion. He was on his third demerit when he'd gone home on holiday and began passing intel from Corporal Haskins to his contact. His father caught him rifling through the corporal's desk on his last visit home.

"Filthy traitor!" That's what Ben's father had called him.

The two nearly came to blows, except Ben's mother, who was neutral by nature, swept between them at the last second and said they were nothing more than a pair of stubborn mules.

"He loved you." Reverend Wainwright's voice prodded Ben back to the present. "You may not think it's true, but it is."

"He turned me in. Had me thrown in prison."

" 'Tis a kinder fate than hanging, don't you think?"

Ben turned away. He and his father had never been cut of the same cloth. His father was a man bred to arms, though he'd chosen to fight from the pulpit instead of the battlefield. He'd been dreadfully unpopular among closet revolutionaries, and well he knew it; he preached all his sermons with a loaded pistol beneath his robe.

More than anything, his father wanted Ben to share his conviction, his standing, but Ben had been unpredictable to a fault. He made friends in unlikely places. He gambled and took risks and, hang it all, he enjoyed it. His father might have forgiven him for joining the Continentals, for there, at least, was a gentleman's commission, punished by firing squad if one was taken by the redcoats. But spying was unscrupulous. Dishonorable. You swung for it like a blackguard.

"The church has more to offer than sanctuary," the reverend said, gently. "I can see you are lost, Ben. Confession would do you good."

Ben tried to smile so he might appear amused, but he couldn't fight an uncomfortable grimace as he turned toward the door. "I'd rather not."

"Are you too proud to admit your sins? Or too afraid?"

Ben wasn't sure what to say. It wasn't that he no longer believed in God. Quite the contrary. He still read from his father's prayer book when he felt the sting of his conscience. He still struggled to do what was right. But years of bitterness had set him on a prickly path, had choked him off from the church, and he wasn't sure he was ready to return. "I'm not afraid, nor proud," he answered. "The situation is simply too distracting."

"You won't always have time," cautioned the reverend. "Nor opportunity."

Repent. His father's final plea. He'd even promised not to turn Ben in if he would only confess his treason as sin and have done with it.

But Ben would not repent.

It was no sin to stand up to a tyrant, he'd insisted, and wasn't sure if he'd meant His Majesty or the kind of father who would betray his only son in that same sovereign's name.

"I'll be the first to admit my sins weigh as heavy as any man's, but they will have to keep until the world is right again."

And as Ben slipped through the door, he heard the reverend speak this answer to his retreating back. "The world will never be right."

CHAPTER 14

By the time Rebekah headed back toward the boardinghouse, it was nearly midnight. Having skipped breakfast and the midday meal, she could only pray there might be some scraps left from supper. She was halfway up the mist-shrouded road, dreaming of such delicacies as Coffey's autumn apple tarts, when she heard a strange commotion from within the boardinghouse.

Music, she realized after a moment, tilting her head to listen.

When she slipped into the parlor through the front door, she found no semblance of respectability. Tables and chairs had been shoved to the room's perimeter, the rugs rolled up and propped in random corners. A trim officer sat at the harpsichord, his fingers dancing along the keys with a proficiency Rebekah envied. Beside him, two men in homespun sat low near the hearth. One played the fiddle, the other a worn fife.

Couples were already dancing back and forth across the floor as the rest of the assembly kept time by clapping. On the other side of the room, Coffey milled about with a tray of food hoisted to the height of her shoulder, her hips swaying in time with the music as she stopped to set down a platter of Scotch eggs at one of the tables.

Stunned by the scene and wondering what Mrs. Pendergrass might say when she saw it, Rebekah slipped her cloak from her shoulders and nearly smiled at the foreign-sounding peals of genuine laughter.

Hattie was not nearly so reserved as Rebekah. Ribbons flying, she danced in the center of the throng with a ruddy-faced gentleman who swung her about three times so fast the poor girl stumbled breathless to a stop and blushed a full shade deeper than crimson. Then off they went with a start, moving about the scant length of the room, nearly bumping into the wall before they had time to pivot and turn.

Shaking her head, Miss Ward stooped to poke at the fire in the grate. "What a shameless lot." Her mobcap gave her the appearance of a disgruntled pastry. "Dancing around like a bunch of—"

Before she could properly land the insult, her hand was snatched by a cheeky young boarder who flounced her twice up and down the length of the room. The whole time, Miss Ward huffed and puffed and called him a rascal, but a wayward grin belied her bluster.

When the song ended, Hattie emerged stumbling from the fray, her brow sheened with sweat. "Oh, Rebekah!"—she hooked Rebekah's arm and shouted over the din—"You simply must come and dance! I can't remember the last time I had such a wonderful frolic, and—*oh!*"

Hattie's words tripped to a halt as she spied something over Rebekah's shoulder.

Rebekah could tell from the urgency of Hattie's sudden primping that it was a man, and a handsome one at that. She turned with a sigh, glancing at the door, and then felt herself sway.

The spy.

Of course it was him, she thought, with a peculiar tick of despair.

The other girls noticed him as quickly as Hattie, and no wonder, for he was clean and polished, wearing a fine gray coat over a bottle green waistcoat, his hair tied neatly back with a black ribbon.

Rebekah wondered where his money came from, this spy who gave no hint of having respectable employment.

Did treason pay so well?

One of the other girls squeezed between the dancers to take his coat, another to collect his bag.

Ben didn't seem to notice either girl. He scanned the room until his eyes settled, rather intently, on Rebekah. His lips twitched upward as Hattie tugged eagerly on Rebekah's arm. "He is devilish handsome!" Hattie hollered over the music. "Don't you think?"

"Devilish," Rebekah echoed dimly. "Aren't they all?"

• • •

The song ended to boisterous applause. As the dancers bowed and scrambled to secure new partners, Rebekah broke away from Ben's notice and slipped deeper into the crowd, finding a corner on the other side of the parlor where she could safely avoid him. As she slid into an open seat, the fiddler struck up a tune she remembered from her own dancing days. She kept time with her foot despite herself, tapping steadily until all at once the skin at the back of her neck prickled. A second later, she became aware of someone standing beside her.

"You're worse than a bad penny," she said without looking up.

His voice hinted at a smile. "Well, that's a fine way to greet a customer."

"A *customer?*" The muscles in Rebekah's shoulders tensed as she glanced upward.

He'd already removed his coat and now turned to observe the dancers, extending a hand toward her. Reading his intention, Rebekah shook her head, too late, for he hooked her fingers before she could utter a word and pulled her from her seat and backward with him into the frivolity.

Once they took their places on opposite sides of the aisle, Rebekah's head cleared a bit. This was only a dance, she reminded herself, and he was only a man. If she thought of him as a customer and nothing more, it would be easy enough to dismiss him and be done.

Though it had been years since she'd danced in a formal setting, she forced herself to recall the steps. She skipped once, stepped forward, then accepted his hands as they circled.

"How long will you be staying with us?" She asked the question in a proper, cordial tone.

His lips curved. "Spoken like a woman who can't wait to be rid of me."

"In my defense, our first encounter did little to recommend you."

"It certainly recommended *you*."

She tilted her head at the compliment, supposing he was alluding to her beauty, as most men did.

"I've rarely seen anyone think so quickly on her feet."

She frowned. This was not the kind of praise to which she was accustomed, but the dance forced them to separate before she could respond. He offered his hand to the girl beside them as Rebekah accepted the lead of the man adjacent. This man was older, more reserved, though his eyes slid appreciatively over her curves. She kept an absent expression as she went through the motions with him, skipping in step and circling the other couples before her hand was claimed, again, by the man she knew only as Ben.

He moved her deftly about the narrow space, always anticipating the next move so she hardly had to worry about remembering which way to turn.

"It seems you're rather quick on your feet as

well." Rebekah spoke this compliment with an uninterested air but could not help adding a playful smile, at which he barked a laugh.

"Minx," he called her.

They separated again. Half a dozen skirts swirled around Rebekah as the couples weaved about, the tight crowd infusing her with warmth. She watched as Ben ushered Hattie up the row—the younger girl stood on tiptoe, speaking quickly in his ear, and he smiled readily, dipping his head close as he answered.

Rebekah frowned, wondering if he was like other men, as much at ease in one woman's company as another's, or if this was simply a game he played for the benefit of his cover.

A moment later, he was reunited with Rebekah, his hand curving warmly around her hip. "You look like you have something on your mind."

"I can't help wondering"—her words were cut as another couple swept briefly between them—"that is, I can't help wondering why you've remained in Haverstraw."

"I work the merchant circle. I have a bit of negotiating to do with one of the business owners nearby."

He spoke his answer casually and efficiently, though they both knew she wouldn't believe a word. More than anything, she wanted to catch the spy in one of his lies, if only to see him startle. "Really?" she said. "Which business?"

"I can't answer that. My clients demand discretion."

"The London Trade, I take it?"

He chuckled but didn't answer. How could he, she thought, when no less than six redcoats danced nearby?

"The London Trade" was well-known slang for the black market. Granted, the soldiers were as likely to make friends with him as they were to arrest him for it. Both sides profited from the trade, and so both sides, for the most part, turned a blind eye. He played a dangerous game, though, for one had to know exactly who they could bribe—and who they couldn't.

After that, the musicians quickened the pace so that Rebekah could hardly remember where she was supposed to step. Ben firmed his hands as he guided her, and she followed his lead though she felt a growing twinge of suspicion she couldn't fully account for.

His hand brushed her waist, her hip, and then—

Without missing a step, she caught him by the elbow, preventing him from reaching his hand into her pocket. In the moment, she was too stunned by his nerve to be the least bit angry.

"Looking for something?" She smiled, glad she'd had the foresight to sew his letter into the hem of one of her curtains so as not to carry it on her person.

Ben let the music guide him a bit closer than

necessary, laughing lightly against the curve of her neck as he reeled her around with the other dancers. "Can you fault me for trying?"

Her heart skittered as she pushed back to look at him. Their previous encounters had set them at odds, and she wasn't exactly sure why. She didn't really mind so much that he was a traitor. After all, she'd made bedfellows with men from both political camps. Perhaps it was because he'd made their standoff personal, in a way, by mentioning Mason, by trying to rile her into cooperating with him. Until that moment, he'd been an opponent, an adversary to be bested, but as she stared at him now in the flickering light, it was hard to see him as anything but a roguish young man with thoughtful blue eyes.

She edged away even farther at the thought, nearly bumping into the couple behind them. "The dance is ending," she observed as the musicians finished the song.

"Oh, but I don't think it is," Ben countered, a faint smile playing about his mouth even as she snatched her hand from his and turned into the crowd.

June 28, 1779

This time, when Ben entered The King's Ferry Tavern, he was greeted with an enthusiastic wave from the elder Mr. Eldridge.

"Mr. Clarke!" Jotham's uncle hobbled across

the parlor, his stooped weight slanted to the side as he leaned into his cane. "How long it's been since we've done business. It's a thrill to see you again, lad. A *thrill!*"

Ben clasped the proprietor's extended hand and smiled, grateful that Jotham, though a grudging partner, had agreed to settle his cover.

Silas gripped him by the elbow and tugged him toward a small gathering of officers. "Gentlemen," he greeted throatily. "What a fine customer we have with us today. Mr. Clarke here went to school with my nephew. Old chums as they are, he's been known to offer our humble establishment the occasional bargain."

As far as introductions went, Ben's was over as soon as it had begun. One of them smiled, but the rest nodded uninterestedly and returned to their cups in less than a second. Before Ben could insinuate himself into the conversation—an awkward undertaking, to be sure—Silas set a hand on his shoulder, pressing him down into the last open seat as he lowered his aging voice to a conspiratorial whisper. "Oh, but I have the finest jars of mustard down in the cellar if any of you are interested in an afternoon tuck. Bit of bread, it's the very thing for His Majesty's finest."

The men glanced at each other in silent counsel before one of them shifted, setting down his tankard. "Mustard, you say?"

"All the way from Germany," Ben answered.

Silas jabbed the air with his cane. "Some upstart tried to sell me some last spring. Prices so high I thought we'd have to fight a duel. I begged Clarke to keep an eye out, for I have such a weakness for the stuff. Always back and forth to the city on other business, aren't you, boy? Most of it is aboveboard, I don't have to assure you, gentlemen, but he's always happy to make a trade on the side . . ." Silas trailed his words, and Ben was examined with far more interest.

"How do you get it out of the city?" one of the officers inquired.

"I have an arrangement with an old friend."

"What friend?"

"A fellow schoolmate. Can't share his name, of course, but he has access to all kinds of shipments out of the city."

Most of this was true. Thomas Millington had been at Yale at the same time as Ben and Jotham, though he was the caretaker's son. Since then, he'd been known to sell Ben the occasional cache of smuggled goods for a fraction of the cost. He didn't know Ben was a spy, but he knew Ben was a Patriot and of otherwise reduced means, and that was enough. Though Ben found it helpful to ground his covers in reality, it was frightfully dangerous; any offer of such services could just as easily be taken as a confession of guilt.

The soldiers were glancing at each other again.

One of them took a swig of his drink. Another shook his head.

"My wife's been desperate for tea," a portly man sitting to Ben's left broke in. "Supplies running so low, she's been brewing it with basil for flavor."

"Basil?" Silas interjected, scrunching his nose. "Horrid what we've come to. *Horrid!*"

Ben didn't answer straightaway. How strange, he thought, that the whole of one's cover could be so easily settled with a single jar of mustard.

Once he was sure he had them all hooked, he grinned and inquired, lightly, "What kind of tea does she prefer?"

Silas banged a hand on the table. "Splendid to do a bit of business, isn't it? Splendid!" Then, noticing Jotham behind the bar. "Jotham, my boy! What are you doing skulking about over there? His Majesty's men are hungry, can't you see? Bread, my boy, quickly, and do bring up some of that *delectable* mustard."

CHAPTER 15

June 29, 1779

For nearly ten minutes, Rebekah stood on the step, staring forward at the green door without announcing herself. She felt like a coward for not knocking straightaway, but she didn't know what to expect, not of Mason, nor of herself.

He'd already abandoned her with a child. He hadn't meant to do it, exactly, and yet there was nothing she feared now more than false promises. She knew how easy it was to lose herself to him—how blissful the night, how bitter the morning.

The last time she'd come to the Davies house, she'd not been sent for or even announced. An errand boy had delivered his note early in the morning, while she was brewing a cup of tea for her father, who was still abed.

> *Duty has called me into the fray. I will write to you as soon as I am able and remain loyally yours.—M.D.*

The words were aberrantly stiff, dispassionate, nothing like the fond, feverish notes he'd been known to slip into her hand as they passed on the road or, once, on the church steps after service. It was not the kind of good-bye a love like theirs deserved. Rebekah had repeated this to herself as she saddled her horse and sped toward his family's estate, hoping only to see him once before he departed.

Then she'd lost her senses and entered the house without knocking, calling his name from the bottom of the staircase. A servant in the hall squeaked in shock at seeing her there and turned quickly into the room from which she'd come.

Rebekah's embarrassment only intensified when she caught her reflection in a looking glass on the wall to the right. Goodness, no wonder the servant had fled. She looked nearly feral with her windswept curls askew and cheeks chafed red and raw from a wild ride through the bitter March air.

Before she could straighten herself, Mason had appeared at the top of the stairs. "What are you doing here?" he'd demanded, his voice an uncomfortable, angry crack of sound in the otherwise empty hall.

Rebekah shifted back on her feet as he descended the stairs. She'd never seen a man in any state of undress, but Mason wore only his breeches and shirtsleeves, his unbuttoned waistcoat flapping down the length of his torso. It occurred to her that he might have been finished with their romance altogether, wishing to make a clean break of things, and here she'd come like a lovesick chit to press him.

Yet, the man was bound for war. What if he was shot down? What if this moment was the last in which she could truly call him her own?

"I couldn't—" Her voice broke, betraying her, and so she licked her chapped lips and tried again. "I couldn't let you go without a proper good-bye."

"I'm not going forever."

"Yes, but I had to see you first."

"Why?"

"Because I love you."

As soon as the words passed her lips, Rebekah's cheeks flamed hot with embarrassment.

Mason merely stared at her, blankly, as if he hadn't understood the words.

Horrified, she spun to leave, but he snatched her hand before she reached the door and pulled her into his arms, tucking her face tightly against his chest.

At first, his embrace offered comfort, security. She felt abler to stand on her own two feet.

But then the air between them shifted. The depth of his breathing shallowed as his lips moved from her face to her neck, his kiss gentle at first, then urgent, pleading for an answer she thought herself ready to give. By the time he kissed her lips, Rebekah could hardly stand. She'd been lonely for so long, tired of passing evening after evening in silence. The only time her father voiced his thoughts in her presence was to grumble against the Patriots. Even then, he was more or less speaking to himself.

Mason had brought laughter back into her life. He'd made her feel excitement and companionship, made her heart beat twice as fast when she thought of seeing him, but even that was nothing to the pounding pace of her heart as they climbed the stairs together, as he kissed her again, more fiercely, walking her backward into his chamber—

Rebekah shook her head, rattling herself back to the present. Hardly knowing what she dared hope with a history such as theirs, she lifted her hand and knocked briskly on the door.

No one answered.

She balled her hand into a fist in frustration, nails piercing her palm as the silence lengthened. She nearly left, but she couldn't go. After all, Mason *was* expecting her. She had a place with him there, however fleeting. Emboldened by the moment they'd shared in the grove, she pulled the door open and stepped silently inside.

This time, no servants were about, and the whole house smelled ancient, like dust. Though not as fine a house as her father's, nor as large, it was a respectable brick structure with tall windows on the second floor and green shutters all around. Mason's late parents were farmers in name, but his father had nonetheless received a sturdy inheritance with which to run the estate.

The fields beyond were well tended in Jacob Davies's absence, but the halls and front room were silent, the furniture draped in faded white coverings. On the wall to the right, Rebekah found the same looking glass which had greeted her on her last visit. She drew herself up as she studied her reflection, but she could do nothing to alter the passing of time. In her deep burgundy gown, she seemed a good deal paler, a good deal thinner, a good deal less the girl who had stared back from the mirror all those nights ago.

She trailed her fingers down her cheek and turned away, facing the stairs as she called out, "Hello!"

Her voice didn't echo as she hoped but was swallowed up by the heavy drapes and rugs, a deadened sound. She waited for history to repeat itself, but Mason didn't appear at the top of the stairs, and so she pivoted, peering through the nearest doorframes on either side. The sitting room was empty. So, too, the dining room.

With a sinking feeling, she thought she might have misunderstood Mason's invitation, or else he'd changed his mind about meeting her there. She pressed forward anyway, quiet as a cat as she tiptoed down the hall, peering through doorframes left and right as she went. At last, she located him in a small library near the back of the house. The drapes were closed, the room as dark and dusty as a tomb. A faint halo of candlelight swathed Mason's features as he pored over a stack of papers at his desk, his lips thinned to a thoughtful line as he lifted the missive in his hand for closer scrutiny.

Rebekah, who couldn't help thinking he had the kind of profile history remembered—the kind men sometimes carved into statues—stiffened when Mason looked up without warning and locked eyes with her. "Spying, are we?"

Spying.

The word set Rebekah on edge, but then he slid the missive out of sight, his lips softening into a grin.

Though she was embarrassed to have been caught watching him, she returned the smile and stepped into the room. "I couldn't help it," she said. "I've always thought you have the handsomest crease between your eyes when you're thinking *very* hard."

"I see." He rose from the desk and crossed the room, standing so close she could smell the clove-scented soap on his skin. "Then I shall have to think very hard much more often."

Her heart tilted as he bent and pressed a warm, lingering kiss to her mouth. For years, wanting any man had frightened Rebekah more than entertaining all the men she hated, yet she was only seconds in and already sinking in his presence. If she wasn't careful, affection would lead to adoration, and that could only lead to something far more bewildering, something she wasn't sure she dared touch.

A vigorous knock at the door scattered all thought.

Mason's lips broke from Rebekah's at the same moment she turned to find no less than ten red-coats standing bottlenecked in the hall beyond.

Rebekah's face turned scarlet as the one in front strode into the library.

"Lieutenant," he greeted, removing his hat with a grave expression. "Forgive me for intruding, but there's an urgent matter. You're needed at once."

"Yes?" Mason demanded. "What is it?"

The soldier was making a commendable effort of not looking at Rebekah, but he tugged a bit at his collar, more visibly abashed than the rest of the men who were muttering and snickering in the hall. For his part, Mason stood as tall and unbending as ever, waiting for his subordinate to continue, but his shoulders were tellingly stiff, and no wonder. If his superiors learned he'd been alone with a single woman at his family estate, he faced serious censure.

And if the truth came out that the woman in question was a prostitute?

Rebekah clasped her hands, praying his men were loyal enough to cover for him.

"There was a raid," the soldier answered soberly.

"Rebels set fire to a Loyalist home to the south of Haverstraw. Poisoned all the horses. There's nothing left."

Embarrassment forgotten, Rebekah lurched forward, grabbing a table edge to remain upright. Fear strangled her for a moment. Then, with horror, she blurted, "South of Haverstraw?"

She could hardly believe she'd interjected her voice into such an official conversation, but she couldn't help it. Her father's estate was to the south. Had the mob burned his house? Had he been *inside* when they did it?

Mason ignored her outburst but demanded of the soldier in a tense voice, "Which estate?"

"Heston's place."

Rebekah's breath shuddered out of her. Caleb Heston was a man with deep pockets and loud Tory politics. He'd been known to shuffle crops and cattle to the British cause, which made his estate more of a target, but he and Rebekah's father were close neighbors. Though her father had grown quieter about his allegiances in recent years, if the rebels wanted to strike another blow against Loyalists, his home would be a practical mark.

Mason dismissed his man with a clipped nod. He reached for his hat, then his sword, giving a slight huff when he realized Rebekah was already six paces ahead of him and gaining on the door.

"Where do you think you're going?" he asked.

Rebekah hardly heard him. An inner army of images had assailed her, and she could think of nothing else—rebels marching up the drive to her father's house, pulling him from bed as they set his house ablaze. Tarring and feathering had not happened anywhere near Haverstraw, but it *had* happened, and far worse.

"I must return home," she answered. "To make sure my father is safe."

After everything that had happened between Rebekah and her father—after everything he'd done to her—this crack of fear, loud as thunder, confused her and overwhelmed her senses.

She remembered running into his arms as a child when he'd return home from business. She remembered him sitting with her through the night when she was once sick with fever. She remembered the garnet earrings he'd brought from one of his trips to the city—they weren't the finest jewelry in her box, but she'd worn them until the hooks were loose and they were nearly falling apart. Time and again, she'd told herself that these memories meant nothing, that they could never erase all the years of stiff silence and disapproval.

Even so, her father loved her. Perhaps not as well as he could, but insofar as he was able, he'd tried.

She made it down the hall but no farther, for Mason strode forward, hooked an arm around her waist, and pulled her back. "The roads won't be safe," he said. "You can't go."

"I must."

"I forbid it."

She glared until he sighed and took her by the shoulder, ushering her out onto the lawn where his men waited for him. "Escort her to the fort," he ordered one of his underlings. "Take her to my tent and keep her there until I return."

Panic rose up to replace Rebekah's earlier indignation. Some five hundred men were posted at the fort. Surely, one of them would recognize her. And when she was recognized—when she was seen in Mason's *tent*—it would look to all as though he was housing a harlot on His Majesty's grounds. Such a scandal would ruin his reputation, if not his entire career.

"Mason, wait." She planted herself and lifted her hands imploringly. "I need to speak with you. Right now."

"There isn't time."

"Yes, but—"

"It's only a minor precaution, until I know the roads are safe enough for you to return home."

"In which case I can just as easily wait for you here."

He shook his head, his voice growing terser. "If the rebels mean mischief, my home is no safer than your father's. Even now, they could be marching this way."

"Will the roads be any safer if I walk with a single escort?" she argued. "I tell you, it isn't necessary."

"*I* decide what's necessary," he answered, then signaled to one of his men, who stepped forward and took her by the arm.

Without another word, the soldier steered her up the path toward the road. She turned at the fence, catching one last glimpse of Mason, who stood framed in the doorway and surrounded by all his men. They listened intently, nodding at his orders without question. If she went to the fort, she had no doubt the truth about her occupation would come out, and Mason's superiors would make an example of him. They had trouble enough with men sneaking off to find bawds, let alone someone in Mason's position. His reputation, his position—all might be forfeit, and it would be entirely her fault for deceiving him.

Desperation made her dig her feet into the dirt, compelled her to say that which she would never have otherwise dared utter to a man in uniform. "Who do you think you are to order me about, Lieutenant Davies? I won't have it. I demand to be released at once!"

There was silence then.

One of the soldiers coughed under his breath. Another shuffled his feet.

When Mason lifted his head, his eyes were more severe than she'd ever seen. "If it's a choice you'd like, then here it is, Miss Stanton. My man may either escort you to the fort, or I can have him take you into custody. The choice, of course, is entirely yours."

CHAPTER 16

Rebekah's lies nipped and gnawed at her the entire way to Stony Point.

Her escort, who strode a few paces ahead, offered no distraction, but walked quickly through the woods, forcing Rebekah to straggle miserably behind. He was much younger than Mason, and somber, with rounded cheeks puffed out in a petulant scowl. She wondered if he was insulted by Mason's directive, if it was a slight against his pride to convey his superior's sweetheart about as if he was of no more use than a common errand boy.

Thankfully, they met with no resistance along the way. Muddy roads near the marshes were the only peril, and Rebekah's dress hem the only casualty. She hiked her burgundy skirt to the tops of her boots as they began ascending the road which led up to the fort.

Stony Point was the topmost jewel of a towering precipice, some hundred and fifty feet above the Hudson. The triangular peninsula was a veritable island in high tide, which made her wonder, after several weeks of intermittent rain, if they'd be forced to swim across. To her relief, the narrow causeway was clear, and so she and the soldier followed the worn path onward as tangles of mist rolled up over their feet from the marshes.

By the time they reached the gateway, her breath was coming in sharp gasps, and a few wispy curls had blown free of their pins, circling her head like a windswept diadem.

"Lieutenant Davies wanted her brought to the fort," announced her escort as they approached the sentries.

All the men in earshot shared a pointed, dubious look before the guard nodded and waved her through.

Rebekah entered a few paces ahead of her escort, feeling like a captive as she was prodded into the camp. To the right, the British flag rippled triumphantly on its high post. As she shielded the sun from her eyes to glimpse it, she couldn't help considering what Ben wouldn't give to see it torn back down and hurled into the nearest fire.

Ahead, clusters of triangular tents fanned out on either side of the hilly path. While Haverstraw's mountains were robed in summer green, the grass here had been tromped down, matted by hundreds of boots, and worn to brown. Given the scenery, Rebekah wouldn't have been surprised if she'd seen actual skeletons lumbering about. The British had cleared the trees from the top of the promontory and fashioned them into a spiked fence around the perimeter, which left the whole place sun-bleached and eerily void of shadows. Rocks and stumps jutted out of the ground like bones shouldering up from the earth, and the muggy air stank of sweat and ash.

The fort's inhabitants added life, thankfully, but little cheer. Women teetered beneath baskets full of produce and laundry, and, of course, there were soldiers as far as the eye could see. Many stooped tiredly over their fires as they prepared the evening meal. At the end of the row, a drummer boy had fallen asleep with his chin propped on his hand while watching an uninspiring game of checkers.

As Rebekah passed through the throng, she saw the Hudson River stretching out into the distance. All her life, she'd seen that river either from the safety of Haverstraw Bay or from the woods behind her father's house, but the deep gray water seemed vast beneath the fog, reaching from one shore to the next as if struggling to bring two sides together.

Rebekah kept her eyes on the horizon as she and her escort climbed up one hill and stumbled down another, ending at a rocky ledge on the far tip of the peninsula. There was only one building to be seen, a rickety shed tossed in next to a circular arrangement of wagons, which were covered with tarps and slick with the afternoon rain. "Hurry up," the soldier grumbled behind her, and so Rebekah set her hand on one of the wagons to keep her balance as she picked her way down the ridge ahead of him. Before long, they came upon another formation of tents on a narrow plateau. These looked larger than those they'd passed near the entrance, though no less drab. Here, Rebekah's escort pulled her to a stop.

At her questioning look, he thrust her forward, toward one of the canvas shelters, then turned on his heel without a farewell and marched off. Stomach clenching, Rebekah watched him go, then pulled back the flap he'd indicated and ducked inside.

Mason's tent was larger than it appeared from the outside and finer than she might have expected, with a slim cot, well upholstered, and a desk as befitted a promising officer. A crate had been overturned into an end table, which was flanked by a spindly, high-backed chair. Above her head, the canopy of canvas was just tall enough for her to stand in the middle. Beneath her feet, a sad patch of dead, brown grass. She leaned forward, lifting the lid off his traveling trunk and found all of his articles carefully sorted and folded in place.

She lowered the lid carefully, then straightened. How easy it was to imagine Mason occupying such a space, small though it was. He was trim and efficient about everything, and though his wealth was more modest than most, it was noteworthy, and he had a way of not flaunting it, exactly, but displaying it in the details.

With wary eyes, Rebekah lowered herself into his chair and watched the tent's entrance. The first hours were filled with anxiety as a hundred questions contended for attention. Was her father safe, or had he been shot down by the rebels before Mason could reach him? And what of Mason himself—was he in any danger?

She gave herself a vigorous shake to stem the tide of panic. Before the day was done, Mason would return for her. And when he did, she'd tell him the truth.

Yes, all of it.

She'd tell him about Eli, about her father, about Pendergrass House. Then, perhaps, they could move forward together. He would forgive her, and she would forgive him, and the truth would draw them closer together.

She was resolved.

Rebekah was hunched in the chair, dreary and half-dreaming, when voices stirred the silence. Realizing she'd slept through the night, that a new sunrise had replaced the last, she pushed up onto her feet—

And swayed.

Why had Mason not returned? Was it really possible he'd been killed by the rebels?

She paced twice but couldn't bring herself to

leave the tent. She wasn't sure she could bear the mortification of asking his men, not when they were sure to wonder who she was to him.

As the fires outside were lit, she could smell the sausages and potatoes boiling in their kettles, and her stomach seized. Given the hour of her rendezvous with Mason, she'd missed supper the night before but dared not ask a soul at the fort for breakfast. Rations were for soldiers and camp followers, those who pulled their weight; surely, no crumbs would be spared for the local prostitute, even if she had somehow ingratiated herself to the lieutenant.

Even as she thought it, footsteps moved in her direction. She wrung her hands but set her jaw, determined to tell Mason of their child while she had the nerve. She'd throw herself upon his mercy and pray he would deliver her. The words were all there, waiting within her as the flap was thrown open and a shadow cut the sunlight to loom silently before her.

Swinging around in a rush, Rebekah grabbed hold of the desk and blurted, "Mason, please, I must tell you—"

It was not Mason who stood in the opening, but the surly young man, her escort, holding a trim square of white paper in one gloved hand. His voice held more of an edge as he strode forward. "The lieutenant asked me to deliver this to you."

The letter was placed in Rebekah's hand before she realized she'd reached to receive it. She nodded her thanks, waiting for the soldier to leave, but he stood by the entrance, illuminated from behind by sunlight. Resigned to an audience, she opened the note with a slight air of hauteur, as if she was not in the least affected by the situation.

Miss Stanton,
My man has been instructed to return you at once to Pendergrass House. I thank you not to speak of this to anyone.
Dutifully,
Lieutenant Mason Davies

Rebekah stood in a trance as the note fell from her hand. One of Mason's men must have recognized her. She'd known this was a risk and could well imagine how the conversation had gone—the poor devil had been tricked, they likely said, trapped by a trollop, and what else could he have expected from a light-skirt?

She turned away from the soldier, wishing he would go away. Her feelings for Mason and all the hopes she'd placed in him had been rewritten by snide and idle gossip, her name and good intentions ruined before she'd ever had a chance to explain.

Yet, there was nothing to explain.

Not really.

Whatever gossip Mason might have heard was likely true. She'd done so many despicable things, had become every inch the woman her reputation suggested her to be. How foolish to expect things to have ended any differently. She'd fallen, was falling still, this time away from him, into a dark place where even the dimmest dreams of deliverance offered no solace.

The corners of her eyes burned with tears, but she allowed them to slip no further. Dragging in a measured breath, she smiled at the soldier and followed him out of the tent, squinting as she stepped beneath the bright shafts of harsh, unforgiving sunlight. For a moment, she stood startled, shielding her face with her hand as she waited for her eyes to adjust.

Passing soldiers glanced her way but otherwise paid her little mind. She recognized some from the boardinghouse. Others she'd seen loitering outside the tavern near the ferry. They were men of the world, cultured in the ways of women, and so would never have clutched at their Bibles in her presence.

Oh, but the women.

They froze in their work and stared openly, whispering among themselves, their eyes darting over Rebekah's gown as if they could read every inch of her dishonor in the seams and the stitching.

There was nothing for it but to retreat to Pendergrass House.

A job was a job, after all, Rebekah reminded herself.

And Mason had nothing to do with it.

CHAPTER 17

By the time Rebekah returned to the boarding-house, the kitchen had been cleared of its usual breakfast bustle.

Only Coffey remained. Stooped over the fire, the cook wiped a sleeve against her sweat-sheened brow, frowning when she lifted her eyes to Rebekah. "You're pale as a corpse." She gestured for Rebekah to sit. "Not taking ill, I hope?"

"I was at the fort all night," Rebekah answered. "Only just returned. The whole ordeal has left me awfully tired is all."

Coffey shook her head and plated some pickled eggs and mutton. "Men make us tired, and don't I know it?" She set the food in front of Rebekah, then poured a cup of tea and slid it across the table as well.

The steam coiled upward, warming Rebekah's face in a cloud of citrus and cinnamon. She smiled her thanks as she tucked into her breakfast, ravenous despite the circumstances. Pendergrass girls lived off a pittance, but Coffey made sure they were well-fed, and this was as silver a lining as Rebekah had ever seen.

Coffey set to humming after that. It was a sorrowful tune, accompanied only by the clatter of cutlery in the next room, where one of the other girls was busy polishing.

Rebekah sipped her tea, lulled half to sleep by the warmth in her belly and Coffey's honeyed voice.

All turned cold when Miss Ward strolled into the kitchen with a pewter cup cradled in her claw-like hand. "Well, Your Majesty!" She curtsied crudely as she fixed her eyes on Rebekah. "At last, you've rested yourself enough to grace us with your presence!" The woman snorted at her own quip, then shoved the cup into Rebekah's hand.

Any remaining appetite withered as Rebekah stared down at the familiar tincture—juniper, black hellebore, and other herbs mixed with a bit of milk. All the girls drank it twice a week. The mixture was intended to keep them from *begetting any brats,* as Mrs. Pendergrass was in the habit of saying.

Rebekah thought of Eli as she lifted the cup nearly to her lips. She remembered brushing his hair with the tips of her fingers and the way his cheeks puffed as he nursed. If she closed her eyes, she'd see the flutter of his petal-sized eyelids as he awakened in her arms. Desperate to forget him, to guard against ever hurting that way again, she tossed back the contents, blenching through the piney aftertaste as she slid the tankard back on the table.

By the time she opened her eyes, Miss Ward had already forgotten her and was circling the kitchen, poking her bent nose in various tureens. "That's going to burn," she snapped, directing Coffey with the spoon.

Though Rebekah was quite certain Coffey had never burnt a dish in all her life, the cook nodded and pulled the offending pot off the flame.

Miss Ward threaded her way to the other side of the kitchen. "I've told my sister you'll be making white pot pudding tonight. And don't forget to peel those potatoes over there. Captain Haggerty will be dining with us, and you know how he likes our chowder."

"No, ma'am. I won't forget."

"See to it you don't, or you can just as easily be on your way." Miss Ward tossed the spoon onto the counter with a clatter and was gone.

In the older woman's absence, Coffey hauled the basket of potatoes onto the counter. Beads of sweat had gathered at the back of her neck beneath her scarlet wrap, but she looked otherwise unruffled.

Miss Ward's threats against Coffey were frequent, but they held no clout. No doubt, Miss Ward thought she could do Coffey's job well enough in a pinch, but her sister was more practical. Men requested Coffey's food by name, especially her tarts, and she was well compensated by Mrs. Pendergrass because of it. Of course, that didn't mean Miss Ward's condescension didn't sting, or that Coffey couldn't see that her value was measured only by her usefulness.

No longer interested in breakfast, Rebekah pushed back her plate. "Do you want any help with—?"

"Don't you go pitying me," Coffey warned. "She may not think it's true, but you just remember I know how to run my own kitchen."

Rebekah sighed. "It must be impossible for you here. How can you stand the way she talks to you?"

"Her ways are rude," Coffey allowed, more evenly. "But her sister's money saves up as well as anyone else's."

Rebekah tilted her head, considering Coffey's osnaburg gown. Made of scratchy, coarse linen, it was the usual mark of an enslaved person. While it was not illegal, in New York at least, for slaves to dress above their station, Rebekah had never seen Coffey, a free woman in her own right, wear anything else. She never donned the slightest piece of finery, nor wore a finer dress even for Christmas. Rebekah used to think it was because the quiet cook wanted to pass unseen in a house full of harlots, but now she wasn't so sure.

"Are you saving for something in particular?" she wondered aloud.

Coffey laughed as she snatched the first potato off the heap. "So many things," she answered.

She worked deftly with the knife, the peel spiraling off as neatly as a ribbon.

"Do you have family waiting for you?" It was the most natural question in the world, and yet they both knew it wasn't.

Coffey finished with the first potato. She set it down and reached for another without looking up. "I have a husband."

Rebekah's breakfast curdled in her stomach. "How did you come to be separated?"

"He worked in the stable," Coffey answered. "I worked in the kitchen. We married in secret. When I was freed, he went off in our master's stead to serve with the militia. Two more years, he says, and he'll give him his freedom." She leaned against the counter and touched her fingertips to a thin wooden bangle on her left wrist. "Two more years," she said, more deeply. "That is, if he keeps his word and truly lets him go."

"I'm so sorry," Rebekah said. "It must feel like an eternity."

Coffey pursed her lips, nodding tightly.

Rebekah went back to staring down at her breakfast. How awful, to have never asked about Coffey's family before. She couldn't imagine being married to a man, knowing he was forced to fight, to kill in a war which was not his own. All Coffey could do in the meantime was work and pray he wasn't killed before they could be together, pray that the word of one man truly granted his liberty. Coffey's master may have freed her, but she wasn't really free.

Not in any of the ways that mattered.

When Rebekah glanced up again, Coffey had blinked away any trace of tears and was staring, pointedly, at Rebekah's right hand. Spirit sinking, Rebekah followed the cook's gaze down to Mason's ring; she didn't realize she'd been twisting it around and around her knuckle.

With quiet grace, Coffey set down her paring knife and reached into her apron pocket, sliding a scrap of paper beside Rebekah's plate. "I need some things from market," she said. "Take your time with it, you hear? Whoever he is, a bit of distraction is a fit remedy, if you don't mind my saying so."

An unspoken exchange passed between the two women; they saw each other clearly and recognized themselves in what they saw.

Smiling weakly, Rebekah took up the list.

A bit of distraction—sensible advice, but she wasn't sure if her heart would allow it. Thus far, she hadn't admitted to herself that Mason was the same as the men who called on her at Pendergrass House, but he'd smiled and charmed as easily as any man, taking everything he could without offering anything more in return.

For too long she'd hoped he'd reappear to deliver her, but now the truth was plain.

He didn't want her.

And, surely, no decent man would, she thought with a pang, while she could still be bought by the hour.

As Rebekah slipped around the house in her straw hat, she could hardly breathe through the muggy heat. Mosquitos hummed about her ears and neck, but all was otherwise quiet and still, free of the acrid stench of whiskey and old furniture which permeated the house. Overgrown treetops converged near the back of the building, forming a canopy of shadows and sunlight.

Rebekah froze mid-step when a chorus of whinnies sounded in the stable. She told herself it was probably nothing. A curious fox lived in the neighborhood and sometimes found his way inside with the horses. Yet, the attack on Heston's house had her on edge. Lifting her skirt off her boots, she turned toward the stable, was nearly through the door when she heard the soft, reassuring croon of a man's voice.

"Easy, girl," said the voice. *"Easy . . ."*

Rebekah leaned against the edge of the door-frame. She'd brought a basket for her trip to the market and nearly gave herself away by dropping it when she saw Ben standing in one of the stalls, running a gloved hand down their strongest mare's spotted muzzle.

All at once, the terror of a hundred rumors stole upon her. Raids. Tarring and feathering. Tories forced at gunpoint to run naked through the streets.

Had Ben been involved with the burning of Heston's house?

She imagined him setting upon her father next, if he hadn't already. Or burning Pendergrass House after he was done using it for refuge. According to Mason's subordinate, the men behind the attack at Heston's house had poisoned all the horses on the estate.

Her stomach soured as she watched Ben cajole Hecuba in her stall.

"It seems you're waiting for me to do something suspicious," he observed without turning.

She ought to have known it would be impossible to surprise him. Impossible, indeed, to sneak up on a spy. "I'm wondering if you already have," she admitted, strolling toward him in what she hoped seemed an airy manner.

He half turned. His smile was there, a lazy lift to his lips, but his gaze remained as impassive as ever. "An accusation, then? Very well. Let's hear it."

"Where were you last night?"

"I was here." He removed his hat and tossed it on the barrel as he met her eyes, all but daring her to refute his claim. "All night."

Rebekah didn't trust him. He'd answered the question too quickly, didn't seem a bit curious or suspicious about what she might be driving at.

Before she could form her next question, though, he turned her previous one back on her. "And where were *you* last night?"

Judging by his tone, he already knew the answer, but she told him what any of the other girls might have shared the previous evening and refused to sound embarrassed. "I was at the fort."

"All night?"

She shifted her basket from one arm to the other. "And all morning. Yes."

If she planned to take satisfaction in his discomfort, she was mistaken. He hardly registered what she said. Giving Hecuba's nose a final pat, he stepped back. "I didn't torch Heston's house. I was here all night. Ask Mrs. Pendergrass."

"Who burned it, then?"

"A passing mob from the north. The British will hunt most of them down by sundown, I'm sure. Enough to make an example to the ones who got away."

"Do you support what they did?"

"Old man Heston came to no harm."

This all came down to semantics, of course. As if burning a man's home wasn't harm enough. "But if he had?" she pressed. "Would he have had it coming, I assume?"

Ben's smile was gone. Along with it all pretense. "I could have been out at Heston's, if I wanted to be. But I wasn't, and that's more than answer enough."

He stood much too close to her. Whereas Mason was refined, there was something rougher about Ben, something raw. She detected none of the rose water Mason favored, nor the cloves or bergamot oil common to his particular pomade. With Ben, she was reminded of leather and pine and something deeper, harder to qualify, as if he was always walking through the mist to find her.

Beside them, Hecuba must have sensed the tension, for she pawed the ground and knickered, her glassy eyes darting.

Before Rebekah could grab for the bridle, Ben took it in his hand and quieted the beast with a soft click of his teeth. He gave the horse another lingering pat. "What do you call her?"

"Hecuba."

"Your mistress said it would be all right if I borrowed one of your horses. This one seems the sprightliest." He turned and took up his hat, then a riding crop from a peg.

As he shifted, Rebekah spotted the glint of a pistol tucked beneath his coat. "Where are you going?"

"You sound concerned."

"Only . . . curious."

His lips twitched like he wanted to smile. "If you must know, I'm off to see a rather portly gentleman about some tea. Dreadfully dull business, but I'm afraid it must be done."

Supposing this was a lie, or perhaps code for

something more political, she matched his gaze and held it, searching him for the truth.

He held up a hand before she could press him, this time smiling in earnest. "You and I must come to a truce, and soon, Miss Stanton. For as much as I enjoy your interrogations, I fear you are getting altogether too skilled at them for my own good."

He swept up into the saddle before she could speak again.

She ran a thoughtful hand between Hecuba's glassy eyes, effectively blocking his exit. "If you can manage it," she said, casually, "do try not to get shot this time. It would be a wretched shame if you were."

His only answer was a low laugh, which Rebekah heard but did not see, for she slipped her hand away and stepped aside, listening to the pattering of Hecuba's hooves, which rose to a rolling clatter as Ben gained the road beyond.

CHAPTER 18

Later That Night

From the other side of sleep, Rebekah heard a child's laugh, and she knew—

Eli was playing about her dreams again.

As soon as she thought it, the slip of laughter flitted away like a scrap of paper in a heavy wind. She wrestled inwardly to hold on to the dream, to make it last, but consciousness beckoned.

With a tired groan, she rolled onto her side, blinking the space around her into focus. Her candle had nearly guttered, the low, flickering light barely illuminating the stranger sprawled on the bed beside her. He was near her age and a bit of a dandy despite the mud-spattered boots he'd kicked off by the door. He'd called himself Tobias. Or was it Thomas? Rebekah had seen so many customers that evening that for the life of her she couldn't remember.

She shifted sideways, propping herself on her elbow so she might see him better.

Just passing through, he'd said of himself, with a speck of sorrow in his eyes.

Weren't they all?

For years, it had been easy enough to call men beasts and be done with them, and many of them were. But as Rebekah studied the man beside her, she couldn't help but wonder who worried about him the most when he traveled. He was someone's son, wasn't he, as surely as Eli had once belonged to her? Too well, she knew what it was like to be blown off course, how it felt to do the very thing you hated because you didn't know how to stop.

Her thoughts shifted, regretfully, to Mason.

Their first meeting had been five years before. At that time, the war had not quite reached Haverstraw but was a distant drum of politics in the background of tavern chatter. In the midst of this, Rebekah and her father had been invited to a party at Caleb Heston's house. The rooms were crowded that night with gossips trying to be heard over the music as the players tried to keep time with the rapid flirtations unfolding throughout. At supper, Rebekah was seated next to the family's oldest son, Robert, who was as spindly as a banister rail and prattled endlessly, recounting all of his accomplishments and travels without leaving her the slightest gap in which to interject a single word.

Robert didn't dally about securing Rebekah for the first dance and proceeded to crush her toes three times before the song was done. Before she could flee the dance floor, he leaned in very close to her.

Dreading some awkward bit of flattery or,

worse, another dance proposal, Rebekah smiled, pretending not to hear him as she slipped into the crowd.

But Robert was not the kind of man to give up so easily. He parted the couples behind her, calling her name as if she truly hadn't noticed his attentions. Dodging the simpleton's pursuit, Rebekah stumbled down the first hall she passed.

The room to the right, a parlor, was occupied by older gentlemen who filled the high ceilings with curls of pipe smoke and frenzied political discourse. The next room was filled with quibbling matrons. At the end of the hall, she spied a heavy door slightly ajar, leading to what seemed an empty library.

Without stopping to knock, Rebekah pushed inside.

Mason had been perched against the corner of a desk, nursing a glass of amber liquid. He turned his head as she entered.

"Oh!" cried Rebekah, flustered by the sharp, impeccable lines of his uniform. "Forgive me, I was only trying to—"

He didn't stand, but his smile arrested the flow of her words. "Come in," he said. "If you're trying to escape that imbecile, Robert Heston, I am more than willing to share my sanctuary with you."

Rebekah stepped back. Her neck prickled as she realized they were entirely unchaperoned. "I couldn't possibly," she answered, and turned to leave.

Mason's smile broadened. Before she reached the hall, he crossed to the patio doors and flung them open, leaning against the doorframe so anyone mingling on the terrace below would be able to see him. "There," he remarked. "Quite safe, you see."

It had all seemed such a happy coincidence. Perfect timing. They talked for a while, then danced together twice. In Rebekah's narrow experience, Mason Davies was as gallant as men came. She'd been a respectable girl, then, from a respectable home, with a future worth dreaming about.

Now?

Without warning, the stranger in the bed beside her shifted, grunting as he awakened. Rebekah could still feel his sweat on her skin. Unable to face him after thinking of Mason, she slipped her eyes shut and pretended to be asleep, waiting as the stranger dressed and placed his coins quietly upon the table.

Rebekah couldn't sleep after that.

In truth, she rarely could.

She slid out of bed, wrapping her shawl tightly around her shoulders, and crept downstairs to make a cup of tea. Such midnight vigils were common for her, though this time she had to pass Ben's room on her way down and found herself stepping all the more lightly.

His tea business, whatever it was, had not kept him long that afternoon. He'd returned shortly after sunset. Rebekah had been speaking with a young man when he entered the parlor, but he'd hardly glanced her way, seeking out Coffey instead. He'd asked for a bit of supper and took it up to his room, leaving Rebekah to wonder why she was so discomfited by his presence when he seemed entirely unflustered by hers.

Voices stopped her in her tracks before she reached the kitchen.

It was an unusual hour for customers to mill about, unless they'd arrived by carriage in the middle of the night, but Rebekah hadn't heard any noise outside to signal their arrival. Feeling more than a bit nosy, she peered around the parlor doorframe and saw two of His Majesty's men lit by the glow of the fire. Their coats had been slung over their chairbacks, their collars loose as they leaned over the dwindling embers. One was familiar—Captain Haggerty with his thin, serpentine nose, who'd knocked her down the night he'd been hunting for Ben. The other was new, freshly arrived from the sight of the traveling trunk beside the castaway scraps of his supper.

Rebekah arrived in time to catch a handful of the second man's words. ". . . to oversee the withdrawal of troops."

"Johnson's not concerned in the slightest,"

Haggerty replied. "The fort is secure, and the remaining men more than capable to hold it. Do you think you'll have enough men to carry out the campaign?"

The stranger dropped his voice to the scantest murmur. "Strong on men, short on time," he answered. "Tryon wants us to reach our mark by the end of next week. The raids are to begin at once."

"I'm surprised General Clinton is letting him off his leash. I thought he despised warfare of such a—rigorous nature."

" 'Tis a ghastly business by any standard. But if a brute will answer only to brutality, then so be it. A few burned homes and churches will be a price well spent if it means drawing Washington onto the field."

Rebekah drew back, a sharp breath seizing in her chest. *Tryon*. He'd been the governor of New York a few years prior but had since been made commander of the British forces in Long Island. By all accounts, he was a vicious man who wanted nothing more than to pillage rebellious towns into submission to the crown. If raids were coming, as these men claimed, Rebekah had no doubt homes and churches would be razed, stores and homes looted, women and children made an example of for the sake of their seditious husbands.

Perhaps this was justice.

Perhaps this was what traitors deserved.

This was what Rebekah had been taught as a child.

But the lines no longer fell as clearly within her as they once had. In this matter, at least, she owed no loyalty to a king whose men would sanction such tactics, neither could she turn her back and ignore the fray.

Hardly daring to breathe for fear she might be heard, she shrank back into the shadows and stumbled away from the parlor. She scurried upstairs, grateful when her bare feet did not fall upon any creaky floorboards as she found her way to Ben's room. Softly, so as not to alert the men in the parlor, she opened the door and ghosted inside, closing it behind her with barely a *snick*.

Ben slept at a sprawled angle, fully clothed though significantly disheveled as if he kept himself ready to run at a moment's notice.

Barefoot, Rebekah padded across the floor and reached out a hand to jostle his shoulder.

His eyes flew open.

Before she could scream, before she could move, her wrist was seized in one of his hands, and a pistol appeared in the other, jammed tightly against her ribs. Her pulse ratcheted at the cold, unpleasant press of metal against her chemise.

Just as quickly as he'd pointed the weapon, he drew a sharp breath and lowered it.

"Rebekah?" Eyes flashing with recognition, he shuddered and let go of her hand.

Horror-struck, she stared back. It wasn't the first time she'd wondered what Ben was capable of, but it was the first time she thought she might not want to know the answer. What had the man seen, experienced, to instill in him that kind of impulse, ready within a moment of waking to shoot or to die?

She swallowed hard and then, in a hoarse voice, said, "I must tell you something."

Ben shoved himself up from the bed and lit the lamp, wanting to see her more clearly. "What is it? What's wrong?"

Rebekah paced away from him. Uncommonly pale, she clasped her hands together and closed her eyes. From the moment he'd met her, she'd never given the slightest impression of fear in his presence, nor distress. Now, she looked terrified.

He went cold all over, wondering if one of her so-called customers had hurt her. "What happened?" he demanded. "Are you all right?"

"Yes, yes, I'm fine." She paced again, clutching the ends of her shawl tightly in her hands. "I couldn't sleep, you see, so I went downstairs, and two officers were in the parlor, and they didn't see me, but—well, I thought you ought to know what they said."

She glanced down at his gun as she turned to

look at him; he set it on the table to put her more at ease. “Well?” he pressed. “What did they say?”

She chewed the inside of her cheek and turned toward the window. Though Ben was not unsympathetic to her struggle—for, truly, he’d felt much the same the day he’d first turned traitor—he was growing impatient. She lifted a hand to brush the hair out of her face, and he caught her by the wrist, tugging her attention back to him.

Sighing, she pulled out of his reach and lowered her arm to her side. “They’re pulling men from Stony Point.”

“Yes,” he answered. “We’ve heard rumors to that effect.”

“Have you also heard that some of them are to carry out a campaign of raids?”

Ben blinked. Whatever he’d expected of Rebekah, it was hardly to be granted such precise, vital intelligence. “Who’s leading them? Did they say?”

“General Tryon.”

The name hit Ben like a blow and sent him staggering back. Desolation warfare wasn’t formally sanctioned by the British, but it was no secret Tryon wanted nothing more than to slip his leash and be given free rein to bring Patriot sympathizers to their knees. “You’re absolutely sure?”

“Positive.”

He stared at her for a hard moment. He couldn't think of a single reason she'd feed him false intelligence of this nature. If she wanted to destroy him—and he'd thought a time or two that she might—she had only to speak to one of the redcoats in the parlor, and he'd have been clapped in irons before he even knew what she was about.

Thoughts roiling, he stepped around her, collecting his boots and coat from a chair in the corner. Over his shoulder, he asked, "Did they say when he plans to strike?"

"End of next week."

"Did they say where, exactly?"

"No."

"Did they—"

"That's all I know." Her voice came out pleading, tired. "I swear."

Ben stuffed his few provisions into his bag. When he turned again, he found Rebekah leaning against the bedpost, her hip a soft, striking curve. "It seems you'll need to borrow Hecuba again," she observed, and tried to smile.

"What you've done tonight is very, very dangerous," he said, stepping closer. "I am grateful."

"How long will you be gone?"

He wavered. Rebekah's information was critical, the kind that could change the whole course of a war. There was no telling what Wayne might do with this kind of news, or Washington.

They might wish to abandon all plans against Stony Point entirely, which meant Ben might be sent to join with the rest of Wayne's men. He could be sent anywhere, at any time, at another man's behest.

When he didn't answer, Rebekah set her hand on his sleeve. The room was stuffy and warm, but her fingers were startlingly cold.

"Wait here," she whispered then opened the door and vanished into the hall.

Ben paced the room until she reappeared a few minutes later. Closing the door soundlessly behind her, she stepped close, took his hand, and pressed a small square of paper into his palm.

He smiled despite himself. "You didn't give it to Davies."

She held his gaze when he looked at her. Now that all the banter was stripped away, it was easier to sense just how much of herself she concealed from others, as if behind a towering wall. She was silent a moment. But then, offering him a candid smile, said, "You knew I didn't."

Of course, he knew, but he found her quiet sincerity a welcome change, oddly enticing. "I don't understand," he said. "Why are you helping me? I thought you and the lieutenant—"

Her smile sharpened. "If you don't go soon," she warned. "It might be too late."

He pocketed the note, trying to read her but finding himself oddly not up to the task. He wondered if something had happened between her and Davies, an argument perhaps, or if she wasn't as close to the lieutenant as he'd previously thought.

But was she helping Ben because she felt a kinship to the Patriot cause—or to *him?*

He shook his head and crossed to the window. From prior experience, he knew it best not to get entangled with anyone on the road, least of all a woman, but rather to say good-bye and be done. And yet, he had no wish to say his farewells now.

Neither, it seemed, did she.

"They'll hang you if they catch you," she said, stopping him as he shimmied the window open.

Though she'd spoken the words evenly enough, he detected the slightest note of genuine worry in her wide, luminous eyes. He took up her hand and pressed a firm kiss to it, smiling briefly against her knuckles. "I do not doubt that they will try."

CHAPTER 19

July 1, 1779
Sandy Beach

"Someone get this chickenhearted milksop out of my sight before I have the simpering wretch flogged!"

Ben, who'd been pacing outside Wayne's tent, paused as a no-account soldier was escorted out, roughly, through the flap. With one glance, Ben could see what had so incensed the general, for the young man's uniform was wrinkled, short one button at the cuff, and he wore a look of angry, youthful impudence as he was marched up the drive, away from his superior.

Silence followed. Then a tapestry of colorful oaths. A moment later, an officer ducked through the canvas flap and cleared his throat. "The general is ready to see you."

Ben straightened his hat and collar before ambling into the tent, where a young man with a high forehead and a patrician nose was holding court from behind a desk littered with maps and correspondence. Though Wayne didn't bother looking up from his papers, his presence was enough to set a lesser man than Ben on edge.

At thirty-four, General Anthony Wayne had refined himself into an unlikely marriage of dandyism and quiet ferocity. His temper ensured that his men followed orders without debate, and his valor, which they'd witnessed firsthand, decided their loyalty. Intelligence glimmered in the man's eyes, and passion, both of which had made him popular with the ladies despite the young wife waiting back home.

His reputation as a conqueror had as much to do with strength as with bearing. Namely, in that he dressed the part. Even now, in the middle of a field, his hair was meticulously powdered, his coat trimmed with white facings and fitted over a shirt with innumerable ruffles. Wayne expected his men to dress themselves in similar fashion, as if they were prepared to ride unto their deaths like gentlemen at his personal request.

Many proudly had.

At last, Wayne spoke, though remaining focused on his papers. "Aren't you supposed to be keeping eyes on Stony Point?"

He sounded annoyed, which meant he was angry, and no wonder, as Ben's presence was a serious breach in protocol. Informants worked with couriers to protect them from exposure, and Wayne was in no position to eschew necessary caution. After the massacre at Paoli—which many had blamed on Wayne—he was desperate to re-prove himself to Washington. The Light

Infantry corps had been granted to him as a token of good faith.

For weeks, Wayne had been training his men, all the while keeping an eye on the glimmering mark of Stony Point. Reclaiming the fort for Washington would be the perfect victory to strengthen the general's limping reputation. To this end, he'd been receiving reports from Jotham's courier ever since the British takeover, passing them on to Washington only after every detail was authenticated.

Caution was paramount.

Even so, Ben wasn't willing to entrust Rebekah's information to anyone else, not even a courier. The situation was far too urgent, too volatile, and he didn't want anyone to find out she'd been the one to aid him.

"Tryon's planning raids," Ben announced without preface or hello. "Some of the troops they're pulling from Stony Point are meant to aid him."

Wayne's jaw tightened to a handsome, chiseled square. "Tryon," he spat, then poured a knuckle of brandy and held it out to Ben. "I don't know why Clinton puts any stock in him. The man's a beast even by redcoat standards. Though I can't help wondering why you brought this news to me directly. What of the courier?"

Too distracted to drink, Ben palmed his glass. "I didn't trust anyone else."

Wayne's eyebrow dipped. "How did you discover it, exactly? From Eldridge's contact in the city?"

On this, Ben needed to tread carefully. He had no wish to expose Rebekah as an informant, even to Wayne. If he thought she was a liability, she could be snatched in the middle of the night, held in custody until their mission was over and the danger had passed. And if he thought she was a useful asset? Well, there was danger, too, for she might just as easily be enlisted as an informant, strong-armed into a battle she had no wish to fight.

"We both know that well's been dry for several months," Ben answered.

Wayne exhaled loudly. "I do hate to repeat myself, but I must ask again. This intelligence. *Where* did it come from?"

No use arguing. Wayne had diffused enough mutinies to snuff the slightest spark of insubordination with a glare.

"I heard it from a woman," Ben admitted. "She works at the boardinghouse where I was staying. She overheard the conversation and shared it with me."

"What kind of a woman? A servant?"

"In a . . . manner of speaking."

When Wayne spoke again, his voice was much lower. "You mean to tell me I'm to take military action on the word of a strumpet?"

"I trust her."

Wayne laughed derisively, sliding back in his seat. "And I'm to take your word for it, then? I suppose it's safe to assume she's a handsome wench."

Ben ignored the taunt.

Wayne turned back to the matter at hand. "I don't suppose she heard where Tryon's men are being sent?"

When Ben shook his head, Wayne shoved a stack of papers back from his hands, staring up at the canvas ceiling until, gradually, his lips twitched closer to a smile. "Perhaps this is fortuitous."

"For Stony Point, you mean?" Ben leaned closer. "Does this mean you have a plan?"

"There's a time to plan, Renshaw, and a time to strike and precious little time in between. Washington trusts me to act decisively, which is precisely what I intend to do. I told the man I'd invade hell itself if he but asked me to."

"I can only imagine what he said to that."

Wayne gave a devil's grin. "He said I ought to start with Stony Point."

Ben blew out a breath and stood. There was a chance this conversation had happened. Yet again, there was a chance it hadn't. Hyperbole was Wayne's favorite medium. "I can return to Haverstraw if you wish me to," he offered. "Keep you abreast of any changes."

Wayne thought then shook his head as he took

up his pen. "I need you to track down Eldridge's contact in the city first. You're to ask her to pass on a small bit of intelligence on my behalf."

Ben stared at him, momentarily confounded. "I'm to ask—*her?*"

Wayne laughed again, the amusement in his eyes making him appear somewhat younger, nearer to his true age. "Jotham didn't tell you, did he? Skittish thing, your friend. His girl works in the home of a Loyalist family. They have a captain staying with them at present, and shall we say the girl's grown rather 'close' to him?"

At the insinuation in Wayne's voice, Ben thought again of Rebekah, of Lieutenant Davies, and prayed the general would not demand a similar arrangement if the idea ever presented itself. "What do you need me to do?"

"She has a brother in the Continentals, though she's thus far renounced any relationship with him. I need her to tell the good captain that she's heard from this brother. Something about me being sent with my men to head off these rumored incursions."

"You really think a simple diversion will work?"

"We have to keep General Clinton's eyes off Stony Point for as long as possible. I put trust in Jotham's contact to flesh out the details. Do be on your guard, though. Security into the city has tightened. We're having a devil of a time getting old bachelors like you past the checkpoints."

Ben laughed. "I'll make it through."

"Yes, you always do." The general thought for a moment then settled into a sharp, scheming smile, one he'd spent years refining in ballrooms and on battlefields alike. "Though I am, as ever, ready to offer a solution."

Later that evening, Ben, who'd been waiting in the tavern cellar for nearly thirty minutes, couldn't conceal his amusement when Jotham appeared in the doorway looking as put-upon as a servant.

"I've been ordered to find a certain lady friend of yours," Ben said by way of greeting.

"Of course, Wayne told you about her," Jotham muttered. "The man's looser about his gossip than a kitchen girl."

"It was a surprising development, I'll admit, though I understand your discretion. As I've been tasked with finding her, though, you might as well tell me who she is."

"I knew her years ago, before I met Agatha."

Ben couldn't help but laugh. "You wretched hypocrite," he said. "I do believe you once criticized me for putting my trust in a woman."

"That's different," snapped Jotham.

"I'd like to know how."

"Don't think I don't know *exactly* why you've been staying at Pendergrass House. All the soldiers in my parlor say as much, that they all have a rare bit of competition where Rebekah

Stanton is concerned. Of course, I can't begrudge you a bit of pleasure when it becomes so easily part of your cover."

Ben's amusement was doused by the implication. "Your contact," he said crisply. "How do I find her?"

"She works in the kitchen of a Loyalist family, is bedfellows with one of the captains who has been staying with them. Like I said, I've not had word in months. She's either been arrested, or she's being careful. I dared not reach out for fear of exposing her."

"What's her name?"

"I wouldn't tell Wayne, and I certainly won't tell you."

Ben sighed. "I suppose you won't tell me which family either?"

Jotham stared at his boots. "Track down our courier," he said. "That's the safest way to contact her."

"How do I find him?"

"He sells at the fish market down by the East River. He's there every Tuesday. Three tables down. Woodsy fellow with bristly hair. Terrible temper, so mind your step."

"How do I signal to him why I'm there?"

Jotham rifled around the crates until he found a spare bit of paper. "She always folded her list in the exact same way, to signal she had a message for me in particular."

He flattened the sheet on a nearby barrel, pulling the lantern closer to his hands. He flipped the edges toward the center, each side folding over the next, and then in half the other way. When he finished, he held up the inconspicuous paper. "Doesn't matter what you write on the paper so long as it's folded like this. If he's convinced, he'll meet you in the alley behind Mulligan's Clothing Emporium."

Ben slipped the paper into his pocket, to be studied later, as Jotham took up his lantern.

"I'm sorry for what I said before," muttered Jotham. "About the woman."

"Think nothing of it."

Jotham nodded, clenching his jaw before setting a hand on Ben's shoulder. "Just remember that it's her job to be beautiful. It's her job to smile and make you think you're the only man in the world. You know that, don't you?"

Ben grimaced. He didn't feel taken in by Rebekah, for he could still tell where her false smile ended and her real one began. Nor could he judge her too harshly for her circumstances, whatever had led her to them, when he was in plenty of ways a prodigal himself. He'd been angry with his father for trying to fashion him into the kind of man he wasn't, angry enough to curse him, to turn his back on his entire family.

Not much had changed in four years.

Ben was still angry, still battling, and how

easily he found he could still play a part. He'd strolled into Pendergrass House without any qualms and settled right in, cozied up to a prostitute without the slightest flicker of hesitation, and was planning, even now, to pull her deeper into his world. He was comfortable anywhere, always had been, and this made him wonder which parts he was truly playing at and which had always been a part of him.

No, Ben wasn't one to claim the moral high ground where Rebekah was concerned. If she was to help him, he could but appeal to her good sense, and perhaps this would be enough.

If not, perhaps a little begging would do.

CHAPTER 20

July 2, 1779

Rebekah's fingers hovered an inch over the ivory keys as the storm, which had been gathering outside since the first flicker of dawn, broke free of its fetters. Rain drummed against the roof as a slash of lightning fragmented the sky beyond the house's dirty windows. Rebekah ignored the noise, squeezing her eyes shut, her nose crinkling as she tried to remember how to play.

Her hands shifted, then shifted again, correctly framing a minor chord on the harpsichord. She waited for another clap of thunder before pressing the keys, conjuring a deep, sepulchral noise. Swiftly, she realigned, waited for another clap of thunder as she struck the next chord.

She played like that, beneath the storm, for some time. She was by no means an expert, playing more by touch than by memory, and despite the occasional false note, she picked her way competently through a familiar refrain.

When she felt a presence behind her, her hands dropped from the keys, and she turned. "Mrs. Pendergrass," she exclaimed. "You startled me."

The older woman had once mocked Rebekah for trying to play the sad, old instrument. Now, something else shimmered in the older woman's dim eyes. It came like the lightning. There one moment, gone the next.

Mrs. Pendergrass crossed the parlor and knelt on the hearth, preparing the fire. "When did you learn to play?"

"I was twelve, I think. I told my father it was a useless waste." Rebekah plinked a single key and sighed. "It seems I was right."

"We know more when we're young than when we're old."

Rebekah glanced curiously over her shoulder. She'd never heard Mrs. Pendergrass speak so candidly, in a voice nearly wistful. "Were you very wise, then," Rebekah asked, "when you were young?"

Mrs. Pendergrass laughed into the soot. "I married a good man. A foolish man, I'll admit. He'd have run this place into the ground if he'd lived long enough to do so. But I was smart enough to look ahead. Smart enough, when he died, to become my own mistress."

Rebekah, who harbored no hopes of ever having the means to become her own mistress, swiveled to stare out the window. Though dawn approached, the storm clouds kept the parlor cloaked in shadow, all except a soft crown of lantern light hovering over the instrument.

There was silence, then a crackle as Mrs. Pendergrass brought the fire to life. From one end of the room to the other, flickers of light jumped to attention.

"There," said Mrs. Pendergrass with a satisfied smirk, sitting back on her heels. She brushed her hands on her apron, then rose in her indolent way. "Now to wake my sister, who was not a bit wise in *her* younger years, but very like she is now—a lazy slugabed."

When Mrs. Pendergrass's smile grew unexpectedly, Rebekah returned it.

Then the moment was gone.

Three steps from the landing, Mrs. Pendergrass turned, her hand on the banister as she looked down on Rebekah. "Do try not to be playing that horrible thing when the men come down. They aren't looking for accomplished women, are they?"

Rebekah's smile turned wan as her mistress went out of the room. She stared down at the keys again, then at Mason's ring. She ought to have thrown the wretched thing away or sold it. How had she learned nothing in all her years of falling for him and falling again?

She sat up a little straighter, placing her hands back on the keys. This time, she didn't wait for the thunder, but played, truly played, as she'd long wanted to. The performance sounded far from perfect. She hit a few wrong notes as before, and her pacing lagged, but a strange clarity came upon her as she stumbled through to the end of the song and, at last, struck the final note.

A flicker of pleasure grew within her breast. She thought she'd forgotten, but she remembered how to play. It seemed even the things she'd abandoned were still a part of her. If only she didn't have to remember them alone.

As if hearing her silent wish, a warm, masculine hand brushed the back of her neck.

She supposed a customer had been roused from bed by her playing and no doubt desired a more private performance. Suppressing a sigh, she slipped her hands away from the keys and folded them demurely in her lap. Then, fixing her lips into a coquettish smile, she glanced up over her shoulder—

And faltered.

Ben stood behind her with sopping hair, his coat drenched two shades darker from the rain. He seemed to be waiting for her to speak, but she struggled, for there was something remarkedly becoming about him, what with the music and the rain, and she found no heat in his eyes such as she found when other men looked at her.

Only warmth.

Rebekah hesitated. Mrs. Pendergrass would never forgive her if she didn't offer herself to him at once. Two shillings, she thought out of habit, but the words wouldn't come.

Instead, she said, "You're back."

He removed his coat, shaking it free of rain

before slinging it over a nearby chair. “You sound surprised.”

She was about to answer when he slid onto the bench beside her. Their shoulders touched, and Rebekah fought the strangest urge to scuttle away.

“You didn’t take Hecuba,” she explained. “I assumed you weren’t planning to return for quite some time.”

He reached forward, rattling a few notes from the instrument, which made her wonder if he’d received lessons once as well. “I wasn’t sure myself,” he replied. “Now, tell me.” He dipped his head nearer to hers and arched one eyebrow over his bright eyes. “Aren’t you a *little* glad to see me again?”

She pivoted off the bench and stood. “I’m glad to see you’re safe,” she said, diplomatically. “What business brings you back to Haverstraw?”

“As chance would have it, I’m in the business of acquiring a wife.”

Silence hung between them.

He’d said the words so casually, with the barest brush of a smile, and not even bothered to stand. Of course, this wasn’t a proposal. Rebekah wasn’t so agitated by his presence that she couldn’t see straight when it mattered. He was either speaking of some other woman or else playing with her, though she couldn’t imagine why.

She rebuffed him with a laugh, settling into a

chair by the fire. “If this is your idea of a proposal, I’m afraid ’tis somewhat lacking in passion.”

Ben crossed the space to claim the seat opposite her. “I have business in the city,” he said in a lower voice, keeping an eye on the staircase beyond her shoulder. “Pressing business. But the sentries are stopping anyone who seems the least bit suspicious. Bachelors, you see, face extra scrutiny. I can’t risk drawing any extra attention to myself.”

“So, naturally you need a wife.”

“No.” He leaned closer, the firelight warming his blue eyes. “I need someone to *pose* as my wife.”

It would have sounded radical, like downright lunacy, if Rebekah wasn’t so amused by the whole ridiculous scheme. “Oh, come now, you can’t possibly be considering me.”

“Why shouldn’t I consider you?”

She laughed again. “Because it’s absurd. You hardly know me. Besides, how do you expect me to explain my absence to Mrs. Pendergrass?”

“All she needs to know is you went off with a customer who wishes to remain discreet. I’ll pay you for your trouble, of course, however much you deem appropriate for the task.”

Rebekah’s laughter died in her throat. The banter had been enjoyable, but this mention of payment planted her firmly back in the reality where men bought her one night at a time. His proposition was different, but somehow it still made her feel cheap.

She lifted her eyes and realized he awaited her answer. "What is this business, exactly?"

"It'll be safer for you if I don't answer that."

"If you want my help in any respect, then you *will* supply an answer. Does this have to do with the raids I heard those men talking about?" For the last several days, she'd been watching the papers carefully for any mention of General Tryon's name, any hint that he'd begun his assault, but there had been nothing.

Ben paused, staring into the fire as he answered. "We can't head off Tryon's raids without more information. But we can make the most of the information you've given us, use it to strike back in our own way and in our own time."

Rebekah sank back in the chair. But of course, she couldn't go. The thirty miles from Stony Point to the city was an unpredictable strip of no-man's-land, where they were as likely to be accosted by British raiding parties as by privateers prowling for passing carts to rob.

And if they did make it into the city?

"They'll hang you if we're discovered," she said. "I'll spend the rest of my days in prison."

She meant this to be her final say, but Ben took her hand before she could escape. "I won't let anyone hurt you." He spoke the words firmly, with conviction, the timbre of his voice an uncanny echo of the harpsichord's solemn hymn.

Floundering, Rebekah tried to remind herself that the man lied for a living, that he couldn't be trusted as easy as that.

Then he tightened his hold on her hand. "You have my word, Rebekah."

She searched his eyes for any hint of duplicity but was met with a frankness uncommon to him. He needed her help. Badly.

Though she was inclined to wrench her hand away, she couldn't. She was so tired of being wanted—of being desired—that she was drawn, desperately, toward the possibility of being needed for once, of being truly useful.

If pressed, she wasn't sure who held the highest or most rightful claim to their country. But if a man like Tryon was allowed to carry on in pursuit of winning that claim for his king, then perhaps the war needed men like Ben, if only to balance the scales of decency every now and then.

If he needed her help to do it, then no matter the danger, she'd help.

CHAPTER 21

July 3, 1779

Whichever way Ben turned, he saw red. One soldier was speaking with the carriage driver ahead. A cluster of them marched up the next street over. More loitered outside various storefronts. Ben wasn't necessarily anxious about getting caught on the way into the city. Their pass was an expert forgery, and Rebekah the perfect distraction. The true risk was being recognized within the city itself, in which case escape became a far more complicated matter.

He and Rebekah had crossed King's Ferry without incident, then ridden nearly eight hours, stopping only long enough to rest the horses. To her credit, Rebekah gave no indication of being nervous. She sat beside him in her straight, thoughtful way, her eyes studying every field and hillock as if she'd never seen a patch of grass before.

For the first while, she inquired about his family and his past, but she spoke in what could only be called a parlor voice, as if she was merely going through the paces and expected him to answer vaguely, which he did out of habit. After that, they settled their story. How they'd met.

How long they'd been married. Rebekah embellished some of the details herself—such as the subject of their first marital argument, on the matter of a burnt pudding—and insisted their passes be left with her after crossing into the city. Whether this was extra caution, as he was the more likely to be arrested, or if she expected him to cut and run when her back was turned, he couldn't tell.

Overall, her fortitude impressed him.

If the jarring of the carriage wheels made her uncomfortable, she never said so. If she was tired or conflicted or even afraid, Ben never would have been able to tell. Not until their carriage approached the city border did he feel her stiffen beside him.

"Easy," he muttered, placing his hand on her knee.

She nodded faintly and smoothed a trembling hand over her bodice. She'd insisted on changing before they left, so instead of her usual frippery she wore a homespun gown, dove gray, with a straw hat pinned at a jaunty angle atop her curls. He was so used to seeing her done up in all her baubles and paint that he'd been half-silenced at the sight of her. Even when all the rest was stripped away, when set against nothing but itself, her beauty held its own.

He forced his thoughts to the present as a redcoat strode forward. He was a squat man with a forgettable face, except for a hooked nose which might have been broken a few times. "Papers?"

Ben produced them at once, trusting Wayne's man had stolen the right set.

The soldier's eyes moved in an efficient line down the length of paper. "It says your wife's sister is having a baby?"

"That's correct."

The soldier *hemmed* under his breath. "Where does she live?"

"Elizabeth Street. Due any day now."

"This her first?"

"Fourth. They've three girls already." Ben smiled broadly. "My brother-in-law's been on his knees for weeks praying for a son."

The soldier's attention lifted from the papers and settled on Rebekah. He squinted against the setting sun to see her better. "Any little ones of your own waiting back home?"

This was the moment Ben had been dreading. He knew Rebekah was quick-witted. He knew she was brave. But even the keenest spies, even the most daring, could betray themselves if they weren't careful.

Without the slightest flinch of uncertainty, Rebekah hooked her arm through Ben's. "We haven't been so blessed," she answered, offering a shy, fond smile.

Ben sat stunned. She'd spoken the words so naturally, so pleasantly, even he might have believed her if he didn't know she was lying. Though impressed on a professional level, he was suddenly more unsure about her. Would he ever know, truly, if she was playing him for a fool?

The soldier folded Ben's papers and returned them. Then, shouldering his musket, he stepped back. "I hope all goes well for your sister, ma'am."

The road ahead was open.

Ben tipped his hat, his smile turning a bit smug as they rounded the corner to safety.

"You lie well," Rebekah observed once they were clear of the soldiers.

He angled her a look as he slid their pass into her hand, as promised. "You're quite proficient at it yourself."

They rode in silence again. Ben hadn't visited the city since the British had imposed martial law three years prior, which had prompted thousands of Patriots to flee in mass exodus. Homes where Ben had once been welcome, where he'd dined with like-minded families and courted their daughters, were now occupied by British and Hessian troops who would shoot him on sight if they knew what he was.

Though he'd read reports of the great fire which had ravaged the streets on the heels of Washington's retreat, he wasn't prepared for the near wasteland which greeted him. Every fourth building or so bore the blackened marks of a vengeful fire, some of the buildings razed to their foundations like men cut down at the knees.

"What is it?" Rebekah asked beside him. "What's wrong?"

Ben shook his head, watching people move about their business, greeting one another in the streets as if nothing had happened, as if nothing had changed. Poverty had been given free rein, but if the rumors were true, that didn't stop those with deep pockets. Beneath the stench of squalor, officers glutted themselves with wealthy families who went on with their glittering dances and dinners as if the rest of the city didn't lie beneath their feet, begging for crumbs.

"It never should have come to this," he remarked bitterly, then urged the horses to match pace with the cart ahead.

They crossed over at Chambers Street, onto Broadway, before turning south toward the East River. To the left, people promenaded across the Commons, a wide patch of lawn where Patriots had once gathered in feverish protest of the Stamp Act. Ben's knuckles whitened over the reins as he thought of all the men and women who'd been erased from their own city, forced to pledge allegiance to the king or else to live in exile. In the end, all pleas and protest had been drowned beneath the deafening refrains of "Rule, Britannia!"

He might have grown in anger and indignation had Rebekah not drawn a breath. "I've never seen a church such as that," she confided in a hushed voice.

He followed her gaze across the street to St. Paul's Chapel. With its tall pillars and towering portico, the dark stone chapel stood proud and firm amid the otherwise emaciated streets, untouched by both flame and rebellion. The same could not be said of Trinity—the chapel's mother church—which had burned along with everything. Ben closed his eyes, reminding himself not all had been lost; sometimes, even in war, beautiful things were spared.

Spirits buoying, if only slightly, he rode the rest of the way to Dunmore Tavern without stopping. There was a good deal of stretching and wincing as he and Rebekah clambered down from the seat. Ben's stiff legs took some coaxing as he called for the hostler and circled the carriage to gather their bags.

They stepped into the dim, narrow parlor, where one squat window split the space in half with a shaft of dwindling sunlight. On either side of the door, tables had been crammed in tightly. Ben and Rebekah had to walk sideways to squeeze past the first two tables, then turn the other way to avoid colliding with a gentleman who was leaving. The room was clean enough, though, and a tureen above the fire smelled strongly of gravy. More importantly, Ben had gleaned through Jotham that the landlord was of secret Whiggish leanings, and so unlikely to turn them in if they were discovered.

A moment later, the man himself pushed out from the kitchen to lean against the bar. A gusty fellow with heavy jowls, he seemed to bellow whenever he spoke.

"Why, yes, my boy! Yes! We've a room!" He turned back toward the kitchen. He bellowed for his wife to scrounge up some provisions, then bellowed for a boy named Tom to tote the bags to the room at the top of the stairs. He turned back around. "Sit, *sit!*" he bellowed at Ben. "Supper won't take but a moment!"

Ben spoke his thanks, then stepped away from the bar. He found Rebekah already sitting at a table by the window. Head propped on her palm, she stared at the street beyond, her eyes wistful. Not long ago, she'd seemed little more to Ben than a siren with a sharp tongue and mocking eyes, but the perils they'd faced had softened the image and revealed the kind of woman she really was. Clever and calm, though she had little experience in Ben's world, she matched his pace with commendable ease.

He was loath to admit it, given her profession, but, heavens, she suited him.

"I've ordered supper," he told her, dropping into the seat across from her.

Her attention remained fixed on the street beyond. "So many people." She shook her head as she watched the crowd hurrying about.

"I take it you've never traveled."

"I was supposed to visit my cousins once, in Philadelphia."

"But you didn't?"

"No." She dropped her hand from her face, turning from the window. "I didn't."

Ben couldn't quite name the look that had shadowed her gaze, but it made him tense. Rebekah had seen so little of the world, nothing at all beyond Haverstraw, yet she'd somehow managed to see and experience only the worst.

"Bless me, man, if you don't have the prettiest wife!" The landlord boomed the accolade as he crossed the room, showing all the teeth of his crooked smile as he waved toward the bar. "Except for *mine,* o' course!"

At that, a reedy woman glided forward. She had a dusting of flour on her cheek and a tray balanced on her hip. She shouldered past her husband with an exasperated smile, swatting his arm in such a fond, familiar way the man chortled under his breath and pinched her waist.

Rebekah sat a little straighter as a number of platters were arranged on the table between them. There were two deep bowls of oyster stew and cold veal cutlets paired with boiled eggs. The platter of peach tarts smelled strongly of cinnamon and cardamom, but Ben noticed Rebekah had eyes only for a short stack of warm corn cakes, pulled fresh off the fire and steaming.

"I feel like I haven't eaten in three days," she exclaimed as her eyes raked over the feast.

Ben was inclined to agree. Lunch had been hours ago and consisted of only a few strips of dried meat, a stump of bread, and a thin wedge of cheese split between them. Even so, Rebekah didn't move. A practiced courtesan, she sat patiently with her hands folded primly before her as she waited for Ben to serve himself first.

"There's no need to stand on ceremony with me," he said, with a bit more irritation than he could fully account for. "If you want to eat, then eat."

A flash of surprise lifted her brows as she leaned forward and began filling her plate.

In that moment, small and fleeting though it was, Ben saw exactly what Rebekah had come to expect of men, that they would see to their own wants and needs first without any consideration for hers.

She asked him something about their room, but Ben barely heard.

How many men, he wondered suddenly?

How many men had used her because she was convenient, because they didn't care to find out if the smile she offered them was real or not?

He ought not to mind if it was the life she'd chosen, if it was the life she wanted, even now.

But he minded.

He minded terribly.

CHAPTER 22

Rebekah took two helpings of everything. Ben followed suit, pausing only once to ask if she cared for a glass of wine. Rebekah accepted, feeling nearly respectable as Mr. Benjamin Clarke's would-be-wife.

For once, not a soul knew who she was nor where she came from. None of the men they'd passed stared or scrambled for their pocketbooks, eager to secure her for the night. She almost felt like no one at all, a blank slate in the eyes of the world.

By the end of the meal, the sun had bent lower, dappling the street beyond in soft blue shadows. When at last Ben stood from the table, he took her arm, gently, and threaded it through his.

Rebekah's heartbeat quickened at the contact. Thus far, the idea of sharing a room had been the least troubling part of his proposed plan, yet she felt unsure of him.

With any other man, especially one who was paying for her time, she'd have known exactly what to expect that night. But Ben wasn't any other man. At least, she didn't *think* he was.

As if to prove this very point, he ushered her away from the stairs and toward the front door, escorting her into the street.

Rebekah fell in step beside him, confusion quickening her words. "Where are we going?"

Without pausing to ponder a direction, he turned left. "I thought you might like to see a bit of the city."

They turned another corner. Then another. She peered up at him, at that dry smile of his, and thought for sure he was up to something, perhaps venturing out to meet a contact. She squinted over her shoulder once to make sure they weren't being followed. "Does this have something to do with your assignment?" she whispered.

He chuckled. "We can call it reconnaissance if that makes you more comfortable."

This set her so much at ease she smiled, but then a group of rowdy boys scampered down the street in breeches and open-collared shirts, hair half wild in the wind as they went to search among the bric-a-brac of market stalls closing for the day. Out of instinct, Rebekah gave the boys a glance, as she always did when she came upon small children. Searching for her eyes. Mason's chin. Something that would jump out at her and whisper, *"I'm him. I'm him."*

She felt Ben watching and adjusted her gaze, reminding herself, as a blush stole up her cheeks, that she was nowhere near Haverstraw.

Her son was not here.

To evade Ben's lingering scrutiny, she stepped up to one of the stalls, fearing he might have spied a hint of the truth.

From the other side of the cart, a withered old

woman in a short gown leaned forward. “Care for a ribbon?” she croaked. “I have such the prettiest colors yer ever to see.”

Though Rebekah had no inclination to buy anything, she smiled politely and looked through the menagerie of ribbons, shuffling the various colors until a scarlet one caught her notice. Satin and two shades brighter than all the rest, it would stand out handsomely in a crowd.

“A most charmin’ color!” the vendor cooed, her hollow cheeks pulling taut as she smiled. “Yes, very becomin’!”

Rebekah brushed the ribbon between her fingertips, considering. “How much?”

“Oh, a penny is all. A pretty color for a penny, don’t you think? It would look mighty strikin’ against yer dark tresses.”

Inclined to agree, Rebekah reached for her pocket, but Ben had stepped forward, a coin proffered in his hand. “Allow me.”

Surprised by the offer, and more than a bit flustered, Rebekah laughed and shook her head. “Oh, come now, you really needn’t—”

But Ben had already stepped closer, his chest pressing against her back as he dropped the coin into the merchant’s hand. As the woman turned away, dropping his money in the till, Ben brushed a finger through one of Rebekah’s locks. “You have the most beautiful curls I’ve ever seen,” he murmured.

Flushing all the way up her neck, Rebekah folded the ribbon quickly and slipped it into her pocket. In general, she'd learned that such gifts and compliments came from men who wanted special favors and were trying to set themselves apart from the rest. Though Ben's gift was of a trifling cost, it felt warmer, more personal. Yet, she wouldn't allow herself to think too much of it. After all, he needed her as much as any other man did. Not in the same ways, perhaps, but they had an understanding.

"Thank you," she said, with crushing politeness. "Now, I do think it's time you told me the rest of your plan since we've made it into the city. You've been rather scant on the details."

He lifted one shoulder in a shrug as he gestured her down the road. "It's simple, really. In the morning, I'll be off for an hour or so. There's someone I have to track down, but it's best if I go it alone. I want you to wait for me at the tavern. You'll keep our pass with you, of course. If for whatever reason I'm not back by noon, you're to take the cart and get out of the city."

He explained all of this quite casually, and Rebekah might have been reassured if she wasn't already carrying the memory of his blood-soaked form falling half-dead at her feet. "So, it won't be *very* dangerous, then?" She squinted up at him.

His smile hitched again. "You know, it is oddly refreshing to be worried over by someone."

"What about your family?" she asked, with genuine curiosity. "Do they not worry over you?"

"No." His answer was clipped, far less cordial, and Rebekah stiffened accordingly.

They were now nearing the harbor. Though Rebekah was no stranger to watching the occasional ship sail along the Hudson, this was something entirely different. A floating city of spires and British flags stretched as far as the eye could see. The scope made Haverstraw feel even smaller, and Rebekah felt smaller herself because of it.

Ben paused when they reached the pier, following her gaze across the purpling horizon. And though Rebekah had lost any expectation of further conversation, he sighed roughly and tugged her toward a bench at the end of the wharf. "I come from a Loyalist family," he confessed in an undertone, guiding her to sit. "I have a hard time speaking of them, so you'll have to forgive me for being prickly."

She kept her voice twice as low as his. "Do they know about you? About your position in the war, that is?"

"They know enough."

"Do you ever hear from them?"

"Not a word," he said. "Not in nearly three years. They were in Boston when the city fell to Washington."

Rebekah clasped her hands in her lap, keeping

her eyes on the water. As far as captured cities went, the Continentals had taken Boston in a fairly nonviolent exchange. This was how the newspapers told it, anyway. Washington's men had surrounded the city at night, having drawn British attention to a battery firing from the opposite direction. The Loyalists surrendered peacefully before any of the troops could fire a shot, but this didn't mean some had not paid a steep price for their refusal.

"Did you ever find out what happened to them?"

"My mother and sister were shipped to Nova Scotia with the rest. I've not heard from either since they were exiled, nor do I expect to."

"Were you already a—"

Ben slipped her a look, before she dared utter the word *spy*.

"What about your father?" she amended quickly.

He turned his face away, into the shadows. "He was the first to realize I'd turned. He informed against me. I was arrested shortly after."

"So, he wasn't sent off with your mother?"

Ben's expression was strangely static. He stared ahead for so long Rebekah abandoned any hope of receiving an answer. When he spoke again, his voice was choked, less controlled. "He was a clergyman. So devoted to his king he wouldn't yield even when Washington's men marched up to his parish. There was a fight, got out of hand.

In the end, one of them lost his head and shot him. My father didn't live long enough to board the boats with the rest."

Rebekah gaped at him, too horrified to speak.

Patriots had murdered Ben's father. In his own church. Ghastly. Inhuman. Too well, she remembered the terror when she thought rebels had marched on her father's house. She'd wanted to believe she hated her father, but fear had awakened her to the bitter truth: she loved him still.

As Ben stared at the ships in the water, Rebekah sensed a similar conflict within him, the silent warring between grief and anger. She could think of no words to comfort him, no solace. Nothing she said would ever be enough. "I'm so sorry, Ben." Her voice broke as she slipped her hand over his. "Truly, I am."

Without looking at her, he took her hand and slid his fingers between hers, pulling her palm flush against his.

Rebekah stared at his fingers locked with hers, her heart striking a strange new rhythm. She knew how it felt to lose loved ones, to lose oneself in the process, but more than shared sorrow connected her to Ben, and she knew it as soon as he looked down at her with that sharp, searching gaze.

Her cheeks warmed when he drew closer. She closed her eyes and felt his breath against her temple, then her cheek, moving downward toward her lips.

Her thoughts, which had been spinning a moment ago, had frozen, balanced as if on the thin edge of a coin. Memories of Haverstraw, of Mason, of Pendergrass House—they all ebbed away, became somehow less a part of her as she waited to feel that first warm brush of Ben's lips against hers.

CHAPTER 23

The stillness lengthened, then shifted. Before Rebekah could register what was happening, Ben had drawn back and stood up from the bench. Dazed by his distance, and more than a bit embarrassed by her behavior, she scrambled to her feet.

In Rebekah's trade, knowing what men wanted was second nature. Ben was more inscrutable than most, but she didn't doubt for a moment what she'd seen in his eyes. Even now, his smile was tighter than normal as he offered his arm to escort her back. "It's getting late," was all he said.

Tucking a few windswept curls away from her face, she slid her arm through his, careful to exude nothing but dispassionate poise. Inwardly, though, she struggled. Aside from Mason, she'd never desired for any man to touch her, let alone kiss her. She was good at her job, of course, could make men think she fancied them, and aside from the occasional flicker of revulsion felt nothing whatsoever during the whole exchange.

If Ben wanted to kiss her, there was nothing surprising in it. She was far more bewildered by his restraint and equally unsettled by her reaction. What had made her so weak, so muddled in the mind, as to lean forward when she ought to have pulled back?

Perhaps it was because Ben had not used her casually, nor treated her as a means to an end. She'd told herself before that this didn't signify anything, that it didn't make him any different from other men, but now she supposed it did.

Was *this* why she wanted him?

All at once, Ben stiffened beside her, so abruptly Rebekah wondered, with horror, if she'd blurted that particular question out loud. When she dared a glimpse of his face, his profile bore its usual pleasantry, but his eyes were sharper, more concentrated. Without warning, he walked a bit faster, tugging her against him.

"What is it?" she asked. "What's wrong?"

"Nothing." He shuffled a passing glance across the street, where a bewigged redcoat with laughing eyes escorted a fine young lady in a green satin gown. "Don't look. Keep walking."

Sweat collected on Rebekah's back, but she followed Ben's lead. They passed the couple without incident, after which Ben released an unsteady breath.

"Who was that?" Rebekah whispered.

"No one." He loosened his hold on her arm but still held on. "A gentleman from my past, and I'd prefer to keep it that way."

"Did he recognize you?"

"Very unlikely." He smiled and pressed her hand.

Though Rebekah wanted to take comfort in the gesture, she couldn't banish a peculiar niggling sensation between her shoulder blades. As they reached the end of the street, she darted a cautious glance over her left shoulder. She spotted the crimson uniform, the impeccable wig. She wondered if the officer had turned back to look at them, for she saw the quickest flash of his profile—the smooth ridge of his nose and a high, chiseled cheek—before he said something to the lady beside him, laughed at her reply, and continued on his way.

As they made their way back to Dunmore Tavern, Ben found himself in an uncommonly gray mood.

Corporal Haskins was in the city. Devilish timing.

Ben had kept a brave enough face for Rebekah's sake, but there was a chance he'd been recognized or, worse, followed back to the tavern. He circled the street twice before returning, just to be sure, and was tempted to pack their things at once and send for the cart.

Even as he thought it, he knew this wasn't an option. Not yet. Wayne would be livid if Ben abandoned his post without good reason, especially as there was no telling what, if anything, Corporal Haskins had seen. The streets were fairly shadowed, and Haskins had never been particularly sharp-eyed. After all, Ben had been able to operate directly under the corporal's nose in Boston.

Boston. He nearly groaned as all the old frustrations bubbled to the surface. He felt like he was sitting at the family table again, watching the self-important corporal dance attendance on his smitten sister.

Was Meg still smitten?

To his chagrin, the question had not occurred to him until now. Of course, the corporal's relationship with the lady in the street had seemed more than comfortable, nearly intimate, but such a dalliance didn't necessarily mean Haskins wasn't married to Meg, who might have been awaiting her husband's return to their home in Nova Scotia.

Shaking his head, he entered the parlor two steps ahead of Rebekah and held the door for her. They climbed the stairs in silence as his thoughts shuffled from one inconvenience to another.

He'd nearly kissed her down by the river.

He wasn't sure what had come over him, exactly. He'd always thought it best to keep his hands to himself where Rebekah was concerned and managed well enough, but it had been a very near thing.

It wasn't only that she was attractive. He'd thought as much before, about her and about other women, and kept his wits. But then she'd taken his hand, offering quiet words of sympathy. It was a point from which he feared there was no coming back, for in that moment he'd seen beneath the courtesan smile and found a soft, somber soul and a spirit of loyalty despite any claims she'd once made to the contrary.

Together, they entered the chamber. The room was dark except for the candle she held steady in her small, pale hand. She cupped her other hand gently around the flame to keep it from guttering, but it danced like mad in the upstairs draft. Ben's heart beat faster as he closed the chamber door behind them.

He couldn't touch her. He knew this now and thought he'd armored himself sufficiently, but then Rebekah set the candle on the table and hooked him with a slight, inviting smile.

He considered the curve of her lips a moment longer than necessary, then forced his gaze back to her eyes. As soon as he looked at her, she settled upon the bed, studying him with a look of shrewd expectation.

Ben wasn't sure what she meant to prove, but her smile only sharpened the longer he stared. Did she really think he was the same as all those other men, or did she merely want him to be?

Perhaps it made things easier if she knew what to expect of him. Or perhaps his nearly kissing her down by the river had shaken her composure as surely as it had shaken his, and she was ready to prove to herself that he was nothing more than a man.

In his frustration, Ben nearly called her bluff. He wanted to pull her from that bed and into his arms, to kiss her so determinedly she'd forget all other names but his. He'd never forgive himself if he did. He wasn't the sort to take advantage of a woman, even if she was willing.

By the barest thread of self-control, he stepped back, swallowing a curse as he tugged some slack into his neckerchief. "You take the bed," he muttered.

Her chin jerked up. "Where will you sleep?"

"The chair is comfortable enough for my purposes. After all, one of us should keep watch." He shrugged out of his coat and slouched in the chair without further discussion.

Rebekah held the candle aloft. "You can't stay up all night," she protested. "You'll be dead tired on your feet come morning. We should take turns."

"No need for any concern on my account. I have a good deal of experience with this sort of thing."

"Yes," she replied. "I'm sure you do."

"*Goodnight,* Rebekah."

She pursed her lips and blew out the candle.

Across the room, garments rustled as she prepared for bed. Once Ben was sure she was settled, he kicked off his boots and tipped back in the chair, staring into the shadows as he wondered, for several hours, if she was truly asleep.

• • •

After a fitful night, Ben awakened to find Rebekah curled up tightly in the middle of the bed, her hair strewn over the pillow. It certainly wasn't what most men might have expected of spending the night in a tavern with a woman—least of all one of her profession—but now that daylight filled the room, the whole evening before seemed as hazy as a dream.

Stiff and out of sorts, he pulled himself up from the chair.

Though asleep, Rebekah shifted on the bed as if she'd heard him, pulling the cover with her as she rolled from one side to the other. Ben had heard her turn over a good number of times in the middle of the night. She'd muttered restlessly but never stirred enough to answer when he stood to ask what was the matter.

He studied her closely as he gathered his clothes. Her features weren't peaceful, exactly. They were blank, unreadable. He might have thought she dreamt of nothing at all had he not drawn near enough to notice her right hand was fisted up in a pitiful grip. Frowning, he reached down and brushed his fingers gently across her knuckles until her grip relaxed and her hand fell slack upon the bed.

Ben drew back. He couldn't imagine the kinds of memories that might have preyed upon her, and, of course, he dared not ask. The day ahead was to be long and perilous, and he needed to focus if they were to survive the worst of it.

Stepping away from the bed, he forced his thoughts from Rebekah and began readying himself. He shaved in the basin and pulled into his boots, then he tucked his pistol in the usual place beneath his coat.

Without making a sound, he stopped at the table by the door. There he took up a quill and leaned over a blank sheet of paper, composing an inconspicuous list of random grocery items. He sprinkled sand over the ink to dry it, then blew it off again. With great pains, he folded the paper according to Jotham's careful instructions. Flipping the finished product over several times in his hand, he inspected each crease until he was satisfied with his work. Then he slid it into his pocket and stepped toward the door.

"Where are you sneaking off to?"

Ben turned sharply on his heel. Still abed, Rebekah had propped herself up on one elbow, studying him with dark, sanguine eyes. He had no idea how long she'd been watching him, was beginning to think she'd have made a capable spy after all.

"I have to meet my contact," he admitted. "At the fish market. I won't be long."

A wrinkle knotted in the center of her brow as she considered his words. Then she sat up abruptly, pulling the covers up to her waist. "I should go. Not you."

Ben laughed tightly as he took up his hat. "Have you taken leave of your senses? Or perhaps you've forgotten I had a bullet inside me the first time we met."

"I've not forgotten anything," she answered tersely. "But, of the two of us, I'll blend in far better at the market, as well you know."

Ben set his jaw, wanting to argue, but he had to admit that she was right. From a strategic standpoint, a woman filling her basket would draw far less scrutiny than a single man. He'd thought as much on the ride to the city but hadn't wished to compromise Rebekah's safety more than was absolutely necessary.

She rose from the bed before he'd fully conceded. Though she wore nothing but her thin chemise, she cut a strong, striking figure as she drew herself up. "Come now," she said, reaching for her dress with an arch smile. "A wife would do as much for a husband, wouldn't she?"

He watched her slide into her petticoat, smiling at her nerve though he also wanted to scowl. "As it seems your mind is made up on the matter"—he slid a dagger from his boot and held it out to her by the hilt—"the least I can do, as a good husband, is see to it you're decently armed."

CHAPTER 24

Rebekah struggled to breathe evenly as she moved down the street, her basket bumping her hip in tandem with her heart. *"You'll find him at the fish market. Three tables down. Woodsy fellow with bristly hair."*

Dunmore Tavern was a few blocks away from the slips, where a long line of merchant vessels had been tied up along endless alleys of water. Rebekah would have been lost among the wharves twice over were it not for Ben's careful directions. He was particular on every point and made her swear she wouldn't deviate from the plan unless absolutely necessary.

She was to work her way through the meat market first, then continue on by Hanover Square to the Old Slip Market. Ben wanted her to fill her basket before she approached the courier at the fish market. She would draw far less suspicion with a basket full of goods.

The streets and stalls were abuzz that morning, vendors bellowing prices as the crowds swarmed. Rebekah had been to the Haverstraw market countless times, usually filling orders for Coffey, but this was an entirely different experience. There were countless stalls and far too many people crammed together as they circled them.

If Rebekah was discovered, she might have to make a run for it, but where would she go? To the right, the streets all jogged to meet one another, intersecting in strange patterns, and the docks and waterways to the left were an expansive network teeming with people, the sails of clippers towering in the distance.

Rebekah might have panicked at the scope of it, but she lowered her head, narrowing her thoughts to the task at hand. All she had to do was go shopping for a while. This was done easily enough.

She slipped into the meat market first. Inside, she inspected a cart full of hares. Blunted claws, dry ears. Much too old. Coffey would never have forgiven her if she'd returned with such a pathetic specimen. She selected some veal instead, her heart drumming erratically when the salesman said hello. All the while, the memory of Ben's voice guided her. *"Don't talk too much to anyone. Don't be overly friendly, but don't frown either."*

She offered the man in front of her a modest smile, tipped her head in a distracted farewell, and slipped back out into the fresh, open air. The next market was less busy, but the merchants shouted twice as gustily across the center aisle, their clamorous voices joining in what sounded like a foreign language. Wincing through the racket, Rebekah inspected a crate of turnips to steady her nerves. She purchased two, followed by a loaf of brown bread.

By the time she stepped in at the fish market, her basket was full, as Ben had instructed. Almost instantly, she spotted the table he'd described, and the man with bristly hair. *"All you have to do is hand over your list,"* Ben had told her. *"Take whatever fish he offers, and then make your way to the meeting point."*

Rebekah drew a slow, staid breath and stepped forward.

The man was in the process of descaling a herring, but he lifted his head when he noticed her observation. He was no older than Mason, though not nearly so cultured. Patriots and redcoats alike shaved every three days or so, but his chin and jaw bore a defiant patch of stubble. Tossing down his knife, he wiped his slimy hands down the length of his apron and sniffed. "Yes?"

Rebekah glanced down at the barrel of fish beside her. A host of glassy, dead eyes studied her, daring her not to tremble as she pulled out the list. "I have an order here," she said. "For a—a party. Very particular."

She pressed the note into the man's hand and stepped back. If she hadn't been watching for a reaction, she might have missed the quick flare of his nostrils as he tore into it. With gruff disinterest, his eyes moved down the list. Then, crumpling the paper in his hand, he pulled three fish, seemingly at random, from nearby barrels and set to wrapping them. As Rebekah waited, she fought the urge to shuffle back and forth on her feet.

Keep your wits about you, she told herself. *You're nearly done.*

"Here." The man shoved the parcel into her hands. The cold, wet fish seeped through the paper, sticking against the front of her dress.

Rebekah stared at him. Was that really all it took? Was there nothing more to say, to do?

From limited experience, she knew Ben's world was fast and dangerous, but this was so quiet, so easy. It was an insidious whisper drowned out by a city filled with shouting.

The man's eyes hardened. "Is that not all?"

"Yes!" There was a lot of awkward blinking on Rebekah's part as she slipped the fish into the last remaining gap in her basket. "Yes, thank you." She paid him, and then off she went, holding her breath as she waited to hear the first cold shout of soldiers advancing to detain her.

No one came.

Stunned by her success, she circled the street twice to ensure she wasn't being followed, then wound her way back toward Dunmore Tavern. She was a few blocks away when she slipped into the narrow alley Ben had indicated behind a tailor's shop. She set down her basket to wait.

The courier made her loiter a good long while.

She wasn't sure if he had reservations about meeting with her, or if he was only being careful, or if, perhaps, he'd ignored her signal and had no wish to meet at all.

Her answer came all at once when, without any warning, the courier materialized out of the shadow of a nearby doorframe. Rebekah's lips parted in greeting, but he thrust her back against the wall, so hard her head struck the stone. Her ears were ringing when he shoved his face next to hers, close enough she could smell stale ale on his hot breath. "What are you playin' at?" he snarled. "Who told ye to give that cursed note to me?"

Pain ravaged Rebekah's head, but she ignored it as she shifted her hand, grasping for Ben's dagger tucked beneath her skirt. "Your man in Haverstraw," she hissed, stifling the urge to scream when she couldn't reach it. "He sent me."

This was, admittedly, more than a bit of a fabrication. Rebekah didn't know the exact identity of the other spy in Haverstraw—Ben trusted her, but only so far.

The courier didn't release her, but his grip loosened marginally. "I've no reason to believe ye."

"The note was folded in just her way, wasn't it?"

She wasn't sure whether the note itself swayed his opinion, or that she'd acknowledged his informant was a female, but he shuffled back a step, granting her an extra inch to breathe. "What's he want now?"

"He has a task for her."

The man snorted. Dropping his hand from her arm, he turned away. "Well, she'll have a devil of a time completin' it, won't she?"

Rebekah stared at him, dumbfounded by his bitter reply. Ben had warned her that the girl might have gone quiet out of fear, that the courier might refuse to meet with her, or that they might have both been arrested. Yet, there was something fatal about the courier's words.

"What do you mean by that?"

The courier mopped a hand over his face, leaving finger-shaped streaks of grimy perspiration. "Wench weren't no older than you," he muttered. "If yer smart, you'll leave off with this, whatever it is you're doin', whoever yer involved with."

Rebekah dropped her gaze and thought of Ben. She recognized something in him, something that reminded her of herself. Perhaps it was that fruitless, senseless scrambling for freedom, like watching a moth trapped in a net. He may not have been right on every point, but she understood him. And yet, what would his life look like when at last the war was over? If Washington won, would he truly feel free?

Would any of them?

"Thank you anyway," she said to the courier, her voice drifting out of her. "It was most kind of you to meet me."

She sidestepped him to leave, but he seized her arm and gave it a powerful shake. "That captain of hers found her riflin' through papers she had no business riflin' through," he said between his teeth. "He flogged the wench himself, jus' outside the barracks, until she couldn't but hardly stand."

Rebekah's throat spasmed, threatened by the sudden movement of bile in her belly. Too well, she remembered the day that Peter Nelson had forced her to stand upon the barrel, starving her, humiliating her, making every nerve in her body feel the full terror of his power over her. It had been a destructive experience, unforgettable in its anguish. She could hardly imagine what would have happened if the monster had been granted a whip. "Where is she now?" she whispered.

"Didn't make it even three weeks in prison but died of festerin' wounds." With an unexpected laugh, the courier spat on the ground as if to christen her memory. "A fine service to the cause, don't ye think? But men like Washington won't even bother to learn her name."

Rebekah pulled back, wanting to leave and yet rooted to the spot. She thought of Ben's father, shot down in his own church. She thought of Heston's place, burned to rubble. She thought of what might happen to her or to Ben or to any of them if their connections were found out by the opposite side. She was beginning to believe the color of one's coat hardly mattered anymore. Both sides were willing to do unspeakable things. Willing to kill. To torture. To die.

The courier released her with a grunt. "They'll do the same to ye if yer caught. Ye'd best leave off like I did, or you'll go the same way. That's a fact."

CHAPTER 25

By the time Rebekah returned to the tavern, an unnatural tightness tickled at the base of her throat, exactly where one might loop a noose. She swallowed a few times, struggling to dispel the pressure as she pushed through the front door. Smiling for the landlord's sake—and restraining herself from sprinting—she slowly mounted the stairs.

Ben must have been watching for her from the window because he opened the door a second before her fingertips brushed the handle. He tugged her inside, nearly knocking the basket of market wares off her arm. His eyes were fierce, urgency humming through him as he guided her, a bit roughly, across the room.

"You're all right?"

Too overwrought to answer rightly, Rebekah set down her basket and dropped onto the bed.

"Did he meet you?" Ben pressed, hardly giving her time or space to think. "The courier?"

Rebekah's head was tender from the knocking it took. She leaned it back against the pillow and answered him with a simple, "yes."

Ben paced twice. He squinted out the window, then back at her. "Well?"

"She's gone."

"Gone?" He froze mid-step, face stripped of all color. "What do you mean she's gone?"

"The British found out what she'd done. They flogged her, quite brutally by the sounds of it, and tossed her into prison. She died of infection."

At those words, all the breath seemed to slip out of Ben like a wind-abandoned sail. His knuckles turned bone white as he grabbed the bedpost for support. Leaning there, he stared at the floor and struggled to find his voice. "Did he say anything else?" he rasped.

Rebekah bit down hard on her lip as the courier's warning echoed in her mind—*you'll go the same way*. No doubt, Ben had already considered the possibility. To him, at least, it seemed the risk was worth it. "He wants nothing more to do with these schemes," she said, climbing to her feet. "He wishes to be left alone. He was very persuasive on that point."

Ben's eyes sharpened as he lifted his head. He scanned her face, her arms, hoisting a brow as he pushed back from the bedpost. "Persuasive *how?*"

A peculiar look on his face made Rebekah shift back on her feet, but before she could answer, the door to their room was flung open.

"Have a care, sir!" Ben shouted, jumping in front of Rebekah as the landlord entered.

But when the landlord spoke his voice was unnervingly soft, calculated, not anywhere near to his usual shout. "Take it easy, my friend," he said, holding up both hands in surrender. "I thought you might like to know a band of redcoats is fast approaching."

Unable to hide her panic, Rebekah stared at Ben. She didn't want to go to prison. She didn't want to be flogged. And she certainly didn't want to see him hanged.

He looked back at her a moment, his brows bunched close together. Then he shrugged at the landlord. "Why should such news matter to me?" He sounded offhand, but he stepped to the window anyway and scanned the street below.

"I have a lad back and forth from the docks, who keeps an ear out for me. He heard the strangest bit of news this morning, that one of the gentlemen in my inn—well, I can hardly believe it myself—but he said that one of the men in my inn has been informed against, and I have every reason to believe, good sir, that man is you."

Ben moved so fast for his gun that Rebekah nearly screamed, but the landlord laughed before Ben's finger found its place on the trigger. "Deuces, boy, if I wanted to see you swing, I'd have waited by the door to let them in. Besides, I've the strangest notion you chose my inn deliberately. Perhaps as a bit of—insurance?"

Ben smiled tightly. "I've heard rumors," he admitted.

"Quite right, sir, quite right. Some of us are obliged to play a part, as you well know, but not all of us have laid down with the enemy."

Laid down with the enemy. Rebekah felt sick at the man's phrasing and watched Ben's profile for any hint of panic or concern. When nothing moved in his expression, she told herself this was a good sign, but her stomach lurched despite her, utterly unconvinced.

"Go out the back way, through the stable," the landlord was now saying to Ben. "I'll hold them off as long as I can."

Ben clasped the man's hand in unspoken thanks while the landlord patted him on the shoulder. "Yes, yes," he said. "I wish all the best of luck to you and your pretty wife." He struck the word "wife" in a funny voice, tipping his head to her as he swept out of the room.

As soon as they were alone, Ben took Rebekah's hand. "It seems we're in for a bit of a jaunt," he said, smiling gravely.

They seized their half-packed bags and took the stairs two at a time.

Down in the parlor, the landlord was back to his usual business, his laughter nearly shaking the rafters above them. Ben pressed a finger to his lips as he and Rebekah crept out through the kitchen. They dashed along the path to the stable, where one of the horses, the fastest of the bunch, was already saddled.

“I quite like that innkeeper,” Ben remarked as he sprung up into the saddle. He cast a regretful glance at the cart, which would have to be left, then lowered his hand to help Rebekah.

She stood frozen beneath his gaze, the blood rushing in her ears. She thought she could hear redcoat boots advancing in a rolling drumbeat up the street.

If Ben heard the same, he didn’t say as much. He leaned sideways when she didn’t take his hand, grabbed hold of her arm, and wrenched her up into the saddle before him.

Ben’s heart banged against his ribs as he wheeled them around the stable and bolted for Queen Street. A series of angry bellows hurtled up the street behind them, followed by cracks of gunfire. Grabbing hold of Rebekah’s neck, he shoved her head down, deftly steering them between passing carts and horses. The faces of startled travelers, the buildings and the trees, all swept passed at full tilt until the buildings became sparser and there were fewer crowds to jump aside for fear of being trampled.

“Nearly there!” Ben shouted and flew past the last point of passage, spurring the horse so fast the sentries barely had time to unshoulder their weapons.

Another chorus of shouts echoed behind them, another overture of gunfire, to which Ben paid little heed. He rode at a breakneck pace until wilderness replaced city all around and the poor horse could take no more. He yanked to a stop deep within a knot of towering pines, the horse's hooves scrabbling over tree ruts as it settled itself.

His hands shook when Rebekah slumped forward. He dropped the reins and gripped her shoulders, pulling her upright. "Are you hurt?" When she didn't answer, he ran his hands over both her arms, over her back and up her neck, praying his shaking fingers would come back clean of blood. "You weren't hit, were you?"

"No," she gasped, trembling in his arms. "No, I wasn't."

Ben released her. *"Curse that Haskins!"* he spat savagely under his breath.

This time, when Rebekah spoke, her voice sounded stronger. "The officer from last night?"

"I didn't think he noticed me. Obviously, I was mistaken."

"We've outrun them, though," she said, setting a hand upon his sleeve. "We're safe now, aren't we?"

He angled in the saddle, dashing one last glance in the direction of the city before pulling her back against his chest. "Best not to chance it," he muttered and gave the reins a vigorous *thwap*.

He stopped only twice to rest the horse, and then all the way to King's Ferry without halting again. He and Rebekah boarded and crossed the Hudson in silence, watching as the mountains rose out of the mist to greet them from the other side.

From the dock, he rode until they came to a clearing near the boardinghouse. By now, dusk had painted the sky a rich indigo, and the horse was panting miserably from the heat, a thin layer of foamy spittle gathering about its teeth. Ben dismounted with a grimace, tugging the horse's face down to his level. He patted her between her wide, glassy eyes. "Well run," he murmured, then reached for Rebekah, who sagged down from the saddle beside him. She didn't speak a word, but her legs shook as she lifted the corner of her sleeve to wipe the grit from her face.

As soon as her feet were under her, Ben withdrew his hands. He didn't know what to say to her now that they were both safe. He thought of Jotham's contact, that poor young woman whose only crime was getting tangled up in their cursed cause. He'd heard of some women being flogged for consorting with the enemy or else arrested, but he'd never quite faced the reality of it. He tried to imagine what the woman had looked like when Jotham knew her, when he'd first enlisted her help, but every time he tried, he saw only Rebekah, her gaping eyes lit with terror as the whip connected with the delicate skin of her back. He twisted away to banish the ghastly image, leading the horse to the creek as he collected his thoughts.

He reminded himself that he'd been in close scrapes, many times over, and rarely minded. In fact, he'd once relished the breakneck pace of a few such chases. His mission with Rebekah had hardly been his most dangerous, but it bothered him more than all the rest.

He glanced at her over his shoulder.

She brushed her hand over her skirt, but it was a hopeless gesture, for she was caked with dust from waist to hem, and her hair had blown free of its pins. She lifted her chin before he could look away, her eyes forming a question he couldn't decipher.

He wouldn't blame her if she hated him, if she called down curses from on high to smite him. From the beginning, he'd known it was dangerous to involve her. Still, if she was a willing accomplice, what did it matter? This had calmed his conscience to a point, but he no longer felt certain. After all, she served Mrs. Pendergrass willingly, too, but was she really free to do as she liked?

He stared at his boots.

Freedom.

The word meant something different to everyone, and yet he hadn't the dimmest idea what it meant to Rebekah. He stiffened as she joined him at the stream. She knelt on the bank and splashed a palmful of cool water against her face. He stared, watching the beads of water run down her temples, unnerved she could exude such poise after such a narrow escape.

"You were very brave," he said.

She peered up at him, the edges of her hair dripping, and smiled. "I didn't feel very brave, but I thank you anyway, Mr. Clarke."

Though she'd only spoken his alias, there was a note of fondness, of familiarity he'd never heard in her voice before. More than anything, he wished he might correct her, tell her to call him *Mr. Renshaw* instead—or, far more suitable to his wishes, *Ben*.

Instead, he pivoted away. They'd gotten too close. He saw this now and the danger in it. In his line of work, there was always a risk of suffering collateral damage, and he'd accepted that. Some of his superiors might think little of a prostitute captured in the name of the cause, or even one killed, but Ben wouldn't risk it. He had enough sins that he couldn't bring himself to confess without adding one of that magnitude to the list.

"You should go it on foot from here." He motioned up the hill. "It's not far."

"And you?" She straightened and stepped closer, her hand half-reaching toward him before falling back to her side. "You won't come in to rest? To dine?"

Though Ben's eyes were gritty from lack of

sleep, his heart was pounding again as he looked down into her dark eyes. What had he proven to her except he was just as selfish as all the other men who'd used her to see to their own passions? His had been of a political bent, perhaps, but that didn't make them any nobler where her welfare was concerned. He'd used her. Might have gotten her killed. He hadn't really thought it would come to that, but war made monsters of them all.

Desperate to clear her from his conscience, he dug in his pocket, pulled out a few notes, and held them out to her. "For your trouble," he said, trying to sound dismissive for both their sakes.

Her eyes widened as soon as she saw the money, then narrowed when she snatched it from his hand. "You aren't coming back."

He searched her for any sign of disappointment, but she was far too practiced for that. The glow in her eyes already had disappeared behind the blank mask she donned for every other man she served. Feeling he ought to offer some sort of farewell, some bit of consolation, he took her hand, feeling her fingers stiffen beneath his.

"You've been very useful to our cause." The words emerged in a tumble, impossibly trite, and perhaps that's what gave him away in the end.

For, although Rebekah nodded, she didn't step back or pull her hand from his as he expected. She drew closer. Without speaking, she lifted her chin and pressed a warm kiss to the edge of his jaw, torturously brief. “Good-bye, Ben,” she whispered against his skin.

His pulse thundered. He felt a roiling wave of frustration as she turned to leave but assured himself she’d be far safer in Haverstraw—far safer away from *him*. He watched until she was clear of the trees, then heaved himself into the saddle. “Inconvenient woman,” he muttered under his breath, then rode hard in the opposite direction.

Ben did not ride straight to Wayne’s camp, as were his orders, but first to The King’s Ferry Tavern. He spotted Jotham at his usual post behind the bar, the only black coat in a throng of crimson. The man was in the process of drying a tray of tankards, his rag working in tight, efficient circles, though he paused a second when Ben strode into the parlor.

Ben took his time closing the door behind him. The whole way there, he’d toiled over how he might convey the terrible truth to Jotham, how the woman who had aided him, who had trusted him with her life, was dead.

Though failing to find his nerve, Ben stepped up to the bar.

Jotham’s brow inched up as he waited for Ben to say something.

With renewed remorse, Ben stared gravely at his friend, the code words nearly catching in his throat. “Sherry, if you please.”

To Ben's relief, his voice cooperated, sounded as cavalier as ever it was, entirely composed.

Jotham, who'd known him since boyhood, stared at him as if he'd shouted, his face gray as stone as he somehow surmised the unspoken truth. Jotham cleared his throat but didn't speak. He filled a glass at random and shoved it across the bar.

And that was all.

Jotham's coloring returned as he lowered his eyes and went on drying his tray of tankards as if nothing had happened, as if death had not come whispering its wretched taunts against his ear.

Ben's words of comfort, such as they might have been, sat heavy within his chest, even as a growing rage burned within.

Around them, the British chattered and chortled. They recounted their victories over drinks Jotham himself had poured for them and left no slip of silence in which a woman might have been rightly mourned or remembered in any of the ways she deserved, even if she was a spy.

CHAPTER 26

July 5, 1779

Settling back into the way of things was hard, but Rebekah saw no alternative.

Mason was done with her.

So, too, was Ben.

The men were as starkly different as crimson and blue, but it didn't much matter the color of their coats; they were both deserters where she was concerned.

Of course, it was unfair to expect them to keep promises they'd never actually made to her. Most people shook the dust of Haverstraw quite willingly from their heels and always had. But after her time in the city—and those warmer moments she'd shared with Ben—Rebekah was beginning to feel like dust herself, brushed and blown aside as soon as she was no longer suitable or convenient.

Unfortunately, Mrs. Pendergrass had a sharp eye for moping and no patience for it, so as soon as Rebekah returned, she was put through her usual chores at a far more rigorous pace. She served in the kitchen. She scrubbed the filthy windows. She delivered trays of food and ale. She was dead on her feet by the end of her first evening back, but she nonetheless stooped over a gentleman's shoulder at the end of supper, her fingers grazing his stiff, white collar.

"Two shillings," she whispered in her most dulcet tone, hoping Mrs. Pendergrass would be satified with the performance.

"Soon," the man muttered, tapping his plate with a finger even as his eye roved along her curves.

Rebekah's hand teased a slow line from one shoulder to the other as she stepped away.

Hattie caught her by the elbow as soon as she was clear of the table. "I just heard," she whispered, her voice squeaking at the end, "that a gentleman paid *ten* pounds for you."

Rebekah sighed. Mrs. Pendergrass had made no secret of her escapade in the city, so she was forced to confirm the truth of it, for the fourth time that day, with a clipped nod. What Mrs. Pendergrass didn't know was that Ben had really given her fifteen pounds; Rebekah had secured the extra in the hem of her curtain where his note had so recently been kept.

Hattie bit her lip, trying to conceal her excitement. "Who was he?"

"A man of no account," said Rebekah.

"Do you think he'll call for you again?"

Rebekah scanned the room to keep from answering. A fair number of customers had shuffled in that evening, seeking solace from another storm about to roll through. Most of the girls moved about the parlor in their skirts and stays and little else, sweating under the oppressive heat as they cleared the supper plates.

"Was he very rich, then?" Hattie persisted, helping Rebekah along, as if she'd merely forgotten how to gossip.

"I've no idea."

"Very handsome?"

"Not in the least."

Thunder gave a disagreeing grumble outside the window.

"Do you think he'll—"

Rebekah was spared answering when a band of officers pushed through the front door. Hattie abandoned her present line of questioning to primp her hair and trimmings, but Rebekah couldn't have lifted a single finger to straighten herself.

There, in the middle of the throng, stood Mason.

Rebekah's world narrowed, suddenly fixed to the point of his smile. And, oh, she thought miserably, but he smiled well. As sociable as ever, he was listening to the chatty ensign who was standing beside him. Though Mason didn't miss a beat in answering the other man's questions, his eyes were pulled to Rebekah, and there, for the moment, his attention remained.

It was the first time Mason had looked at her

knowing exactly who and what she was, and yet, aside from a flicker of what might have been pain, his gaze didn't look so very different. He'd always been able to read her, could tell when she was angry or somber without her saying a word about it, and so she prayed he couldn't see how confused, how devastated, she'd felt at losing him again. Nor, she realized with a start, was this the only secret she was keeping from him.

What if he learned about her recent trip to the city?

Her stomach seized at the thought. He would never forgive her if he knew what she'd done for Ben, was as likely to arrest her as he was to ever forgive her, and he had the power to make her pay for everything she'd done, for all the ways she'd lied. She was so focused on him, foolishly so, that she nearly yelped when someone pinched her leg beneath her skirt.

"I'm ready," grunted a drunken voice as clammy fingers shoved two coins into her palm.

Ignoring the press of the customer's sweaty chest against her back, Rebekah managed not to break stares with Mason. To her satisfaction, he looked away first, but a moment later he was laughing heartily at something one of the other men had said.

At the sound of that laugh, searing anguish took hold of Rebekah, followed at once by bitter loathing. She wanted to hurt Mason. She wanted to hurt him, and she wanted him to want her, and she knew very well that these two ends could be met in much the same way.

She spun into the stranger's arms and offered him a beguiling smile.

The man was a lanky nobody with eyebrows so pale they might not have been there at all, but he smiled readily enough as his eyes roamed over her.

"Follow me," Rebekah whispered, trailing her hand from his shoulder down to his hand.

As she led the stranger toward the stairs, Mason's gaze seared a point between her shoulder blades.

Somewhere in the last second, her throat had gone tight, but she ignored the pain of it and tugged her customer by the hand, all the way up the stairs. She wanted to leave it at that, to allow Mason to think she really was that cold, but she couldn't help herself. At the very last moment, she glanced down from the landing and immediately cursed herself for it.

Mason had moved to the base of the stairs, his right hand curled around the banister, his other resting on the hilt of his sword.

Rebekah smiled to twist the dagger deeper but only succeeded in wounding herself as she suddenly imagined the stranger's hands roving along her clothes, her skin, tugging at her, pulling, wanting all of her and yet none of her. She told herself it didn't matter, that men could do whatever they wanted with her, but the trembling in her hands told her otherwise. More than anything, she wanted Mason to step forward, to snatch her back from the precipice.

"She's with me." That was really all he had to say, and perhaps all the unspoken things between them might finally find a home.

But Mason didn't move.

Hand on his sword, he watched, unblinking, until Rebekah turned the corner and disappeared from his sight, where only the shadows of her chamber cared half enough to shield her.

Rebekah wasn't surprised when Mason sent for her the next day, but she was disquieted. He wasn't the kind of man who tolerated loose ends in general, so she suspected he wanted to make sure she held no ill will against him, perhaps even apologize for his previous conduct.

He met her in the entrance to his tent before she was able to announce herself. He sighed as soon as he saw her. "Rebekah," he called her—*not* Miss Stanton—and steered her inside.

She fortified herself with a smile. "How pleasant it is to see you again, Lieutenant."

Lieutenant. This was not a promising introduction, and well he knew it. With far more presence of mind than Rebekah felt, he took up a beveled decanter and set to pouring drinks. "I've been meaning to call after you for some time," he admitted, handing her a glass of wine. "I stopped by the boardinghouse a few days ago, but they said you'd gone off—with a customer."

An unspoken question tainted his tone. A bit satisfied by his jealousy, she set her drink on the table untasted. "You are attentive as always. I appreciate your concern."

A scowl escaped him, but he swallowed his drink despite her flippant tone.

"Is there anything else?" she asked before he'd made it to the bottom of the glass. "If not, I should be getting back."

"Getting—back?"

"To Pendergrass House."

"Are you punishing me?" He plunked down his empty glass. "It seems a bit unfair, don't you think, when *you* were the one who misled *me?*"

"On the contrary. You've done your duty remarkably well. And I thank you for it."

Formality was a painful pretense with Mason, but Rebekah felt she carried it off well.

Until he poured himself another drink, that is, and settled into his chair. "I have no intention of sending you back to Pendergrass House," he answered gruffly. "Not now. Not ever again if I can help it."

Hope had become rather a hard sell for Rebekah, but her mind nonetheless whirred as she wondered at his meaning. "But Mrs. Pendergrass—"

“Can go to the devil. I haven’t brought you here to make pleasantries, Rebekah, or even amends. I’ve brought you here to make an offer.”

She swayed on her feet, hardly daring to imagine that he might propose marriage after so many years, and yet—

“What kind of an offer?”

“I thought I could be done with you. I told myself it was for the best. That it would be easy. But then I saw you there. In that place.” He finished his second drink, palming the glass as he raised his head to address her more directly. “I want you to live here, at the fort. I’d find a suitable position, of course. Cleaning, mending. You’d earn rations and wages and keep to your own tent. No other men would touch you.”

She stared at him, aghast. “What, as a camp follower?”

“Yes.”

“What would we be—to each other?”

He waved a hand at the hesitancy in her voice. “You needn’t worry. I’ve spoken with the colonel. Everything is settled.”

This was not exactly an answer—nor, she noticed, was it a proposal. But if Mason had spoken to his colonel on her behalf, perhaps one was in the making. To take her on in any respect was a considerable risk on Mason’s part, and the colonel would only have allowed it if he believed there was some kind of understanding between them. If their relationship was deemed anything less than respectable, Mason could lose his position, and she'd be drummed from the camp in shame.

Even so, she could not help but doubt him.

Mason had always cared a good deal for appearances, for reputation. If he wouldn't propose marriage outright, nor even mention it, then a part of him must have thought it was impossible. Without the assurance of a formal offer, Rebekah would be living on borrowed time, a passing whim until he found a more suitable match and, someday, married.

Then where would she go?

Back to her father, to be forever despised for her poor choices, or back to Pendergrass House, where she'd be nothing more than used goods to every man who wanted a go with her.

There was, of course, another option. She might leave Haverstraw entirely, to live in an exile of her own making, cut away from every person who had once been part of her—her father, her first love, her child, who didn't even know of her existence . . .

Adrift in her thoughts, she didn't see Mason stand or cross the tent but flinched when he touched her arm, the heat from his hand sinking into her. "Don't keep me in suspense. What have you to say?"

"I hardly know what to say," she owned.

Mason's eyes flashed with astonishment.

Rebekah understood his disbelief. Two weeks ago, she'd have accepted him without pausing for breath. But if Mason took her on only to leave her again, if he cast her aside as he'd done before, she feared she might never recover. "I need time to think," she said, moving to leave. "To decide."

Mason stepped in front of her. "I'm trying to give you a better life. You know that, don't you?"

"And I thank you for it, but I cannot give you an answer yet. Unless you wish to reserve me for the evening, I must return to Pendergrass House."

With an incredulous scowl, he stepped forward. Then, cupping her chin, he tipped her face and covered her lips with his.

It was a convincing final appeal, wore her down as he no doubt intended. By the time she pushed back on his chest, she could hardly draw breath. "Give me two days," she pleaded, fearing she wouldn't take much convincing if he decided to be more persuasive.

He smiled wistfully, pushing a stray hair back from her eyes. "For you, Rebekah, I'd wait twenty years."

CHAPTER 27

July 5, 1779

Ben didn't often feel out of place in his unpowdered hair and civilian garb, but he almost did in Wayne's camp.

A fair number of the Light Infantry had been assembled near the ruins of Fort Montgomery, the rest dispersed in other camps nearby to evade suspicion. They wore freshly laundered uniforms and plumed hats in various styles, their hair powdered to meet the hawk-eyed general's satisfaction. These troops were seasoned, all the officers chosen by Washington himself, and deadly with weaponry.

The men ignored Ben's arrival as they gathered around their fires, settling in for the evening meal. Ben glanced over the various tin kettles of salt pork and turnips. Everything was boiled, as encouraged by Washington, to keep the men healthy and fit. Occasionally, troops were caught frying their meats on the sly, especially after an inspection, but not in Wayne's camp. If he caught the barest whiff of grease, he'd have had them whipped.

Before Ben could request a formal interview, Wayne stepped out of his tent. Dressed in his usual fashion, hair powdered with flour and tallow and hat angled over his brow, he shot Ben an ungenerous glare. “You need a shave, Renshaw.”

Ben smiled. “I beg pardon. I didn’t have much time to see to my toilette.”

Wayne turned away but at the last minute gave an idle wave.

Ben obeyed the summons, falling in step beside him.

“I take it you have news for me.” Wayne didn’t look at Ben but scrutinized the men, always searching for infractions.

“The girl in the city is dead.”

Wayne swore as Ben explained. “So, we’ve reached the point of war where the dogs will kill our women.” The spark in his eyes dimmed a fraction, and he sighed. “Well, no matter. Washington has other eyes in the city, far more efficient. A tight little ring.”

Ben swallowed a curse. Was this all the thanks Jotham’s woman was to receive? She was dead and gone, and *no matter*. A fit price for a glorious cause, barely a footnote, it seemed, on the general’s conscience.

“What other eyes?” he asked.

“A fair bit above your pay grade, that.”

Ben bristled at the insinuation. Those who spied for money were always suspected of disloyalty, easily turned if they were offered enough coin. Because of this, Ben was reimbursed any expenses accrued on missions but was otherwise an unpaid agent. He was no mercenary.

"What news *is* within my pay grade?" he challenged. "I take it your Light Infantry has been moved here for a reason. Is the attack at hand?"

"Not a single one of them knows of the attack, so don't you dare utter a word about it."

"You seem fairly confident you can take the fort."

Wayne's eyes turned thoughtful. "It is an alluring challenge, you must admit. A fine feather in Washington's cap."

"So, you're to pluck it for him."

"Those detestable lobsterbacks have been sitting comfortably long enough. Whatever they may say in the city, their 'Little Gibraltar' is *not* impenetrable." Wayne's voice deepened. "One of our own has already made his way inside."

Intrigued, and more than a bit impressed, Ben leaned closer. "How did he manage that?"

Wayne all but grinned, a rare bit of boyishness shining through. "He rode in under a white flag, escorting a local woman who wished to see her sons, who have enlisted with the British of late. They didn't think him much of a danger, but he saw enough. There's a weakened side of the western wall, easily exploited, and their artillery will be less than sufficient in an all-out attack."

"So, the attack *is* imminent?"

"An operation like this requires a deft hand.

Washington has surveyed the fort with me and agreed that Stony Point can be retaken. But he's urged me to tread carefully. He won't risk compromising our secrecy by sending reinforcements, so we're ensuring we've allowed for every potential calamity. I won't gather the rest of the men together until the time has come."

This sounded very like Wayne. He planned meticulously for every contingency, but when the time came to draw blood, he hurled himself into the fray with the best of them. It was how he'd risen to general so quickly, been called a "modern Leonidas" after his valiance at Monmouth. He was a gentleman and a rabid dog. He led from the front and went for the throat.

Ben's thoughts darkened as they drifted to Rebekah. If she was, as he'd once suspected, entangled with the lieutenant, she might find herself in the thick of it if such an attack unfolded. He remembered his final farewell to her, spoken in the interest of keeping her safe, and realized he might have left her dangerously exposed.

Wayne recalled his attention. "I want you to help us," he said, clapping him on the shoulder. "You've had a hand in this from the beginning and know some of the British in the area."

"You wish me to camp here with your men?"

"No. Return to Stony Point. Take up your cover and keep an ear to the ground. Let me know if anything changes, and I'll be in touch when I'm ready to lead the assault." Wayne glanced at Ben's pistol, which was tucked, as ever, into the side of his belt, and smiled dryly. "Oh, yes," he added, "and you'll be wanting to get your hands on a proper musket, won't you? When the time comes."

CHAPTER 28

July 6, 1779

Rebekah had to pass her father's house on her way to the Sawyers' farm. At first, she had every intention of pressing on, but her feet slowed to a halt, the pebbles on the road crunching beneath her shoes. Tired, she couldn't help but stop to lean against the fence, just once.

The place was familiar to her in the way of dreams.

The gravel drive was lined with dogwood trees, which formed a wide, pink canopy in the spring and an eerie procession of skeletal limbs in winter. Gardenias and hydrangeas crowded the front gardens, all of which had been first planted by her mother long ago. Every line of the towering house beyond was as straight and stately as she remembered. There was her father's green Windsor chair in its usual place on the porch. And there, two stories up, was Rebekah's window, which had once been shuttered and barred, entombing her in darkness as Eli was ushered into the world.

Her father had been at the tavern on that night.

He'd never been much of a drinker, not even in the long, bleak months after Rebekah's mother died, nor did he enjoy the kind of company taverns generally provided. But there he'd been, sitting in some dim corner with brandy or rum while Rebekah screamed alone in her chamber with the midwife.

It had taken more than twenty hours to deliver the baby. At times Rebekah was certain she was dying, as if her body was splitting right down the middle and no one would be able to patch her up or make her whole again. Even her most strident screams weren't enough to hold the pain or give it direction. The midwife whispered patiently to her in these moments, brushing the matted hair back from Rebekah's sweat-soaked brow. At one point, the older woman went wretchedly silent, pacing from Rebekah's bedside to the door and back again as though preparing to call for help. But then Eli arrived, the little screamer, and was placed into his mother's arms.

Rebekah's father lumbered in a few hours later. Smelling stale, like whiskey, he gave the child a single peck on the crown of his head, then disappeared into his study. Bedridden, Rebekah did not see her father again for days.

As she eyed her childhood home, Rebekah realized she'd grabbed hold of the gate latch, as if to enter. She dropped her hand and stepped back. It wasn't her home anymore, hadn't been for some time, yet how swift and piercing her panic when she'd thought a mob might have burned it.

If she knocked on the front door, would her father jump out of his chair in the hope it might be her? Or would he refuse to answer the summons, fearing it was?

She didn't try for an answer. Though her heart twisted at the thought of pressing on, she couldn't bear the thought of facing him after all she'd done or of forgiving him for all he hadn't. And so, she banished the memories and walked away, finding it was becoming easier and easier to leave the things she loved the most behind.

The rest of the walk took upward of an hour, but she counted each step as penance and paid little mind to the blisters. When at last she arrived, her first thought was that the Sawyers' house was much smaller than she had expected, but the structure appeared sturdy and the grounds well-kept. From within the barn, came the baying of dogs and cattle alike, no doubt sensing her approach. Feet aching, she pressed against the fencepost and scanned the property for any hint of the child.

Voices came from the other side of the property, and she had to dig her feet into the topsoil to keep from fleeing. She'd come too far to turn back now. She had to see the child, and she wouldn't leave until she did.

Mrs. Sawyer circled the house first. She wore a homespun short gown for working out of doors and a straw hat with an enormous brim.

As soon as Rebekah saw her, all the hollow, empty places in her heart filled with sudden loathing. Not for her father or for the reverend or even for this woman, this stranger, who was presumably raising Rebekah's child as her own. No. As Rebekah looked upon Mrs. Sawyer, it was as though a curtain within her was blown aside, and all the shame of who she'd become awakened her to the kind of woman she might have been if things had gone differently. If she hadn't gone to Mason's house that day. If she hadn't loved him or turned to Mrs. Pendergrass when her heart was broken over him.

Again, she looked at Mrs. Sawyer. The woman was homespun linen. Rebekah was crushed satin, made over and over into something different for every man who didn't want her.

Mason would never marry her. She knew this distinctly. Still, to refuse him was to remain at Pendergrass House.

As soon as that thought came, a small boy with blond curls scampered around the barn in search of his mother. He wore a grass-stained cotton shift, which fell past his knees.

Rebekah watched him leap into his mother's arms, and her lips parted—

"Eli." She spoke his name like a benediction.

Any doubt about whether or not he was hers vanished as she watched the little mite dash across the yard. He favored his father's fair complexion, but his dark eyes and dimpled grin were unmistakably her own.

"Eli." She spoke his name again, louder.

But, of course, the child did not hear her. Eli already had a mother. He would never dream of Rebekah as she dreamed of him. He would never wonder about her or wish things had happened differently.

Stepping back from the fence, Rebekah shook her head and forced herself to think reasonably. She'd robbed herself of her own child. This much was true. But his father cared for her, wanted her. With time, he might love her enough to offer marriage.

She'd wanted to see her child, just once, and now she had. It was time to leave him behind, truly behind, and get on with living.

Closing her eyes, so she might not see him again, she turned back toward Haverstraw.

Late that night, after everyone in the fort was already in bed, Rebekah ignored the muffled sounds of guards murmuring in the distance and sneaked into Mason's tent.

Neither of them spoke.

He stepped away from his desk, lifting a single brow as she peered up to study his face.

She sensed the question in his gaze and felt her answer balanced precariously within her chest. She couldn't speak it. Mason didn't know there was a child out there, somewhere, who looked like him or that Rebekah wanted everything he'd once promised her. He knew only what she let him see, and even that was a piercing sadness which he likely didn't expect.

She sometimes wondered if he suspected the truth, given what had become of her, even if he didn't allow himself to admit the possibility.

"We have a son."

Inhaling slowly, she opened her mouth, but her lips fastened on the words.

If Mason knew the truth, there was a chance he would be obliged by duty to protect her, perhaps even propose marriage. Once, the possibility might have encouraged her. But now that she had him within her reach, she feared news of the child was just as likely to drive him away if he thought she was entrapping him.

Or if he was angry enough that she'd given Eli away.

She looked into Mason's eyes more closely and found the deeper emotions he so rarely showed. Hope. Doubt. A thread of desire.

She mattered to him, despite it all. This was promising. It was what she'd always hoped to see, and so she allowed his gaze to fill her with warmth. It had been so long since she felt loved, cared for. Truly wanted.

Silently, she stepped forward.

He touched her chin.

She rested her head upon his chest, and his arms circled around her. Strong, dependable Mason.

Feeling his lips brush her neck, she shivered, sensing his desire with an eagerness that unnerved her. Was it any better to be one man's mistress than mistress to many?

She pushed back once more to read his eyes, struggling to draw breath at the flush she saw on his skin. He wanted her as much as ever, and yet a day was coming when her eyes would grow tired, and her cheeks would turn pale. What if he decided then that he wanted someone else, a woman who hadn't given so much of herself away already? He might cast her aside, into the steady line of faceless lurches who took what they wanted, who crushed her against her bed without bothering to look into her eyes.

No. She couldn't bear it.

Whatever she spied in Mason's expression—and she prayed it wasn't doubt—made her close the space between them. She brushed her lips against his once, twice, before he clutched her against him and made her forget everything else but the warmth of his touch.

CHAPTER 29

Wearing only his breeches and shirtsleeves, Mason sat on the edge of the bed, his fingers brushing Rebekah's skin as he cinched up her stays. With every tug, she sucked in a breath, until she felt she was sewn together as slender as a reed.

When he was finished, they both stood, and he stepped behind her, burying his face in the curve of her neck. "How I've missed you," he murmured.

Rebekah smiled, turning into him, brushing her lips once more against his before reaching for her petticoat and gown. As Mason poured two glasses of wine, she fixed her hair and smoothed the creases in her petticoat, fussing with an uncooperative pleat as a swell of rain pattered the canvas walls.

She wasn't sure what she'd expected to feel, but her time with Mason was nothing like her encounters with customers. More than once, she'd found herself reaching for him, inwardly, wanting him as much as he wanted her. Beneath it all, the old aches lingered, the same sorrow, and yet they were dulled, muted in the moment so she felt she could, at last, catch her breath.

Mason did not send her off straightaway. Instead,

he asked if she'd eaten. When she answered with a startled *no,* he summoned his servant to procure them leftovers from supper—beef stew and a few hard biscuits. As soon as it was delivered, Mason sat Rebekah down and told her how it was going to be.

"I've reserved a tent for you on the other side of camp. You'll be comfortable there. The colonel has given permission for you to be here, but only on the strictest understanding that you conduct yourself respectably. I am responsible for you."

Between intermittent bites, Rebekah listened. The beef was mealy, not up to Coffey's standard, but the rest of the meal was adequate, especially with as fine a wine as Mason poured, presumably to mark the occasion.

"I meant to ask if you can sew," he said as an afterthought.

Rebekah nearly laughed. At Pendergrass House, she'd remade her own gowns so many times there was no deciphering the original pieces. Lower bodices. Longer sleeves. Higher waists. Whatever the fashion deigned to be, she could make a passable copy. And, of course, she could sew secret notes into curtains if the situation required it.

"I can sew," she answered.

"Excellent." Mason topped off her wine as soon as her glass was empty. "I'll see you're set to work tomorrow. Laundry and mending with the other camp followers. The work might seem menial, I know, but if you earn your keep, you'll fit in well here. As for us—" He swallowed with a bit more effort. "If we are to repeat the events of tonight, I know I need not tell you we must be careful and entirely discreet." He stood before she could reply. "So, shall we send for your things?"

"I don't want them." The words rushed out of her so fast, so unexpectedly, she cringed.

She didn't want Mason to think she was vain, waiting in expectation for her lover to supply her with a whole new chest of finery, but every dress she owned, every shift and petticoat had been stripped off her by countless other men. She'd worn them in back halls and stairwells and in the haystacks behind the stable. As for the men themselves, she rarely remembered their faces, but the gowns—

At Mason's look of curious surprise, she shook her head. "It may sound trivial," she said. "But those gowns—I can't. I can't stand to wear them ever again."

She didn't think he'd understand, not fully, but he leaned forward, resting his hand over hers on the table. "Not to worry. What sort of gentleman would I be if I didn't see you dressed properly?"

"I don't need much."

He pushed back from the table to retrieve his pocketbook. "Nonsense," he said, placing far more than the usual two shillings in her hand. "I intend for you to be perfectly comfortable here. You must order some things at once."

As Mason stepped back, Rebekah stared down at the money he'd left in her hand. She reminded herself that he was not like all the other men who had paid for her, but it was an empty, inglorious moment.

"It's drizzling," he observed, touching his hand to her cheek. "Won't you take one of my coats to keep you dry?"

"My cloak will do."

She smoothed her hair. He kissed her hand.

And off she went, alone.

July 7, 1779

There was a general store on the western side of Haverstraw. Though the selections were generally sparse, nearly anything could be ordered from the larger cities. In name, the establishment belonged to an enterprising young farmer named Mr. Thomas Guthridge, who'd opened the shop out of his farmhouse some five years prior. But his mother, a withered old widow, worked the counter while he saw to the fields and property beyond.

The woman was nearly blind behind a thin pair of wire spectacles, and her fingers had turned hard and knobby in recent years, but she was the best seamstress for miles. Customers often found her wandering agitatedly, inspecting the store and complaining of dust, and so her son supplied her with piles of fabric to keep her hands busy. She was particularly skilled at designing gowns and hats, but she also was known to produce stockings, shirts, breeches, and all manner of haberdashery at a fraction of the usual cost.

Rebekah rose before anyone else was awake at the fort, waved down a passing cart, and caught a ride out to the Guthridge store.

Thomas Guthridge was washing windows when she arrived, his sopping sleeves rolled up to his elbows. He offered a lopsided wave as she pushed through the front door and, to her amusement, nearly dropped his bucket.

The shelves in the side parlor were, as usual, sparsely stocked, but there wasn't a speck of dust anywhere to be found. Near the back of the room, Mrs. Guthridge was clad all in black and stooped like a ponderous crow over a table full of linens.

"Good morning!" greeted Rebekah, stepping forward. "I need a few dresses. Have you any new fabric?"

"Pick whatever you like," croaked the old woman, gesturing distractedly.

Rebekah studied the small pile of samples. She had no wish to stand out at the fort as Mason's mistress, so she thought it best to err on the side of unassuming. Three of the gowns would be linen, good for working—one brown, one taupe, and one a dusty blue, nearly gray—with narrow skirts and simple silhouettes. She requested petticoats in several patterns, a new neckerchief, and a checkered apron.

Mrs. Guthridge jotted everything down in scrawling lines, nodding her sage approval to the commission.

Rebekah rounded out her order with a few chemises and a new pair of gloves. She felt, at last, as though she'd left the grit and grime of Pendergrass House well enough behind her.

"I can have one of the dresses the day after tomorrow," said Mrs. Guthridge, pushing her wiry glasses the rest of the way up her nose. "I have a few petticoats at the ready, just need to take them in a bit. The rest I'll have to order."

"That will do well," Rebekah said, handing over the entire sum of Mason's allowance. "I thank you."

When she returned to Stony Point, she retired to her tent. Though Mason's was tall enough to stand in the middle, hers was squat, with room enough only for a mattress on the ground and a chipped washing basin. She sighed as she stooped inside and plopped down upon the scratchy straw mattress.

She was in the middle of unfastening her cloak when a shadow darkened the narrow entryway. Rebekah turned to face the newcomer and nearly shrieked when Mrs. Pendergrass stood over her with a wrathful expression.

"You unscrupulous *hussy!*" hissed the older woman.

Rebekah's heart hammered in her chest, but she fixed a bland smile upon her face and folded her cloak in a tight square before placing it, very calmly, at the end of her mattress. "How did you get in here?"

Mrs. Pendergrass offered an oily smile. "Oh, these men know me, girl, and I know them, all their dirtiest secrets. I had only to mention the colonel, how interested *he'd* be to know how often they do me patronage, and they granted me a brief interlude."

"As scheming as ever."

"Yet, not as scheming as you. So, tell me. What do you think will happen to you when your Lieutenant Davies, fine catch as he is, decides to marry?"

Refusing to give credence to the very same doubts which already had assailed her, Rebekah gestured toward the entrance. "You might as well go back to the boardinghouse," she said, praying none of the other camp followers would notice her former mistress loitering there. The last thing she wanted was more tangible proof of the kind of woman Mason had brought to the fort. "There's nothing you can say that will change—"

"As if I didn't pluck you up out of nothing,"

Mrs. Pendergrass went on, talking straight over her. "As if I haven't fed you, lodged you, defended you against the kind of men who might have knocked you about. Have you so soon forgotten Peter Nelson? Lecherous fool came sniffing around for you often enough, and I sent him on his way."

"You have my unending thanks and gratitude," answered Rebekah, caustically.

"Disloyalty," Mrs. Pendergrass sneered in reply. "Why, I sometimes think it's the lowest sin of them all."

"I can think of a few that are much, *much* lower," said Rebekah, laughing without humor.

Mrs. Pendergrass swooped forward, clear of the entrance, and struck Rebekah hard across the face.

More stunned than hurt, she staggered back, tripping over the mattress as a swell of blood rushed to her cheek.

"Insolent girl," Mrs. Pendergrass jeered before Rebekah could push herself back up. "You may have a pretty face, but I tell you you're nothing to that man but a loose skirt. Mark my words, your lieutenant will toss you out on your ear within a year's time. Then what will you do? Certainly not come crawling back to me, for I've done with you."

Fury clouded Rebekah's vision, but she wasn't so naïve that she couldn't recognize her fears staring back at her from within Mrs. Pendergrass's hideous words. For that, a tremulous kind of sadness stole upon her.

Before she could answer the indignation glittering in Mrs. Pendergrass's waiting eyes, someone behind them cleared his throat. "Miss Stanton, are you all right?"

Rebekah glanced up to find a burly, old soldier peering down at her through the entrance, studying her stinging cheek before turning his glare on Mrs. Pendergrass.

The man's intervention grounded Rebekah. It reminded her that the narrow borders of that simple tent were her home for however long she was allowed to stay, and that Mrs. Pendergrass had no business there.

Drawing herself up, Rebekah smiled and, for once, felt every inch her own mistress.

"Everything is fine," she answered, with composure. "Mrs. Pendergrass was just leaving."

CHAPTER 30

Later That Night

The moon was full when Ben ambled through the front door of Pendergrass House. All the lanterns were lit and the fire raging in its hearth, tinging the room in a familiar collage of tawny light and shadows. Twice as many officers as usual crowded around tables, and they were in high, boisterous spirits, bellowing back into the kitchen for another round before the last was even finished.

Ben slid his bag from his shoulder as he scanned the crowd. Wanting to explain his sudden departure to Rebekah, he'd rehearsed an expressive apology all the way from Wayne's camp, but she was not in attendance to hear it.

His gaze shifted upward, toward the rooms upstairs. Perhaps she was seeing to a customer?

The thought gnawed at him as he lowered himself into a seat by the fire to wait.

A moment later, Coffey stepped into the room. She passed a tray of ales around one of the tables and a platter of tarts at the table beside. Swiping her hands down her apron, she stepped up to Ben's place, her teeth flashing in the shadows. "Safe to assume you'll take the usual?"

Ben smiled. Coffey made the finest Shrewsbury cakes, very like the ones Ben's mother used to serve for afternoon gatherings in the parsonage. "You know your customers well," he praised. "If you have some at the ready, I'll gladly accept." He motioned to the side, where several men hooted over a game of checkers. "What has them so deep in their cups?" he asked in a quieter voice.

Sadness pooled in Coffey's eyes. "Raids in Connecticut," she said in an undertone. "They've been very—successful—from the sounds of it."

Though Ben had known such news was coming, he sat up a little straighter, attention fixed. "Where?"

"Fairfield. They burned more than eighty homes and some fifty barns or so. Two churches, last I heard, and a school."

She spoke straight-out, narrating the events without the slightest tone of criticism. But Ben saw the look in Coffey's eyes. She deplored it as much as he did, this warfare turned on civilians, many of whom would have been women and children, now without homes. Nodding his thanks for the information, Ben watched Coffey lift her tray and go into the kitchen before he resumed studying the officers.

Fools. They celebrated prematurely. If homes and churches had been burned, a whole new wave of recruited militia would be prodded into action by the desire for swift and painful retribution.

Tryon's own superiors were as likely to renounce him as they were to give him accolades, for even General Clinton, devil that he was, upheld the military limits of a gentleman.

With renewed disquiet, Ben thought of Wayne's designs on Stony Point. When the rebels landed their next blow, many of them would feel they had a score to settle. Vengeance was dangerous in battle. It made men unpredictable, more vicious toward anyone who might step in their way.

When Coffey returned with his order, Ben set a hand on the table to stay her. Leaning in as if to request something else, he dropped his voice. "Where's Rebekah?"

An unsettled look swept across the dark swoop of Coffey's brow. She looked nervously over her shoulder, ensuring the soldiers weren't eavesdropping, then back at him. "But Mr. Clarke, I thought you already knew."

Though panic shot through him at her ominous words, Ben held his composure. "What do you mean?" he demanded tersely. "Where is she?"

"The fort."

Ben, who had never once flinched while holding to a cover, flinched now. "Why, you cannot mean with Lieutenant Davies!" He might have laughed to hear himself sound so much like a jealous suitor, and yet there was no humor in the possibility.

Coffey's frown confirmed the worst.

"And all the better for us to be rid of her," rejoined a voice from over his shoulder. "The vile little traitor."

Ben swiveled and stood, looking down on Mrs. Pendergrass, who wore a thin smile of silent satisfaction. For a moment, he stood paralyzed by that word—*traitor*—realizing Coffey had not said anything to indicate whether Rebekah had gone to the fort willingly.

Had Rebekah been found out for what had transpired in the city?

Had she been *arrested?*

His thoughts turned to Jotham's woman. Flogged into submission, the poor creature, and carted off to die in prison.

Oblivious to his terror, Mrs. Pendergrass smiled. "I know she was a favorite with you, Mr. Clarke, so you will please accept my apologies. It seems she was available to the highest bidder all along. After all, the lieutenant was quite taken with her."

Ben felt a volley of relief go through him, followed by a quick charge of confusion. She'd moved into the fort, a position no doubt arranged by Davies. But was she glad to have been taken on by the lieutenant, or had she gone with him out of necessity, seeing no other option at hand?

Mrs. Pendergrass gestured across the room. "I have other girls who are just as pretty, sir, and more than willing to keep you company this evening."

"A tempting offer," he replied. "Though unnecessary. I find myself uncommonly tired this evening."

Mrs. Pendergrass smirked as she turned away, no doubt reading the truth of his partiality.

Rumpling his hair in his hand, Ben sank back in his chair and ignored Hattie, who was offering him a coy smile as she wiped down a table in the corner. He was in no mood for the slightest flirtation, even in the interest of maintaining his blasted cover.

As the redcoats cavorted around him, Washington and Wayne were plotting their assault on the impregnable Stony Point. If Wayne was at the helm, it would be a calculated strike, both brutal and effective.

Rebekah stood, unknowingly, in the middle.

The laughter around him grew sharper, more drunken, and Ben couldn't decide which unnerved him the most—that Rebekah had moved into the fort with the lieutenant, or that he minded half as much as he did.

Rebekah's fingertips throbbed as she threaded her way through the camp. Never had she held so many ripped stockings in one day, so many shirts with fraying sleeves. Her back ached after hunching for long hours over her knees as she worked, and the hot, sticky air was not helping anything for comfort. She had to stop every five minutes to wipe sweat from her neck and shoulders with a rag she kept in her pocket.

Her basket felt heavier with each step she took toward the rear of the camp, where the officers' tents clustered close together near the abatis. All answered to Lieutenant Colonel Henry Johnson, a man who boasted to have served beneath a British flag since the tender age of thirteen. Rebekah hadn't seen the man directly, but she sometimes heard traces of his Irish accent, which he tried to conceal, when he shouted at someone in his tent.

She pulled back the flap to Mason's tent and ducked inside. He was in the middle of drafting a letter. At first, as she laid a set of mended shirts upon his trunk, she wasn't sure if she ought to linger. Plenty of people were moving about the camp, enough of a crowd that someone might have seen her enter and notice if her departure was by any means delayed.

As Mason didn't look up from his letter, she moved to leave, but then he held up a hand, signaling her to wait.

Nerves humming, she set down her basket and perched on the edge of the bed. She was beginning to wonder more frequently what kinds of intelligence a man of Mason's rank might have been privy to, if he could predict the passing tides of the war or perhaps the outcome of any given battle, which she would only read about in papers weeks after the fact. She squinted, discreetly trying to make out the address but couldn't distinguish a single word.

When he finished, he slid the letter out of sight and adjusted the lantern on the desk to see her better. She waited for him to stand, to approach, quite possibly to kiss her, but he only leaned back in his chair. "How have you been settling in?"

"Well enough."

"You get on with the other women?"

The other women said little to Rebekah. Most were married to soldiers, or else engaged, so they glanced at each other knowingly whenever Rebekah stepped out of her tent to join them.

Rebekah hated those glances.

Though all the women worked in much the same ways, Rebekah's past made her an outsider, somehow beneath everyone else in rank. Shaking her head, she stood and brushed off her skirt. "I'd rather not talk about them," she said with a disinterested air, setting herself upon Mason's knee.

His arm curled around her waist. "What should you like to talk about instead?"

She touched his collar and tilted her chin. "About nothing in particular." She flashed a smile. "After all, 'tis the topic I most enjoy."

She leaned down to kiss him, trying to keep things comfortable and amiable.

He pressed back on her shoulder a half second

before their lips met. "I want you to be happy here," he said, looking her in the eyes. "You know that, don't you?"

A whisper of unease threaded through her, but she nodded.

"And you'll never be secure here, with me, if you can't be honest. You know that, too?"

Again, she nodded, but lowered her eyes, and so he caught her chin and swiveled her gaze back to his. "Are you sure?"

There was something in his tone, something he wasn't saying because he wanted her to say it first. Alarm triggered, she wondered if one of his men had learned of her trip to the city, if she'd been spotted with Ben after all.

She wasn't sure how effectively she could lie to a man who knew her as well as Mason. She opted for silence and smiled her reassurance, pushing her fingers through his hair, hoping to put the issue, whatever it was, to rest. "What are you going on about?" she said in a laughing voice.

He caught her by both wrists, tightly, then put her away from him. "You're not going to tell me, are you?"

She trembled on her feet as he rose to tower over her. Somehow, he knew about Ben. The realization drained her of all color. Would they wait until morning to flog her, or would he tear her from the tent by her hair and get it over with?

She felt she ought to throw herself at his feet,

grovel for mercy, but she was paralyzed. All she could do was deny it, which she promptly did in a quavering voice. "I'm not sure what's upset you. What do you want me to say?"

"That wretched woman had the nerve to come here." He waved an arm toward the camp. "One of the men saw her strike you."

Confusion nearly bowled her over, but then she was struck by a piercing sense of clarity. He was speaking of Mrs. Pendergrass.

Rebekah was so relieved she didn't know whether to cry or to laugh. From the outset, she'd never intended to tell Mason about the altercation with her former mistress. Then, after a long day of strenuous work, she'd forgotten all about it.

"I didn't think it was important," she said, not untruthfully.

"Yes, well, I've told the men she's not to be granted admittance ever again."

"She won't come back," Rebekah answered. "She's only angry because she feels cheated. She hates feeling cheated."

"She's angry because she's lost her prettiest girl." He was vexed with her, for those words weren't spoken as a compliment to Rebekah but as a matter of hard fact. Even so, she was glad to see some of the tension go out of his shoulders as he asked, "What else did she say to you?"

She recalled Mrs. Pendergrass's warning, that Mason was only using her, would toss her to the side if ever he married. If she told him this, she had no doubt he would lavish her with fervent assurances, but these could so easily be proven empty with time, and she didn't want to appear insecure about him.

"Nothing of importance."

The rest of Mason's anger melted away as he took her in his arms. "You must not allow anyone to trample you," he said, with feeling. "You belong here. You belong with *me*. I'll be hanged before anyone—least of all Mrs. Pendergrass—makes you think otherwise."

CHAPTER 31

July 9, 1779

"My, but 'tis lovely." Rebekah's fingers slid appreciatively over the pale blue petticoat. "Just as I hoped it would be."

Mrs. Guthridge set at once to wrapping the dress and a few other articles, her knobby fingers struggling with the paper and twine. "It does my heart good to know you approve of it, Miss Stanton."

Rebekah's answering smile was cut by a cool, masculine voice behind her. "Let us hope Lieutenant Davies likes it as well."

Rebekah couldn't move, couldn't speak.

A second later, his hands were on the counter beside her own, his fingers impatiently drumming. "I'm here to pick up my new gloves," he said to Mrs. Guthridge.

The older woman croaked a reply as she slid Rebekah's parcels across the counter and slipped into the back room.

Rebekah wished she could disappear as easily. Gathering the other packages clumsily in her arms, she lifted her chin. "Good morning, Father."

"Good morning," he answered.

She hadn't heard him speak a word in two

years, and yet his voice rumbled with its understated importance, a tradesman through and through. Taking his words for the dismissal she expected, she cut to the door, but far too quickly. One of the parcels tumbled out of her arms and onto the floor.

Heart pounding, she stooped to retrieve it, but her father got there first, plucking it up and tucking it beneath his arm. A hostage.

With no choice but to engage, she looked into his eyes, and the expression she found was heart-rending. No anger held court in his deep, serene eyes. No sadness. Just a foreign detachment, as if he hardly recognized her. He held her package in the same arm which had once cradled Eli.

This realization snapped her back to her senses. "May I have my package, please?"

"You're living at the fort," he noted without relinquishing it. He waited pointedly, perhaps hoping she might deny the claim.

" 'Tis common knowledge," she answered.

He swore so bitterly, then, that Rebekah merely stared at him. Not once in all her years had she heard him use such language in her presence. Stunned by his response, she went on in a gentler voice. "You needn't worry about me. He's a decent man, you know."

"Decent," sneered her father. "Decent enough to take you to his bed when I told him—I *told* him—to leave you alone."

Rebekah shook her head, confused, then set her armload of packages on the table beside her. "When? When did you say this?"

"The night they burned Heston's house. Lieutenant Davies came around to make sure my property was secure. Arrogant swine had the nerve to smile and flatter me as if I didn't know who he was to you. I thought he knew what you'd become, but the idiot gaped when I said as much. I told him he ought to marry you outright or else stay away from you or I'd put a musket ball through him."

Here, at last, was the truth. The real reason Mason had abandoned her the night of the raid. All sensible thought was eclipsed by a flash of anger.

Mason had kept this conversation from her.

He'd carried on with her despite her father's wishes.

Now, Rebekah looked at the man who'd turned his back on her when she needed him most, the one man who was supposed to love her regardless of how far she strayed. She had no idea he cared so much, that he would have stepped in and interceded on her behalf.

He shook his head at her stricken expression. "I've seen you around town. Miserable and frail. All those men lusting after you. I knew it was only a matter of time before—" His words caught, and then his voice hardened. "When I heard Davies was back, I knew he'd send for you eventually. Set you up *comfortably*."

"Why?" she pressed. "Why should that matter now?"

He pinched the bridge of his nose between two fingers, closed his eyes as if summoning patience. "Confound it, Rebekah, if you would only—"

Come home.

He stopped short of saying the words, and Rebekah stopped short of wanting to hear them. She laughed so she wouldn't cry. "What could ever tempt me to return to the man who took my child from my arms?"

"I was trying to help you."

"By taking my son."

"By giving you a *future*."

If only he had apologized, Rebekah thought she might have relented. Deep in her heart, she wanted to forgive him if only it meant feeling like a daughter again.

Instead, he shook his head and grumbled. "Lot of good it did me."

Rebekah's face flushed with anger. Did he think she'd *wanted* all those men to touch her? Did he really think she could bed man after man out of spite alone?

"I despise you." She spoke the words softly, slowly, as if testing their shape and weight, trying to decide if they were true.

Face red, her father thrust the package back into her arms.

She caught and clutched it against her chest.

I didn't mean it. I didn't mean it! She tried to speak the words, but her heart was too stubborn.

She'd gotten that trait honestly, from him.

As soon as that thought crossed her mind, she remembered what Ben had told her of his father, how hatred had separated them until it was too late. She'd seen the grief in Ben's eyes, the uncontrollable anguish that came from knowing his father had been murdered by Patriots who shared his own zeal. And yet, Ben's mission was the same as it had been then—to wrest the nation from those who cried *God save the king!*—no matter the cost.

Once again, the story of Ben's father loomed as a ghostly harbinger of what might very well befall her own if tensions rose to another tempest. Given the chance, would the Patriots force Haverstraw Loyalists from their homes? Would they shoot them down if they refused to leave?

She opened her mouth, wanting to warn him, but her father would not hear a word.

Spinning on his heel, he marched back up to the counter and called in a rough voice, "Mrs. Guthridge! My gloves, if you please!"

When Rebekah returned to the fort, she hurried to her tent and closed the flap, wrestling the urge to confront Mason. She had no right to be angry with him for lying, not after everything she'd withheld, and yet his betrayal dealt the most venomous sting.

With vigorous strokes, she washed in her chipped basin, then changed out of her old gown and into the fresh one from Mrs. Guthridge. The linen was a cloudy blue, a style far more subdued than those she'd typically worn at Pendergrass House. Feeling more herself—put together, at least—she perched on the edge of her mattress and stared bleakly down at her hands, which were red and rough from working.

They were the same hands she'd brushed against Mason's chest as they lay abed, the same which had once cradled Eli's tiny body, the same hands which had scraped countless shillings off her bedside table for the last three years. They looked so hideous to her now. So foreign.

"Blue becomes you."

Rebekah's hands constricted into fists as, glancing up, she found herself once again the center of Mason's gaze.

"May I come in?" he asked with a mannerly bow.

Finding a smile despite the jump in her nerves, she answered. "Of course."

He ducked into the tent. He had to bend at the waist, nearly in half, in order to fit into the tiny space.

“What brings you here in daylight?” She shifted sideways on the mattress to accommodate him. “People might see.”

“I heard you’d left the fort.” He sat beside her, offering a tired smile. “We’ve received some concerning warnings about rebels in the surrounding areas. I was worried about you.”

She thought of Ben, of his business in Haverstraw. Was it because of him that Mason looked so drawn, so tired?

“I had an order to fetch,” she said.

He toyed with the modest bit of lace at her cuff. “So I see.”

He leaned forward before she could stop him, his lips touching hers so gently, so tenderly, that all the old aches faded, diminished nearly to nothing. She forgot she was angry with him. She forgot she was confused. She could trust Mason. She could love him. Everything was as it was meant to be. But then, just as she leaned into him, giving herself over to his kiss, her father’s cold reproof sounded in her head. *“I told him to leave you alone . . .”*

Rebekah fought the intrusion, concentrating all the more on Mason. She focused on the strong grooves of his hands as he brushed the hair back from her neck, the warmth of his lips as he parted her own. He was the one she’d always wanted. The one she wanted still.

Even he was not convinced.

He angled back, a swift flicker of doubt clouding his bright, clear eyes. “Is anything the matter?”

His concern pierced her. Despite it all, Mason deserved the truth. They both did, even if she had to scrape the words off the back of her throat to admit it. “I saw my father this morning.”

She stared at him, waiting to see if he would willingly confess.

There was a tic in his jaw, but otherwise nothing. “Did he say anything?”

Disappointment firmed Rebekah’s voice as she answered. “Of course he did.”

Mason’s expression shifted. He grasped her by the shoulders and turned her to face him directly. He took one look at her face before his fingers tightened, as if she was slipping through his hold. “God help me, I tried to stay away from you. But I couldn’t do it. I love you, Rebekah. I do. I *do*.”

With a strange, frightening sense of detachment, Rebekah thought this might be true. But what did it matter? Mason was an officer with an otherwise pristine reputation. She was a prostitute who’d entertained many of his fellow officers in her chamber. How could they ever respect him fully if he married a woman like her?

She shook her head, bitterness mounting. Though she understood his predicament, this did not make it any easier to accept. All of Mason’s valor on the field, his valiance in battle, it all meant nothing to her if his love was not brave enough to overlook her situation, nor selfless enough that he might deny himself of her. Her father had pleaded with him to marry her or to step aside, but here, at last, she saw the truth for what it was, the crux of their relationship.

Mason would do neither.

He dropped his hands to his lap. "I tried to respect your father's wishes," he said. "But I couldn't stand it, the thought of not seeing you anymore."

"Neither could you propose marriage," she added in a hard, cynical voice.

As expected, he had no answer, but leaned forward, his arms resting flush on his thighs. "I never meant to lie to you. I swear I didn't. This hasn't been easy, you know."

At those words, something raw and rebellious snapped inside her. A strangled laugh climbed her throat. "It hasn't been *easy* for me either," she hissed. "It wasn't easy when you left me here without word, without promise. It wasn't easy when my father turned his back on me. And it certainly wasn't *easy* when I gave birth to our son."

The truth struck a furious blow, first to Rebekah, who hadn't meant to speak the words, and then to Mason, who turned whiter than his shirt.

His hand shot out, grabbing hold of her arm. "What do you mean?" he demanded.

"What do you think I mean? I had a child. *Your* child."

"You say you *had* a child. Why? What happened to him?"

Rebekah dropped her gaze, trembling as the truth, which she'd concealed for so long, ran its full course. "He's with a mother who can take care of him in all the ways I cannot."

A throated sound escaped him. "And you consented to this?"

Rebekah nodded, but the empty gesture was a half-truth at best.

Mason must have sensed the pretense, for all at once he swore violently under his breath. "Why didn't you tell me?"

"Would it have changed anything, if you knew?"

He bit the inside of his cheek and fisted his hands, and, despite it all, Rebekah fought the reckless urge to touch him. "I wasn't sure how you'd feel," she explained, more measured. "I was afraid you'd be angry with me for giving him away. Or, worse, that you'd think I was trapping you into marriage."

There was that word again, the one word he wouldn't speak—*marriage*.

"There's not a day I don't wish I'd come back sooner," he said instead, in a stripped voice.

Before it was too late, Rebekah finished inwardly, her tired eyes pricking with tears. She turned her face away from him. “It does not do to dwell on the past.”

“And the future?”

She parted her lips to answer, but he cupped her face and slanted his mouth over hers, silencing the words before she could speak them.

Rebekah floundered in his hold. She tried to convince herself he was the same man, the one she wanted, but she sensed an echoing note of anguish in his kiss, which made her fear he wasn’t strong enough, nor brave enough, to love her in any of the ways he’d once promised.

CHAPTER 32

After Mason left Rebekah's tent, she lay huddled on her mattress, staring at the faded canvas walls around her. Since coming to the fort, she'd grown accustomed to this colorless palette—gray like the Hudson, like a sunless sky in a place of fog and mist and moonlight. The rest was dead grass and squat stumps, where trees had once grown, and the faded laundry hanging out limply to dry. Even her new blue dress seemed grayer in the shadows than it was blue. Most days, the only swatch of color was the marching about of uniforms, which made her think only of war, of blood.

Of Mason.

Her lips tingled from his kiss as she reached for her packages from Mrs. Guthridge. Trying to distract herself, she tore into them, shaking out the chemises as she set to folding them. She leaned across the bed to a trunk Mason had scrounged up for her use, stacking the new articles neatly inside.

Coffey had only been able to smuggle a few of Rebekah's personal effects out of Pendergrass House: the garnet earrings Rebekah's father had given her, which she never wore anymore; a faded miniature painting of her mother with her wide, country-girl eyes and modest smile, both so unlike Rebekah; and there, at the very bottom of the trunk, was the knife Ben had given her in the city—

And the scarlet ribbon.

So soon after her fight with Mason, thinking of Ben filled her with quiet affliction, but she unfolded the ribbon and straightened it reverently in her lap. She'd come to suspect that Ben had only left her behind to keep her safe, that the events in the city had unnerved him. In a way, she could respect him for it. In other ways, it caused a deeper pain she couldn't understand.

He'd abandoned her. Gone to live his life while she suffered through her own.

She twisted the ribbon around her fingers. Time and again, she'd tried to put Ben from her mind, to pledge herself to her place at the fort, but memories of him snuck up at odd times, much like himself, as if he was leaning close, brushing the hair from the back of her neck as she played the harpsichord in the boardinghouse parlor.

Breath catching in her throat, she reached up, pulling the pins from her hair and beginning to smooth out her rumpled tresses.

As she did this, she wondered if Ben was still dashing about in the shadows, still scheming, if he smiled upon other women as he'd once smiled upon her, or if his partiality for her had been genuine.

She would likely never know. He'd made it no secret he wouldn't return.

But after everything that had happened, and amid everything that was happening even now, there was a place in her heart for him. She would be foolish to pretend otherwise. She would not think of him, she told herself, but perhaps she could remember him, even so.

Sweeping the hair back from her forehead, she gathered all of her curls in one fist. She worked quickly, with grave determination, braiding and knotting the tresses down the back of her neck, securing the waves at the bottom with a few determined twists of the scarlet ribbon.

For the second night in a row, Ben took supper at the tavern. The food wasn't nearly as appealing as that which he had enjoyed at Pendergrass House, but the company was more favorable, and that was counting the presence of some dozen or so of His Majesty's finest.

He was finishing a bowl of lamb stew when Jotham stopped by his table to collect the empty dish.

"I have some of that sherry you favor," he said, wiping a damp rag over the table.

Sherry. An edge in Jotham's eyes assured Ben the code had been used deliberately.

Ben smiled, but his nerves were strung taut. "I should like some very much, thank you."

A few moments later, Jotham appeared with a short glass and his usual glower.

Ben quaffed the contents, paid his bill, and stepped out onto the path. The cellar entrance was at the back of the establishment, the view obscured from the road, and so he was able to move freely as he yanked open the door and stepped down into the dank cellar, pulling the door closed atop his head.

Jotham didn't keep him waiting amid the cobwebs for long. Within minutes, dust drifted down from the rafters above Ben's head as his friend descended the stairs with lantern held aloft.

"Where are you?" Jotham grumbled into the shadows.

Ben stepped clear of the stairs and, despite the uncertain circumstances, smiled.

Jotham grunted when he saw him, sliding his light onto a nearby barrel. "When's the last time you slept?" he asked under his breath.

Ben chuckled. "Did you request this meeting to inquire after my sleep habits?"

Jotham dug a letter out of his pocket and handed it to Ben. "A courier left this for me this morning."

Brow crooked curiously, Ben opened the missive, tilting the paper toward the lantern until the scrawl became legible: *three ales; two meat pies; two rounds of rum for His Majesty's men . . .*

"A sizeable bill," Ben observed.

"Oh, get on with it," Jotham snapped.

Ben leaned closer to the paper, carefully inspecting every inch.

Some spies had been granted a particular chemical compound for writing invisible missives, which could only be deciphered if one had the particular counteragent. These were the rumors Ben had heard regarding a few of Washington's favorite informants. But the circles Ben worked in were far less established, and so they used more rudimentary means.

He pulled the lantern closer and removed the candle, hovering the paper above the flame until a lighter scrawl appeared between the items listed.

> *I'm ready to pluck that feather. We will convene at the Springsteel Farm on the 15th, after supper. I expect you to be there.*

Ben stared at the words well after he'd registered their meaning, then touched the paper to the flame, watching the corners of the page blacken and curl as they ignited. He glanced up in time to see a soft bolt of light brighten Jotham's features before the flames withered and all that remained was a small pile of ash on the top of the barrel.

"They're ready to take the fort," Ben announced,

sounding far more resigned than he felt. "On the fifteenth."

Jotham watched him closely, his eyes narrowed to slits. "So soon?"

Ben didn't answer. His thoughts marched ahead even as he stepped back, away from Jotham and out of range of the lantern light. Not for the first time, he reminded himself that he couldn't allow Rebekah to compromise Wayne's plans, nor his cover. Yet, if he did nothing, she might find herself in the middle of the fray. He'd heard stories of civilians struck in the crossfire of battle. Of women rounded up and either sent to Britain or relocated to American prisons.

"I know what you're thinking," Jotham said. "But you can't warn her. She's far too unpredictable."

"She saved my life."

"I understand that. And I know you're partial to her. Really, I do. But it's time for you to see reason, Ben. She's a *whore*."

A storm of fury swept through Ben. He'd fisted his hands before he even realized he'd done it, wanting nothing more than to strike until Jotham could no longer stand.

"Don't call her that," he warned.

Jotham threw up his arms. "What else am I supposed to call her? She's already made her bed—with the lieutenant, mind you—and now she has to lie in it. What if she goes to Davies, if she tells him what she knows?" Jotham was pacing now, restlessly, sounding increasingly alarmed by the possibilities. "If you want to slip your head in the noose over some secondhand hussy, then have at it, man. But I won't be dragged to the gallows on account of her, even if she was more than a bit useful."

"And what of the woman *you* used?" Ben bit out the words before he could stop himself, taking keen satisfaction in the wounded look that crossed Jotham's face. "You knew what might happen if they found out, didn't you? You used her anyway. And now you'd have Rebekah pay the same price, and all because you think you're so much better than her? Well, I'll tell you here and now, Jotham. You're not."

Jotham swore so viciously that Ben barely made out the words, though the blow to his jaw removed any doubt of his meaning.

On instinct, Ben levered back an arm, ready to return the blow, but Jotham dodged back on his feet before Ben could land it.

"Get out!" snarled Jotham. "Get out of here before I break your neck!"

Ben loosened his fist and leaned against the barrel, catching his breath and, very slowly, leashing his temper. He knew Jotham's anger had little to do with him and more to do with his guilt about what had happened to the woman in the city. Even so, he nearly loathed his friend. It was far too easy for people to dismiss Rebekah, to trample her and degrade her.

To call her a whore.

He straightened coolly, brushing the remnant ashes of Wayne's letter off the barrel as he collected his hat. Without a word, he turned away from Jotham. He took the stairs quickly and shoved through the door.

By the time Ben reached the road, an evening fog hovered densely over the grass. It reminded him of musket smoke, thick and suffocating. Though he knew it was nonsense, he quickened his pace, half-fearful that, if he strained his ears, he would hear the strange, inhuman roar of unseen men dying in the darkness.

CHAPTER 33

July 10, 1779

Morning arrived slowly, bleakly, with no promise of a true sunrise.

As Ben stepped through the church door, he was struck by a strange mindfulness of his father's church in Boston, like parting a veil into the past. He remembered sitting in the front box of the narrow white sanctuary, the window light trailing the floor in front of his feet as he listened to his father preach on the importance of giving to Caesar what was rightfully his, and the particular evils of anarchy.

"Repent of your inconstancy to those whom God has appointed to guide you through this valley of woe. Repent of your ingratitude, of your self-importance, of your arrogance to think yourselves kings in your own right. There is no honor in anarchy, for it breeds nothing but bedlam within . . ."

Flinching inwardly, Ben wrestled his thoughts back to the present, to the small, worn sanctuary that was every inch as modest and understated as its under-shepherd had proven himself to be.

Ben's footsteps echoed up to the hollow balcony as he made his way to the sacristy door. He let himself into the cramped room which had once, for a brief while, been his home. He found the reverend stooped over the narrow table, reading, with spectacles perched low on the bridge of his nose. The older man didn't hear his guest's arrival, not until Ben shifted sideways and closed the door behind him.

The reverend settled a finger on his page to hold his place as his eyes rose to greet his visitor. "Mr. Clarke!" the reverend exclaimed, dropping his hand altogether. "I did not realize you'd returned to Haverstraw."

Though relieved to see the reverend again, Ben had thin patience for pleasantries. "I need your help," he said without preamble.

The reverend sank back into his chair and gave Ben a more measured inspection. His eyes, which were watery from reading in the low light, narrowed slightly on the bruising along Ben's jaw. "Dare I ask?"

Looking rather like a ruffian, Ben smiled as he dragged his usual chair back from the table. "I've not been brawling, if that's what you think. Just ruffled someone's feathers."

The reverend chuckled. "I'd say I'm surprised, but it wouldn't be true. So, tell me. What is this help you need?"

"I need you to go to the fort and speak with Miss Stanton."

The reverend drew back, his bushy brows inching upward. "To what end?"

"I can't tell you the particulars. It's a precarious situation, but the short of it is that I must speak with her."

"I fail to see how I can help. Miss Stanton has washed her hands of me and the church." The reverend's lips twitched. "Much like you had, by point of fact."

"Yet, here I am. I need you to give her this." Ben pulled a note from his pocket and held it out to the reverend. "I need you to stress that it's important, that she *must* meet with me. I'd go to the fort myself but can't risk drawing notice. Please, Reverend. You're the only person I trust."

The reverend's eyes flicked to the folded paper. He tapped his fingers on the table. "Nothing that amounts to treason, I trust?"

Ben hesitated. Of course, Jotham's concerns weren't without merit. It was downright dangerous to hint to anyone, reverend or otherwise, of the coming attack. But he couldn't leave things with Rebekah as they were. Too many words were unsaid, too many unseen dangers rising up around them on all sides.

"It pleads only for an interlude," Ben assured him. "No one reading it would think otherwise."

The reverend took the note, turning it over in his hands as he stared across the table at Ben. "If I'm to agree, then I must question you on one final matter. Namely, I must be assured that your intentions toward Miss Stanton are in every respect honorable." He paused. "You've not taken advantage of her position, I trust?"

Ben's neck mottled at the implication. "I fail to see how that's any of your concern."

"She is one of my flock, wandering though she be. I cannot share particulars any more than you can in your line of work, but I can tell you she's suffered greatly. I would not help you add to that suffering, not for all the world. So, if your intentions are in any way selfish, if you have any aim of using her carelessly, then you must find someone else to assist. Are we understood?"

Ben tensed. He'd never asked how Rebekah came to be at Pendergrass House, trusting she would share as much if she wanted, and now felt guilty for never having questioned her. Had someone hurt her in the past? Was that why she'd fled to the fort, to the supposed safety of Davies's tent?

Of course, the reverend would never tell. The man was sworn to silence by the principle of his calling, but this didn't mean Ben wasn't tempted to question him as he might an enemy spy.

"She's not safe at the fort," Ben replied. "I want only for her to be safe."

With an air of finality, the reverend nodded and slipped the note safely into his pocket. Then he gave Ben another once-over. "You look awful, you know. Like you haven't slept in weeks."

Though Jotham had said as much, the observation was somewhat better received coming from the reverend. Ben laughed softly. “In truth, I can’t remember the last time I did. The war weighs somewhat heavier upon me than usual. Which brings me, I’m sorry to say, to yet another request.”

The reverend scowled outright. “The church is here to offer far more than favors of this nature, I’ll have you know.”

“Really? Here I thought this was the kind of favor you’d be more than willing to grant.”

“And what kind of favor might that be?”

Ben’s tired smile tilted a fraction. “I’d have you hear my confession.”

CHAPTER 34

Ben had killed five redcoats in his time. He'd lied to Loyalist families who opened their homes to him and flirted heavily with their women as he culled them for information. Once, while living in Boston, he had kissed a married woman while her husband, a British officer, was out of the house. At the time, he told himself it couldn't be helped, for the woman had found him far too near the study where he'd been rifling. He'd never made such advances again. Not all of his father's sermons had fallen on deaf, defiant ears.

Now, there was Rebekah.

He told the reverend all of it. How he'd carried her off to the city and very nearly gotten her killed. How he'd deposited her at the edge of Haverstraw and left her with no explanation, so it was likely his own blasted fault she'd moved into the fort with the lieutenant. He'd ached to kiss her in the city, more than he'd ever ached for any woman. This was a shameful wish, he thought, when every man she knew used her for such pleasures. *Paid* her for such pleasures.

And Ben had done nothing to help her.

When he finished his confession, which took a good long while, he sat silently in his chair, wondering if he'd shocked the good reverend with the colorful range of his exploits.

The reverend merely sat, pondering for a minute, his hands steepled together, until at last he removed his spectacles and set them on the table between them.

"And your father?"

Ben's eyes narrowed. "What *about* my father?"

"I wondered if you had anything to share regarding him."

"I was nowhere near Boston when the city fell," Ben said defensively. "His death was not my fault."

"I didn't say it was."

Ben shifted in his seat, discomfort mounting. "You want me to say I've forgiven him for informing on me? Is that it?"

"I'm in no way telling you what to say, Ben. I'm only asking you to consider which thoughts weigh upon you, the ones you can't speak of so freely."

Ben stared forward. He'd learned about his father's death three days after Boston fell. He'd gotten more than a bit drunk that night. Even aside from the loss of his parent, Washington's "glorious cause" felt considerably less glorious after his fellow Patriots had shot an unarmed reverend for spite. Yet, Ben himself had killed redcoats, hadn't he? It had been unavoidable, for he'd have swung for treason if they'd apprehended him, but still. War was every man for himself, though this didn't mean a few ghosts wouldn't haunt him for the trouble.

"If you want the truth of it," said Ben, "I sometimes think none of us are on the right side of this miserable war."

"An interesting supposition," replied the reverend, relaxing back in his chair. "One I'm inclined to agree with."

Ben shook his head, discontented by his own answer, wanting to amend it. "But is it really so wrong to desire liberty?" he asked with heightened zeal. "Is it so wrong to demand that soldiers not be forced into our homes if we object to it? Is it wrong for you to be able to preach as freely as your conscience wills you to?"

The reverend shook his head. "I would never suggest any of those wishes are inherently wrong. They are good, but even good things can pull your eyes from God. You see, your true captors are within you, Ben. The sins of your body. The sins of your soul. You must look to those first. Christ is your liberator. His forgiveness is freedom. *True* freedom."

"Yes, but—"

"Countless other nations have come and passed long before ours," the reverend went on. "Many will follow long after we've gone. But we are the new Jerusalem. It matters little to God the color we wear on our backs. And so, as much as we might fight for liberty—rightfully so, at times—we ought to desire unity insofar as we are able."

Ben laughed more scornfully than he intended. "That all sounds well and good," he allowed. "Yet, do you really think preaching of this heavenly Jerusalem is enough to end this war?"

"Perhaps not. But do you really think, if Washington prevails, all will be as free as you wish?"

Ben frowned. "What do you mean by that?"

"Only this. That it is the way of humans to subjugate those they consider inferior. Look at the slaves who fight in this war, for example. Shall they have an even stake in this new liberty when all is said and done?"

Ben sat silent. His family had never kept slaves, but he knew many who did. Once, Ben's father had been offered a houseslave from a minister who was grateful to him for reconciling some trifling conflict in his parish. Ben's father had staunchly—and in rather rude terms—refused the offer, one of the few and only moments Ben had admired his grit.

Since then, many slaves had flocked to the city of New York. Both armies, finding themselves too evenly matched for comfort, had grown desperate enough to promise freedom to any slave who fought for one side against the other.

But the reverend was right. Not all would be free.

"What would you have me do?" Ben asked, more subdued. "Defect?"

"Stop thinking in shades of blue and scarlet," the reverend corrected. "Pursue only what is right. If we've learned anything from history, it's that there will be more than enough evils to survive this war, whichever side claims the victory."

Ben shifted forward in his seat. Rebekah had said something similar at one of their earlier meetings, though in far more cynical terms. *"It matters little to me who puppets the strings of this country. My life will look much the same as it does now regardless of the outcome."*

Troubled, Ben stood. He needed to step outside, to clear his head.

The reverend stopped him before he could beg his excuses. "As to Miss Stanton—"

Ben lifted his chin abruptly, unsettled to imagine the reverend could identify the direction of his thoughts so easily. "What about her?"

"You've assured me your conduct toward her has been, thus far, above reproach. I'm glad to hear it. But I must offer this caution if your feelings for her are as strong as you say. Love as God ordained it is sacrificial. It strengthens and sustains. It is a picture of the love Christ has for us." He lifted a brow. "If you offer her anything less—anything *baser* than that, you understand—you will only hurt her. And in doing so, you will hurt yourself."

Ben dropped his gaze, feeling as though the reverend's weathered hand had gripped his windpipe. "You think I ought to leave her alone."

"Did I say that?"

Ben stared at the reverend. What, exactly, was he suggesting?

That Ben ought to marry her?

Unnerved by the idea, Ben held out his hand in parting. "I'm grateful to you for listening," he said. "And for your—advisements."

The reverend glanced at his proffered hand but didn't take it. "I have heard your confession, Benjamin," he said. "Hear, then, what comfortable words Christ our Savior says to all who turn to Him. *'Come unto me, all ye that travail, and are heavy laden, and I will refresh you.'* "

He gestured for Ben to sit, then placed both hands upon his head, bending it forward as if guiding him down into prayer. "Almighty God, our Heavenly Father, who of His great mercy hath promised forgiveness of sins to all them that with hearty repentance and true faith turn unto him; Have mercy upon you; pardon and deliver you from all your sins; confirm and strengthen you in all goodness; and bring you to everlasting life through Jesus Christ our Lord."

Ben, who for years had wondered whether confession would do his soul a shred of good, could barely find his voice as he closed his eyes and quietly rasped, *"Amen."*

CHAPTER 35

July 11, 1779

The other women said the only thing worse than mending shirts was washing them, but Rebekah didn't mind it.

Washing was an all-day affair.

It kept her busy and wore out her body until she had nothing to worry over except the work of her hands. The shirts, which had been soaking in the copper kettle all night, brought murky bubbles rising to the surface of the water as she boiled them over the fire in the morning. Sweat collected on her forehead and temples as she leaned over the fire, stirring the linens with a long washing bat until the color of the water swirled into a filthy gray.

One by one, she used the bat to fish shirts from the kettle, splatters of steaming water running over her boots as she plunged the clothing into a nearby tub of cool water.

Then came the hardest part. Each of the shirts was molded into a ball. She kneaded them roughly on a wide board, like bread, before beating them with the laundry bat and plunging them back into the water, working the stains out between her hands. Again and again, she did this, repetition of the mind and of the body until, at last, each shirt came out clean. Her right shoulder ached as she worked, almost as painfully as her lower back, but she furrowed her brow and kept at it, refusing to appear frail in front of any of the other women.

Her rhythm only stalled when someone coughed lightly behind her.

She turned at the hip, both hands submerged in the water. "Reverend!" she cried, unable to mask her surprise.

He removed his hat as he stepped nearer.

His presence reminded her, as always, of that horrible night, of Eli, and so she wiped her sopping hands down her apron and greeted him with a mocking smirk. "Have you come to convert me?"

He gave no answering smile. "A mutual friend wondered if I might speak with you."

The hairs on the back of Rebekah's neck prickled. Ben, she thought, a bit breathlessly.

At first, she could hardly believe he would have manipulated a reverend into passing her a message. Yet, if she really thought about it, she could believe it very well.

It wasn't wise to speak with the reverend. After all, she'd accepted a place with Mason and given him her loyalty in every sense of the word. But she saw the fatigue in the reverend's eyes. The wariness. He'd walked all that way, with his

Bible tucked in the crook of his arm, just to speak with her.

Too late to stop herself, she swiped her hair back, away from her face. The strands clung to her temples, soaked with soapy water. “There’s a small clearing,” she said with a sigh and gestured. “Just over here.”

The reverend nodded and followed, waiting until she’d settled on a small wooden bench at the base of a wagon. “Our friend needs to speak with you,” he said without looking at her.

Stunned and confused, she stared down at her hands. She couldn’t imagine why Ben had returned to Haverstraw or what he thought he might have to say to her. Bitterly, she realized he might have learned of her new position at the fort. Perhaps he needed her again. Perhaps he wanted her to rummage through Mason’s things, to pass him information. Or, it might have been another matter entirely. Something *had* passed between them in the city, a mutual understanding, and it was foolish to pretend otherwise.

Perhaps Ben regretted leaving as he had.

Perhaps he missed her.

“Why does he need to speak with me?” Suspicion sharpened her words. “What does he need me to do now?”

“He’s concerned for your safety.”

“My safety? Really?” Rebekah laughed dubiously and shook her head.

"You'll only know for sure if you let him speak with you."

Before answering, she glanced behind them to ensure they were alone. "But, how can I? You know what he is, Reverend. If I get too close to that man in any way, it could ruin everything."

"And what is *everything,* exactly?"

Rebekah struggled to answer.

For the longest time, life with Mason had seemed an impossible dream, one she'd finally attained, but their last argument had filled her with doubt. To complicate matters, she'd not stopped thinking of Ben. She still wore his ribbon. Still worried about him. The confusion was enough to make her want to scream, to weep, and a more unfamiliar part of her nearly wanted to pray, though she stopped herself short of saying so.

She'd prayed in the early days after Mason had gone. Too many times, she'd reached into the stillness, yearning for an intercession that, for her, never came. Perhaps it was far better that her son was not there to see her. There was nothing strong in her. Nothing faithful or courageous or dependable. If he ran to her now, he would see all she was lacking and refuse to call her his mother. He would run straight out of her arms, and she couldn't stand the thought.

"I named him Eli." This admission emerged on a whisper, and, though she hadn't answered the reverend's question, she'd answered the one he'd asked three years earlier.

Without the slightest twitch of surprise or unease, the reverend leaned forward, folding his hands with a prayerful expression. *"It is the Lord,"* he recited quietly, from the first book of Samuel, in which Rebekah had found and chosen her son's name. *"Let Him do what seemeth to Him good."*

The pool of anguish, which had been growing within Rebekah's chest for many years, deepened. "I wanted him," she said in a choked voice. "More than anything, I wanted him, and yet more than anything I didn't. Now it's too late, isn't it? I went there, to the Sawyers. I saw them, and I saw him. How could I ever take him away from the only mother he's ever known?"

"A good mother would do whatever was best for her child, regardless of the cost to herself."

"What, by abandoning him?"

"You must not only ask what might have been best for Eli then, but also what is best for him now. That is what a mother—a *true* mother—would do."

He'd called him Eli.

It was the first time Rebekah heard her son's name spoken by another person. Stricken by the sound of it, she bent and buried her face in her hands.

"Your child will always be yours," the reverend

said in a gentler voice. "Cradle him in your prayers, Miss Stanton, and take comfort that in Heaven, he *will* recognize you as his mother."

In heaven. For Rebekah, those words inspired nothing but dread. Far more often than she'd ever felt God's love or protection, she'd experienced His wrath. There had never been a moment of peace, never a moment when she looked at the cross and didn't shudder.

Why should she be loyal to a God who'd never been loyal to her?

He'd been there, she knew, in every ugly, wretched moment, when men had preyed upon her at her weakest, but He'd done nothing to stop it, and so she felt nothing, feared nothing. Heaven was just another barrier, another wall that would someday stretch between herself and those few faraway souls she dared to love.

"I'm put in mind of Solomon," the reverend said in a firmer voice, perhaps emboldened by her silence.

She looked up at him doubtfully.

"You see, two women were brought before him. One held a child who was living. The other child was dead, smothered by accident in the night. Both women claimed the living child as her own. But when Solomon suggested the child might be divided between the two—cut in half—the true mother fell at his feet and bid him give the child to the other woman to save him."

He met Rebekah's eyes. "He acknowledged her as the child's mother because she was willing to do anything—even part with him—to save him."

Rebekah remembered the story better than she realized. Dryly, she responded, "Incidentally, they were prostitutes, weren't they?"

His lips curved. "And mothers, yes."

Rebekah's sarcasm withered. It was hard to think of herself as a mother, and yet the reverend seemed to harbor no doubts whatsoever that she was. "It was right, then, for me to leave him behind?"

"Commit your child to God," he answered, his voice filled with compassion, "and to the family you have entrusted him to. I'm afraid anything less, in this case, would tear him in half."

She lifted her eyes once more. "And if it tears *me* in half?"

"You may not believe it, but you can be whole, Rebekah. In your baptism, Christ Himself has already made you so."

His words did not settle within her. They felt strange and incongruous when placed alongside everything else she'd experienced, but she felt, somehow, that their meaning would remain with her for a good long while. "I should be getting back," she said, and tried to smile. "Laundry waits for no woman."

The reverend humored her by chuckling at the tired joke, shuffling a small square paper out of his Bible and into her hand. "From our friend," he said. "Shall I tell him to expect your reply?"

Rebekah wasn't sure whether this was wise, so she didn't answer straight away. And all the better, she thought a second later, when the risk was fully embodied by a chillingly pleasant voice behind them. "I wouldn't advise it."

Rebekah recognized the voice, but the terror made it impossible for her to place it. She whirled on the bench and lurched up onto her feet when Captain Haggerty strolled from behind the wagon to block their path, with a musket at his side.

A single breath of silence, in which the captain extended a gloved hand toward her, revealed a straight line of even teeth as he smiled. "I'll be taking a look at that note, if you don't mind."

Rebekah fisted Ben's note into a ball and said with a voice imbued with frost. "I fail to see how my personal correspondence is any of your business."

Haggerty leveled his sneer on the reverend. "Who is it from?"

"As the lady already said, it is of a personal nature."

Haggerty strode closer. "We shall see," he clucked, seizing Rebekah's arm and wrenching it down.

Rebekah hissed as pain clawed up to her

shoulder. Realizing the wretched man would have his way regardless of her struggle, she loosened her fingers.

Haggerty dug the note out of her fist and shoved her back down onto the bench. Impatiently, he unfolded the note. He read silently at first, and then aloud. "I must see you. Meet me in the parsonage orchard at ten o'clock."

Haggerty lowered the note to his side, his brows gathering in the center of his forehead. "Who is this from?" he demanded, his gaze darting from Rebekah to the reverend and back again. When neither answered, his smile returned, a dangerous twist to the corner of his lips. "I will repeat myself only once," he warned. *"Who is this from?"*

Rebekah sat silent. If she confessed, if she told him about Ben, she had no doubt they'd all be arrested.

Perhaps the reverend feared the same, for even as the captain prowled closer, his grave countenance gave nothing away.

Haggerty's smile barely twitched as he took up his musket, twisted it around, and dealt the reverend a cracking blow to the temple.

A raw scream hurled its way up Rebekah's throat as the reverend staggered back, a dazed expression clouding his features as his hat slid backward off his head and fell to the ground.

Haggerty circled them, poised to strike again,

even as the reverend dabbed shaking fingers along the thin seam of blood pooling at his temple.

Rebekah leapt forward before Haggerty could touch him, swinging herself like a door in front of the reverend. “Leave him alone!” She raised a hand, fearing another crack from the musket. “He’s done nothing wrong!”

Haggerty did not mark her protest. “Who are you meeting?” he demanded again. “Is it a rebel?”

“No,” she lied.

“Are you passing secrets out of this fort?”

“Certainly not.” She threw up her hands in a ruffled affront, feigning irritation. “What utter nonsense.”

His voice turned to a growl. “Then you will explain yourself.”

A dozen soldiers gathered around, no doubt drawn to the skirmish by Rebekah’s scream. “What’s going on?” one asked, lending a hand to Rebekah as she guided the reverend down onto the bench.

“I’m finding that out for myself,” Haggerty answered, brandishing Ben’s note. “I’ve just confiscated this, and I intend to get to the bottom of it.”

The note was passed from man to man. “It’s hardly incriminating,” said one. “She could be meeting anyone.”

“But why work in secret?” Haggerty pressed.

"Why use the reverend as a courier? And why won't she tell me who she's meeting?"

Rebekah's stomach turned. He had fair points all around, especially where the reverend was concerned. Even to her, his involvement sounded awfully suspicious.

But then she was struck by a flash of inspiration. The idea came so quickly, so unexpectedly, that she could only pray the reverend would someday forgive her for suggesting it.

"The reverend and I share a mutual acquaintance," she said. "As for my silence, I maintain discretion where all my clients are concerned. As some of your men here can attest."

At that, there came a stir of the most uncomfortable shuffling, but Haggerty would not be led astray so easily. He shot a whip-fast glance at the reverend, who had, to Rebekah's horror, turned noticeably pale. "You expect me to believe the reverend has been arranging liaisons on behalf of a harlot?"

One of the other men cleared his throat. "If what she says is true—well, Captain, then she's a tart, not a traitor, and, therefore, it's none of our concern."

"*If* what she says is true," Haggerty echoed, but sounded doubtful. He glanced at the reverend, who stared coolly back at him.

Rebekah held her breath, terrified the man would feel compelled by his position to counter her claim. After all, if he only called Ben a spy, and himself an unwilling accomplice, he could easily clear his name.

"*Is* it true?" piped one of the soldiers, his voice pinched with surprise.

"You've heard her answer," said the reverend.

Haggerty snorted. "Take them both to the barn," he ordered. "Hold them there for questioning."

Rebekah's heart rate tripled as two redcoats crowded forward to collect them. "This is ridiculous," she said, struggling to root the panic out of her voice. "I demand to speak with Lieutenant Davies."

This was a foolish plea, of course. Even if Mason did not suspect she was a traitor, he would surely believe she'd betrayed him. At the moment, though, she could think of no better alternative.

"Yes, I'm sure you do," Haggerty sneered in reply. "But he's away for the day, and so you'll have to deal solely with me." He glanced at the men behind her. "If she puts up a fight, you have my blessing to subdue her."

Rebekah stiffened as her arms were seized from behind. "Easy," said the soldier in her ear, his voice tinged in regret. "If it is as you say, then what harm can there be in answering a few more questions?"

More harm than he could imagine, Rebekah thought, watching helplessly as Haggerty slid

Ben's note into his pocket. Now, he knew exactly where Ben would be, and when, and could easily lay an ambush for him.

If Ben was caught, it wouldn't take much pressing to realize he was not what he seemed, not now that he'd used the reverend to pass notes into Stony Point.

Men were killed for far less.

As, she'd lately learned, were women.

CHAPTER 36

The door to the barn was locked and barred. Shafts of early evening sunlight spilled between the boards, revealing every particle of dust in the manure-scented air. One of the soldiers had been kind enough to slip a handkerchief to them before leaving, and so Reverend Wainwright sat upon a pile of hay, holding the cloth to the side of his head with an uncomfortable grimace.

"I'm sorry for what I said," Rebekah whispered once they were alone. "Your reputation—"

"Is expendable," he answered steadily. "Our necks are not."

"You might lose your parish."

"It was a necessary sacrifice. I did it to protect you. To protect Ben. Someday, perhaps all will be remedied. After all, we know the truth."

"I've ruined you," she disagreed. Then, thinking of all the foolish things she'd done to lead them to that moment, rested her chin on her knees and added in a muffled voice, "I've ruined myself."

"There is nothing in either of us, ruined or otherwise, that God is not using for His will." The reverend spoke these words softly, humbly, and with far more confidence than Rebekah could bring herself to feel at the moment.

Even so, she was glad she'd not been locked

in the barn alone. Though Reverend Wainwright was quiet and reserved, his presence became oddly comforting as the hours trundled on. Not once did he grumble. He never paced or shouted or demanded to know when they'd be released.

Someone came, eventually, to feed the horses, but Rebekah and the reverend were granted no food, no water. Haggerty's orders, no doubt. Even then, the reverend made no pleas, merely lowered himself upon the straw to rest his head while the animals chomped their dinner.

Rebekah could not help remembering the day she'd stood upon the barrel. The reverend had been quick to plead for her, bargaining with the magistrate to give her something to eat. She felt a renewed flicker of gratitude, to realize that he'd made such intercessions on her behalf when it was clear he would not make them on his own.

By the time the door was thrown open, the barn was cloaked in darkness, and Rebekah had long suffered the itch of tiny insects crawling over her, which no amount of scratching had relieved. She stood, plucking straw from her flea-ridden hair as a tight formation of soldiers stalked into the barn beneath a lantern's glow.

Mason stood at the front, with the lantern held aloft in his hand.

Given his occupation, Rebekah knew he'd killed men before, though he'd never spoken of it. It had always been relatively easy to separate

Mason the man from Mason the soldier, but there was no separating any of it now. His eyes glinted, cold and dispassionate, without the slightest hint of fondness or familiarity when he spotted her in the corner.

He addressed his men without taking his eyes from her. "Remove the reverend."

At this, they dragged the reverend up by his arms and prodded him out of the barn like a mule.

He glanced back once at Rebekah, alarm lighting his eyes before the door thumped shut between them. Wordlessly, Mason turned to set down his lantern. He moved slowly.

When at last he advanced in her direction, Rebekah pivoted back on her feet. A faint buzzing in her head made her wonder if he might not murder her there in the barn.

"Mason, please—"

He stopped mid-step, his eyes full of simmering wrath. "Haggerty has all but knotted your noose," he said in a voice that chilled her. "I would choose your words very carefully."

She threw back her shoulders. "What did he say?"

"That I ought not to put my faith in a whore."

It was a familiar word, as familiar to Rebekah as her own name, but it smarted to hear Mason say it so carelessly. Face burning as if he'd struck her, she turned away.

Before she made it two steps, he caught her

by the arm, his hand twisting so forcefully as he struggled to pull her back that she panicked and began to thrash against him.

He growled in frustration, the rest of his restraint slipping as he wrestled her into the corner. “What have you *done?*” he snarled, shaking her until the blood pounded in her head. “Tell me the truth. Have you turned traitor as Haggerty says? Or traitor only to me?”

Rebekah fought a sob, thinking of the woman in the city who’d been whipped until she could no longer stand, and by her lover no less. At the moment, she hardly knew which answer would enrage Mason more, so she merely shook her head as if to deny both of his accusations and grasped him by the front of his shirt. “Please, Mason. *Please!*”

He shook off her touch roughly, sending her sprawling in the straw.

Her arms thrummed as she put them out to break her fall, but she turned fast, so he wouldn’t catch her by surprise if he intended a stronger attack.

“You’ve made a fool of me,” he seethed, his shadow looming over her. “Even now I haven’t the dimmest idea what to do with you. Everyone knows you ought to be drummed out of camp.”

“I never wanted to hurt you.” She inched up onto her knees. “That’s the truth, I swear.”

“Who is he?”

"A customer from the boardinghouse."

"Oh, he's a good deal more than that," Mason spat, ripping Ben's note from his coat pocket and pitching it on the ground in front of her. "A man doesn't risk—" he broke off before he could finish. In a tighter voice, not quite controlled, he asked, "Do you love him?"

Rebekah blinked. It occurred to her that if she turned on Ben now, if she exposed him as a spy, there was a chance, however faint, that Mason would forgive her. If he thought she'd been coerced, if she told him she'd been afraid, he might care enough about her to believe her against his better judgment.

But Rebekah couldn't give him Ben. She wouldn't, no matter what Mason did to her, and because of this she couldn't help but wonder—*did* she love Ben?

The question robbed her of all reason. She shook her head. "No," she said firmly. "I don't."

"And me?" Mason ran a hand over his face. "Do you love me?"

How was Rebekah to answer such a question?

If she said yes, she might be permitted to remain with him. But even as she thought it, she knew it wasn't true. However much as she wished she did, she didn't love him.

Not anymore.

"I've lived like this for so long," she answered bleakly. "Men come, and they leave, and I feel so empty, Mason, so empty that even the idea of love makes it worse, makes me sick. Don't you understand?"

Mason's face drained of all color.

For a moment, they merely stared at each other, both stunned by her candor. Rebekah shook her head, trying to put the pieces of their conversation back together, but she was exhausted, covered in stench, and very much afraid. She buried her face in her filthy hands. It was the only retreat she could muster.

The straw crunched as Mason dropped to his knees.

When he drew closer, she shrank away, but he jerked her hands down and away from her face. "You'll stay here until I figure out what's to be done."

"Have I no choice in the matter?"

"I hardly need give you one," he answered disparagingly. "Who else would have you now?"

Here, at last, he caught her at a loss. Her father had made it perfectly clear he wanted nothing to do with her, as had Mrs. Pendergrass. She could think of only one other person to go to, and he had a noose to dodge himself.

Of course, she could leave Haverstraw altogether, start fresh in some town that knew nothing of her exploits. Nearly nothing tethered her to Haverstraw, and yet, somehow, the idea of moving away from her son was unbearable.

Reading her defeat, Mason stood to his full height, looking down on her. "You aren't to speak to that reverend anymore, nor any of the men from Pendergrass House. You are to have an escort at all times. You won't go anywhere unless I explicitly give you leave to do so. Are we understood?"

Though Rebekah was loath to play the part of prisoner, she picked herself up from the ground, brushing straw from her skirt. "Perfectly."

"Then back to your tent." Mason bit out the words as if she was no more than a common foot soldier then plucked up the lantern and stalked from the stable.

He slammed the door behind him. The sound cracked on an echo before leaving her, once again, in silence.

CHAPTER 37

Buzzing with flies, the orchard air smelled cloyingly sweet, the palpable tang of overripe cherries overpowering nearly every other scent. In the darkness, Ben paced beneath the branches for ten minutes, then twenty, then spat a choice oath when he realized Rebekah wasn't coming.

He reminded himself, grudgingly, that it wasn't fair to be angry with her about the snub, not when he'd abandoned her after returning from the city. He'd only been trying to keep her safe, but she didn't know that. For all appearances, Ben had used her for his purposes until he was done.

He only wished he knew if she'd moved to the fort out of necessity or out of desire, if her feelings for the lieutenant were as tender as he'd once suspected. He told himself he was only concerned for her safety given the coming assault, but he wasn't that dense where his feelings were concerned.

He was jealous, ruthlessly so.

He paced again, grimacing as he turned a bit too hard. The bullet wound still ached if he moved too fast, the skin pulling taut as it continued to heal. He pressed his fingers to the welt, feeling the slight groove through his shirt.

Rebekah had kept such a clear head that night,

bandaging him as she did, hiding him in plain sight. She was a quiet presence most of the time, dignified, yet whenever she acted, she was bold, surprising.

He snapped a thin twig from the branch above his head, looking up the worn path toward the church as he turned it twice over in his fingers. It was time he returned to Pendergrass House, but the prospect soured his spirit even more. In the beginning, he hadn't minded taking cover at the brothel, for it was but a means to a much higher end. But now it seemed to him a festering place. The sounds in the upper rooms disturbed him, made him think of all those nights when Rebekah had slipped upstairs with customers as he sat idly by the fire.

He let the twig drop as he walked up the path, then froze sharply. He heard their boots before he ever saw their uniforms—a cluster of soldiers moving beneath a sequence of lifted lanterns.

Soundlessly, Ben skirted the orchard and slipped into the graveyard, drawing his pistol as he crouched behind one of the headstones. His heartbeat pounded in his temples as the soldiers fanned out through the orchard. Their boots pulverized sticks and grass as they moved about, lanterns held high, following a trail of light all the way up to the edge of the graveyard fence.

Ben ducked lower, holding his breath until it burned in his chest.

They were expecting him.

Which meant his note had either fallen into enemy hands, or else Rebekah was not nearly as loyal as he'd previously hoped.

"As you can see," spoke a familiar voice, "there's no one here."

A chill washed over Ben to hear the reverend speak.

One of the soldiers, who had been peering behind a number of headstones to the right of Ben, turned back toward the parsonage. "He must have known we were coming."

"Did you warn him?" demanded one of the soldiers.

The reverend gave a throated laugh. "And how might I have done such a thing," he questioned, "when I've been in your custody all this time?"

There was a shuffling sound, quick and grating, as if someone had been shoved back through the dirt.

"Leave him!" snapped one of the officers. "He'll be out of our hair soon enough."

Ben peered over the edge of the gravestone in time to see the last uniform disappear around the corner of the parsonage.

A single shadow remained, leaning against the doorjamb, a lone figure stooped like a gnarled tree.

Ben waited until the redcoats began their march up the road. Then he vaulted over the graveyard fence and dashed across the yard, sliding in through the door. He found the reverend kneeling by the parlor fireplace, struggling to stoke a pile of flickering embers.

"Reverend!" he whispered, keeping his voice low in case any of the soldiers doubled back.

The reverend gave an uncharacteristic jump. He swayed sideways.

Ben lurched forward, grabbing him by the shoulders to steady him. It wasn't until the reverend saw Ben that relief triggered in his eyes, but Ben felt no such relief. Too clearly, he saw the gash upon the older man's temple, the gritty smear of scabbing blood.

For a moment, Ben couldn't speak. His blood had been up from the start, but now a blistering rage swept over him. He wished he'd fired upon those redcoats when he had his chance in the graveyard. Wished he'd shot them down like the miserable dogs they were.

The reverend set a hand on his arm. "It's not so bad as it looks," he said bracingly. "More than anything, I'm a bit sideways on my feet from hunger. Won't you fetch me some of that bread? And perhaps a bit of tea? We might both do well to steady our nerves before we speak."

Though choked by fury, Ben did as the reverend instructed. He saw the man into his chair then knelt to start the fire. He sliced into the bread with dangerous force, then set the kettle to boil.

By the time the water was ready, he thought he could speak without shouting outright, but his voice shook as he handed the reverend his tea. "What the blazes happened up there?"

"One of the captains intercepted your note."

"He searched you on the way in?"

"No." The reverend's lips twisted. "He caught me passing it off to Miss Stanton."

"Miss Stanton!" Ben nearly fumbled the tea kettle as he tried to hang it back on its hook.

"Yes. She told them the note was from an admirer, but I'm afraid Captain Haggerty suspects she's passing intelligence out of Stony Point."

Ben had to grab ahold of the mantle to keep to his feet, but there was no escaping the shudder that racked his body. Even when he'd been shot in the woods, nearing the domain of death, he'd kept a hold of himself. But now? He knew from experience that interrogations could go in any number of directions, and being a woman precluded Rebekah from very little short of hanging.

"Where is she?" he demanded.

"I don't know." The reverend's voice was reduced to a thready whisper. "I don't know what they've done with her."

The blood in Ben's veins, a moment before boiling with rage, turned to ice. It was his fault, wasn't it? He'd known the danger all along and was far too used to making reckless gambles. If anyone was to blame for what those fiends had done to the reverend—for whatever they'd done to Rebekah—for whatever might happen to her if he didn't reach her in time . . .

He tore across the room, but the reverend was much faster than he might have given him credit for, and stronger, too. He caught Ben before he could reach the door, shoving him against the wall to stay him.

"Leave off!" Ben hissed, forcing himself not to lay hands on the man. "You know I must go."

"I know you to be a reasonable man," the reverend answered in a hard, disapproving voice. "So, you know as well as I that if you go charging out of here, with your blood up like it is, you'll get the both of you killed."

Ben froze. He held back the curse on his lips, knowing full well that the reverend hadn't done anything to deserve it. With shame, Ben glimpsed the bloodied gash upon the man's head, proof he'd braved the British wrath just to keep a dreadful sinner like Ben safe from their gallows.

"After what they've done to you," Ben said in a more measured voice. "Even after what they might do to her—would you have me do nothing?"

"Certainly not. I'd have you sit with me awhile. Drink a cup of tea. And *think*."

CHAPTER 38

July 14, 1779

The sun had set on Stony Point hours ago. Though Mason had ordered Rebekah to keep to her tent, she found the blackness there stifling, unbearably so. And though three days had passed since his cruel interrogation, her arms were still tender from the shaking he'd given her. Rubbing absently at the bruises, she ignited a small fire outside her tent and sat beside it, her knees pulled up to her chest as she listened to the fort's residents rove about.

Most nights, the camp would have been silent and asleep, but the men were in high spirits given a late-arriving shipment of supplies. Ale and cider flowed freely as a few choice cuts of meat roasted over open flames. Laughter pealed from firesides. Somewhere nearby, a man played a fast-paced ditty on a dulcimer, accompanied by a younger lad on the fife.

When Mason and a few other officers moved past Rebekah's tent, he didn't look at her. He didn't stop. He held a tankard in his hand and seemed intent on finding the bottom.

As he passed, Rebekah turned her face toward

the fire. Heat fanned against her cheek as she closed her eyes, focusing on the sound of the dulcimer.

A few officers up the path lent the song their hearty baritones.

> The arch-rebels, barefooted tatterdemalions,
> In baseness exceed all other rebellions,
> With their hunting shirts and rifle guns:
> To rend the empire, the most infamous lies,
> Their mock-patriot Congress, do always devise;
> Independence, like the first rebels, they claim,
> But their plots will be condemned in the annals of fame,
> With their hunting shirts and rifle guns.
> Come take up your glasses, each true loyal heart,
> And may every rebel meet his due dessert,
> With his hunting shirt and rifle gun.
> May Congress, Conventions, those blasted inquisitions,
> Be fed with hot Sulphur from Lucifer's kitchens,
> May commerce and peace again be restored,

And Americans own their true sovereign
lord,
Then oblivion to shirts and rifle guns.
GOD SAVE THE KING!

The song ended with a collective shout and deep quaffs of ale all around. Unwilling to look like a traitor in the slightest respect, Rebekah drank from her cup, but set it aside as soon as the toast was ended, shrinking in on herself as she thought of Ben.

Did men like him really deserve death and hellfire for desiring liberty?

Did *she* for all the wretched things she'd done?

Before she could decide, someone dumped an empty basket onto her knees.

"We need more firewood," barked one of the women.

Rebekah bristled to be bossed about, but she was glad for the distraction. So, she took up the basket, hoisted her lantern, and made her way to the wagons near the back of the fort. Lifting one of the tarps there, she piled the basket at her feet with logs.

With a grunt of exertion, she swung the load up into her arms, but hadn't made a single step when a hand clamped over her mouth from behind. Terror flashed white and hot as she wrenched her body to the side, but she couldn't move an inch. Lantern and basket tumbled to the ground, extinguished on impact and littering the dirt with firewood as she was lugged backward into the shadow of the supply wagon.

"Don't scream," whispered a harsh voice against her ear.

Recognition swept over Rebekah so fast she nearly sagged back into Ben's arms.

He loosened his hand, though only slightly, as if he suspected she might scream. When she didn't, he drew back, turning her by the hip to face him. He lowered his weapon.

She could barely see him in the darkness, just the glint of his gun and a faint flash of pale skin as he angled his head toward her. Yet she sensed a familiar restlessness in him, as if he could feel the silent hunt of several hundred redcoats.

"What are you doing here?" he demanded in a feverish whisper.

"What am *I* doing here?" she sputtered, then shook her head, astounded by his anger. "I might ask you the same question. Of course, I can only assume you need me again. What do you require of me this time, Mr. Clarke? To go through the lieutenant's things? I'm sure, by now, you've heard I have access to his tent."

"No," he hissed. "That's not why I've come."

"Then why?"

He opened his mouth as if to snap something back but closed it just as abruptly, laughing resentfully under his breath. "Of course, you'd think that. I've never given you reason to expect anything else, have I?"

A note of bitterness laced his voice, turned unmistakably inward. It unnerved her far more than his anger.

"You're going to get yourself killed," she decided at last. "You're going to get *me* killed. Whatever it is, I want nothing to do with it."

Ben stepped into her path before she could flee. He drew near enough to search her eyes, then shook his head, his gaze falling from hers. "Why did you move into the fort?"

Rebekah tried to make sense of his question, but it was hard to think straight with the gun in his hand. In the distance, peals of laughter echoed as a pair of soldiers went swaggering past the wagon, whistling and slurring. *"Their plots will be condemned in the annals of fame . . ."*

She waited for them to pass, then looked back up to Ben. "You have to go," she said, her voice stronger. "If Mason finds us together after what happened"—she lost her breath, unable to list the possibilities—"He's furious enough as it is."

Before she could bid him move out of her way, Ben took another step closer, edging her back. "Did he hurt you?"

"It doesn't matter."

"Doesn't *matter?*" he rasped.

Another step left her nowhere to go, her back

flush with the wagon behind her. She looked sideways for an escape.

His eyes flashed above her, holding her gaze. "For the life of me, I can't decide if you're afraid of that wretched man or if you're in love with him. Well, which is it, Rebekah? Which is it?"

"It's not so simple as any of that."

"Then what?"

All at once, her frustration boiled over. "I don't know!" she cried under her breath. "I've only ever wanted to love him."

Ben went so still she might have overlooked him in the darkness if she wasn't already staring into his eyes. A muscle worked in his throat as he swallowed. "What has the man done, such as he is, that he should deserve your love?"

"Very little," she answered, with surprising frankness. "Except my son looks just like him."

Here, at last, was the truth.

As soon as Ben was faced with it, he dropped his gaze again, turning slightly away so she could no longer see his face.

Rebekah stared at her feet, steeling herself for his response. In her experience, the more men learned about her past—about *her*—the less they found to interest them. While a secret love child was hardly the worst indiscretion to her credit, it tormented her the most, made her writhing conscience shriek.

"Are you supporting him?" Ben asked, with a bit

more effort. “Is that why you do this to yourself?”

“There’s nothing I can give him that he doesn’t already have. He belongs to another family now.”

“And the lieutenant?”

“What about him?”

“Has he made you any promises?”

“The lieutenant has promised me nothing,” she admitted, ignoring the pinch in her heart as she, once again, spoke the truth.

Ben exhaled loudly. He turned away as if to leave but spun at the last moment. “What if I could find you another place?” The words rushed out of him, his breath blowing warm against her face as he slid closer once again. “Another position? Would you take the chance if I gave it to you?”

All of Rebekah’s senses snapped to attention. She hadn’t the vaguest idea what, exactly, he was offering, whether a place of sanctuary in another town—such as the reverend might have arranged if she’d ever plucked up enough pride to ask him—or something more intimate.

A place with *him*.

Mason’s earlier wrath slammed a door on this line of thinking. She could hear his angry bellows in the barn, could feel the tightening of his fists around her arms as he all but demanded her loyalty. For as long as she was entangled with Ben, she was a trail Mason could follow back to him. She rubbed at the tender spots on her arms, feeling as though she was still being rattled, shaken about, and was struck then by another fear, far more urgent.

Mason was furious with her, suspicious enough to demand she stay at the fort.

What if he was having her watched?

Terror rising, she tried to turn away, but Ben reached out, his fingers clasping her wrist. “Please, Rebekah. *Please*.”

He didn’t seem the kind of man much inclined to beggary, but there it was. When she didn’t answer, he turned her toward him one last time and pulled her face up. His hands were calloused and warm. “Is there really so much keeping you here?” he whispered.

Nothing at all was keeping her there.

The realization turned her to stone.

She closed her eyes and thought of Eli, that small boy with fair hair and rounded cheeks. She’d spent so many nights wishing she could carve a hole in her heart large enough to hold all the regret she felt from losing him, but her soul was spent. Little by little, she’d frittered herself away on a man who might never love her, on the emptiness that deepened each time she climbed into bed with another man.

In turn, she’d been mocked and degraded. She’d heard the father of her own child—the man who claimed to love her—call her a whore. What if that’s all she was to him—to anyone?

She didn’t realize she was crying until Ben

swore under his breath and pulled her the rest of the way into his arms. He held her tightly, his hands firm against her shoulders as if bracing her against an unruly wind.

In the midst of everything, Rebekah was staggered by his warmth, his steadiness. She reached up, clutching his shirt in her hands.

"Come with me," he murmured, his lips pressed against her hair. "Right now."

Rebekah wavered, hardly able to draw breath let alone to think. A part of her, strong enough to startle her, wanted to disappear, to fly with Ben into the night and never return.

A fine phantom she'd be if she did.

The people of Haverstraw would conjure up all sorts of stories to explain away her disappearance, and Mason would spend the rest of his days wondering what had become of her. A tempting thought, a pretty story, but footsteps were advancing from the direction of the officers' tents. They marched a straight line across all of Rebekah's fine thoughts, scattering them in the wind.

She had no way of knowing who was coming, not really, yet she felt the truth within, as if her soul was tethered to his, despite it all, and could sense whenever he was near.

Mason.

CHAPTER 39

Ben had sensed a moment of agreement in the second before Rebekah twisted her hands free from his. Drawing a rattled breath, she shoved him back so violently he had to grab hold of the wagon to stay on his feet.

Now he heard the footsteps as surely as Rebekah had and held up a hand to stop her, trying to determine how much time they had before they were seen together.

A minute?

Maybe less?

"He's coming," Rebekah whispered. She was inhumanly pale, warding him back with outstretched hands. "You must go! Now!"

Ben stayed where he stood, the window for escape closing fast. If he told her of the coming attack, she might come willingly, but he couldn't warn her. As desperate as he was to ensure her safety, hundreds of men relied on his discretion, would be slaughtered if she let slip what she knew. He couldn't risk it. Even if he could, even if they ran now, together, the lieutenant was sure to give chase. There was a strong chance they'd be picked off by muskets before they could clear the fence.

Chest heaving, Ben turned to flee, but then he looked back for one final glimpse of her. Sudden moonlight, which had been covered by a cloud the moment before, lit the curve of her features, her elegant eyes glimmering with tears as she waited for him to leave. He might have gone, too, if the moonlight hadn't revealed the color of the ribbon twisted up in her curls.

All the breath rushed out of Ben's chest. It was not just any ribbon she'd tied in her hair, but the scarlet one—the one he'd bought for her in the city.

He stepped forward and brushed his knuckles down her tear-stained cheek.

Silently, she stared at him, seeming to hold her breath until he lifted his hand to her hair and tugged that ribbon free. All at once, her curls unwound in an unruly tumble over her shoulders.

Heavens, but she was lovely—unbearably so.

He tucked the ribbon into her palm, waiting until her trembling fingers curled around it, holding fast. "If you're willing to consider my offer," he whispered. "Hang this outside your tent. Tomorrow. I'll watch for your signal, and I *will* return for you. You have my word."

Rebekah leaned closer as if to answer, close enough Ben might have tilted his head and easily brushed her lips, but the footsteps drew perilously close, and so he rounded the wagon and dashed into the shadows beyond.

• • •

Before Rebekah could blink, Ben was gone, and Mason stood in his place, a frigid replacement.

He cast a look around, scanning the shadows. "What are you doing?" His voice was cold.

Rebekah's fingers trembled all the more, her heart pounding in both ears as she slipped the scarlet ribbon, inconspicuously, into her pocket. "I dropped my basket," she answered, crouching to gather the fallen logs. She scrambled to refill the basket, suffering a few splinters in the hurried process.

Only days before, Mason would have jumped to assist her, to prove himself ever and always at her service, but he stood back, his boots at the level of her eyes. He waited for her to finish without speaking.

More than anything, she wished he would leave. His silence as he stood over her was suffocating. She hadn't the faintest idea what she ought to say to him, what he expected to hear. She'd already apologized, but it wasn't enough.

Nothing would ever be enough.

By the time she stood, her hair, no longer secured by the ribbon, had dropped into her eyes. She brushed her fingers through the curls, tucking them behind her ear as, at last, she braved a glance at Mason.

He held his candle low, the shadows making a hollow mask of his face.

She wished he would say something. Order her to leave the fort, or else forgive her. Anything to end the awful impasse. But as the seconds gathered, nothing changed in his features, and so she bent and hauled up the basket, teetering slightly under the cumbersome weight.

Mason sighed from deep in his chest as he lifted the basket out of her arms.

Rebekah shifted back, confusion rising.

She wanted to return to the way they were before she'd lied to him, before he'd come to the barn and made her feel the unbending side of his temper. But he was still Mason, wasn't he? And she was still Rebekah. All that was essential within them remained the same. She stepped closer, placing a hand upon his arm. "Mason, please, can't we—"

He stepped back abruptly, beyond her reach. "Not now," he clipped.

"I know you're angry with me," she said, refusing to drop the matter. "But don't you think we owe it to each other to talk about what's happened?"

"You're mistaken if you think I'm the least bit angry. I'm busy, tremendously so, and haven't the time nor the patience to ensure you keep yourself out of further trouble. So, I will merely advise you to stay within sight of the rest of the camp. Despite my assurances to the contrary, there are those who think you a traitor, Miss Stanton, and would think nothing of questioning you, roughly, if they should happen upon you in the dark."

He bowed his head in parting, a cold courtesy, and left.

Rebekah leaned against the wagon as she watched him go. His warning made her skin prickle, but Ben's words—*"come with me, right now"*—stayed with her through the night.

CHAPTER 40

July 15, 1779
1:45 p.m.

Reverend Wainwright was packing crates of books in the parsonage library when Ben arrived. The windows were propped open on either side of the room, allowing a late afternoon breeze to scuttle across the floor, fanning a few open pages upon the desk. The room always smelled the same, of worn books and ink, but the wind brought with it traces of juniper and white cedar.

Ben hadn't spoken to the reverend since he'd seen Rebekah the night before and felt a pinch of apprehension as he dropped his portmanteau in the doorway as an announcement of arrival. "What are you doing?"

The reverend smiled and went on packing, pausing only long enough to eye the bag at Ben's feet. "It seems we've both been asked to move on."

"Move on," Ben repeated sharply. "What do you mean?"

The reverend took a moment to decide where best to fit a particularly large tome, which he slid into the back of one of the crates. "Word has made its way around about my involvement with you and Miss Stanton. There are those who feel I've behaved inappropriately. I've been asked to move out of the parsonage by the end of the week."

"But that's absurd!" Ben's voice cracked with anger. "You've done nothing wrong."

The reverend now held a small stack of books balanced between his slender hands and, aside from shades of sleeplessness beneath his eyes, seemed as mild and mannerly as ever. "Come, now. Had I come out with the truth of the situation, we'd both of us be in an even tighter scrape than we are. But, tell me, what news do you have to share of Miss Stanton? Is she safe?"

"She's at the fort," Ben reported, his visage grim. "Unharmed, as far as I could see, but scared. I do not think Davies will permit her to leave."

The reverend sighed. "It is my greatest regret, I think, that I might not have seen her more—well, more secure, I suppose I'd call it—before taking my leave of Haverstraw."

"You don't need to worry on that score," said Ben. "I will see to Miss Stanton."

"Yes," the reverend agreed, smiling faintly as he slid another book down from its shelf. "I'm sure you will."

"Where will you go from here?" Ben asked.

"I have a brother in the ministry. He lives in Connecticut. His church was burned recently, and he's looking to rebuild."

"But what will your people do without you? Your congregation, I mean?"

The reverend's eyes drifted to the window. Through it, they could both see the church's gray stone walls. "Oh, I don't have so high an opinion of myself as to think the church will suffer without me. I am but an instrument. One who is, as I am glad to be reminded, easily replaced."

"You make it sound as though you won't miss it dreadfully, but I know you better than that."

"Of course, I'll miss it." A wistful smile pulled at the reverend's thin lips as he took another book from the shelf, fanning the pages a moment before lowering it, too, into the crate. "And I can't help pondering what's to become of you in my absence. I've snatched you back from the gallows more times than I care to think. I would hate for all my efforts to have been in vain."

At that, Ben laughed outright. "Perhaps I'll turn cleric."

The reverend laughed as well, but otherwise did not comment, once again intent on his packing. "And you?" he inquired. "Where are you bound?"

"I can't tell you that," Ben admitted in a more serious tone. "Though a prayer of protection on this particular night would likely not be misspent."

"I shall pray without ceasing."

When Ben stepped forward, taking the older

man's hand in thanks, a regretful look entered the reverend's eyes, far less subdued. The expression of familiarity put Ben in mind of another man entirely. Of course, nothing in Reverend Wainwright resembled Ben's father in the least, and yet, somehow, his thoughts drifted in that direction, perhaps because the two had once been such unlikely friends.

And perhaps not *so* unlikely.

His father had taken to his knees every night, praying for things about which Ben had never dared ask at the time, but now he wondered. Had Ben's father prayed for him? Had he prayed for his son's safety, for his well-being despite all the horrible words they'd exchanged?

"I've appreciated your counsel," Ben said, his throat distressingly tight. "Far more than you know. And for whatever part I've played in your exile, I am truly very sorry. God go with you, Reverend."

"And may He remain with you as well, Benjamin." Reverend Wainwright pressed Ben's fingers, nearly smiling. "Through many uncertain paths, I should think."

July 15, 1779
9 p.m.

Having resolved their previous fight over several shared pints of ale, Ben and Jotham joined

Wayne's Light Infantry at Springsteel's Farm. There they found an assembly of men more than twelve hundred strong and already weary.

The men had gathered in the morning and marched all day, silently, through marshes of sweltering heat and the whole way around the sprawling base of a great mountain. Their clothes were caked in grime, shirt collars yellowed and limp with sweat, hanging uncomfortably about their necks.

They didn't know where they were bound or how long they were to rest there. They couldn't be sure an attack was even imminent. Before arriving at the farm, Ben and Jotham had been instructed not to say a word about their posts in Haverstraw, nor of the coming attack. The orders would be passed down when the time to strike had come.

"We hold fast to the element of surprise," Wayne had written in his last letter. *"Or else we'll die as mongrels."*

Dismounting near the pigsty, Ben and Jotham led their horses to the water troughs. They'd arrived hours after the rest of the men already had settled, and so, as they made their way through camp, they heard a good deal of grousing about the timing of their entrance.

"Worthless coxcombs," one of the men muttered under his breath.

"Good of you to join us," scoffed another.

"Glad to see you didn't have to muddy your boots."

Of course, none of Wayne's men knew who Ben and Jotham were, what the two of them had risked thus far to carry them all to the precipice of battle. As for Ben, he didn't mind a bit of anonymous honor. He'd nearly always worked in secret. But a telling muscle jumped in Jotham's jaw, the very same which had twitched whenever the boys in the schoolyard had harassed him.

"So much for gratitude," Jotham growled under his breath, tugging his horse along with slightly more force than was needed. "You'd think we were here for glory alone, and not to put our sorry necks on the line."

Ben laughed in turn. "I, for one, wouldn't turn up my nose at glory," he admitted. "Though I'd prefer to keep my neck, if it pleases Wayne."

Before Jotham could answer, a man came up behind them saying something or other about someone named Clarke. Surrounded as he was by the crowd of soldiers, strangers all, Ben didn't register the name at first.

The man repeated himself, gawkily. "Erm—Mr. Clarke, isn't it?"

At last, Ben turned, reeling at his error and feeling somewhat less himself. To cover his momentary confusion, he affected a look of irritation. "Yes, yes," he snapped. "What is it, man?"

"Wayne wishes to speak with you, sir. If you'll follow me?"

The man gestured up the rise of the hill, to an old barn with a moldering roof. Ben set a hand on Jotham's shoulder, leaning close. "No shooting any duels in my absence," he said wryly. "Remember, *I'm* your second."

Then he strode after the sentry and entered the barn a few steps behind him.

A row of horses shuffled anxiously at their arrival, their ears swiveling this way and that. Wayne had set up a wooden table on the far side of the barn. It was littered with his usual stacks of papers, a rusty lantern, and a bottle of Madeira.

As the sentry took his leave, Ben slid into the chair opposite the table to wait. He took up the bottle of Madeira, curious about the vintage. A label dangled from a string, which had been tied around the neck of the bottle, and as Ben perused the markings, his gaze landed, entirely by chance, on a letter that had been pinned beneath it.

In truth, Ben didn't intend to read the letter. His eyes had traced a few words on impulse, but he found them so startling that he craned his neck and read ahead before he could stop himself.

> *This letter will not reach your eye until the Writer is no more. I know that friendship will induce you to attend to the*

education of my little son and daughter—I fear that their tender mother will not survive this stroke—do go and comfort her . . .

Ben sat back, bemused.

It was hard to think of Wayne as a man with a family waiting for him, that the "modern Leonidas" thought one way or the other about being slain in battle. The prospect of death had certainly never rattled Wayne's bars before, neither had the memory of his tender wife inhibited him from entertaining a constant ring of female admirers. Wayne was larger than life in nearly every respect. To some of his men, even larger than death.

But Ben knew as well as anyone that there was always someone left behind. Someone to mourn or be mourned.

He thought regretfully of Rebekah, then, of the blood-red ribbon he'd tugged free from her curls. If he should fall in battle before he could reach her—

An abysmal thought. He wished he'd had the foresight to have penned such a letter, something to pass the truth safely into her hands.

By then, he knew better than to read any more of Wayne's letter. A man's dying wishes were private territory, doubly so if the man was still alive. And yet, as if somehow doubting the letter's authenticity, he couldn't help jumping to the last paragraph.

> *I am called to sup—but where to breakfast—either within the enemy's lines in triumph—or in the other world—then farewell my best and dearest friend and believe me to the last moment,*
>
> *Yours Most Sincerely,*
>
> *—Anthony Wayne*

Ben had barely reached the end when a hand clapped down upon the paper, smothering the signature. Then he heard the cold, choked fury in that venomous voice. "What in hellfire do you think you're doing?"

CHAPTER 41

Ben jumped up from his chair and stood at attention. He looked to his boots and tightened his jaw until his teeth ached in his head. How foolish he'd been, to be caught spying on his superior—on a *general*—the very man who had instructed him to spy in the first place.

He knew from experience that facing a temper like Wayne's was no comfortable task. He suspected he was about to be flogged, if not bayoneted where he stood, but he lifted his gaze by the slightest inch, resolved to be a man about it, at least.

The general did not seem entirely himself, more like an unhappy spirit conjured there against its will. He wore a clean uniform, neatly pressed, and smelled strongly of fresh powder, but there were circles beneath his eyes and creases at the corners of his lips that had not been there at the start of the war. To his men, he was a bulldog. To Washington, a champion. And yet, he'd been greeted often enough by death's whispered flirtations to have penned his final wishes to his dearest friend.

Ben cleared his throat. "General, forgive me. I didn't mean—"

As if nothing had happened, Wayne slid the

paper away from the desk, folded it once, and tucked it into his pocket. "What news from Stony Point?"

Knocked off his poise by the turn in topic, Ben struggled to remember his report. "The redcoats suspect a counterattack, of course, but nothing immediate." He paused. "May I ask when you expect to advance?"

"Midnight. When the tide goes out, there's a narrow sandbar at the base of the fort. We can cross easily from shore."

This was a good plan, Ben thought, but he couldn't stop thinking of Rebekah. Even now, she was likely retiring to her own tent, turning over on her mattress to sleep. He wondered if she was waiting for him to return, if she'd tied the ribbon outside her tent as he'd instructed.

As always, he became more uneasy the longer he thought of her. There was a chance, however slim, she might be hit by a stray bullet in the scuffle. After the brutality of Tryon's men in Connecticut, there was an even more frightening possibility of reprisals from his own men. How easy it would be for her to be rounded up with the rest of the camp followers and sent off into exile, or else prison.

"I have a request," said Ben.

Wayne's eyes snapped upward. "An impertinent one, I take it?" He shook his head before Ben could answer and sat abruptly. "Speak it."

“The woman I mentioned, the one who assisted me in the city—”

“The harlot, you mean?”

The word set Ben on edge. “Yes,” he answered, with quiet restraint. *“Her.”*

“Well, what of her?”

“She’s been useful to our cause,” Ben said, laying his groundwork cautiously. “At tremendous peril to herself.”

Wayne sighed, rubbing his tired eyes. “Oh, do be a man and spit it out.”

“Very well. I think we owe her some measure of protection.”

“You think that, do you? Shall I hand Washington’s plans off to you, then, so keen you are to plan? Shall I allow *you* to lead our little campaign?”

Ben stepped closer, refusing to be cowed by the warning flare of Wayne’s rising temper. “I wish only for your permission to marry her. If she’ll have me, that is. And I would have you assure me that she’ll not be gathered up with the rest of the camp followers. She ought to remain with our people.”

There was a silence.

Wayne swore, then laughed. “Have you gone howling mad? Are you truly asking my permission for you to wed a whore?”

Fury nipped at Ben, but he stifled it before he could give it utterance. He couldn’t risk another scuffle like what he'd gone through with Jotham, and certainly not with one of Wayne's rank. Though he was disinclined to admit it, he needed the general's approval.

In the past, he'd laughed at the expense of men who found themselves in similar predicaments. Several had pleaded with their commanding officers for permission to marry a woman who had been deemed less than suitable to reap the benefits and rations of regiment life. But none of those women had been prostitutes. And Ben wasn't a common soldier. He was a coin in Wayne's pocket, and, as such, was answerable to both his whims and his wrath. To move even one step closer to Rebekah, Ben needed the general's blessing, or else he faced serious censure.

"Miss Stanton is at the fort, under heavy suspicion," Ben answered, careful to use her name, subtly correcting Wayne's vulgar epithet. "She's put her neck in the noose for me on more than one occasion. Are we to have used her in the name of our cause and now leave her in such dire straits? Such is not the conduct of gentlemen, surely."

"What are you suggesting?" Wayne barked. "That *I'm* not a gentleman?"

Trusting his instincts, Ben stood his ground. A man like Wayne was hard to peg. He cornered his enemies with meticulous foresight. He cursed more creatively than any man Ben had ever met.

He was terribly fond of drink and vain about the attentions of attractive women, and yet, despite it all, Wayne fancied himself a gentleman above all else and disparaged any man, any *soldier,* who conducted himself beneath the title.

Silently, Wayne dragged the bottle of Madeira closer. He poured a dram and drank the contents in a single swallow.

"You're an idiot, of course, but you nonetheless have my blessing." He plonked down his empty glass and waved a haughty, dismissive hand, toplofty to the last. "Now, get out. As you can imagine, I have far more pressing matters to attend than your current state of bachelorhood."

July 15, 1779
10 p.m.

Come with me.

Ben's words haunted Rebekah. They followed her into her dreams. They shadowed her through the day and as she muddled through her chores. She didn't know what he meant by them. There was a world of difference between pity and a true home, a place of belonging, which she was now beginning to desire above all else. She kept slipping her hand into her pocket, running Ben's ribbon through her fingers and almost praying—as she had not done for years—for clarity.

A moonless night was falling upon the fort, the ground chilly and damp beneath her shoes. She held fast to the ribbon in her pocket, drawing silent strength, wishing she could reach, instead, for the hand of the man who had given it to her.

Thoughts miles away from camp, she didn't notice Mason advancing from the other direction until they had nearly collided.

He stiffened like he'd stumbled upon an enemy in the night. "I haven't the time to speak with you," he grumbled, trying to maneuver around her.

She caught hold of his arm. "I'm not letting you go until you do."

He looked down at her hand then into her eyes. His jaw was rigid, expression forbidding, but she could read the truth in his gaze as clearly as if he'd shouted it. He was lost to her. Had been for some time. Yet, she couldn't leave him without explanation, for he'd done as much to her once, and she'd been wrecked by the agony of it.

Could they set aside the past and speak honestly together?

He was the father of her child, after all. She owed him that much.

"I'm not the same girl you knew four years ago," she said quietly. "Perhaps it was foolish of us to pretend I was."

"Don't," he said. "Don't do this."

"Why shouldn't I? It's no sin to speak the truth."

"The *truth?*" He snorted, yanking his arm from her hold. "I'd be very much surprised if you're familiar enough with the truth to speak it."

She sighed, frustration flaring. "I know I've done wrong. But you aren't being fair. You haven't had to change, Mason, but I had no choice. I've *changed.*"

"As you've made abundantly clear."

"You needn't go on punishing me!" she spat out. "I feel truly wretched for what I've done. The truth, if you'll hear it, is that for four years now I've been surviving on the dim hope you might return and marry me. *That* hasn't changed. It never did, you know."

Speaking those words took more courage than Rebekah had left, but she felt she'd carried it off well. That is, until Mason's laughter lanced straight through her, so cruel and cutting she recoiled.

"I was never going to marry you," he said.

After four long years of waiting for him, of fruitlessly hoping, Rebekah blanched at his words. "*Never?* Not even before I—"

"Once, maybe." He sighed. "But then I learned what you'd become . . ." He shook his head, the anger melting away to regret. "I have my reputation to consider."

The horror of those words rose like gorge,

choking her. "More palatable to keep a prostitute than to marry one, is that it? Yet you've rebuked me for *my* scruples?"

She closed her eyes to clear away the tears, then forced herself to look at him. If he felt any stab of shame for what he'd said to her, for his hypocrisy, she found no evidence of it.

"Is that all?" he asked her.

"I suppose it is." She yanked his ring from her finger and held it out to him, hardly feeling the loss. "If you can't find it in yourself to forgive me, then I see no reason to stay."

"Oh, really?" The amusement in his voice was nearly too much to bear as he snatched the ring from her hand. "Where will you go?"

"Perhaps the reverend can find me a place."

Again, he laughed. "I find that highly unlikely."

His sarcasm set her on edge. "What do you mean by that?"

"Only this. That your good friend, the reverend, has been deemed unsuitable for service after his involvement with you and your young man. He's leaving Haverstraw, and I very much doubt he'll have the connections to see a woman like you set up anywhere."

Rebekah swayed, stricken by the news.

Reverend Wainwright had done everything he could to help her. He'd offered her counsel about her child. He'd protected her from Haggerty, and because of her words—her foolish, thoughtless words—she'd played a hand in the poor man's exile.

"No," she sputtered, disbelieving. "That isn't right. He never . . . what I mean is, he didn't—"

"He did enough," Mason cut in sharply and turned to leave.

Rebekah stared at Mason's back, at that familiar crown of blond hair, which was secured neatly with a ribbon at the nape of his neck. Everything about him was the same, so handsome, so ordered, yet he was nothing at all like the man who'd once gathered her into his arms.

She jogged to catch up. "If you will but write my pass," she said. "I shall pack my things and be off."

"You aren't going anywhere." His voice was low, menacing.

She tried to read his eyes, but he was no longer looking at her. Despite everything that had happened, she couldn't really imagine Mason would keep her against her will for spite, but there was a threat in those words, something he wasn't saying.

"Why shouldn't I?"

He exhaled a long-suffering sigh, as if she'd finally broken him, then grabbed her arm and propelled her off the path and into the shadow of the blockhouse. "It's the most curious thing," he said, in a quieter voice. "But I recently learned of a rebel spy who was recognized in the city.

Nearly two weeks ago. Officers got the drop on him at an inn, but he rode off with a young lady before he could be apprehended."

He caught Rebekah's chin when she tried to look away and swiveled her gaze upward. "Turns out she was posing as his *wife*."

CHAPTER 42

Rebekah stared up at Mason, her heart thrashing until she realized that somewhere in the middle of his story she'd forgotten to breathe. Now, she drew in a breath so slow, so shallow, she feared it sounded suspicious. "Whatever you're talking about has absolutely nothing to do with me," she managed at last.

"Yes, it would seem that way, wouldn't it? Except—coincidentally, of course—this was on the *exact* day I came to call on you at the boardinghouse and was told you had gone off with a client. You were gone for two days, I believe." His brows flattened to a grim line. "So, tell me, Rebekah. Who was your *client?*"

"You have no right to ask me such questions."

"As a lover, perhaps not. But as a lieutenant? I certainly do."

Rebekah waved a hand. "Oh, but I hardly knew the man. He was a traveler of sorts, wealthy enough, just passing through. He wanted discretion, and I obliged. I don't recollect his name."

"Where did he take you to enjoy your services?"

Services. She detested the word but answered as composedly as she could. "An estate to the west of here. It was dark when we arrived."

Mason smiled sharply. "The more you say, the less I believe."

"You are free to believe whatever you'd like," she said. "Though I can't help wondering who else you may have told of your . . . your *suspicions*."

"Not a soul."

This was promising, to a point. If Mason thought she was guilty, if he truly wanted to punish her, he'd have gone to his captain already, if not all the way to Colonel Johnson himself. Circumstantial or not, the evidence was damning.

"What is your plan from here?" she demanded. "Will you not be satisfied until I'm languishing in a British prison? I never would have imagined you to be so revengeful."

His face paled, then flooded with color. "I have no designs to see you locked in a cell," he answered coolly. "I wish only to discover where you stand—or rather with whom you *lie*."

He might have struck her for all the force he put behind the final word, and so she was forced to face it. Most days, Rebekah had tried not to think too deeply about the woman she'd become. She skated across the surface, reassuring herself that she'd been surviving, and that was all—that it hadn't been entirely her choice, her fault. Yet, here she was, still standing on that barrel outside the church doors, weak and alone, hearing the soft chorus of chants, only now they came from within herself. "Harlot! Harlot! Harlot!"

Mason loosened his fingers, but he didn't let go of her. "These are uncertain times," he said. "And dangerous. So, I intend to keep you here until I get to the bottom of this, until I know where you stand. Until I know who, exactly, has been working against us."

Needing room to think, to plan, Rebekah stepped back until she bumped into the rickety wall of the blockhouse.

Mason advanced farther.

She felt his warmth, so familiar, but his eyes turned her to ice.

"And if you find me guilty?" she whispered.

"Give me his name, and it need never come to that."

Rebekah closed her eyes.

So, this was his game. It was her own fault for drawing him onto the field when he'd been avoiding her for days. She'd thought he was angry, brooding over what was to be done about their relationship, and yet here was the truth of it—he knew *exactly* what she'd done. Likely, he thought she had no choice but to bend to him.

"A prisoner, then. Is that what I've been reduced to?"

"Rebekah—"

She didn't let him finish. She couldn't, for the long-faded lines within her were being erased, violently redrawn, and it made her skin crawl.

"Shall you lock me in the barn? Deny me food and water? Send your men to knock me about until I prove more cooperative?" She thought, again, of the woman who'd been flogged in the city and fought a desolate laugh, pressing her hands to her eyes. She was nothing to men but a body, she realized, to be used for pleasure or else to be broken, made more pliable.

Mason seized her by the shoulder when she would have wept, the grip of his fingers biting tight as he held her firmly against the wall. For a moment, he didn't move.

She closed her eyes but felt his cheek brush hers, and then his lips, his touch reminding her of all the tender moments which had passed between them, all the fond, fragile dreams she'd once placed in his hands.

"Just give me his name," he whispered, his lips grazing hers.

Rebekah jerked sideways, flying out of his arms so abruptly he pitched forward and nearly collided with the wall. He regained his bearings quickly and rounded on her, but she was already gone, fleeing to the safety of her tent.

As long as she lived, she'd never give him Ben.

There was nothing Ben wanted, nothing he desired that merited death, and, aside from that, she knew this implicitly: she didn't have to lie to Ben in order to feel safe with him or to know he would do everything in his power to protect her. She might have told him she was a devoted Loyalist, that she'd told Mason everything about what they'd done, and, somehow, she knew he'd still come for her, would defend her against his own if it came to that.

She ought to have gone with him when she had the chance.

The thought didn't distress her as it once would have. She could see now, clearly, that as long as she remained with Mason, she would always be subject to his whims, his orders, to the high walls he'd built around her.

Always a mistress, never a wife; easily used, more easily discarded.

The rest of the fort had retired to their beds, so no one was awake to see Rebekah unwind the scarlet ribbon from her pocket. No one was there to watch her tie it to the post of her tent and step back.

The ribbon hung for a moment before it was caught on a small gust of wind. Then it jumped as if to attention, leapt sideways, and rippled freely, a defiant flash of color in a place of gathering darkness.

CHAPTER 43

July 15, 1779
11:30 p.m.

"Muskets are to remain unloaded!" With a broad stride, Colonel Febiger paced among the men, passing down the orders as Wayne had given them. "Bayonets only. We can't risk giving away our positions. The general says any man who discharges his firearm or shouts out ahead of the siege is to be run through with the nearest bayonet."

The men stood at the ready, collectively nodding their understanding. They'd already been divided into three groups. The center column would go in through the western side of the fort and draw the brunt of the British fire, ensuring the remaining two columns could sneak in along the northern and southern cliffs undetected.

Jotham and Ben had joined a group of six hundred men under Wayne and Colonel Febiger. They were to form the right column, storming in as soon as the British were suitably distracted by the center.

"We also need a small group of pioneers," Febiger went on. "To go in ahead of the next vanguard and chop through the abatis. For this forlorn hope, I respectfully ask for volunteers."

Forlorn hope.

The term was used for any group of soldiers sent in ahead of all the rest, into the deadliest part of battle. Most would not return.

Once, Ben might have volunteered. He was just the sort to catapult to the front, axe in hand, to court sentry fire as he cleared the fence. It sounded bold and glorious, but he had to make it through to Rebekah—he'd given his word that he would—and to do that, he had to survive the assault.

All around him, hands went up. Febiger nodded his silent approval, counting off the men until a small group of twenty or so stood apart from the rest. Then he moved down the ranks, passing forward slips of white paper from a stack.

"It's a dark night," he explained. "Fasten these to your hats so you may distinguish yourselves from the enemy."

Ben slipped his hat from his head, pinning the white parchment to the brim as Febiger continued with his orders. "If you should pass anyone on the road, you are to secure them. We can't risk anyone raising the hue and cry against us."

One of the men near Ben gave a rusty-sounding laugh, leaning close to his friend and murmuring under his breath, "What else? Think they'll want us to bayonet any dogs that happen to bark?"

"Don't be insolent," warned an imperious voice from behind.

The soldier spun on his heel, his face going as white as the paper in his hat when he came face-to-face with none other than Wayne himself.

The general brushed past the man in the middle of his apology to address the rest of the assembly. "Once we have the fort," he said. "We'll turn the guns on Verplanck's Point across the way. They'll have no choice but to surrender. A prize of five hundred dollars and immediate promotion to the first man who enters the fort. As soon as you're in, cry the watch phrase. *'The fort's our own.'* Tonight's mission will be perilous for all. Be on your guard, all of you, and as brave as befits a true Patriot."

Ben fell in line behind the rest of the men, his hands clasping his musket, the bayonet tip gleaming like a diamond in the shadows above him. He thought of all the perils that lay ahead as if waiting to consume them. Five hundred British troops, fifteen cannons, and another fort of British reinforcements less than a mile across the Hudson.

What did he and the rest of Wayne's men have, in turn, except raw nerve and years of growing indignation?

He was reminded, as they branched off, of the twenty men who'd volunteered to enter ahead of the rest. The stakes were high for all, but so too the reward as the fragile hope of freedom whispered like a siren through the ranks, beckoning them on. No man there was sacrificing himself for nothing. But while most thought of freedom, of liberty, Ben could think only of Rebekah, of the ribbon she'd worn, of all he'd risk if it meant having her safe in his arms on the other side of battle.

If she'd have him.

In this respect, perhaps he was no better off than the poor souls who'd volunteered to leap headlong into the fray, most of them doomed to die before they ever cleared the fence.

But he had to try.

No moon shone, but the wind was of an unruly spirit. It roared, then whistled shrilly in Ben's ears as he and the rest of Wayne's men scaled the rocky cliff. From a distance, Ben thought they must have looked like hundreds of spiders skulking steadily up the incline. At one point, he felt sure the wind would blow him off course, send him careening backward into the Hudson, but he firmed his grip with a savage spirit and climbed even higher.

They'd been promised a sandy bank on which to easily pass but had been forced to huddle together under the base of the cliff, waiting for the waters to recede. Ben's breeches were soaked to the thighs after those long slogging hours tromping through the marshes. What's more, their mission had been christened with an unseasonable chill. Were it not for the sweat breaking out on his brow from the exertion of the steep climb, he might even have shivered.

A breath hissed past his teeth as another rock sliced his hand, dagger sharp. He kept his grip though both palms ran slick with blood. Rock by rock, he propelled himself alongside the rest of the men, higher and higher with those aching, bloodied hands.

Wayne was a good distance ahead. It was too dark for Ben to see him, or anything much for that matter, save the endless wall of rock in front of him and the flutter of white papers in the hats of those beside him. But he could sense Wayne's silent headship, the courage and fortitude he inspired in the men now buzzing with hushed anticipation.

By the time Ben reached the top of the promontory, his breath was sharp and painful in his chest. He tried to subdue it, could hear the two men on either side struggling in a similar fashion, and said a small prayer of thanksgiving that, if nothing else, the wind masked their sighs.

There was nothing to do now but wait.

He settled on his haunches and closed his eyes, a spring wound dangerously tight. More than once, his thoughts turned to Rebekah, to their last encounter, but he banished her to the back of his mind with careful, vicious restraint. He needed to stay focused. He needed every nerve in his body honed, narrowed in on what was coming.

A moment later, the first musket blast cleaved the silence. Responding shouts echoed from the top of the treeless promontory. The first column had made its advance and was swiftly spotted by British sentries.

Now, they all waited to see if Colonel Johnson—the poor wretch charged with defending Stony Point—would fall for the bait.

CHAPTER 44

July 16, 1779
Shortly After Midnight

The first shot rang so loud that Rebekah felt as though it had passed straight through her body. With a seizing gasp, she sprang up and prayed she'd been only dreaming.

But then she heard the voice of Colonel Johnson, his cultured tones reverting to their native Irish lilt, as he screamed himself hoarse in the distance. "Come up, you rebels! Come up and fight!"

Blood rushing, Rebekah scrambled up from her mattress, fumbling to find her shoes. In the time it took to secure them, the gunfire had tripled. So, too, the shouts. Her fingers shook so violently it was all she could do to hold on to her shoes, and she fumbled them twice to the ground before she managed to slide them on. Then she ducked forward, crouching on hands and knees at the entrance to her tent, trying to make herself as small a target as possible as she peeked through a thin crack in the canvas.

The night was thick and black, so there wasn't much to see, just a bunch of shadows dashing about, dark as wraiths against the moonless night.

Cannon fire rattled the ground beneath her, reverberating up through her hands, shaking her arms. As a line of men went tromping past, yelling to each other over the commotion, she thought at once of Ben. Then, almost as quickly, of Mason.

She didn't want either to die, yet she knew the ways of war. One side would win, and the other would lose, and she had no way of knowing, after Tryon's hideous raids, if quarter would even be granted to those who surrendered.

What, she thought dizzily, would happen to her?

If the rebels made their way into the fort, and if they managed to secure it, she might very well be herded off with the rest of the camp followers, marked as another Loyalist sympathizer. Her situation would be no less desperate if the British held the fort. Mason already thought she was suspect. He might not wish to see her tossed in prison, but this didn't mean he wanted to protect her either.

If Ben couldn't come for her as he'd promised, might she not be carted away, never to set eyes on him again?

She could think no further. A shot had just gone off a few paces from her tent. She threw herself flat on the ground, pressing her face against the coarse edge of her mattress as someone outside hollered an obscenity.

A moment later came a vigorous shout. "The fort's our own!"

Rebekah wasn't sure what was happening. Surely, there hadn't been enough bloodshed to merit one side claiming victory, nor had she heard a clear surrender.

Yet that single shout was picked up and echoed, repeated by dozens of voices at once, rising to a deafening clamor. "The fort's our own! The fort's our own!"

She stuffed her hands to her ears, blocking out the cries, wanting it all to be over as fast as possible. As she thought of Ben and Mason entering the fray, she hardly dared imagine how such an unholy confrontation might end for either of them.

She hadn't bent her knees in prayer in years.

Not since Eli had rested warm and safe in her arms had she pleaded with God in the darkness. But now, as she pressed her hands to her face, the words sprang up from somewhere deep and vital. "Father, keep them safe," she pleaded. "Preserve them. *Preserve them*."

The only answer to be heard was Colonel Johnson's voice, which rose once more above the din. "Turn! Turn!" he thundered, his voice thick with terror. "The devils are coming in from the other side!"

At Wayne's command, the lines in front of Ben surged forward, men flowing like sand through the spaces in the abatis. The gunfire, which had been mostly isolated to the front wall, changed course immediately to intercept them. Ben bent forward, a bullet ringing wildly past his ear as he charged faster up the final length of the slope.

A few paces ahead, Wayne was shouting the watch phrase with lusty ardor. But just as quickly as the general reached the fence, he reeled back as if he'd run headlong into a stone wall. There was the quick, startling flash of muzzle fire. In it, Ben could see Wayne's handsome, chiseled face, now dripping with blood, illuminated for barely a second.

As darkness dropped again, Wayne's letter flashed through Ben's mind. *"I am called to sup—but where to breakfast—either within the enemy's lines in triumph—or in the other world . . ."*

The next flash of light revealed Wayne slumped on the ground, unmoving.

Ben and another man jumped forward to assist but were cut off by a cluster of advancing redcoats. One was in the last frantic fumble to aim his weapon when Ben lunged forward and sank his bayonet into him. Warm blood pooled against Ben's hands, but he twisted his weapon deeper, trying to make it quick.

His opponent choked in answer, gurgling as he swayed forward to cling to Ben's coat. Ben heard a slight grunt, and then the man drooped forward, body severed from soul before he'd even hit the ground.

Ben clenched his teeth and withdrew his weapon, ignoring the weight of anguish as he pressed onward.

To Ben's relief, Wayne was trying to rise by the time he reached him. The side of the general's face was florid bright, wet with blood. " 'Tis only a scratch," he insisted, though gasping like a man half-drowned. He tried to step forward but sank against Ben's side, dazed.

"Confound it!" Wayne barked. "Lead me forward, men! If I'm mortally wounded, so be it, but let me die in the fort!"

Ben hooked an arm under his shoulder. The other man jumped forward and braced him on the other side. Together, they hefted the general, half dragging him the rest of the way into the fort, where carnage unfolded around them, the battle illuminated by stray sparks of light as the musket muzzles flashed in the night.

Weaving through the smoke and strewn bodies, Ben and his comrade deposited Wayne at the base of the flagpole. The British flag had already been torn down and sat like a heap of dirty laundry at the feet of the Continental colors. Propping himself there, Wayne hoisted up his musket, swearing in masterful form.

Ben leaned forward, trying to examine the gash on the general's temple.

Wayne flinched like a provoked animal and thrust him back. "Leave me be!" he spat. "I've given myself shaves closer than this! Go, now! *Go!*"

Ben heard no more. As soon as he turned, two redcoats rushed straight at him. He stiffened as they advanced. He didn't want to kill them. He knew there was goodness in freedom, in liberty, true honor in standing firm against a tyrant. All these things flitted through his mind in an instant, as fleeting as a muzzle flash. But though he hoped for the glorious things which might be reborn of that night, he felt no glory in killing. They were all men in essence.

Yet, in that moment, what else could he do?

As they lifted their weapons to strike him down, he pleaded with God for mercy then threw himself forward with a roar and attacked. He did not stop until they were dead.

CHAPTER 45

With every moment, death prowled closer to Rebekah's tent.

At first, the worst sounds were in the distance, on the western side, but in a matter of minutes they'd channeled a straight course to the center of the fort. A muffled groan, deep and tormented, sounded close enough to her tent that she might have stretched a hand through the flap and touched the poor soul where he lay dying. He might have been a redcoat, or he might have been a Patriot. It struck her that she couldn't tell the color of a man's coat by his dying screams alone.

It was then she recalled the knife Ben had given her in the city and crawled across her tent, praying she wouldn't need it even as she dug it out of her trunk. Settling down in the corner, she smelled the tang of blood beneath the thickening cloud of gunpowder. She flexed her fingers anxiously against the knife's hilt, drawing her knees up to her chest. She whispered another prayer, trying to drown out the sound of musket fire, but it was impossible to mask the screams, let alone stifle her own, when a dark form entered her tent.

Rebekah held her breath as she waited for the man to move. She couldn't tell much from even that short distance, couldn't make out his face or the color he wore. The shadow moved forward, then paused as if listening. A faint glimmer of white, a small piece of paper, she realized, might have been tucked in his hat.

Without so much as a sound, Rebekah scuttled back. What if he was a Patriot who thought her nothing more than a Loyalist doxy? What if he'd heard of her arrangement with Mason?

He bent to lean what might have been his musket against the edge of her trunk. All the better, she thought, firming her hold on the dagger.

Then he spoke a soft appeal. "Rebekah?"

Gunshots echoed all around, but Rebekah dropped her knife and flew into his arms so fast he grunted and went down on a knee, nearly dragging her down with him. She wondered if she'd hurt him, if he'd been wounded in the attack, but his arms engulfed her before she could question him, holding her tightly to his chest.

"Oh, Ben," she gasped, pushing back to look at him, but he didn't let her speak another word, nor draw a single breath. He took her face between his hands and kissed her soundly.

Rebekah's heartbeat roared in her ears as she clung to him. A moment before, she'd been crouching bone cold in her shift, but Ben was warm, decided, his hot breath ragged as if he'd run all the way across the camp to reach her. She could hardly hear the gunfire now, was aware of nothing beyond the shocking bliss of his lips against hers.

A gunshot at close range, followed by a scream, shocked her back to the present.

Just as quickly, Ben tore himself away, dragging in a deep, unsteady breath. "Forgive me," he said. "I shouldn't have presumed to . . . what I mean is—oh, hang it all! I've been wanting to do that ever since I made you that downright appalling marriage proposal."

Raw with emotion, Rebekah nearly laughed. How strange to hear such words even as the war bellowed on the other side of her thin canvas walls. She wanted to assure him that he'd presumed nothing, that he'd done nothing she hadn't wished for a great while herself, but then she touched his face and felt something wet and sticky on the side of his cheek. She angled back to catch a closer look. What she saw stopped her cold.

Ben looked unnervingly feral, covered all over in dirt and streaks of blood. His clothes were sopping wet, and his hair had worked free of its cord, framing the hard angles of his jaw. A slice on his right cheek looked truly terrible, though she suspected much of the blood on his hands and clothes was not his own.

How many men had he killed that night?

As soon as she thought it, his gaze shuttered.

He turned away and crept nearer to the entrance, lowering his head as he listened to the bloodshed beyond.

Rebekah came up behind him and rested a hand on his shoulder. He flinched, but she didn't move away. His presence, as always, brought a steady calm, made her feel safer, more secure.

"I have to go," he said, very quietly. "But I'll come back. I promise. I only wanted to know you were safe."

"Have the British surrendered?"

"Not yet," he answered, taking up his musket. "But make no mistake—they will."

His words settled ominously in the silence they'd created.

Rebekah wanted to blurt a great many things in that moment, not the least of which was that she was terribly afraid she was in love with him. Afraid because he might die, because he might very well be shot down before she could ever call him her own. She reached forward, capturing his hand tightly in hers. "Ben, please, I must tell you, in case—"

"Don't."

He spoke the word so harshly that Rebekah drew back, but then he reached forward before she could turn away, placing his fingers gently against her cheek. "Wait here," he said. "I'll return when it's done."

Rebekah nodded as he slipped out of the tent,

but she felt a worrying wave of anxiety, strange as a premonition, and couldn't help securing one final glimpse of him as he went. She crouched low in the entrance, folding back the flap and peering out into the night.

It all happened in a matter of seconds.

A thin fragment of moon moved from behind the clouds, enveloping the path in a soft gray shroud of light. The worst of the fighting had moved again, echoing from the other side of the colonel's tent. To the right, Ben dashed off to join the skirmish. There, to the left, stood Captain Haggerty, lifting his musket, with sights trained on Ben as if he was nothing more than a deer dashing across a clearing.

Rebekah went cold all over as she threw herself forward, out of the tent. Before she could think the better of it, she screamed Ben's name.

Rebekah saw Ben tense a second before Haggerty fired. He staggered at the blow but kept to his feet.

She prayed the bullet had merely clipped him.

The real danger was in the distraction, for by the time she realized what was happening, Haggerty had tossed aside his musket and was grabbing for her. She could hardly think, could barely move. She stumbled instead, half-falling back into her tent as he advanced. Though she fought hard, Haggerty scrabbled for her hands only a moment before pressing the cold barrel of a pistol against her ribs.

Ben had been lunging forward, his bayonet tilted, but he froze mid-stride, with a look of devastation, as Haggerty swung Rebekah forward, tucking her body neatly in front of his own.

Here, Rebekah thought, was the moment. The one she'd dreaded since first meeting Ben. She'd always recognized the danger and feared it might come to this. Yet, she couldn't regret him because that would mean giving up, in which case they were both dead anyway.

As if matching her thoughts, Ben took a defensive step forward and nearly tumbled. He blew out a breath, reaching beneath his coat. Rebekah's own breath caught as she watched him withdraw his hand, covered in blood, this time unmistakably his own. He'd not merely been clipped, but was losing blood, and fast.

Her legs sagged beneath her.

"Afraid?" sneered the captain, venomously low in her ear. "It seems Davies should have listened when I told him you were bedding the enemy."

As though giving utterance to her own crowning panic, voices began pleading in the distance. "Surrender, surrender!" they shouted. "Mercy, mercy!"

The battle was ending, but Haggerty didn't care. He shoved her forward without warning, sent her sprawling to her knees in the dirt in front of Ben.

She jumped up fast and spun to keep the pistol in her sights. From behind, she felt Ben's hands close on her shoulders.

"Get behind me," he whispered.

Both his quietness and warmth were there, just as they always were. He steadied her. Made it easier for her to do what had to be done.

"You're already wounded," she argued, her voice barely quivering as she stared across the clearing into Haggerty's gloating eyes. "I won't let him shoot you again."

Ben's fingers tightened and he spoke more fiercely. "Get *behind* me."

Haggerty gave a crack of laughter. It rang louder in the night, for the gunfire had all but ceased. "Valor," he noted. "Not exactly what you'd expect from one of her ilk, is it?"

He straightened his pistol arm. Rebekah flinched, bracing herself for the shot, but Ben took hold of her with a shout and jerked down on her arms, dragging her to her knees as he wrapped himself over her like a shield.

Rebekah was too startled to shove him away, too terrified even to scream. Ben's heartbeat raced wildly against her back. Focusing on the rhythm of it, she pressed her face down against her knees and prayed God would bring them home quickly.

"Haggerty!"

The sudden shout stunned her, but not as much as the voice itself. She couldn't believe it. *Wouldn't* believe it. But then she raised her head just enough to peer beneath Ben's arm.

Mason stood on the other side of the small clearing.

In many ways, he seemed a mirror image of Ben, a man disheveled and defeated, his hands and shirtsleeves marked with blood. The expression on his face was hard and savage, nothing like the debonair young man she'd once admired.

His musket was aimed—not at her, nor even at Ben—but at Haggerty himself.

"The colonel has called for an immediate surrender," Mason announced, his words clipped. "Put down your weapon, Captain, or I shall disarm you myself."

"I told you she was a traitor," responded Haggerty, relishing the sound of the word. "See how she clings to him?"

Mason's jaw tensed, but he otherwise didn't move. "The colonel has called for a surrender," he repeated.

"And who are you to command me?" Haggerty laughed, delighted, as ever, to hold the upper hand. His arm straightened before Mason could answer.

Ben pulled Rebekah's face tightly against his chest, locking her there.

A loud bang reverberated all the way into her chest, but she felt no pain. Instead, she heard a soft thud at a small distance then nothing else.

Ben remained still a moment after it was done, then straightened slowly.

Rebekah followed the path of his scrutiny to where Haggerty lay lifeless in the dirt, his legs sprawled at an unnatural angle.

Pulse leaping, Rebekah looked at Mason, who stood with his still-smoking musket lowered to one side. Despite it all, she felt a sudden pang of fear for him. If the British learned what he'd just done—shooting his commanding officer in defense of a spy—he'd hang for it, if not worse.

Mason watched her from the other side of the narrow clearing, waiting patiently for her gaze. As soon as she gave it to him, he nodded only once, but steadily. Then he leaned forward, placing his musket on the ground at his feet, and stood back, holding his arms in a slow show of surrender as a mob of Patriots rushed forward to subdue him.

For various reasons, some more central than others, Ben wasn't much inclined to like Lieutenant Mason Davies.

But even he wasn't so churlish that he couldn't respect the man for his well-timed intercession. A fine show of clemency was the mark of a true gentleman, and turnabout fair play. So as

Rebekah pulled Ben to his feet, he stopped one of Wayne's officers and suggested Davies be separated from the rest of the prisoners until his actions could be rightly shared with Wayne.

Now that the danger had passed, Ben released his hold on Rebekah and tried to walk. He nearly vomited at the pain, slumping like a sack of beans to the ground. Heavens, but that hurt, so much that his vision blurred. The shot had gone much deeper than he'd realized.

Rebekah was at his side in an instant. Her face was ashen, her tangled hair spilling over both shoulders. "You're wounded," she gasped. "Let me see it."

The initial shock was wearing off fast. Ben tried to oblige, but his vision swam again, and so he shook his head and didn't answer.

Rebekah fussed with his vest buttons until she reached the shirt beneath, which she ripped open without warning.

Pain slithered from one end of Ben's body to the other. He sunk his teeth into his cheek to keep from bellowing. He'd taken a bad hit, he thought grimly, and it would have been worse, surely, had Rebekah not alerted him to the danger. The white slip of paper in his hat would have made an easy target, or perhaps Haggerty had been aiming for something equally vital—his heart.

Resourceful as ever, Rebekah rushed into her tent and emerged with a wad of fabric in her hand. He remembered the night he'd stumbled upon her outside of Pendergrass House. A fine brute he'd been at the time, all but forcing her into her own chamber to tend him. He hadn't loved her then, but he'd certainly respected her.

He focused on the present and found that her hands trembled, a sheen of tears glistening in her gaze. He couldn't tell if she was remembering as well or if his wound was worse than he thought, but he couldn't find the words to ask.

Pinching her lips together, Rebekah pressed the wad tightly against his wound and held it there.

He snarled so violently that she flinched, but then he grabbed hold of her hand to reassure her, holding her to his side. "This feels familiar," he remarked, forcing himself to breathe more steadily. "Though, this time, I'm afraid I haven't any notes about my person for you to steal."

"You're impossible," she answered.

He laughed his faint agreement, then rested his head upon the ground. That took the edge off the pain. All he had to do now was close his eyes.

When he did, Rebekah said his name.

Then she shouted it.

For once, Ben didn't heed her summons. He was so tired. So spent.

When darkness offered itself to him, he turned eagerly into it, like an embrace, and assured himself he needed only to sleep for a moment.

CHAPTER 46

Slowly, with gentle care, Rebekah wiped every speck of blood and dirt from Ben's skin.

It had taken a long while for the surgeon to dig the bullet out. An eternity, it seemed, for them to stop the bleeding. Ben had howled like a beast through much of it, then collapsed senseless on the mattress and would not awaken. The doctor said the shot had, miraculously, missed all vital organs, so there was nothing to do now but wait.

As soon as the surgeon left the hospital tent, Rebekah had pleaded for a fresh basin of water and a rag. One of the soldiers protested her interference, said she ought to be rounded up with the rest of the camp followers in the barn, but another man, much younger—who was known at the local tavern as Jotham—said she should be granted whatever she needed.

Now it was nearly morning, and Rebekah hadn't moved from Ben's bedside.

Beneath the blood, he was pale as a corpse and unmoving.

She dipped her rag in the water, swirling it around, then wrung it out and placed it, lightly, on his face.

He didn't stir.

Inch by inch, she scrubbed spatters of blood

from his jaw, from his cheek. She sighed into the silence and dipped the rag again, the water swirling redder with each pass of the rag.

If Ben had been awake, he'd have teased her mercilessly for her ministrations, but there was nothing for her to do but work in steady silence, washing the blood from his neck, from his shoulders, erasing every hint of battle as she moved to his hands and his arms and his chest.

She remembered the moment he'd stretched himself over her, guarding her from harm. No man she'd ever met had given so much of himself for her, and now, as she waited to see if he would ever awaken, she saw the truth of how her feelings for him had jumped from a smoldering ember into a steady flame.

But could he love a harlot in turn?

More than anything, she wished all the horrible things she'd done could be wiped away as easily as the blood from Ben's body. It seemed impossible. And yet, she remembered the reverend's words. *"You can be whole, Rebekah. In your baptism, Christ Himself has made you so."*

She dropped her rag into the water and reached over Ben, pulling the blanket back up to his shoulders, so he wouldn't be chilled.

"Oh, Ben," she whispered, leaning forward to rest her forehead against his arm. "What is to become of us?"

"What, indeed?"

Rebekah stood and spun to find a stranger standing in the entrance to the tent. He was a handsome young officer, though formidable, and it took Rebekah a moment to register that his coat was a smart shade of Continental blue rather than the garish red to which she was accustomed. He wore his hair heavily powdered, tied off at the nape, and was outfitted in full military regalia, with a gleaming sword dangling from the scabbard at his side.

Rebekah still wore her chemise, her hair woven in a practical braid over one shoulder to keep it out of the way. Thankfully, one of the soldiers had brought her a blanket, which she clutched about her shoulders, feeling half-naked in front of the man.

All bashfulness was forgotten when she noticed the wound on his temple, which had been bound with a thick bandage at the base of his powdered hair, a splotch of blood visible through the coarse material. Whispered rumors said that General Wayne had led the attack that night and been shot for his troubles—more precisely, a bullet had grazed his temple and left a grisly mark.

Startled, Rebekah drew back. "Good heavens, sir, but I think you are General Wayne!"

For the first time, the man smiled. He was twice as handsome as the rumors suggested, and nearly fashionable to a fault. If Mason had stood beside him, she suspected even he would have appeared a dowdy foot soldier by comparison.

"You sound alarmed, young mistress. Are the stories very fearful?"

Rebekah didn't know how he expected her to answer. By all accounts, he was not the sort to put up with nonsense, and so she had no reason to believe he would tolerate a known prostitute to remain in his camp. Was this why he'd come to speak with her?

"I won't give ear to whatever they say of you," she answered evenly. "If you won't mark what they surely say of me."

His eyes flashed as though charmed by her answer. "He spoke of you, you know."

It took her a moment to realize he was speaking now of Ben.

Wayne drew back a chair and settled by the bedside. "Would you like to know what he said?"

"I'd far rather he wake and tell me himself."

"And if he doesn't awaken? What then? Are you to return to the debauchery in which he first found you?"

He sounded like he expected it of her, but while she wanted to bristle, she also felt she had no right to do so. Dozens of nameless men hissed within her conscience, but she banished them with a scowl and shook her head. "I shall never return to that," she said roughly. "Never."

Wayne put up a hand. "I believe you," he said, a

bit more delicately. "But let us do give Renshaw the benefit of the doubt, shall we, and presume he'll pull through? He usually does, you know."

Renshaw.

Rebekah had never heard Ben's true surname. It suited him far more than Clarke ever had, she thought, rough sounding yet somehow refined. "For his sake, I hope you're right, General."

"You needn't keep a constant vigil," he went on, glancing down at the basin of bloodied water with regretful eyes. "Though any man would be affected by the care you've shown to him, I must urge you to return to your tent. Take some time to wash and dress and set your nerves right."

"My nerves are in no danger," she insisted, sitting back down in her chair. "And I have no intention of leaving his side, even if I am doomed to look a bit wild when he awakens."

"You don't look wild."

"I shall become so, sir, if you start ordering me about."

Wayne barked a laugh. "My dear girl, if I didn't have a wife waiting for me back home, I very well might have made you an offer myself, while poor Renshaw here lies senseless."

To this particular remark, Rebekah had no immediate retort. She sensed the general was not speaking entirely in earnest, but hinting at something, trying to fluster her into admitting her true feelings for Ben. This was not easily done.

With a flush, she recalled the feverish way Ben had kissed her in her tent. From experience, she knew such gestures didn't make promises in and of themselves. He might have been swept up in the moment, brought to the brink of frenzy by the battle, and merely lost his self-control.

Not wishing to give credence to Wayne's implication either way, she smiled mildly and folded her hands in her lap. "I've had enough sparring for now, if you don't mind. Why have you come to speak with me, if not to order me to leave the fort?"

"I wanted to take your measure."

"And what have you decided?"

Wayne shook his head as he stood. "You're both fools," he said, but he looked downright fond of her. "I'll have one of the men fetch some clean garments from your tent. You need not look even half wild to tend to him."

"You're very considerate."

"Among other things," he mused, then bowed with a stately flourish and saw himself out of the tent.

As Ben lay senseless, he listened and dreamed by turns, never fully able to distinguish reality from delirium. Throughout the night, he'd been revisited by all his worst moments and trembled, his body shaking in fits. He couldn't help it. He'd confessed his sins to the reverend, but not exorcised them, it seemed, for Satan spat them back at him now.

The old, familiar tyrant.

And all the while, the soft voice of a woman spoke above him. She prayed incessantly, in a voice thick with grief.

"God help me," she cried in a choked whisper.

God help me, Ben echoed within himself.

There, within that chasm of gloom, he recalled these words. *"Come unto me, all ye that travail, and are heavy laden, and I will refresh you."*

The woman ran a soft hand across his brow, then his chest, the path of her touch followed by a cool, damp rag. Her hands were so careful, so tender.

His body shuddered violently in response, the darkness drawing him deeper. He wondered if he was going to die, felt the precarious writhing of his soul, and, though he solaced himself that Heaven awaited, he tried to catch the woman's hand, to hold fast to it so he might not die alone.

Yet, he couldn't move. Couldn't speak. Could only lay prone, visited by phantoms of his past as that soothing voice rolled over him. Half of her prayers he could barely hear, for she seemed to mutter them into her hands, muffling the sounds of her sins as she spoke them.

At last, he centered himself enough to recognize the voice. To picture the soft curves of the woman's familiar face. She was so brave, perhaps the bravest person he'd ever met, though he wished she didn't have to be. More than anything, he wanted to awaken. He wanted to help her, to shoulder some of her burden, but he couldn't think straight enough to open his eyes, nor even to part his lips to declare that he loved her, utterly.

Just before he tipped back into oblivion, her voice grew firmer, sending a prayer heavenward which might have been wrenched from his own spirit. *"Comfort, comfort,"* she pleaded, setting aside the endless recitation of her sins. *"Oh, God, look not upon me in anger, but give me peace . . ."*

The hours blurred until Rebekah hardly knew how many days had passed. Wayne had had all her things delivered to Ben's tent, so she'd washed and changed into a clean gown, even seen to the riotous state of her long-neglected curls. One of the soldiers delivered her meals, but she left each tray where it was set, hardly able to eat when she knew very well Ben might die.

Thus far, he hadn't so much as opened an eye. She held fast to his hand and talked him through the hours—nothing of substance, really—waiting to see if he might press her fingers, even once, but he never did.

So, she waited. And, when she could wait no longer, she slept.

Her head was bent at an awful angle, the upper part of her body slumped forward on his cot as the rest of her sat in the chair. With her eyes closed, the warmth of Ben's arm, so close, was the only assurance he was a living, breathing man, not yet a corpse, but when she dreamed she became less sure of this.

The men who had stormed the fort were lowering him into the ground, covering his limbs with dirt until only his face remained. They wouldn't let her mourn him but drummed her from the camp, sneering at her all the way back to Pendergrass House. There, she found countless men in the parlor, all staring at her with leering faces filled with lust. She wanted to shove at them, to hurt them, but a young woman in the corner was holding Eli in her arms, rocking him tenderly. Rebekah froze, tears rising to her eyes as the woman placed a motherly kiss to the little boy's crown of curls.

"My son," Rebekah rasped, pleading with outstretched arms. "Please, take care of my son . . ."

The edges of the dream evaporated as a warm hand settled on Rebekah's shoulder. Her spirits soared at the touch.

Ben. She knew it was him and practically flew from sleep to greet him.

But when she opened her eyes and lifted her head from the mattress, she found Ben in the same senseless state in which she'd left him. Only his eyes moved. They roved beneath his lids as if his dreams shifted as rapidly as her own. Woozy from sleep, she brushed a hand to his cheek to reassure herself that he was still warm. That he hadn't died.

"Rebekah?"

The voice stopped her cold.

In the first instant, she was certain she was sleeping, that her dreams had taken on a crueler form. But then she glanced up into her father's eyes and knew she was awake.

He looked the same. Stern, harassed, wearing a fine coat that fit him a bit more loosely than she remembered. His gaze moved from her to Ben, whose arm she clutched, and back again. "So," he said, snatching his hand back from her shoulder. "Here you are."

Rebekah hardly knew what to think of his arrival. She had no idea why he'd come to the fort, nor what his motive might be. He might have come to her as a father, to forgive her, though she hardly dared hope this was the case when it seemed far more likely that he'd come at her worst to finally gloat that he'd been right all along.

She set Ben's hand gently upon the bed and rose, wincing at the stiffness in her back. "What are you doing here?"

"I heard about the attack." He looked down, his fingers fidgeting with the hat between his hands. His throat sounded raspier than usual, as if he'd been yelling far too much very recently.

"I knew you'd come here to be with Davies, and I was afraid—that is, I thought maybe you would have—"

He broke off, swallowing with tremendous effort.

Suddenly, Rebekah understood. She'd overheard a few of the soldiers talking that morning. Washington had offered to send the camp followers, some seventy in number, to join with the British army in New York. All but two had chosen to follow their husbands and would be imprisoned upon reaching Philadelphia. Hunger and disease likely awaited them.

If her father's expression was anything to go by, he thought for sure Rebekah would have followed Mason to the ends of the earth, even if that meant subjecting herself to prison.

If she hadn't been shot in the skirmish first.

That final thought shamed her. The fort had been attacked, and she'd not thought to send word to her father to assure him she was safe. In fact, she'd very nearly died in Ben's arms, and her father didn't even know. Surely, it would have destroyed him. She could see that now in the rare bit of stubble on his jaw, the waxy pallor of his cheeks.

She tried to smile but was far too tired to hold it. "As you can see, I am perfectly safe."

He nodded, frowning once more at Ben. "Dare I ask who he is to you?"

The question carried with it all the old arguments, so she had to bite her lip to keep from snapping at him. Of course, she'd given him no reason to trust her, no reason at all to think she wasn't the same Rebekah. But now, in the presence of Ben, he might have thought she was a turncoat to boot, following a trail of men all the way across enemy lines if it served her purposes.

"It isn't what you think," she said quickly.

"No?"

She swallowed hard, her throat suddenly dry. She struggled to find the right words to explain what had happened, how everything had changed with so sharp a turn.

Before she could speak a word of it, her father looked hard into her eyes, looked as he'd never looked before, and whatever he found in her gaze made him shake his head, nonplussed. "No," he said slowly. "I can see it's not."

Relief flickered within Rebekah's chest, but then she sighed, sinking back into her chair. "I'm afraid you wouldn't care for him very much."

"Really? Why is that?"

"He's a Patriot, isn't he?"

Her father gave a brittle laugh. "Is that all?"

Rebekah narrowed her eyes. She couldn't tell if he was being sarcastic or speaking in earnest, but he'd already donned his hat, the usual signal he was finished with an argument. Only they hadn't been arguing. Had they?

"Do you think he'll live?" he asked.

"I sincerely hope so," she replied.

"Very well, then."

He turned to leave.

If she let him go, everything would carry on in the same way. Never speaking, never meeting, a life of past injuries driving them further apart.

A horrible voice in the back of her head encouraged her to remember all the times he'd hurt her, all the ways he'd turned away and let her suffer. Yet, how many prayers had she spoken that night, pleading to God for forgiveness, for deliverance she wasn't sure she fully deserved?

She wanted to forgive her father. She *needed* to forgive him, but she wasn't sure how to go about doing it.

He was nearly outside the canvas, the flap ushering in a sharp current of crisp morning air. "Do you still have supper at six?" she blurted before he'd fully exited.

Her father paused. He barely turned, but she could see a sliver of his profile as he pondered her question. "Are you requesting an invitation?"

Rebekah glanced down at Ben, then back to her father. "The two of you are likely to argue like mad," she warned.

As dignified as ever, her father slid into his gloves. "I shouldn't mind it," came his quiet reply.

CHAPTER 47

July 19, 1779

After three days, Rebekah left Ben's side.

Wayne all but commanded it. He said she'd be of no use to anyone if she didn't get a decent night's sleep, suggested Ben might faint away in fright if he awakened to find her in such a wild, unkempt state. And so, off she went, to her own tent, to leave the fretting and the fussing to the good doctor.

Rebekah was frustrated by Wayne's interference, thought it a good deal below the general to hold court about such matters. Even so, she obeyed. She washed and changed into a clean gown. She curled up on her mattress, intending only to close her eyes for a few minutes, and fell headlong into a heavy, dreamless sleep. By the time she awakened, she was so inwardly turned about that she hardly remembered her name let alone the battle. She heard men's voices just beyond her canvas walls and leapt up, glancing through the flap.

It was the supper hour. The sun had already slipped low, signaling its slow farewell with shades of purple and blue. Smoothing back her disheveled curls, Rebekah rushed from the tent and across the camp to where they were keeping Ben.

As soon as she reached the entrance, her stomach plummeted.

The cot where Ben had lain, where she'd tended to him and prayed over him, was empty, sheets stripped and carried away.

Rebekah's thoughts spiraled as she turned, searching desperately for any sign of him. She wondered if he'd died in her absence. Perhaps Wayne had suspected he was taking a turn for the worse and sent her away so she might not be there to suffer through the end.

Devilish man, she thought wildly. She would *never* forgive him if he had!

She became aware, then, of voices outside the tent and threw herself toward them. "What's happened?" she demanded, seizing one soldier by the shirt front. "Where is he? What's *happened?*"

The man she held merely gaped, but the one on the right offered her a peculiar smile. "Rest yourself, Rebekah. He awoke in the night. No fever, and he was able to eat. The doctor ordered him to walk about a bit, while the tent is cleaned. Said it would help with healing."

Rebekah was so embarrassed by her outburst that she nearly laughed, but then she dropped her hands and almost cried.

Ben was awake. He was awake, and he was *walking*.

The other man pointed to the farthest tip of the

promontory. "He's just there, you see. Watching the ships."

With a mortified flush, she thanked them and rushed off, tears choking her as she spied Ben standing at the edge of the cliff, which he'd climbed with such brutal efficiency not even three nights before. His coat had been tossed in the dirt a few paces away from him, and he wore no vest. Even so, he seemed far more put-together than he had since storming the fort. He wore clean breeches and a fresh white shirt, which billowed slightly in the wind. He was quite a bit paler than normal, his features hardened into a look of concentration.

Rebekah wasn't sure what to make of that expression. She worried he was thinking of Wayne and the rest of the men, already planning on marching off to the next great, glorious battle, leaving her, once again, behind.

Wanting to catch him off guard, if only once, she held her breath, then announced, "General Wayne seems to think we ought to marry."

A flash of pain crossed Ben's face as he pivoted, but then he blinked, and it was gone. In its place was an impassive expression which set her even more on edge. "Does he?"

Unwilling to give too much away before learning the direction of his thoughts, she spoke casually, half-teasing. "I was your wife once, if you recall."

With a slow, sardonic smile, Ben stepped closer, the toes of his boots coming within an inch of hers. "I recall."

By now, the sun had fallen level with the horizon, casting a light gray shroud over everything, but his eyes were that piercing blue. He stood close enough now that she could feel the warmth of him.

Unnerved by the responding flutter in her stomach, she pressed her hands to the front of her dress. "I'm relieved to see you're on your feet, at last."

He chuckled low in his throat. "An understatement, I think. And you needn't sound so formal when we both know it's all thanks to you."

At this, she smiled, allowing herself to feel more hopeful. Emboldened. "And what are your plans from here?" she asked. "If that's not too formal to ask, of course."

He looked down at her, searching her eyes before setting his gaze back on the water. "It seems there was no escaping my father's wishes, after all." He spoke solemnly, but his lips were curved in a telling smile. "You see, I've become quite determined to join the church."

His words took a long, hollow moment for Rebekah to comprehend. When she did, she reeled back. "As a *reverend?*"

She'd practically scoffed the word, but she couldn't help it.

"Of course, as a reverend," he replied, a bit impatiently.

Too shocked to speak, Rebekah lowered her eyes. It wasn't that she couldn't picture Ben standing in a pulpit. Perhaps it took a *slight* twist of the imagination, given all she'd seen him do in the name of spying, but she also knew enough of his past to know it made sense. And while she felt she ought to congratulate him for this glorious new calling, for an end to his rootless wanderings, the words were like dust in her dry mouth. Ben had forged a clear path for himself, but in doing so had rendered her own path far less certain.

There could never be a place for a woman like her in his future parish. This much was certain. As soon as the truth of Rebekah's past was exposed, Ben's parishioners would be the ones to sermonize. They'd rant against their marriage and rebuke him for his folly and, eventually, toss them both out.

For Rebekah, this was the usual way of things. Ben must have known as much. Perhaps this was what she hadn't been able to interpret in his expression when she found him staring out at the water. Perhaps he felt, as she feared, that there was no place for her at his side. Not anymore, nor in any of the ways she wanted.

He was leaving.

And he wasn't taking her with him.

Of course, she understood his reasons. Her

seedy past notwithstanding, nothing about her even remotely resembled a clergyman's wife.

But what was to become of her now? She'd told Wayne she'd never turn back to the old ways, no matter what happened to Ben, and she'd meant it—meant it still. And while there was reason to hope for a reconciliation with her father, she was too afraid to depend upon him, afraid that moving home would test them both beyond their newfound forgiveness.

If she found a suitable position, somewhere respectable, she might see her father from time to time, often enough to heal what was broken between them. But it would be hard to find such a position on her own, nearly impossible if she was to esape the cold clutches of penury. She would need someone with connections, someone who knew people in other cities and might recommend her.

She looked out at the Hudson so Ben wouldn't see the full depth of her disappointment. She drew a quiet breath and tried to speak candidly, but her voice battled her every word. "You said before that you might find me a position, a place where I might be set up away from Haverstraw." She paused. "Do you think you really could, when you're well again?"

"I'm sure I'll think of something." His voice held the barest trace of humor.

She glanced up quickly, into eyes that might

have seemed roguish if it weren't for the fond smile resting on his handsome lips.

He laughed faintly at whatever he saw in her expression, then caught her chin in his hand, holding her gently as he fixed her with a look. She flushed despite all attempts at poise, but before he could laugh again, which he looked very likely to do, she raised herself up on tiptoe and pulled his face down to hers.

He put a hand to the small of her back, drawing her closer.

As he fitted his lips to hers, Rebekah felt a distinct sense of newness, of belonging. Hope blossomed within her. No man had ever made her feel so cherished, nor loved her so openly. In Ben, she found a man resolved to that which he'd long wanted, and so his kiss was firm, unhurried.

And entirely devoted.

They broke away at the same moment, both of them flushed and silent.

"I think parsonage life would be very bleak without a wife," Ben mused at last.

A strangled laugh escaped her. "Is *that* a proposal, then?"

"Shall I try something a bit more inspiring? Oh, very well." He bent and kissed her again, this time whispering very lightly against her lips. "I would have you and none other for as long as I have breath to call you my own. If you'll have me?"

As he spoke, he pressed something into the curl of her fingers.

Rebekah glanced down at the scarlet ribbon dangling from her hand and smiled. After the chaos of battle and Ben's near brush with death, she'd assumed it had been lost, and yet there it was, as secure in her hand as a promise kept.

How often, since Ben had first given it to her, had she pleaded with God for mercy, for deliverance? Though she hardly dared to ask for more than that, she'd pleaded also for strength. For the strength to believe herself forgiven. For the strength to entrust her son to the faithful parents whom God had provided for him in her absence. For the strength to step out of the darkness of her past and into the light, wheresoever it may lead.

As her fingers fastened around the ribbon, she sensed that first quiet glimmer of answered prayer, of two people woven together and held fast by the grace of God.

"If you're trying to hold me in suspense of your answer, you're doing a remarkable job."

Startled by the unusual hesitancy in Ben's voice, Rebekah blinked up at him, nearly laughing as she found her way back to the conversation at hand.

The poor man *had* proposed, she realized.

And she'd not given him an answer.

"I've always wondered what it would be like to be a reverend's wife," she remarked lightly, answering his first proposal with a playful grin. Then, taking his hand between her own, the ribbon crumpling between the joining of their palms, she brought his hand to her lips, pressing a warm, loving kiss against his battle-roughened knuckles as she softly answered his second. "Yes, Ben, with all my heart."

Dear General [Washington]: The fort and garrison, with Colonel Johnson, are ours. Our officers and men behaved like men who are determined to be free.

Yours most sincerely,
Anthony Wayne

—Letter from Stony Point,
New York
16 July, 1779

ACKNOWLEDGMENTS

This book wouldn't exist were it not for Pastor Ken Ballas, who stopped me at a church picnic shortly after *Shadow among Sheaves* had released to ask if my next biblical retelling was going to be about Rahab. It wasn't, but as my family drove home that day Rebekah's story was already taking shape in my head, and I couldn't stop thinking about her. Thank you, Pastor Ballas, for planting that first seed.

I also owe a huge debt of gratitude to the chief historian at Stony Point, Michael Sheehan, for answering so many questions about the fort and battle. I will also thank you in advance for forgiving any creative liberties that might have cropped up along the way (i.e., the timing of the nickname "Mad Anthony") and sincerely hope you haven't had to stretch your imagination too far.

Heartfelt thanks to those who helped strengthen the story. To Ena, Jenny, and Adria, whose notes and conversations have always been a tremendous blessing to me during the writing process. And to the team at WhiteFire Publishing, especially Roseanna White, Marisa Stokley, Janelle Leonard, and Kim Peterson—thank you for all the work you put into polishing and preparing this book for publication and most especially for believing in the story enough to put it into the hands of readers.

Every book I've written has been a journey of sorts, and with this one my family came on that journey quite literally. To my husband: thank you for being so encouraging that you volunteered to pack up a rental car and drive eight hours so I could see the Stony Point Battlefield Site. Your support has always been boundless. I love you. And to my children: you were both so tiny that day, when we all stood together at the top of Stony Point, and I will always cherish the memory of you climbing across those giant rocks.

Finally, to my readers. I struggled for a long while with the dedication for this book. In the end, I hoped that Ben and Rebekah's story would reach and refresh those who feel broken in any way. If you feel as though you fit that description, as I do myself at times, I want to come alongside you for just one moment, long enough to say this:

Jesus loves you. He forgives you. He makes you whole.

Soli Deo gloria.

Naomi Stephens (NaomiStephens.com) is a bookworm turned teacher turned writer. Her first novel, *Shadow Among Sheaves*, was an INSPY Award shortlist contender and the winner of the 2020 Carol Award in Debut Fiction. Though she has called many places home over the years, she currently lives in New York with her husband, her two children, and a rascal of a dog named Sherlock.

Learn more at www.naomistephens.com

Center Point Large Print
600 Brooks Road / PO Box 1
Thorndike, ME 04986-0001 USA

(207) 568-3717

US & Canada:
1 800 929-9108
www.centerpointlargeprint.com